SHADOW
OF THE
EXILE

THE INFERNAL GUARDIAN: BOOK ONE

MITCHELL HOGAN

47N☀RTH

This is a work of fiction. Names, characters, organizations, places, events, and incidents are either products of the author's imagination or are used fictitiously. Any resemblance to actual persons, living or dead, or actual events is purely coincidental.

Text copyright © 2018 by Mitchell Hogan
All rights reserved.

Published by 47North, Seattle

www.apub.com

Amazon, the Amazon logo, and 47North are trademarks of Amazon.com, Inc., or its affiliates.

ISBN-13: 9781503903227
ISBN-10: 1503903222

Cover design by Zlatina Zareva

Printed in the United States of America

For my wife, who scratches her head at what I do for a living but has never failed to do all she can to help me achieve my dreams

I say to you againe, doe not call upp Any that you can not put downe: by the Which I meane, Any that can in Turne call up somewhat against you, whereby your powerfullest Devices may not be of use.

—H. P. Lovecraft, *The Case of Charles Dexter Ward*

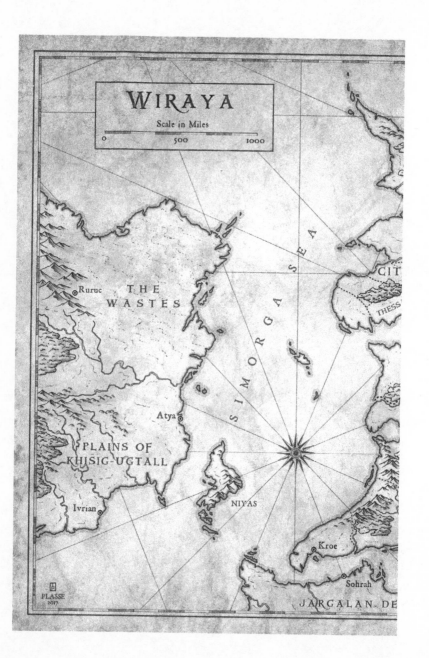

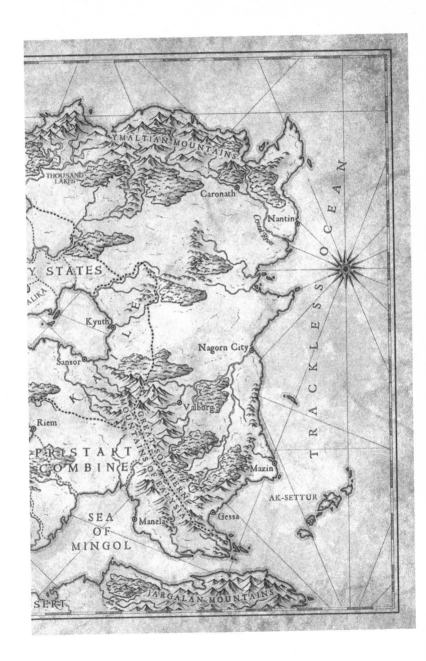

Chapter One

Many centuries had passed since Tarrik Nal-Valim, demon of the Thirty-Seventh Order, had felt the insidious pull of a summons. The warning signs caught him off guard, manifesting as a niggling sensation in the back of his skull, an unseen insect buzzing close by that became more annoying if he tried to ignore the feeling. When he realized what it was, his bowels and stomach clenched. One part of his mind tried to flee while another prepared to fight.

Invisible white-hot hooks jagged into his limbs, torso, and consciousness. Given only an instant to prepare himself, he managed to segregate a portion of his mind and resist the agony. But the hooks sliced and tore at his being, unraveling him no matter how hard he fought. Nausea threatened to overwhelm him. Pain seared his nerves, and his mind swam with disorientation.

With a final nerve-rending jerk, his form was torn asunder, transformed back into his basic essence. He felt himself siphoned through a tear in the veil between his world—Shimrax, the Guttering Wastes—and another, like water down a drain.

The sensation lessened, and his thoughts coalesced. He was standing atop a derelict tower, its roof missing, walls of granite and mortar cracked and broken with only rusted iron supports and rivets remaining. In one corner sat a heaped pile of crushed terra-cotta roof tiles covered in grass and bird droppings, as were the tops of the remaining walls. A half circle of blazing white sun peeked over forested hills to the east, and the air held the scent of rain. The atmosphere was slightly thicker than he was used to and much more humid. A stark contrast to the hot, roaring winds and parched mountains of Shimrax.

As Tarrik took in his surroundings, he noted frost had crystallized on the corroded iron and stonework and crusted over what remained of the timber floor. A swirling mist penetrated every corner and shadow, giving off a sulfurous stench underlaid with rot. Both frost and mist weren't his doing, he knew, but a side effect of the summoning and its tearing of ethereal fabric, a commingling of worlds for a brief moment as the veil between them was ripped apart.

A curious place for a summons. Fraught with danger. So much could go wrong.

Either the sorcerer who'd summoned him was an idiot, which would be good for Tarrik, or desperate, which could be good or bad.

Tarrik's essence and mind prickled as the summons grew in urgency. A hundred needlelike pains pierced his body—his summoner prodding him, reminding him who was the slave and who was the master. He steeled himself and ignored the sensation. He was no weakling. He'd fought abominable creatures inhabiting the abyssal realms that sent others fleeing in fear. He'd endured battles against the Kasonna-Vulur invaders where only a fraction of a fraction survived. He'd walked the hallowed thoroughfares of the ancient ruins of Polas'azar, then climbed the cliffs of Lantrin to guest with the winged Halimir. He'd killed sorcerous masters before and would again.

Only then did he see that his summoner was a woman. Sweat dripped from her brow, and her chest heaved as if she'd just run up the stairs to the top of the tower. She had black locks, reddish-brown skin, sharp cheekbones, and a firm figure clad in worn and stained traveling leathers that showed she was no stranger to practicality. Her clothes were wet, as was the hair plastered against her scalp. No doubt from the rainstorm Tarrik had just missed. Fine lines fanned out from the corners of her eyes, hinting at her age. At her feet sat a small leather sack, out the top of which peeked the corner of a black bound book. Probably a grimoire.

She stood, eyes half-closed, inside a protective circle marked in chalk and blood and seemed to concentrate on drawing his essence forth. The corpse of a small goat lay nearby. Blood wasn't necessary for a summoning, but demons liked to keep that information under wraps. Whatever they could do to confuse sorcerers, they did.

Tarrik stood inside another circle, caged by glittering lines of arcane force that crackled with intensity. A wave of scorching heat flowed across him, creating a tingling agony. Resisting a summons brought pain, but Tarrik had never been one to acquiesce quietly. He hadn't survived so long and progressed in the hierarchy of demons by being timid.

He drew upon a tendril of dark-tide power, which the woman quickly suppressed. Standing his ground, Tarrik fought back, not caring if he hurt her.

Their battle lasted only moments. She was too strong, and he quickly backed off.

Away from the realms of the abyss, he'd need to conserve his arcane energy. Opportunities to replenish it would be few. Tarrik would need to ensure his sorcery would work to his advantage. He'd been around a long time and wouldn't waste his energy like a lower-order demon.

The woman must be a practitioner of great power and expertise to reach through the veil and hook a demon of his order. He hadn't been summoned for centuries and thought—hoped—his name had been lost long ago.

Red-hot spikes pierced his mind, driving him to his knees. Something whimpered, and he realized he was making pitiful noises.

The spikes withdrew slightly, giving his thoughts and body a moment to recover.

Seeking a weakness he could exploit, or better yet an outright mistake, he steeled himself with a growl and sent his awareness pulsing along the edge of the restrictive markings. But he was out of luck. No miswritten runes, no spelling mistakes for this sorcerer.

A simmering resentment in his guts turned to anger. Once again someone was attempting to enslave him.

"Reveal yourself, demon!" she shouted, and Tarrik realized he hadn't filtered fully through the gate. The forceful tug of her summons pulled at him harder, like ropes binding his limbs and torso. The needle-sharp pressure in his mind intensified, on the verge of debilitating torment.

Tarrik gave in and allowed his essence to coalesce into his natural shape. It wasn't so different from that of a standard human male, though the harsh abyssal environment of Shimrax had sculpted his muscles, rendered his fat, and roped his body with sinew. He drew himself up to his full height, knowing he stood a head taller than most humans. His straight black hair brushed his shoulders, his skin sleek and taut.

Tarrik decided his natural form would suffice. After all, demons and humankind were closely related, and it took effort to maintain a different physical manipulation for any length of time.

The summoner's eyes narrowed, and the hot spikes of agony lessened slightly. Her gaze traveled along his body from head to toe. No material objects could pass through a tear in the veil—unless they were summoned separately—so Tarrik was naked.

He raised an eyebrow at her. He hoped she was enjoying the view, because if he found a way to free himself, he was going to rip her head from her shoulders, then suck the marrow from her bones. And when he was done with her body, he would imprison her soul and take her back to the abyss. There she would remain his plaything until her soul screamed for an end, a true death.

She took a deep breath and held her arm out dramatically. Tarrik noted it was trembling with either exhaustion or fear, maybe both.

"I am your master! I command you to reveal your true form!"

"This is my true form," Tarrik said flatly.

That was how all these summoners saw themselves. They were the masters, and the demon was the slave. Minor demons reveled in being summoned, as their base hungers were usually well sated by defiling and slaughtering humans. But Tarrik Nal-Valim was no ordinary demon. He'd evolved past base desires and was now only a few tiers down from the exalted status of a demon lord.

"Do not lie to me, or I'll visit upon you such pain as you've never—"

"This is my true form," he said again with an exasperated sigh. "And I have felt such pain before. I have no desire to repeat it."

She sniffed and whispered a cant under her breath. Tarrik sensed a whiff of power caress his body. He stiffened but otherwise made no move.

He recognized it as dusk-tide power, and that told him which world he was in—Wiraya, so the humans called this realm. Sorcerers here absorbed both the dusk-tide and dawn-tide essence and used the energy to perform their cants. She had timed his summoning to draw on her stored power and also take advantage of the dawn-tide surge. Her reserves were depleted, though—he could sense it. Summoning took a great deal of arcane energy.

His own demon sorcery used the dark-tide power too, but he had no way of replenishing it until the next full dark, when both moons stayed below the horizon. He had no idea when that would be.

"You speak the truth," she said slowly. "Your skin . . . it's silvery gray. You could be of San-Kharr blood."

"But I'm not."

Tarrik searched his memory and came up with a vague sense that the San-Kharr were arid-plains dwellers from the scorching south of this world who spent much of their time living underground, but his knowledge was a little hazy on the races of Wiraya. One human was much like another.

"No." The summoner paused. "You're a little short for a demon, aren't you? Still, you're above average height for a man."

"Did you expect a giant? Horns and talons?"

He'd had enough of assuming monstrous forms to deliberately repulse and alarm humans, though some of his race delighted in such displays.

"Well . . . yes."

"You don't know much, do you?"

"Be silent, slave," she hissed. "I'm not open to your manipulations. I am your master."

"Your first time, is it?"

From her attitude and bearing, he decided it had to be. Despite the position she'd put him in, Tarrik was impressed. To summon a demon like him on her first attempt at breaching the veil showed a talent and knowledge of sorcery few could surpass, not to mention the strength such a feat took, both in dawn-tide and dusk-tide power.

"I said *be quiet!*"

He put his hands up to show he meant no mischief. Besides, bound as he was, he couldn't harm a hair on her head. "You sorcerers are always so sure of yourselves. If you'd just—"

She spoke a cant, one that Tarrik recognized an instant before the Wracking Nerves slammed into him at full strength. His skin burned with agony, and he cried out, collapsing onto the floor.

As swiftly as it had engulfed him, the punishment ceased. He lay curled up, hands balled into fists, the metallic taste of blood in his mouth. He'd bitten his tongue, which throbbed with pain.

After a few long panting breaths, he struggled to a sitting position. When he looked up, his summoner was peering into the distance over the side of the ruined tower, a look of worry on her face.

Something was chasing her. She was desperate. This, Tarrik could work with.

"You sorcerers," he said, pausing to swallow the bloody saliva that was thick in his mouth, "are always too quick to punish. The carrot works better than the stick."

"I have no carrots," she replied. "And you're not a donkey."

Tarrik struggled to his feet, nerves still tingling from the torture. He glared at her but remained silent while she stared at him. Her dark-blue, almost black eyes were filled with fear and despair.

"I think," she said slowly, "I've gone about this the wrong way."

Clearly she'd expected a monster. A creature she could command with no qualms and feel no regret about if it was injured or killed. Tarrik's lips opened for an automatic rejoinder, but he clamped them shut. Better to obey her commands and get this over with, but he didn't like the way she was looking at him.

"First things first," she said. "I command you to tell me your name."

Tarrik envisioned his hands wrapped around the summoner's neck, her eyes bulging and face turning purple as he choked the life from her. The image brought a smile to his face. He decided to play along and offered a deep bow from the waist.

"Tarrik Nal-Valim, demon of the Thirty-Seventh Order. Which you already know since you're the sorcerer who summoned me."

"Sorceress, though that term is archaic. I'm a woman."

"I can see that."

She was quite attractive, in a rain-soaked feral-cat way. He added a leer for good measure. Base behavior was expected from demons, and he was happy to oblige. Whatever got him unhooked from her clutches quicker. And if she was uncomfortable in his presence and thought he was constantly thinking about ravishing her, then she'd want him gone as soon as possible. As far as she knew, all demons behaved like savage animals. His brutal realm didn't lend itself to niceties.

"You *will* obey me, slave. You are bound. My will is paramount."

Tarrik knew she was right. But one slip from her, one misspoken cant, and she'd die quickly. Then he'd be free to return to Shimrax, where he could continue to plan his redemption in the demon lords' eyes and return from exile.

"And what is your will?" he said.

She stared at him for a moment, as if trying to make a decision. Then she bent, took an object from the sack at her feet, and held it out. A gaudy gold-and-jeweled sunburst talisman—used by a sorcerer as a concentration and calculation aid.

Tarrik's gut twisted when he recognized it. The talisman had belonged to Contian, grandmaster of the Red Gate Covenant and carrier of their most potent catalyst, his previous master and a rare type of sorcerer. The two had even become friends in a strange sort of way, demon and human working together. What had happened to the old man that this woman now held his talisman?

Since returning to Shimrax centuries ago, Tarrik hadn't heard from Contian. He'd expected to. He'd even sworn on this very talisman that he'd serve of his own free will for a year and a day if summoned again. After all this time, the old man was likely dead. The thought brought a surge of sadness and grief. He hoped Contian had died well—though trouble had forever followed him.

"You swore on this talisman," the woman said, "many years ago. And your oath still holds true."

"No, it doesn't," Tarrik said.

"Serve me," she pleaded, holding up the talisman between them, "of your own free will. For a year and a day."

"No." Tarrik couldn't think of what else to say.

Possible actions roiled through his mind. He could agree, then kill her when she unbound him. Or disagree—and probably be forced into slavery for an unspecified length of time. What if he agreed and was true to his word? This last option stuck in his craw. Voluntarily serving a master was . . . unpalatable, to say the least. Especially as she hadn't earned his service, not like Contian had.

"Where did you find that talisman?" he said. "How do you know about my oath?"

He doubted Contian had written it down anywhere, in a diary or some such, or his own grimoire. No . . . the old sorcerer was too canny for that.

She shrugged. "I do know, and that's all that matters. You swore by your true name, Tarrik Nal-Valim, outcast among demons, outlawed in many of their realms."

"To Contian," he reminded her. "Not to you."

"You swore on this talisman, which held his catalyst—the thing that made his sorcery possible. It was the possession he held most dear."

Memories flooded back to Tarrik. He saw Contian sitting in his rickety chair in front of the fire, reading, always reading. He saw ash falling like snow after Contian burned a stronghold of dead-eyes that worshiped Andil-tekkur, a wraithe that had lost all reason and urged the creatures to ever greater depravities. He saw Contian walking through an inferno, protected by spherical arcane wards and cradling an insensate black-haired woman he'd saved from ghouls. The sorcerer Delfina, his first apprentice.

Tarrik examined his summoner again. Black hair, those penetrating blue-black eyes, that figure, and an immense sorcerous talent. The pieces slotted into place. This woman was Contian and Delfina's daughter. He knew sorcerers enjoyed a longer life span than normal humans, though nowhere near as long as demons, so it was possible . . . *blood and fire.* He filed the revelation away for another time. She was still his jailor, and he wanted nothing to do with her.

"Just to be clear," he said, "you want me to honor the oath I made to Contian, not to you, all because you happen to have his talisman and catalyst? If I do, you'll release me from your sorcerous bindings, and I'll serve you for a year and a day. Does that about cover it?"

She met his eyes for the count of a dozen heartbeats, then nodded.

"I could just kill you as soon as I'm released," he said.

"You won't."

So sure of herself.

"You believe your sorcery is puissant enough to defend yourself. But you have me bound. Why not order me to perform whatever task you like? I'll be forced to comply. Why—"

Tarrik broke off and smiled. Her nervousness and desperation fell into place. She was on the run. But summoning emitted powerful energies, which would have given away her position. She was looking after her own skin. Still, he was intrigued. And what was service for a year and a day against the possibility of a much longer time of bound servitude? Slave, she'd called him, and rightly so. Why was she insisting on unforced service instead?

"Why are you doing this? Why not just force me to do your bidding?"

She glanced over her shoulder at the woods beyond the tower, as if expecting someone, or something, to appear. Following her glance, he saw the tower stood upon a hillock with a fast-flowing river on one side. To the south and west, the forest stretched to the horizon.

"I don't want a slave," she said, turning back to him, "demon or not. I'd have to be too careful, too . . . vigilant. I have enough to worry about."

I'll wager you do. She was definitely scared and expecting some kind of attack.

"Set me a single task then. Once it's completed, I'll be free to return to my realm." Except she'd still know his name and could summon him again when she had the strength. He'd better head off that idea. "After that, you can summon other, lesser demons who would suit your purpose better than I."

She shook her head, strands of hair sticking to her damp cheeks. "No. I've decided on you. Lesser demons might be more malleable, but I require someone with a little more finesse." A slight upturn of her lips.

Had she just given him a compliment? How much did she know about him?

"Very well. Undo your bindings, and I'll swear service to you."

A tinkling laugh broke from her lips. "I don't think so. You swear, by your true name—then I'll release some of them."

It had been worth a try, but she'd been testing him already. "I will not serve you willingly. You are not Contian. You will have to keep me bound to prevent me from returning to Shimrax. Our relationship will be as master and slave, as you so easily called me."

That should do it. No mention of how quickly she'd die if her bindings slipped. This woman deserved no respect from him. What she deserved was to be defiled and to die a painful death—as did all humans who made slaves of demons.

Curling a finger around the strands of hair stuck to her face, she tucked them back over her ear, her eyes narrowing as she stared at Tarrik, assessing him anew. After a long moment, she let out a resigned sigh. "Then our bargain is struck." Disappointment tinged her words. "I wish . . . I didn't have to, but I will keep you bound. Serve me well, and I'll not mistreat you. You'll find me a hard master, and my path may be a difficult one. Perhaps . . . I will release some of the bindings to give you more freedom than others would. Is this acceptable?"

"It is," Tarrik said, and her shoulders slumped with relief. "I'm not doing this for you," he added. "I'm doing it out of respect for Contian. What happened to him?"

Her mouth drew into a tight line. "A demon ripped his head off."

"Ah."

"Not a summons of his. He . . . disliked the practice."

"He was a sensible man."

"Not sensible enough."

"What do you mean?"

She looked away. "Never mind. So what's next?"

Uncertainty knotted his stomach, but there could be no other way out of his situation. "I'll swear if you release some bindings. I, Tarrik Nal—"

"Wait." She held up a hand to stop him.

What was it now? He'd agreed to her terms. Let it be done and his service commence. He'd follow her commands to the letter, whether to her benefit or not. There would surely be opportunity to misinterpret the spirit of them occasionally.

"I . . ." She swallowed. Another glance over the tower's edge.

Tarrik could see distant figures atop a ridge now. Her hunters, edging closer. Four, he decided, that his eyes could discern.

She spoke as if her thoughts pained her. "This was a last resort, summoning you. I'd rather not have gone down this dark path. Going over my . . . Contian's notes, I decided you were the only demon I'd be comfortable summoning." She met Tarrik's gaze briefly before looking away. "I'm outlawed as well in certain regions. Running from . . . those who would do me harm. And some of my own people wouldn't shed a tear if I disappeared."

An admission from her, a confession. Did she hope it would absolve her of enslaving him? If so, she wasn't as smart as he'd first thought. She was desperate, and those chasing her were close. Besides, she was a sorcerer. They existed only to use others.

"You want me to kill for you," he said.

Her eyes met his again, and Tarrik was struck by their intelligence. "I want you to save me."

Her words—an echo of Contian's all those centuries ago—chilled Tarrik down to his essence. Were they a trick? He didn't think so, but when dealing with sorcerers, it was best not to take anything at face value.

"Tell me your name," he said.

"It holds no power. I am not a demon."

"Nevertheless, I have to call you something. 'Master' is . . . not palatable, and I cannot serve you freely."

She nodded and clasped her arms around her torso. Tarrik noticed she was shivering in the cold morning air even though she was bathed in sunlight. Her hands and what he could see of her arms bore the signs of a swordsman: calluses, and scars where another's blade had sliced her skin. But no sword hung from her waist.

"Very well. My name is Serenity Branwen."

Before he could stop himself, Tarrik snorted. "Serenity?"

"The times were peaceful when I was brought into the world. That peace was fleeting."

"Why do you need me? Isn't your sorcery enough to protect you?"

"The creatures they've sent after me are immune to sorcery."

Ah, no wonder she needed help. Deciding there was no point in delaying any further, Tarrik knelt on one knee and bowed his head. "Do your worst then. I refuse to serve you freely."

Expecting more talk or delays, he was startled when some of the bindings vanished immediately. The glowing ring that caged him dissipated into sparkles, which faded to nothingness. Only a charred circle remained on the timber floor.

Tarrik raised his arms above his head and stretched his back. He could kill her now, or attempt it. But despite the two of them never having met before, she knew him well. Contian's doing, Tarrik realized. He surreptitiously tested her bindings with a trickle of dark-tide power. They were more than adequate, though not full bindings. He would have to serve until released.

"The name Serenity is too well-known in some parts of Wiraya," she said, interrupting his musings. "Call me Ren."

He nodded slowly. "Did you bring me a weapon . . . Ren?"

He had learned the art of the sword and spear from many masters but didn't actually need a weapon since his demon catalyst was of the shadow-blade variety and secreted underneath the skin of his forearm. Another truth he'd keep from her. Soon he'd have a whole bagful. It was good policy to keep your summoner in the dark as much as possible.

Ren cast her gaze around the derelict tower, as if a weapon might miraculously appear.

"Don't tell me you summoned me to fight for you and didn't bring a weapon for me to use?"

"I thought I'd brought one up here, but . . ." She rubbed her eyes with a trembling hand. "There's a sword downstairs."

She was tired, and no wonder after being chased and backed into a corner, then exerting herself in a major summoning. She'd need to rest soon before she collapsed from exhaustion. He took a few steps toward her, then stopped when her face hardened with resolve.

"I'm not going to hurt you," he said, holding his hands up.

He skirted the dead goat and its pool of gore and stopped an arm's pace from Ren. This close, he could see a paleness to her reddish-brown skin and a darkness around her eyes. Behind her, a half-rotten staircase led down.

"How close are your pursuers? I mean, how long until they get here?"

Tarrik had seen them in the distance, but he had been away from this world for many years. He couldn't yet judge travel times.

Ren picked up her leather sack and tucked the book inside, along with Contian's talisman, all the while tilting her head to keep one eye on the demon. Tarrik could sense the pulse of her incantation as she maintained her grip on his bindings. She didn't trust him, and she was right not to.

"Half an hour maybe," she said. "They'll stop to plan. Some of their hunters found me a few days ago and must have gotten word to their masters. I sensed them closing in and tried to outrun them, but somehow they tracked me. I holed up here, not wanting to stay at an inn or anywhere someone might recognize me, but two men found me last night. That's when I decided I had no choice but to summon you."

A puissant sorcerer always had choices. Was she feigning helplessness? And she clearly hadn't run from the men who'd found her.

"I assume they're downstairs, the dead men?"

Ren nodded, and Tarrik descended the decrepit staircase. Ren followed more slowly.

The ground floor was in better shape than the top of the tower, and the sorcerer had obviously been living there for a few days. The floor was mostly clean of dead leaves, and there was a bed of green ferns covered with a blanket. The remains of a small fire lay against one wall, ringed by blackened river stones.

The two corpses had been dragged against another wall. They were hard-looking men, lean and weatherworn, garbed in sturdy brown pants and shirts, standard wear for trackers and hunters. Two bows rested against the wall beside them with two quivers of broadhead arrows and one sheathed sword. The weapon was short but would do.

There were no visible wounds on the bodies apart from the life-blood that had dribbled from their noses and ears. Ren had killed them with sorcery.

She moved to a set of saddlebags next to the makeshift bed and deposited her sack next to them. Against the bed rested a sheathed sword with a hilt fashioned to resemble feathered wings and a silver snake entwined around the orichalcum pommel. The blade reeked of power, though it looked too long and heavy for Ren to wield effectively.

"Cover yourself, demon, for decency's sake," she said.

"A dead man's sword and a dead man's clothes. How gruesome."

"I didn't know I'd be forced to summon you or that you'd be naked."

"Call me Tarrik," he said. "Or I'll call you Serenity."

She sniffed, then nodded. "Very well . . . Tarrik."

"What else do you know about these creatures coming after you?"

"One stumbled across me a few weeks ago. I barely managed to escape with my life. My sorcery didn't work against it; somehow my power twisted around the creature. I lost it in the dark, then circled back for my horse."

Few creatures of this world were immune to sorcery, the same as in the abyssal realms.

"Doesn't sound too dangerous," he said flippantly.

She glared at him. "When I said I lost it, I meant two mercenaries I'd hired held the creature off while I ran. They died for me."

"They died for money. That's what mercenaries do. You didn't force them into their chosen careers."

The subtext was obvious: not like she'd forced him into this arrangement.

"Still, if I hadn't hired them, they'd be alive," she said.

Tarrik shrugged. "Maybe. Maybe not. Who set these creatures on you?"

Ren looked everywhere except at him. "I don't know."

Lying. She'll get us both killed.

The bigger of the two dead men was still smaller than Tarrik, but he would have to do. He grabbed the corpse under the arms and hefted it to a sitting position. The carcass was cold and stiff, and Tarrik grunted with effort as he forced its limbs in directions they didn't want to go. Eventually he managed to remove the man's shirt and pants and donned them himself. The coarse material was damp and cold and scratched his newly created skin, which would take a few days to firm up. The pants didn't cover his ankles, nor the shirt his wrists. He must look like a boy who'd outgrown his clothes.

The boots were too small for his feet, so he discarded them. Shoeless was the preferred method of hunting in his realm anyway, and his soles would be as tough as old leather soon enough.

Checking the sword, he found its blade spotted with rust, but the edge was still keen. Shaking his head at the lack of care the man had taken with the weapon, Tarrik buckled the sword belt around his waist.

"You said these creatures are closing in. You can sense them?"

"Vaguely. I can sense the ripples surrounding them. Whatever was done to make them immune to sorcery creates a . . . vacancy. That's the best way I can describe it."

"How many of them?"

"Three, and they're approaching from different directions."

Tarrik grunted. He thought he'd seen four figures on the ridge, but maybe his eyes hadn't adjusted to this world yet. He drew a breath in and considered their options. He would prefer to leave Ren here and hunt alone, but he doubted she'd allow that. The other option was for her to stay inside the tower and fight from within rather than just hide, to take advantage of the protection its walls offered. That way he wouldn't have to worry about her when the fighting started.

"I'll fight them outside," he told her. "You stay in here and block the door and hope none get past me."

"I . . . thank you," she replied.

Tarrik drew the sword and unbuckled and discarded the belt. The blade was crudely made and heavier than he was used to for its size.

His bare feet crushed soft leaves and twigs as he took a few steps away from the tower to give himself room for warm-up exercises he'd learned from a master swordsman centuries ago. With slow movements he moved the blade through various positions: tip almost touching the ground, vertical with the hilt at eye level, forward thrusts and sideways. It was a measured dance designed to stretch and loosen muscles and instill efficient footwork and lethal strokes.

As he moved through the exercises, he tried to stay relaxed in body and mind. He sensed a headache fast approaching—a consequence of the summoning. He needed food, and soon, if he was to cope with the settling pains, his newly materialized body would endure. But there was no time to eat, not until the threat to Ren was dealt with.

Tarrik shoved and kicked at the tower door. There wasn't much give, so it would probably do. If Ren were killed, he'd be free. But the power she held over him prevented him from leaving her to a grisly fate.

He scrounged a mass of dry twigs from underneath the trees, then piled pine branches heavy with sap on top. When the mound reached his waist, he stopped, sweat pouring from his skin. He swiftly crafted a makeshift torch, then set himself to wait. Not knowing what these beasts were that had been set to hunt Ren—or their abilities—put him at a disadvantage. Fire would scare away some; with others, he could use the flames for cover and as another weapon.

The creatures came when the sun had traveled a finger's width across the sky. Their shadows moved among the trees, furtive and liquid.

Tarrik used the barest trickle of dark-tide power to light the torch, then shoved it into the kindling, which crackled with flame immediately. He took a few steps back and ran through a final sword form. Good enough, he decided, though he'd prefer a spear rather than a sword.

Holding the sword close to his leg, he stood very still alongside a tree and kept an eye on the woods. His innate demonic talent of concealment would keep him hidden unless he made any sudden moves, and he hoped surprise would give him the edge. To his left, the fire blazed. He trusted it would be enough to deter an attack from that side.

A musky scent reached his nostrils, underneath it a hint of stagnant water. He frowned. Marfesh, a rare type of Twenty-Seventh Order demon, resistant to sorcery. Their immunity made them peerless sorcerer killers but also complicated any summons. Tarrik was in luck, as although they were vicious, they weren't particularly intelligent. What worried him more was that a sorcerer must be controlling them, a sorcerer hidden from Ren's senses, which was why he'd seen four figures but she'd only sensed three.

Killing his own kind didn't bother him. It was how things were. Three more demons that wouldn't ascend to the next stage of their existence. Like uncounted others. Once, Tarrik himself might have been a marfesh, though he hoped he'd begun higher up in the natural order. Only when you advanced to the Thirty-Third Order did you retain your memories. Something to do with the development of the brain.

A twig snapped behind Tarrik's tree. He held his breath and kept still as a marfesh's scaled head and long neck emerged to his right. Its lidless, orange eyes swiveled back and forth, its purple, forked tongue darting in and out. Fortunately for Tarrik, his concealment held as the marfesh's senses were dull, and its focus remained fixated on the tower.

He was never one to spurn a gift when offered. Tarrik shifted his weight and drove the sword into the marfesh's neck. Green blood spurted, splashing the ground, but the demon leaped back. Its mouth opened wide, and Tarrik threw himself to the side as the marfesh sprayed saliva. The soaked leaves began to smoke and wither, sending fumes into the air.

He rolled to his feet and rushed the marfesh, dodged a swipe of its talons, and hacked at its neck again. The demon collapsed, its body flopping like a puppet whose strings had been severed, its clawed hands scrabbling in the dead leaves. The marfesh shook with a violent tremor and was still.

Tarrik raced around the other side of the tree as another marfesh scurried toward its fallen companion. Before the demon realized he was there, he plunged his blade into its chest behind its foreleg and skewered its heart. The marfesh uttered a piercing shriek, sending a distant flock of birds cawing into the sky.

He jerked the sword free and ran, keeping within the cover of trees. Movement was the key now. The element of surprise was gone, and there was still another demon and a sorcerer to kill.

Tracks in the leaves made him pause: long strides, as if the marfesh was running. He followed them quickly—then they narrowed as the demon slowed its pace. The marfesh was somewhere close by, but he couldn't see it. All was silent. Even the disturbed birds had flown away or settled down again.

He pressed his back against the rough bark of a large tree and willed himself to blend in. A drop of water landed on a leaf by his foot. A curl of smoke rose from the green.

Tarrik lunged to the side. Too late. His frame erupted in pain as the demon's talons sliced into his shoulder and down his back. His legs tangled, and he tripped, falling onto the leaf-strewn earth.

A shriek filled the air as the marfesh dropped from its concealment in the tree. Tarrik scrambled to his feet and backed away, looking
around for any sign of the sorcerer. The demon's tongue flicked, and
its mouth opened. Tarrik ducked and rolled forward. Venom sprayed
overhead, and droplets burned his clothes and exposed skin, tearing a
cry from his lips.

He clenched his jaw and thrust his sword at the marfesh. The
demon dodged back, hissing as it rose on its hind legs. Tarrik leaped
forward, avoiding its sharp talons, and sliced a shallow line across its
chest. He caught a hammering blow to his side for his trouble and
staggered back, breath coming in harsh gasps, sweat stinging his eyes.

He felt dusk-tide sorcery building behind him. He cursed and
dodged around the marfesh until the beast was between him and the
sorcerer.

Tendrils of violet crackled through the air, hissing with virulence.
They slammed into the marfesh, causing its scales to glow a furious
crimson before rolling off, the demon shedding the harmful incantations like water.

Tarrik heard the sorcerer curse but couldn't spare him a glance. He
ducked under a vicious swipe from the demon's talons and drove his
blade into its chest up to the hilt. Green blood spilled over his hand
and spattered the ground. The marfesh fell, dragging his sword down.
He tried to pull the blade free, but it was stuck between two ribs. The
hilt slipped from his blood-drenched grip.

Tarrik grabbed it with both hands and pulled to no avail. Sorcery
flared again behind him, and he flattened himself on the ground, pressing against the marfesh's tough skin. The beast offered some protection, but not enough. Violet threads cascaded around him, searing his
exposed flesh and burning his clothes.

When the attack subsided, Tarrik leaped to his feet and rushed the
sorcerer before he had a chance to draw more power. He was a slender
fellow, short, with oiled-back brown hair and a scraggly beard peppered

with gray. One hand clutched what looked to be a stone statuette—his talisman.

A perfect sphere of protection materialized around the man. He gave Tarrik a sneering look before glancing at the tower.

"Run, little man," goaded Tarrik. "She's coming for you now that your pets are dead. Flee while you can."

If the sorcerer required the help of three marfesh to take Ren down, she was obviously his better when it came to the arcane arts.

The sorcerer swallowed, and a flash of fear crossed his face. Then he set his mouth into a grim line. "I will not. I . . . cannot."

Only the pain in his shoulder and back and the feel of his blood trickling down his side prevented Tarrik from rolling his eyes. Humans were too timid. The sorcerer probably thought he'd be killed if he let Ren escape. And from the fear he displayed, he was probably right.

The door to the tower opened, and Ren strode out. She gave the sorcerer a contemptuous glance, then ignored him as if he were of no consequence, focusing instead on the dead marfesh. But Tarrik knew she would still be weak from the summoning. He hoped she had a plan, as he couldn't get through the looming arcane shield.

"Why not leave and enjoy the remaining life you have," he said to the man, "before she kills you."

The sorcerer shook his head. "He will find me. Better a quick death now than one at his hands. Failure is not tolerated."

"Then skin one of the marfesh. Make some armor from it to deflect sorcery."

The skin would degrade quickly no matter what was done to preserve it and thus would only offer limited protection. But this man was probably ignorant of such matters.

"Who are you?" the sorcerer asked. "How do you know what the demons are called and the properties of their skin?"

Tarrik tried a nonchalant shrug, then grimaced in pain. "I'm just a man like any other."

"Your blood is purple."

Oh. Yes.

"He has the blood of demons in him," Ren said. "A useful trait, as you saw. Now, who sent you?"

The man licked his lips, eyes shifting nervously. Tarrik felt him begin drawing dawn-tide and dusk-tide power.

"Don't," said Ren flatly. "You know who I am."

Tarrik gave her a sharp look.

"You know you're no match for me. If you try to kill me, I'll send you to the abyss as a plaything for the demons. It is within my power. Instead, leave with your life, and be thankful."

For an instant Tarrik thought the sorcerer would attack, but the energies he'd gathered dissipated. He backed up a step, then turned and ran. Once into the trees, he dropped his spherical shield.

"That didn't go too badly," said Tarrik.

Ren passed a weary hand over her face, then slumped to the damp ground, her eyes closed.

"Back in a bit," Tarrik said, and sprinted after the sorcerer. The man couldn't be allowed to live, not now that he'd seen Tarrik. Someone might put together his origins. Ren was obviously up against powerful individuals, and Tarrik would need all the advantages he could get to survive.

"No!" Ren called after him.

As he ran through the forest, plotting an arc to intercept the sorcerer, bonds tugged at him—Ren trying to restrain him. She clearly hadn't thought of simply countermanding her order to kill those who hunted her. That, combined with the looser bindings, gave Tarrik a certain amount of leeway.

His bare feet brushed over the damp leaves and pine needles with scarcely a sound. If the sorcerer was still running, he wouldn't hear or see Tarrik until too late. And as Tarrik ran, the stresses of his summoning, of being made a slave again, came crashing down. He wanted to kill someone for what had happened to him. To scream and burn and murder, to wash away his rage with blood and violence.

Just as the man paused to glance fleetingly over his shoulder, Tarrik caught sight of him.

The sorcerer slipped, stumbling down the bank of a stream and splashing across it. On the other side, a gray horse was tied to a branch. The animal whuffed as Tarrik approached from the side. Its ears swiveled uneasily.

The man looked behind him again before stopping to catch his breath. Tarrik stepped out from behind a tree and cut his throat with the sword. A gurgling sound bubbled through the blood, a disgusting red color, and the sorcerer clutched at Tarrik's clothes.

Tarrik waited until the light left the sorcerer's eyes, then let him slump to the ground. He picked up a rock and hammered the man's skull again and again until his arm ached.

He sat back on his haunches, panting, and dropped the gore-spattered rock. *One less summoner in the world.* He felt a certain amount of satisfaction in killing one of the humans that enslaved his kind.

Would Ren thank him? Probably not. She was a summoner herself. She probably thought slavery wasn't abhorrent.

Tarrik took a few moments to steady himself. His shredded back and shoulder stung, but he'd survived much worse. Still, he'd have to see to the wounds soon.

He rifled through the horse's saddlebags, ignoring the way the beast stared at him. *Horrible creature. Only good for its meat.*

He found mostly useless belongings: clothes, too small for him; a bundle of fire sticks; a pot and a pan; other cooking utensils; provisions. His stomach growled. Maybe there was useful stuff here after all.

Tarrik slung the saddlebags over his shoulder and knelt next to the dead sorcerer. The man's purse was full of coin. He had a gem-studded knife too—which gave Tarrik an idea.

He cut open the man's shirt, then felt for a lump next to his heart, the area where sorcerers' catalysts were usually implanted. He sliced open the skin, grasped the blood-slick gem, and wrenched it out. The process was much easier after death, when they didn't bleed so much.

Striding to the stream, he washed the blood from the catalyst. The gem was illuminated from within by a silvery glow, with dark threads fracturing the surface. Tarrik slipped it into a pocket. The crystal might come in handy.

The horse snorted again.

Tarrik untied the beast's reins and led the steed through the stream and back to the tower. Ren might have a use for the animal, and if not, they could always eat it. His stomach rumbled at the thought.

"Did you kill him?" Ren asked when Tarrik handed her the horse's réins.

"No, we had a conversation over a cup of tea. Of course I killed him."

"Why?"

"That was your original command, and I don't like loose ends."

"He wasn't a danger anymore."

"Treat me like a demon slave, and that's how I'll act."

"I offered you freedom."

"Oh, so it's all my fault? And what freedom? Freedom to serve you?"

"No. I didn't mean that. Just . . . forget it."

"As you wish, *Master*."

Her mouth drew into a thin line at his words. She considered the horse, then the rapidly diminishing bonfire. "You keep the horse. Mine is at the back of the tower."

"I don't want it. I'll walk."

"Don't be so stubborn. We have a long way to travel."

"Don't worry about me, *Master*. I'll keep up. Besides, I hate horses, and they hate me." He gestured toward the fire. "I'm going to cook—I need to eat before we leave. I assume we are leaving soon?"

She nodded. "We can't stay here now. We'll head out once you've eaten." She disappeared around the side of the tower.

Tarrik took the cooking pot from the saddlebags and walked to fill it from the brook nearby. When he returned, Ren was securing both horses to a tree, the gray and her brown one. Tarrik ignored her and poked around inside the tower until he found a sack of grains. He added several handfuls and some sort of dried meat from the dead sorcerer's provisions into the pot along with finger-size green vegetables that he broke into pieces. He found a long stick and placed the pot in the fire.

"That was for the horse," said Ren.

"What?"

"The grain. It's a mixture of corn, oats, and barley."

Tarrik shrugged. All food in this world was terrible, apart from the meat. And he hadn't exactly been eating well on Shimrax, where food was scarce and sometimes all he could manage were baked riven-grubs. He hadn't had a decent meal since being exiled. "But it's edible?"

"Yes . . . but I'll do the cooking from now on." She gestured to his shoulder. "Let me take a look at your wounds. I have a salve and some bandages."

Her touch was gentle—and disturbing. Having a human's hands on him wasn't a new experience, but the sensation was as unsettling as he remembered. It took all his willpower to allow her ministrations and not attempt to tear her throat out. When she probed a tender spot, he inadvertently drew on his dark-tide power, which Ren ruthlessly tore from his grasp as her own power flared—another reminder that she was his master.

Chapter Two

They traveled west for a day, Tarrik walking while Ren rode. The temperature grew cold as the sun descended, and Tarrik guessed the season was either side of winter, but which side he couldn't be sure. The air smelled too damp and washed clean to him; he preferred the dry and odorous demon realms.

They made camp beside a small cliff with enough of an overhang to provide shelter in case it rained again.

"Fetch wood for a fire," Ren said as she dismounted and found a suitable branch to secure the horses. "No one will be following us yet, so we may as well be comfortable while we can."

Tarrik wasn't so sure—she hadn't sensed the sorcerer hunting her, after all—but he gathered a hefty pile and set it ablaze using one of the dead sorcerer's fire sticks. He was hungry again despite having eaten all the stew he'd cooked in the morning and quite a bit of bread and cheese on the trail. Ren seemed to eat sparingly.

As the sun set, she left him warming by the fire and disappeared into the forest. When the sun dipped below the horizon, the dusk-tide came. Tarrik felt the surge of power as a tingling in his skin. He could sense Ren absorbing its energy.

Human sorcerers drew on the eldritch forces that swept their world at sunrise and sunset and stored the dawn-tide and dusk-tide energy in their repositories. Both sources of power needed to be replenished regularly; if they weren't, the sorcerer's repositories would eventually drain to empty. The sorcerer could shape and control the energies using a combination of his or her mental abilities and cants based upon geometric calculations and the ancient Skanuric language—one of the first tongues of this world, now spoken only by scholars, sorcerers, and priests. Demons, on the other hand, used dark-tide energy for their innate talents and their own cants. Unfortunately for Tarrik, the dark-tide was only available in this world when both of its moons remained below the horizon.

Ren's accumulation of the dusk-tide continued for some time. Her ability to absorb the energy was greater than that of most other sorcerers Tarrik had known. He wondered how much of Contian's talent she'd inherited.

A short time later he felt two minuscule surges of dawn-tide sorcery. When Ren returned, she carried two dead birds.

Sitting on the ground away from the fire, she began plucking them, starting at the legs, then moving to the back and breast. Tarrik suppressed a snort. With their bare torsos and feathered wings and tails, the birds looked like miniature grebsuls, lower-order demons usually hunted for food.

Ren hacked the wings off, then took a burning brand from the fire and scorched the remaining tufts to ash. She cut off the legs and heads, placed both carcasses into a cast-iron pot, added some dried herbs and a splash of water, then put the lid on and shoved the pot into the coals.

"I noticed you're eating quite a lot," she said. "Is that normal?"

"It will only last another day or two. A summons takes a lot of energy from me. And my wounds are healing."

Ren frowned. "Why does the summons take your energy? Doesn't the sorcery do all the work?"

"I don't know." He stood and gathered their canteens. "I'll fill these." Her questions irritated him, and he didn't want to engage with her.

He wandered off in the direction of the sound of running water and stopped at a clear stream flowing over rounded pebbles. Tarrik scratched the bandage on his shoulder but couldn't reach the itchy wound on his back. The flesh was healing swiftly and should be almost whole in a day or so. He contemplated the movement of the water and his predicament, even though the wind chilled him. The truth was, he had little room to maneuver with Ren and her hateful bindings. Which meant, as usual, he needed to remain calm and cunning and search for any weakness.

When he looked up, it was dark. Filling the canteens, he returned to the camp.

Ren had dragged the pot from the fire and was sitting cross-legged on a blanket with a sorcerous light hovering above her shoulder. She was reading a book.

She looked up at him and smiled. "We'll need to find you some new clothes at the next town. We can't hide your size, but we can at least make you less conspicuous."

That suited him. The less trouble he ran into, the better. Usually sorcerers only summoned a demon for violent purposes. Maybe this time would be different—except it hadn't started out that way.

"I'll find you a proper sword too," she added. "If you're to pose as my bodyguard, you'll need to look the part, and act it. That sorcerer and the demons aren't all that's following me."

"Care to elaborate?"

"There's . . . a presence I've felt. It will strike soon—I'm sure of it." Her eyes searched the night around them before returning to the fire.

Vague.

"What kind of presence?"

"I've told you all you need to know."

Tarrik tried another line of questioning. "I need to know how powerful you are. What you can and can't do."

She'd summoned him unaided, which spoke of great power and control, but if he had a better idea of how skilled she was, he might be able to figure out a way around her defenses. And then she'd be dead, and he'd be back on Shimrax. There, he could continue to plan. He couldn't live in his austere cave forever, hunting merely to survive the arid wastes. It was either escape or go mad.

"I didn't take you for an expert in sorcery," she said.

"I'm not. But the more information I have, the better prepared I'll be."

Ren poked a stick into the fire, and Tarrik thought she was ignoring him. Then she spoke, her words slow and reluctant. "Do not think I don't know what you're doing, demon. But you are right. You do need to know *some* things. I can generate a fifth-tier shield, effective against physical force, heat and cold, sorcery, and various other attacks. I trust you understand what that means?"

Contian had only managed a fourth-tier shield, and he'd been a grandmaster. Tarrik had seen him walk unharmed into sorcerous conflagrations over almost molten rock radiating heat that would melt flesh from bone. Every arcane shield had its weakness, but he knew from experience that a fourth-tier shield was impregnable to any power he could muster. A fifth-tier was . . . he had no idea but nodded as if he did.

"As for my other abilities, I imagine you'll see them for yourself soon enough," added Ren. "No more questions."

Tarrik seethed at her peremptory tone but was smart enough to bide his time. Unfortunately, time wasn't his friend. The longer he was in this world, the greater the chance he'd be killed.

Ren took the lid off the pot, and the smell of the roasted birds was overwhelmingly good. She gestured for him to join her as she began carving the meat.

Later, after picking the bones clean, the warmth of the fire and the food spreading through him, Tarrik felt strength returning to his body. He shivered in the cold-edged wind. Ren was cocooned in a blanket, staring into the diminishing coals. Not a word passed between them, almost as if the other did not exist. He wanted to question her about many things: what season it was; how dangerous things were for her— and, as a consequence, for him; and most of all, when and how Contian had died. But he held back. He didn't know her and wouldn't be able to tell if she was lying.

Tarrik fetched a blanket from the saddlebags and found a soft spot of earth on which to lie down. His feet were freezing, and he wrapped the blanket around them.

Ren shrugged off her blanket and leaned forward to add some thick branches to the fire. Tarrik watched the play of muscles beneath her clothes and the way her black hair moved in the wind, all too aware that she was attractive. Feeling lust stir within him, he looked away and ruthlessly suppressed desire.

"Are you feeling better after eating?" she asked.

Her face was hard to read in the flickering light. He supposed she was concerned whether her slave was functioning properly.

He nodded. "Though a drink or three would round out the meal and do wonders for my well-being."

And help to suppress the wildness of his blood.

"I hope my summons didn't take you away from anything important."

"To be honest, I was a bit bored. This will make a nice change. A holiday."

Tarrik had been in the middle of three-player Croix, a complex board game. When the summons had begun to draw him away, his opponents had laughed and then stolen all his money. Vadik-Karrina and Omolt-Abbami. He'd remember them when he returned and make them pay.

"You jest with me." She rummaged through her gear and drew out a bottle and uncorked it. "Contian wrote you had a fondness for strong spirits. Wine is the best I can do."

Anger surged through Tarrik. Contian had said he'd expunge Tarrik's name from all records, but he had lied. To a human, a promise to a demon probably wasn't worth keeping. Blood pounded in his head, and all he could hear was the beat of his raging heart.

Restraining the urge to kill Ren, Tarrik took the bottle from her. He swallowed a mouthful and, finding the wine not too awful, drank more. It was better than the fermented, bitter garotte-beetle milk he usually drank—all he could obtain by bartering his kills on Shimrax.

"Go easy," Ren said with a laugh. "It's the only one I have."

Tarrik handed the bottle back. The wine would help for a time, until he could get something stronger. Alcohol had a numbing effect on demon desires, and he'd need it to maintain control. At least he didn't have to worry about becoming drunk—his organs limited the effects of spirits. The amount it would take to get him drunk was enough to kill a human.

"Would you like to know more about what happened to Contian?" she said.

Tarrik met her eyes. "No."

"You're stubborn. He wrote that about you too."

He remained silent. She would never gain his trust the way the old sorcerer had, and the first time she slipped up would be her last.

"There's a town not far from here, a few days' ride. It's sizeable enough, and we shouldn't have any problem finding you clothes and a decent weapon. Failing that, another few days on is a city. I have business there."

Tarrik looked up at that. "I thought you were on the run?" The marfesh and the sorcerer had seemed to confirm this.

"There are certain places where I am not welcome. But there are others where I can move about freely without fear of reprisal."

"But someone wants you dead."

She nodded as she poked at the coals with a stick. "There are many who want that. Some within the . . . organization I belong to. There are different factions . . . it's complicated."

31

"What does your 'organization' do?"

Flames crackled while Ren hesitated. She stared at him, a fire in her eyes as if she might burn him on the spot. When she spoke, her voice was low and tight. "We, ah, we're called the Tainted Cabal."

Tarrik laughed softly, for he couldn't help himself. But his reaction wasn't mirth, rather a bitter and hateful acknowledgment of the name.

This woman who had summoned him was one of the worst enemies of demonkind.

The members of the Tainted Cabal were worshipers of Nysrog, a demon lord driven to insanity by a summons gone wrong. He had eventually been defeated, but only after raining down death and destruction on Wiraya for decades. Human sorcerers were weak and always drawn to easy power. Many lusted after the gifts and abilities Nysrog had bestowed upon his most ardent followers. The Tainted Cabalists were the most prolific users of demons as slaves, more than any other sorcerers. And they'd forced many demons to fight and die for their mad schemes.

Tarrik had figured out Ren was dangerous, but now he knew she was crazed. He hated her for what she and her ilk had done to thousands of his kind.

She turned back to the fire and took a sip of wine. "I'm not aligned with those who desire the return of Nysrog. That undertaking is nigh impossible, and only the most zealous adherents believe it will happen. We aim for something that's achievable. And Nysrog thrives on chaos, while we prefer order."

Despite himself, Tarrik was intrigued. He wondered why she was telling him so much, then remembered that as her summoned slave, he was bound to keep her secrets.

"Nysrog was defeated . . . when?" he asked. "Close to two hundred years ago?"

"One hundred and eighty-three."

"And after all this time no one has been able to summon him again?"

"He grew immensely powerful. Some say too powerful to control."

A combination of the demon's insanity and the human essences he had subsumed. Probably hundreds of thousands of them. "If you do not work to return the demon lord, what do you work toward?"

"Nysrog brought into this world others of your kind. Lieutenants of a sort, lesser demon lords subservient to him. Most were killed or returned to the abyss during the many battles and their aftermath. But not all. One demon chose nine human sorcerers of great power, and to them he promised greatness. Some agreed to follow him; some did not. But in the end it didn't matter. The demon bound them all, much as I have bound you. Except . . . worse. He invaded their minds, broke them, dominated them. And after that, they all served willingly."

A coldness washed through Tarrik. He ran through the list of demons he knew had died or returned. But he needn't have done so, for one name stood out among all the others: Samal Rak-shazza, whom many demons named the Adversary. A manipulator and deceiver. Nysrog hadn't been the real danger. He doubted these humans had been aware of the reality at the time.

Decades ago, the other demon lords had caught Samal imprisoning and absorbing the essences of his peers in order to increase his power—with plans to kill them all and make himself ruler of the abyssal realms. The lords had tried to capture him, but he was already too strong. He had escaped, then disappeared, and later rumor put him on the human world. Samal had followed Nysrog and ensconced himself as the conqueror's lone adviser. From what Tarrik surmised, Samal Rak-shazza had been the true power behind Nysrog and the cause of his fall into insanity. He had also been the cause of much of the trouble between demons and humans and had subjected both to countless depravities. He hadn't been seen in the demon realms since the defeat of Nysrog.

"The sorcerers couldn't kill or banish the demon?"

Ren shook her head. "It took all the might of the remaining human sorcerers and their priests to weave a prison strong enough to contain him. More than it took to defeat Nysrog. This is the demon I serve. The faction of the Tainted Cabal I belong to seeks the return of Samal Rak-shazza."

Samal was an abomination, Tarrik knew. Ren's goal was to free the most malevolent demon lord in all of the abyss.

"Why? What role do you play in freeing this demon from his shackles?" Tarrik asked.

Ren gazed at him for a long moment. "That's enough for tonight. We have a long day ahead of us tomorrow. Clean the pot, please, before you retire."

She turned from him then, spread her blanket away from the fire, and was soon curled up, apparently asleep.

Tarrik cleaned the pot in the river, scrubbing it with sand, then wrapped himself in his blanket and closed his eyes. He wondered why she hadn't suggested setting a watch. Sorcerers had their tricks, he knew. And he would sense if anyone came within a few dozen paces, even while asleep.

When morning came, the wind had died down, and Tarrik wasn't so cold. He'd woken a few times during the night, once from the chill and twice because of unpleasant dreams of Nysrog and Samal.

Ren fed the horses some of the grains, which Tarrik thought would be better used in a stew. The creatures had picked the area around their tree bare of grass, and that should be enough. Not only were they stupid, they were also greedy.

Ren saw the clean pot and smiled her thanks. Tarrik did not return it—why thank him for doing something he had no choice about?

He wished he'd accepted Ren's proposal of free-willed service. If he had, he could have killed her and left this awful realm and not gotten involved in this mad plan to free Samal Rak-shazza. Tarrik's own name would go down in infamy—that was certain. He was reviled enough by other demons without this overshadowing him as well.

Ren brought out two small loaves of bread and set them to warm by the awakened fire. After turning them once, she held one out to Tarrik.

"Eat. I'm sure you'll like it. They're my last ones. We can stock up on fresh supplies when we get to the town."

Tarrik reluctantly took the loaf. It was lighter than he thought and, when he bit into it, sweet. Dried berries were inside with fragments of nuts.

He watched as Ren broke small chunks from her loaf and peered at each for signs of dirt before daintily nibbling them. While Ren took her time eating, Tarrik scouted around the campsite to be free of her presence and peered at the cloudy sky. When he returned, she was waiting beside the horses, which were now saddled.

"Ride the gray," she said. "We'll make better time."

"I'd rather not."

"It's not a request."

Tarrik considered the likelihood of her punishing him for refusing. He decided to choose his battles. After last night's revelations, he had much to think on, and being subjected to the Wracking Nerves so early in the morning over a horse wasn't worth a refusal.

He secured his shoddy sword to the saddle where he could easily reach it and mounted. The creature turned its head and stared at him.

"I don't think she's pleased you're so heavy," said Ren. She gave him a curious look before suppressing what looked like a smile and urging her brown along a faint game trail.

Tarrik had to admit he must look an amusing sight: barefoot, with pants and shirt too small and exposing his ankles and forearms.

These stupid beasts required vocal commands, didn't they? It had been so long he'd forgotten much of this world. "Follow the other beast, the brown one," he told the horse, and flicked the reins. To his relief, it plodded along after Ren's.

After they had traveled an hour, the forest thinned. Ren slowed her mount to ride alongside Tarrik.

"That brand on your back, what does it mean? It looks deliberate."

His mouth was suddenly dry. The burning agony of the ensorcelled orichalcum brand came back to him, making his head swim and his heart thump against his ribs. He reached for a waterskin and took his time swallowing a few mouthfuls.

His wrists and legs had been tied to a metal whipping post in the shape of an *X*. His clothes had been cut from his skin and thrown into a lake of lava. And it wasn't enough that the Demon Lord Council had marked him for all eternity. All his remaining possessions had also been thrown into the searing orange lake after the valuables had been taken.

"I am *chiggruul*, outlawed, in most realms of the abyss."

"What for?"

For betraying our society. For loving the wrong woman. "For my dealings with Contian."

A half-truth, and indeed he didn't even know why he told her that much.

"I had no idea the consequences would be so harsh," she said.

"Neither did I," muttered Tarrik. Then louder, "If you plan to negotiate with the higher-order demons, I won't be of any use. Most demons will not associate with me."

A gust of wind blew his hair across his face, and he brushed it away. In the virtually windless realm he'd been living in—if you could call it living—his mane had been less annoying. He remembered seeing a length of leather cord in one of the saddlebags and busied himself burrowing for it.

"I won't be dealing with any demons other than you if I can help it," Ren said.

Curious. If she was telling the truth, there was more to her story than she'd let on. Then again, there was more to everyone's story: lies they were ashamed of; secrets held close; desires they dared not speak of, hidden away in their hearts.

Tarrik found the leather cord, cut a length with the jeweled dagger, and tied his hair back. "And why is that?"

Her response came quickly, as if prepared in advance. "I do not condone what the Tainted Cabal has done to demons. I usually avoid summoning. My colleagues think I am mad, and maybe I am. Instead, I study sorcerous artifacts and their uses, seeking the lost secrets of their creation."

"That seems . . . boring."

Ren offered a short laugh. "It interests me. But it is a quiet existence."

"Then why do people want to kill you?"

"How do your back and shoulder feel?" she asked instead of answering. "I'll change the bandage when we rest again."

"No," he said angrily. "I want no more of your nursing. I can look after my own wounds." He was healing swiftly anyway—another of his innate demon traits.

"As you wish," Ren said, as if unconcerned. "I will not insist." And she guided her horse ahead again.

Later that day they heard horns somewhere far away. Ren stopped and stared in the direction of the sounds for a while before urging them on at greater speed.

That night, they did not light a fire for warmth or food and relied on the light from Chandra, the smaller white moon of the two that lit this world, to make their camp.

Late into the night, Ren cried out in her sleep so violently that she woke Tarrik. He rolled from his blanket, sword in his hand. Ren did not wake, though he heard sobs escape her lips.

There was something . . . a feeling in the air that made him cold inside. He became intensely aware of the silence that surrounded him. No crickets chirped. No grass or leaves rustled, disturbed by nocturnal animals. There was nothing, except a hint of movement above Ren, so brief Tarrik thought he might have imagined it.

A shadow, silvered with moonlight. A scent reached him—a pungent miasma of rock baked under a hot sun—and he knew he wasn't imagining things.

This was dark-tide sorcery.

A faint cracking sound made him start. Ren stirred again but remained asleep.

Tarrik drew on his own dark-tide power, a trickle only, and sent his awareness out. He needed to be careful. Ren was unaware of what was happening, so whatever power this was had penetrated her wards.

He fashioned a scrying, then took it down a few levels. A scrying might be sensed, and subtlety was required. He knew there were creatures in this world that hunted in the night and fed on the living. Could he be so lucky that Ren had become their prey?

A cold breeze touched his skin, but it burned as a fire might. Tarrik looked down at his arms; they tingled, yet there were no marks.

His throat tightened with an emotion he seldom felt. Fear.

Be very careful.

He released his dark-tide sorcery, the barest whisper of power. And he *saw*.

Motes of sorcerous light swirled about Ren, cavorting in a complex dance he couldn't fathom, and yet there was a rhythm to them that echoed in his essence and set his heart pounding. It called to him.

Demon sorcery. *A demon lord's sorcery.* But it had an insubstantial quality, as if an echo.

Tarrik hissed softly. Who of the demon lords was capable of such power—to reach through the veil and send his or her awareness into the human world? It wasn't possible. The lord had to be here, to be . . .

Samal.

The motes changed, became a thousand hues of darkness tied together with tendrils of violet.

Ren moaned, low and long.

Tarrik's dark-tide sight caught a glimpse of an image: a man, hauntingly beautiful.

"Yes," Ren whispered.

The face swirled into darkness, replaced with a knife that shone with reflected moonlight, sharp enough to split a hair.

Ren whimpered. "No."

The knife disintegrated, and faint music filled the night. Delicate notes rang out, somehow entering Tarrik through his skin, his hair. They changed . . . became ominous—and seductive.

"Please . . . ," said Ren.

Tarrik glanced at her and saw she was still asleep.

The shadowy motes re-formed, this time into a hazy, oozing image . . . treacle flowing down a wall. The chill intensified until it became unearthly, something that hungered to consume living heat.

More notes joined the others, silvery, tinkling, emanating from Ren. They entered Tarrik's mouth and nostrils, filling his lungs with a disturbing harmony.

Ren drew her legs up to her chest, hugging her knees. Another whimper.

The presence intensified, a mixture of cold and power so strong that Tarrik had to turn away, trembling. He hoped it didn't notice him.

Samal had opened a door, wherever he was, and reached out to Ren. And his presence was exquisite. Tarrik had the impression he was seeing the barest inkling of what Samal had done to the Nine, how he had ensnared them and taken control of their minds.

Ren cried out, writhing, her fingers clawing at her blanket, one hand digging into the dirt. She coughed, then said something so softly Tarrik couldn't hear. Then again, her voice becoming stronger.

Her eyes suddenly opened, and she snarled and lurched to her feet, mouth speaking potent cants. The shadow motes and music around her dissolved into the night, and she stepped back, as if uncertain. Then she laughed softly, a sound disconcertingly intimate.

Tarrik sensed the despair behind Ren's reaction, and for a moment he could see all too clearly what had happened. Even from his arcane prison, Samal tormented and cajoled those he controlled. The demon lord was a faint, disembodied jumble of desires and emotions, all the more insidious for it.

"Demon," Ren's voice rasped with suppressed anger, "I take it you weren't going to use that on me?"

Tarrik realized he still held the bared blade in his hand.

"No," he said. *Not tonight.*

"What did you see?"

He licked his lips. Was this another test? "A demon lord visited you. A disembodied spirit. I think it was Samal."

Ren glared at him, and Tarrik thought she might blast him from existence. But she looked away, then down at her blanket, now jumbled at her feet. She picked it up.

"Samal was in my dream. I've experienced unsettled sleep before but never imagined . . . well, now I know; I can ward against intrusion." She looked at Tarrik again. "There was a discordance . . . something disrupted his sending. I think it was you or your presence."

That wasn't what Tarrik wanted to hear. He wanted nothing to do with any demon lord—not here, nor back in the abyssal realms. Samal was dangerous, depraved, and malevolent.

What fools these creatures were! Even after centuries of dealing with demons, they still didn't know the truth. Blind and ignorant, they strode forward as if they were all-seeing and all-powerful.

Whatever Ren was embroiled in, he wanted no part of it.

Midmorning on the third day after leaving the ruined tower, they saw smoke rising into the sky from the many chimneys in the town ahead. They crossed another stream and found a worn wagon track following the bank, which made their going easier. Soon the water pooled into a sizeable pond, man-made from the look of the stones damming the stream. Tarrik could see small silver fish darting in the shallows and larger ones deeper in.

"We'll stop here," Ren said, halting her horse.

"Why? The city's not far." Judging by the haze on the horizon, the settlement they were approaching was much larger than a town.

"That's why. We'll rest in case of trouble, and I'll bathe to make myself more respectable."

"Are you expecting trouble?"

She flashed him a smile. "Always. Stand watch, please."

She gathered a towel and a bar of soap and headed down the slope to the pool.

Tarrik's fingers hooked into claws. They were being pursued, and she stopped to bathe? He dismounted and took out the bottle of spirits he'd found wrapped in cloth at the bottom of the dead sorcerer's belongings. A few swigs later he felt better, more in control. Humans didn't understand that demons felt everything so deeply. They angered hotter and quicker, hated darker, and loved . . . with their very souls.

Tarrik drank a quarter of the bottle and placed it back in the saddlebag. He'd had better. When you imbibed so much to cope with this realm, you couldn't help but become an expert.

The horses cropped grass at the edge of the track, and Tarrik let them. No one was coming from either side. He found a place in the shade where he could keep one eye on his surroundings and one on Ren in case some water creature tried to kill her. Maybe a snake. He'd heard they could grow as big as trees on Wiraya. Ren's clothes—clean ones she'd donned this morning while she hid behind bushes—hung on a tree branch above her boots and belt. He caught a glimpse of her shining skin in the water and a faint sound of a song on the breeze.

His thoughts wandered, as often they did, but kept returning to Contian and his first apprentice, Delfina. So the old man had finally found someone to love. At least he'd known that happiness, after all he'd endured. A shame their daughter had turned out so twisted. Contian would be turning in his grave. He had been a reluctant member of the Tainted Cabal, but allegiance to a demon such as Samal Rak-shazza would have horrified him.

Tarrik heard hooves clopping on the road. Soon, from around the bend, a young boy appeared leading a pack mule. As they neared, Tarrik saw the baskets lashed to the beast's sides held various fruits and vegetables, brown and green and purple. He came up blank on their names, eons having passed since he had laid eyes on Wirayan fruit. They probably tasted awful.

Road dust coated the boy's shoes and the cloth of his pants. He stared at Tarrik, his mouth hanging open. His expression led Tarrik to think he'd suffered a serious head wound at some stage in life.

"Close your mouth," he said as the boy and mule passed, "or a bug will fly in." The boy stank of wariness and curiosity.

"What?" said the boy.

"Never mind. How far is the city?"

"Not far. You look funny."

Tarrik sighed. Coming from this lout, he'd take that as a compliment. The young human was no good except as a piece of meat.

The boy glanced toward the pool. His eyes widened, and his mouth dropped open even more. Tarrik smelled the musky scent of lust emanating from him.

Ren had emerged naked from the water and was toweling herself dry. Tarrik stared for a moment himself. He couldn't blame the boy.

"Keep moving," he growled. "Now you have a story to tell your friends."

The boy hurried away with frequent glances back in Ren's direction.

She'd wrapped the towel around herself and waited until the boy disappeared. Then she motioned for Tarrik to turn around. He gave her a shallow bow and did so. Soon she was clothed again, her damp hair leaving wet trails on the collar and shoulders of her embroidered scarlet shirt.

"Maybe you should have bathed farther upstream," he said.

"Have you ever tried to wash properly squatting over a shallow stream? It's awkward and undignified."

"And revealing yourself to the local boys isn't?"

She snorted and mounted her horse, then kneed it along the road. Tarrik followed on the gray. As she rode, she combed her raven hair free of tangles. By the time they reached the city, the wind had mostly dried her tresses, and she plaited them into a single braid.

A market was set up at an intersection outside the city, wooden stalls lining all four roads and filled with goods and produce. Chickens squawked in cane baskets, ducks quacked, and frogs . . . did whatever they did. One stall sold metal utensils and various knives; another, homemade leather goods. Tarrik squinted at them—very homemade. A steady stream of people arrived from the town and left with their sacks and saddlebags full. A thin layer of dust coated most of the goods and the stalls, and not many of the merchants seemed inclined to do much about it. Shouts about products filled the air, along with lies about how one merchant's goods were superior to another's, a human trait he found contemptible. The stench of humans and their emotions—mostly sour greed—was overwhelming, and he tried to breathe through his mouth.

"Ooh, honey," exclaimed Ren. She dismounted and exchanged a few coins for a jar of the disgusting light-amber-hued substance. She wrapped the jar in a spare shirt and tucked it into her gear, and they continued.

When a grubby young boy walked close to the gray and his shoulder brushed against a saddlebag, Tarrik caught the boy's eye and held up an admonishing finger. The potential thief gave a resigned grin and turned aside.

Soldiers guarded the road entering the city, their uniforms a greenish-gray color that reminded Tarrik of pond slime. Each had a shield-shaped red cloth sewn over his right breast, upon which was an embroidered black . . . bird? Only one, a grizzled veteran with a salt-and-pepper beard, wore a sword. The others carried daggers and thick batons of steel-banded wood. They seemed more interested in eyeing the women walking past than preventing trouble. Useless scum who wouldn't last a day in a demon realm.

He and Ren passed the soldiers without incident. Underfoot the road turned from packed earth to stone. Soon they were riding through streets filled with dust and garbage. Narrow alleys to each side were muddy and piled with refuse buzzing with flies and scurrying vermin. A woman emptied a chamber pot from a third floor window without looking below. A pig, tied with a length of rope to keep it from wandering, snuffled toward the waste. Tarrik would never understand how humans could live in such disgusting conditions, though the lower demons were the same.

Ren led them to a shop front with a sign depicting a needle and spool of thread. No prizes for guessing what the owner did. Tarrik scratched his chest where the rough material of the shirt itched his skin. He'd be glad to get out of the dead man's garments.

They tied the horses to a hitching post, and Tarrik felt a brief burst of sorcery from Ren.

"To prevent any would-be thieves," she said when she saw him looking at her. "And could you stop glowering? It makes you noticeable. More noticeable."

The shop was filled with crates of cloth and tables holding folded pants and shirts, underclothes and coats, jackets and hats. A wooden counter dominated one wall with a long metal ruler screwed to its surface and a few pairs of large shears.

A short man blinked at them from behind the counter. He pushed his spectacles up the bridge of his nose as he hurried toward the pair. He wore a linen apron with six needles stuck into it close to his collarbone.

"Good day, my lady. Welcome to my humble establishment. It's a fine day in Ivrian. The rain yesterday cleared the air and—"

"My man here needs some clothes," Ren said curtly. "As you can see."

The tailor stared at her for an instant before letting his eyes roam over Tarrik. He wrinkled his nose with what Tarrik assumed was distaste for his current attire.

"I see. Yes. He's sizeable, isn't he?"

"That's why I hired him."

"A sound policy. Now . . ." The tailor moved to a nearby table on which sat various trousers of fine quality. "This is the latest fashion in all the major cities. See the double stitching along the seams and the distinctive—"

"Three sets of clothes will suffice," said Ren. "One good set for any formal engagements I have to attend; the others are for working. They all need to be loose enough for a swordsman. One pair of riding boots, and another for walking." She turned to regard Tarrik, and he noted a glint of amusement in her eyes. She tapped her cheek with a finger, as if thinking. "Something dark, I think. To match his coloring and make him all the more menacing."

"Indeed, my lady!" The tailor rubbed his hands together. "I have plenty of suitable stock on hand."

Ren held out two gold coins, and the man's face fell. "Whatever these buy. And make it quick—we haven't got all day." She turned on her heel and made for the door.

Tarrik watched until she was gone, then drew another two gold coins from his stolen purse. "Something a bit nicer," he said with a smile.

Chapter Three

Under the watchful eye of the tailor, Tarrik tugged on his new clothes as if he were donning armor. And in a way, he was. He thought of the garments as his first line of defense against Ren and this world of demon enslavers.

The woolen topcoat and trousers were black with a patterned silver trim and cunningly placed slits to allow freedom of movement. The charcoal cotton shirt was almost too tight when he fastened the strange buttons the tailor called "mother-of-pearl." Black leather boots completed the outfit: almost knee-high, with silver side buckles.

Tarrik walked around the shop a few times, squatted, and leaped.

The tailor beamed and clapped at his antics. "A much-civilized improvement, if you don't mind me saying. A masterful assembly. Dark and brooding."

Tarrik glared at him until he looked nervously away.

The clothes were certainly of far better quality than he'd been able to find on Shimrax, a menacing world only fit for exiles and criminals. But that was his lot now. He was unlikely to see again the wondrous cities and sublime architecture of the other abyssal realms: sorcerously woven voidstone towers spiraling into the sky with intricate elder-glass bridges spanning hundreds of paces. Or to attend the Nazgrese Games, where higher-order demons pitted themselves against each other in tests of speed and strength and dark-tide talents, or the extravagant feasts and sophisticated revelries hosted by the demon lords when—

Tarrik ruthlessly crushed his memories from before the shame of enslavement. To dwell on the past would lead to rage and despair, and he couldn't afford to lose himself. Not in this world. Not under the restraints of a sorcerer.

He adjusted himself through the trousers. "They'll do," he said to the tailor.

"I expected nothing less. Now, let me wrap up the other clothes your . . . er . . . employer wanted for you."

The man bustled about behind the counter, wrapping each item in brown paper. Perhaps he thought Tarrik was a plaything rather than a bodyguard.

Let the meat-bag think what he wants. He doesn't matter.

While the tailor was about his business, Tarrik braided his hair in the intricate *grash-bren* style, signifying a shamed demon forced to follow an inferior leader. He had to pause a few times to remember the pattern sequence, and he didn't have a white cord to intertwine with the braid, but no one here would know the difference or understand the style's significance. The pattern was a physical reminder to himself, a motivation to break free.

The tailor approached carrying a pile of flat packages. "I must say you look quite intimidating. My clothes accentuate your . . . er, physique and the air of danger about you. Quite menacing."

Tarrik buckled on his miserable excuse for a sword and took the packages. "That's what I get paid for."

"Indeed! Though I dare say you're not just for show. Now, your collar isn't quite straight. If you'll—"

"I'll fix it."

"I wouldn't want you to leave my establishment with such a small detail—"

"I said I'll fix it." Tarrik turned away, leaving the tailor with one hand outstretched.

He paused at the doorway, letting his eyes adjust to the brighter light outside. The transition from dark to light or light to dark had undone many a warrior, the perfect moment of disorientation for an enemy to attack.

He stood just outside the shop, squinting under his raised hand until his eyes attuned. None of the passersby looked threatening, though he didn't know enough about the characteristics of these humans to make an accurate assessment. For all he knew, there could be a knife under every coat, a blade under every skirt. If any of them made the slightest threatening move against him, he'd cut their throats.

A yelp came from over by the horses. An urchin jumped back nursing a hand, then sulked in the shadows of a nearby shop awning. The child had long hair, but Tarrik couldn't determine if the scamp was a boy or a girl. The thief had obviously tried to take something from his or Ren's horse and been chastised by whatever protective cant Ren had placed upon their belongings. He wondered why the waif wasn't dead. Perhaps Ren thought killing thieves would attract too much attention. Nevertheless, her mercy signified weakness. Something he could exploit if an opportunity presented itself.

Ren lounged against a wall across the street as if nothing out of the ordinary had happened. She raised her eyebrows at his clothes, then took a bite from a pastry she was holding and glanced down both sides of the street before she strode toward him.

"Bought it from a street vendor since you were taking so long," she mumbled.

She didn't ask if he wanted any, which suited Tarrik. Sweet foods tasted foul and disagreed with his guts. He didn't know how humans tolerated such saccharine fare. Contian even used to add honey to his tea. Tarrik shuddered. Bee vomit, of all things.

"You're supposed to be unnoticeable," continued Ren. "Isn't this outfit a bit ostentatious?"

"I don't know what type of bodyguards you've had before, but unnoticeable isn't an advantage. The less you're attacked, the better as far as I'm concerned. It means I'm less likely to be killed."

"Whoever comes after me won't care if you're noticeable or not."

"Then there's no harm done."

Ren tilted her head to look up at him. "Rebellious, aren't we? I'll let it go this once. But do not test me."

She licked her fingers and wiped them on a wax paper bag. There was a smudge of powdered sugar around the corner of her mouth, but Tarrik decided not to tell her about it. After all, he wasn't here to take care of her personal grooming.

"Your collar is crooked." Ren reached up, and before Tarrik could react, her fingers touched his neck.

He grabbed her wrist hard, making her gasp. He had a vision of his hands around her neck, her eyes bulging, face turning blue.

"Let go," she said. "It hurts."

Tarrik's skin tightened, burning under Ren's sorcerous bindings. Automatically they forced him to release his grip. The burning sensation faded.

"I don't like to be touched," he said. "It is ill-mannered in my realms to touch without an invitation, and transgression usually ends in violence. Only a lover's caress is acceptable."

Ren raised her chin and sneered at him. "You impudent slave! You are mine to do with as I will. And your demonic lusts will not be tolerated."

She rubbed her wrist until the whitened skin returned to a normal color.

"You have been warned," he said.

"You cannot harm me—" Ren broke off.

"And yet I just did. Your bindings are not as potent if I react without thinking."

He shouldn't have said as much, but her unfinished remark suggested she had reasoned it out already.

They untied their horses' reins and mounted. Ren adjusted the hilt of her sword to make sure she could easily reach it. Tarrik scanned the street and eyed loitering townsfolk who wilted under his glare. The strictures placed upon him and his desire to stay alive in this horrible world meant performing this bodyguard role to the best of his abilities. He would put on a good show while he bided his time.

"That sword belt and sheath are shabby," said Ren. "They stand out against your new finery."

"Perhaps they are well-worn and serviceable. Perhaps my employer is too miserly to provide better-quality weapons."

"Some people may think that. Those who matter know me better and will draw their own conclusions. Tomorrow we will make a trip to a weaponsmith and see you properly equipped. We've arrived a bit late to make an appearance at the citadel today."

He followed Ren as she led them along cobbled streets, taking turns seemingly at random, but the citadel loomed closer as they rode, its turrets protruding over the tops of the city's buildings. As they neared the structure, the streets and buildings, not to mention the people, improved. Uneven cobbles changed to flat pavers; flaked paint and varnish gave way to fresh whitewash and colorful tones; clothes of rough linen and wool turned to spun cotton, silk, and brushed suede.

The humans smelled too alive; their odor of sweat and musk inflamed him. What was the point of them? They had just the one life. They couldn't be reborn as something else, wouldn't advance to a higher form. They lived, bred, died, and repeated the cycle until . . . what? The coppersmith over there, why did she bother? How did she make her existence bearable for the few years she had in this world? Why didn't she succumb to despair? Why didn't she curl up and weep at the unfairness that was her lot?

Perhaps it was a human trait: the strength to continue when all seemed hopeless.

Lesser demons hadn't the ability to think in such complex terms. They fought to survive and breed just as humans did; higher thought processes were beyond them. Were humans really just smarter lesser demons?

This world had always confused him. It didn't seem like anything was real. And that, he realized, was dangerous. If you thought something was an illusion, or didn't matter, you lost focus and let your guard down.

Such had happened to him with Jaquel, his human wife, who had never flinched in the face of danger, whose razor wit had always gotten the better of him. She was dead now. His heart clenched with grief whenever he thought of her. The only thing in this forsaken world that had seemed so very real.

They stopped in front of a three-story building. Trees lined the street, the scent of their blossoms almost overwhelming to Tarrik.

"Crab apple blooms," Ren said, dismounting. "Can you smell them?"

Tarrik nodded, wary of opening his mouth in case he gagged on the stench.

When he offered no further response, Ren shook her head and led her mount down an alley into a courtyard behind the building. Two shadows emerged from a doorway. Tarrik reached for his sword, stopping when he saw it was only a couple of stable hands, a boy and a girl. Both wore light-gray trousers and shirts, with an emblem embroidered in russet thread on the breast. The symbol looked like a dog next to a horned beast.

Ren began removing her gear from her horse and told Tarrik to do the same. He slung the saddlebags over his shoulder and loaded up with Ren's when she handed them to him. Her sword she kept to herself.

The girl kept glancing at Ren.

"What is it?" Ren said.

"Pardon, my lady, but there's . . . you have something on your lip."

Ren frowned and wiped the back of her hand against her mouth. It came away smeared with powdered sugar. "Thank you," she said, handing the girl a copper coin. "Make sure our horses are given the highest-quality feed. I'll settle the cost with the innkeeper."

The stable hands nodded and led the horses through a large doorway. Tarrik was glad to be rid of the foul-smelling beasts, though both his and Ren's gear weighed heavily on his shoulders. Perhaps horses were good for something.

Ren stood in front of him, hands on her hips. Her eyes flashed with anger, and he could smell its bitterness on her.

"You must have seen the sugar on my face, yet all this time you said nothing."

"Should I have? I wasn't aware that was one of my tasks."

"Don't make this harder than it should be."

"Should my slavery be easy for you? Should I try my best to make sure you're presentable? Bathe and dress you? Braid your hair?"

"A good idea. You seem to have done an excellent job on your own."

"I—" Tarrik stopped. Braiding another's hair was only for children, and lovers.

"Cat got your tongue?"

A cat? What cat? "I am yours to command."

"Then I command we go inside, find ourselves a room, and have a hearty meal."

The entrance hall of the inn was large and well-kept. Tarrik noticed no cobwebs in corners or on the wooden beams crossing the ceiling. His new boots scuffed over polished timber floors that had been recently mopped of dirt and dust. On a side table sat a green glazed vase holding stalks of the white crab apple flowers.

In a corner, two men sitting in padded chairs were engaged in a hushed conversation. A long counter took up the far wall, behind which stood a toadlike fellow with protruding eyes. He also wore a gray embroidered shirt, which Tarrik realized must be a uniform. To his left were a silver bell and an open ledger, an inkwell and a copper pen.

"Welcome to Ivrian, and the Demon and Hound," the man bellowed in a jovial manner. The two men in the corner looked up, disturbed from their discussion, then returned to it. "My Lady Bentina," continued the toad man, "it has been some time since we last had the pleasure."

Ren inclined her head as she approached the counter. "Morten, is it not?"

"Indeed it is, my lady." The man smiled, obviously pleased he'd been remembered.

"I'll take one of the special suites for the night, if there's one available."

Morten nodded and picked up the pen. He licked the nib and dunked it into the inkwell. "You're in luck. And for your man?" He began writing in the journal.

"Bring a cot to my rooms for him. I'll not waste coin on him."

Morten paused an instant before resuming his scribing. "Hardly a waste, my lady! When servants are rested, they provide better service."

Ren placed a gold coin on the counter and slid it toward the man. "I need him to wait on me. Take whatever expenses we incur out of this gold talent. I require a hearty meal for myself as well as my man, but only after I bathe. Have hot water brought to my room."

"Our cooks and the dining room eagerly await you," said Morten. "My girl Pris will show you to your rooms, see you settled, and arrange for the water. Please let her know of anything else you require. Pris!"

A bronze-haired, doe-eyed girl appeared from a curtained doorway behind the counter. She already carried bed linens and a bowl filled with nuts and dried fruit. The girl gave Ren a shallow bow, hesitated, then bowed to Tarrik as well. She ducked her head when he grinned at her gesture.

"See Lady Bentina to the Pheasant Suite, Pris. Then fetch her hot water for a bath."

The suite was on the second floor and comprised two large rooms: a bedchamber and what Pris called the "preparation room," which held a copper tub to wash in and a table upon which stood an assortment of jars containing unguents and oils.

Pris left to fetch water while Tarrik placed the gear he carried against one wall. Ren moved to the oversize four-poster bed and tucked her sword beneath the silk covers. She rounded her shoulders and stretched her neck. She didn't speak, and Tarrik was content to let the silence grow.

He took the bottle of spirits from his gear, considered for a moment, then returned it. The drink had diminished rapidly, significantly easing his demon lusts and urges. Best to drink sparingly now until he could find more.

There was a knock at the door.

"Enter," said Ren.

Pris came in, trailed by three boys and four girls carrying buckets of steaming water. They were followed by two young men lugging a wooden cot, a thin mattress, and two blankets. The water carriers dumped their burdens into the tub while the cot was placed against the only spare wall. One of the young men lit an alchemical fire stick and set it to the pile of wood in the fireplace.

All the servants hurried out, leaving only Pris, who lingered close by Tarrik. She smiled at him, and he saw she'd undone the top two buttons of her shirt so it now gaped open. Blood rushed to his groin.

If nothing else, humans were good for sating carnal desires, and Ren hadn't forbidden his coupling.

He saw a faint look of disgust on the sorcerer's face. "That will be all, Pris."

"Yes, my lady." Pris turned to Tarrik and opened her mouth to speak.

"My man has no requirements," said Ren curtly. "We will be down for our meal once I've bathed."

Pris's cheeks grew red, and she hurried out of the room, head down, no doubt thinking Tarrik and Ren were lovers.

She was probably used to trying her charms on lonely nobles staying at the inn, Tarrik thought. Likely she was hoping to get pregnant; giving birth to the child of a noble—even a bastard child—would raise her standing considerably. To his mind it was an abhorrent practice and set Pris little above a broodmare. Still, if Ren let him outside, he would pay her a visit.

"The Demon and Hound . . . which am I?" asked Tarrik rhetorically.

"The hound," answered Ren with a tight-lipped smile. She took a chair and jammed it under the door latch.

"Are we in danger?" Tarrik asked.

"Always. Best you remember that. But be extra vigilant. Something is awry. There is a presence close by, somewhere within the city."

"Samal again? You said you could ward against—"

"I have. It's not Samal." She looked like she would say something else but shook her head. "I will bathe now. You keep guard."

"You bathed earlier, in the stream."

"Cold mountain water only scrubs away the worst of the dirt. Now I want to relax in a hot-water bath."

Tarrik suppressed a shudder. He seldom washed. Water was scarce on Shimrax—indeed, in most of the demon realms. Before his first summons to this world, the most water he'd seen at one time was a trickle of a stream you could step over. To keep his body clean, he was used to scouring his skin with fine sand, then rubbing down with oil, which was scraped off to remove any remaining dirt.

"Forget about Pris," Ren added. "She is not for you. We must do nothing to reveal your true nature."

"I had not thought to touch her," Tarrik lied.

Ren snorted. "Demons hunger, do they not? Without restraint and without scruple."

"The lowest among my kind do—that much is true. I have evolved above such base cravings." The less she knew the better.

"You were one of those lowest once."

Tarrik inclined his head to acknowledge the point. "As you were once a babe—squalling, grasping, hungry for whatever was placed into your mouth. You pissed and shat yourself without care. We, all of us, had such beginnings. Then we outgrew them."

"But not totally. Demons are volatile."

"We feel more deeply than humans do. Some would say that makes us more alive. After all, can one really experience life without strong emotion?"

"Civilized people hold their emotions in check. To let yourself be ruled by animal passions is to surrender to chaos."

"Is it? Must you suppress your anger toward someone who has wronged you? Must you hide your desire from someone you love? A civilization without passion is a dead civilization. It might as well be populated by rocks. The demon realms are not savage—well, not all of them. We are lettered. We enjoy luxuries. We do not condone those who whip others for no reason, who murder, who steal. Those realms are not a lawless place. Transgressors are punished."

The main law, of course, was that the strong ruled the weak and did what they wanted.

"As you were punished. Exiled, I believe?"

"Yes." He was *chiggruul*, an exile.

"For what?"

For being foolish. Weak. For falling in love with a human.

He did not reply, and Ren glanced toward her steaming bath. "Tell me more about your realms."

"No."

"I could compel you."

"You can do whatever you wish to this slave, Master."

"I know this, and yet I will not." Ren paused for a heartbeat. "Tell me of your exile then. Not the why of it, but the effects."

Tarrik reasoned she must know something of the abyssal realms. After all, she had Contian's notes and probably access to knowledge of demons accumulated by sorcerers over the centuries. He couldn't outright lie, and subtle misdirection was risky.

"Shimrax is the least habitable of the realms. It is arid, desolate. But creatures survive there, adapted to the conditions, and demons are able to hunt for food, and for skin, bone, and sinew to make essential items. There is no order there, not like the other realms. A harsh place, and many exiles go mad from despair."

"And when they do?"

"They are killed, or kill themselves."

"It seems I have saved you from an ignominious fate."

A mere delay only. Although there was redemption for exiles—very occasionally the demon lords might grant a reprieve. Tarrik didn't know how he might earn such a thing for himself, but he had to hold tightly to the hope.

"I am a slave. Do not try to justify what you've done."

Ren pursed her lips. "My bath grows cold. Keep watch."

She left him them, entering the preparation room and leaving the door a few hands ajar. Tarrik's pulse pounded in his ears; his vision narrowed. His jaw clenched; he removed the bottle of spirits from his saddlebag and took a long draft. It took a while, and another mouthful of liquor, before his rage subsided.

Faint singing reached him from the preparation room. He couldn't make out the words, only that the tune was slow, deliberate—perhaps a lullaby—and Ren's voice was pleasing.

Tarrik sneered at his weakness. Nothing was pleasing in this world.

He turned away from the open door and busied himself honing his sword in a patch of sunlight shining through the gap in the window curtains. Nicked and rusty, the blade wasn't fit to kill chickens. He'd take Ren up on her offer of new weapons tomorrow.

He kept his eyes on the edge of the blade as Ren strolled back into the room, leaving wet footprints on the wooden floor. The nicks he couldn't do anything about, but the sharpness was almost to his satisfaction. He placed the whetstone against the metal and completed a few more strokes.

"Tarrik. Stand, please."

He looked up. Ren was clothed in a thin robe that clung in patches to her damp frame, leaving only her neck, hands, and feet exposed. She'd used some of the unguents and smelled of lilac and lavender. What he could see of her reddish-brown skin gleamed with fragrant oils, and her long raven hair had been brushed until it gleamed. His lust flared, his heart hammering in his chest.

"Stand," she said again.

Tarrik blinked, wrenched back to reality. He took a few deep breaths, then did as ordered, unsure why she was making such a command. He licked his lips, needing a drink to take the edge off his emotions. Demon slaves had been used sexually before and no doubt would be again. Perhaps that was what she wanted. Unnerved, he tried to think of something to say to break the silence.

"We would have made it to the citadel before dusk," he said.

"I wanted one more night without observant eyes."

He smelled the lie on her; saw her eyes drop, a hand wiped on her robe. Whatever she was up to, he wished she'd get it over with.

Ren remained by the bedside. "In the citadel, you can't so much as piss without someone knowing," she continued. "You are to stay by my side always and in my room when I'm sleeping. Is that understood?"

Tarrik nodded.

"Many people will attempt to question you. Do not tell them anything about me, or about you. State only that you have been hired as my bodyguard and nothing more. You are to pretend you're from the southern lands beyond the Jargalan Mountains, a wild area people here know little about. Do you understand?"

He nodded a second time.

"Do not disappoint me."

"I am bound to obey you. It is hard to disappoint someone in this situation."

"Nevertheless, it has been done."

She knew that her commands could be misinterpreted or circumvented if their wording or her bindings weren't precise. So far, his probing of her bindings hadn't revealed a flaw, and they hadn't been together long enough for him to discover a loophole. But given time, he'd find one.

He thought it wise not to respond. Ren waited for his reply, staring at him with her almost black eyes, which seemed to know his thoughts and plumb his depths. After a long moment, she looked away, frowning. "Please go into the preparation room while I change. Close the door."

Tarrik did as instructed, disappointed she wasn't going to take advantage of him. There was always a chance, in the heat of passion, that her bindings would slip.

They descended the stairs to an eating room. Wood blazed merrily in a stone fireplace. Several tables with chairs were dotted around the room. A woman wearing a gray apron, again with the embroidery Tarrik now realized was supposed to be a demon and dog, came to serve them.

Ren ordered roast chicken and seasonal vegetables, freshly baked bread, and two berry compotes.

Tarrik put away one and a half whole chickens. The birds had more meat on them than those he was used to in his realm. Then again, everything there was harder and tougher, including himself.

The rest of the food tasted alkaline and too sweet and would likely wreak havoc on his insides. But to make him seem more civilized to Ren, he forced himself to eat some of the bread and vegetables, imagining them to be freshly killed human meat. Lesser demons ate only raw flesh, which was why they could be starved and sent after humans.

Ren seemed amused by his unease at the dining table. Her hair hung loose, softening her face and giving it a gentle appearance, almost vulnerable. But he saw that her eyes flicked constantly to the other diners.

As soon as Tarrik stopped eating, she bade him rise, and they returned to the room. Ren jammed the chair underneath the latch again.

"We'll sleep now," she said. "Gods know we need it. Maybe they won't come for me tonight. The innkeeper knows me by a different name, and I'm not generally well-known in these parts."

Tarrik took off his shirt and began unbuttoning his trousers. This was another opportunity to make her uncomfortable, though there was probably no chance she'd reconsider his enslavement.

"Your pleasure is also my duty," he said. "I will do such things to you as you never—"

"Cease your disgusting talk."

Tarrik felt her bindings constrict around him, forcing him to leave his trousers half undone.

"I rarely dally with men—their touch is seldom as gentle and knowing. And never with demons. Dress yourself, and go to sleep. You *will* obey me."

As the bindings eased, Tarrik turned away and prepared for bed. He left his sword unsheathed on the floor beside him and made sure the blankets wouldn't tangle him if he had to rise swiftly in case of trouble.

He turned to face the wall and tried not to hear the sounds of Ren undressing. Her scent lingered in the air—an expensive fragrance of cinnamon and vanilla. Tarrik wondered if her dreams would again be invaded by Samal and if he could then learn something to use against Ren.

Later, he rolled over to find a more comfortable position. Through half-lidded eyes he saw Ren sitting on her bed, robed, her back to the headrest, knees drawn up. Her eyes were unfocused, as if she were lost in thought, and her teeth worried at the knuckle of the middle finger of her right hand.

Eventually, she lay down, and soon her breathing steadied. Tarrik decided she'd fallen into sleep. He was about to close his eyes when the hairs on his arms stood on end. The scent of sunbaked rock reached his nostrils.

He rolled off his bed and grabbed his sword. Crouching low in a fighting stance, blade held before him, he searched the room, ears pricked for any sound.

Nothing. Just the wind outside. Faintly creaking timbers.

Tarrik remained still, barely breathing. His eyes flicked to Ren. She was asleep, her wards undisturbed.

In a corner a hint of movement, as if the shadows roiled. Between one breath and the next, they somehow took on weight and became solid.

Tarrik took a few steps forward, interposing himself between the shadows and Ren. He wished he could use his shadow-blade, but preferred to keep it from Ren's knowledge for as long as possible.

The shadows flowed like liquid to reveal a humanoid shape . . . a creature such as he'd never seen before. It looked somewhat like a dead-eye, with spindly limbs protruding from an emaciated body. But instead of the usual milk-pale skin, the being was mottled and dark gray, its fingers ending in sharp black talons. The creature blinked rapidly, shaking its head as if dazed.

Then it opened its fanged, lipless mouth and keened—a piercing wail that vibrated Tarrik's bones. The air behind him hummed as Ren's wards erupted. A sphere of energy surrounded her before she leaped off the bed and pressed against the wall.

He rushed forward and lunged with his blade, snake quick, but the thing was no longer in front of him. His sword passed through thin air.

The creature was beside him, its claws ripping at his flesh, scoring long gashes across his arms. Tarrik dropped his blade and grabbed its wrists, twisting, but barely managed to turn them away. The creature fought with immense strength, far greater than a human's.

Tarrik tangled his leg with its leg, twisted, and deliberately fell. They landed with a heavy thump, Tarrik atop the monster. A purple tongue like a serpent's flicked through the gash of its fanged mouth.

Ren shouted cants. Scintillating lines of power streaked past Tarrik but somehow *bent* around the creature. They scored across the floor instead, carving charred lines and slicing timbers. Ren's words became curses.

The creature's talons gashed Tarrik as they wrestled, each attempting to gain an advantage in the thrashing of limbs and slick skin.

Savage snarls escaped the beast as they fought. Its elbows hammered into Tarrik's head. Its fists pounded his torso, yet all the while Tarrik warded off the sharp talons. His blood greased his arms, lending him some advantage. The creature might match his strength and speed, but Tarrik had a master's knowledge of fighting barehanded. He evaded each move and managed to land a few blows that caused it to stagger and grunt in pain.

The creature retaliated with a blow that rocked Tarrik's head. His vision blurred, his breath rasping in his throat. They crashed into a

Shadow of the Exile

table, which toppled over, and Tarrik glimpsed Ren standing to one side, a candelabrum clutched in both hands.

As they writhed and hammered at each other with knees and fists, Tarrik managed to wriggle away from the creature's sweaty grasp. He wrenched its arm behind its back, wrist clasped in an irresistible vice. The creature struggled, tried to rake Tarrik's legs with its talons. He kicked its knee, and there was a muffled crack. He yanked its arm. Another crack followed.

The creature convulsed and thrashed as Tarrik dropped the now useless arm and clasped the other. Ruthlessly, he broke it too. Animal gasps and roars of pain came from beneath him. The creature screamed in agony, its arms flopping grotesquely.

Tarrik seized its throat with both hands and squeezed. Eventually the struggle lessened, then ceased. For good measure, Tarrik slammed its head into the floor. When there was no reaction, he tossed the corpse aside and stood. The slashed flesh of his arms burned with agony, and his purple blood made a pattering sound as it dripped to the floor. His head ached. He reached up and realized his scalp had split, and more blood was trickling down his neck and back. His entire body dripped with sweat.

Ren regarded him without expression.

"What was it?" Tarrik said.

The room was moving. He staggered to his bed and sat. Shouts came from outside the room, and fists hammered on their door.

"A type of dead-eye, rarely seen. It moved through my wards without disturbing them." She glanced at the ruckus coming from the door but didn't move.

"Why didn't you use your sword?" He blinked sweat from his eyes and tried to focus, but his mind kept wandering. He should pick up his own sword. He should bind his wounds.

"Because it's not designed for physical foes."

Tarrik tried to move, but his arms were weak. The room tilted at an angle, became darker.

"What . . . ," he managed to croak before the shadows swallowed him.

Tarrik woke to burning arms and a foul taste in his mouth. He glanced down and saw the gashes were now only thin scars, his blood washed away. He'd been healed somehow, though the wounds still ached. He touched his head; his hair was damp, but there were no signs of injury. Still, his eyes ached, and his mind was cloudy with exhaustion.

Ren sat cross-legged on her bed, her dark eyes watching him. Stars glittered outside the window, and he guessed he'd only been unconscious a short while. All signs of the fight had been cleaned up: no broken furniture, and the floor was spotless.

"Did you do this?" he asked her. "How?"

"No more questions. You were injured, and I still need you."

No human sorcery could heal like this—Tarrik knew that from Contian. The only way to heal was through the gift of a god's power. And he highly doubted that Ren, one of the Nine and a demon worshiper, was favored by any such deity.

What was she? And what had happened to the creature he'd killed?

Ren noticed him looking around. "I arranged for the dead-eye to be removed and burned, though I expect they'll sell its corpse for a few coins instead. There are necromancers and other dabblers who'd pay good money to dissect it."

"Who sent it? I sensed dark-tide sorcery."

"And that makes you think it was a demon? What I do know is that a great deal of energy was used to take control of the creature and send it here. Wasted energy. It will not happen again—that I can guarantee. And that's all you need to know. Go back to sleep."

Tarrik doubted she could guarantee anything.

Chapter Four

As was his custom, Tarrik woke well before dawn, even though he was tired and sore. He'd been in this world for days now, and his internal sense of time had adjusted. Dawn and dusk were prime hunting times in the abyssal realms, and only a fool would remain asleep then. Fools and prey. His thoughts turned to the attack in the night and who might have sent the creature. Was it the same person who'd sent the mercenaries and the sorcerer and marfesh after Ren? Or a more powerful enemy?

His arms still amazed him, and he examined the scars, which looked like they were months old. He dressed himself swiftly as Ren stirred. She rubbed heavy-lidded eyes, and again the bloodied knuckle of her right hand caught his attention. It looked worse than before. No wonder she was worrying her finger raw, after being set upon twice by entities while she was asleep.

He secluded himself in the preparation room while she garbed herself. When she gave him permission to return, he was surprised to see her wearing severe clothes that looked almost uniform-like. He also realized why Ren had suggested dark material to the tailor: so it would match her formal garb.

She wore black leather boots with silver side buttons underneath a slim charcoal skirt and short coat, with a silver-buckled and silver-studded belt. The only color was the deep crimson of her silk shirt. Her hair was simply braided, but already a few strands escaped.

Her sword was strapped to her back, and she'd pinned to her breast two brooches fashioned from orichalcum: one, a nine-pointed star; the other, a square face divided into four smaller squares, each containing a rune. Only a sorcerer would wear such rare artifacts in the street. The metal alone was worth a fortune, and even a veteran warrior would have to worry about arrows and bolts. And you couldn't dodge those if they came from behind. Neither could a sorcerer raise a shield against what was unseen . . . he would keep that in mind.

The nine-pointed star had to signify the Nine, the sorcerers who served the demon lord Samal Rak-shazza. They would surely know each other, so the brooch must be to identify them to outsiders. The four squares and runes . . . had they something to do with the Tainted Cabal?

"Gather our gear," Ren said. "Let us be gone."

When Morten saw Ren enter the reception hall, his mouth opened, and a croak came out. Pris, who had been about to disappear behind the curtain with dirty glasses, gasped and dropped one. It shattered on the floor, and all four denizens of the inn froze.

Tarrik noted a grim smile on Ren's lips as the two others recognized her as a Tainted Cabalist.

"Uh . . . Lady Bentina, we, uh, I, had no idea." Morten bobbed his head like a bird pecking for seed while Pris backed through the curtain. "There were better rooms available. If you'd said—" He clapped a hand to his mouth, realizing he'd admitted to renting her a substandard room at top price.

"If I'd wanted you to know, I would have told you," Ren said. "I prefer privacy. We will not require a morning meal, and we're leaving now. No change from the gold talent is necessary because of the disturbance last night."

"Yes. Of course. I mean . . . thank you."

Ren left the man standing there, mouth open like a fish. Outside, the two stable hands rushed to prepare the duo's horses. Tarrik heard them whispering urgently to each other and to the older hands inside the stable. A short while later the animals were saddled and led out.

After mounting, Ren fished out a copper talent and flicked it to the boy and girl. They let the coin clink to the pavers without any attempt to catch it.

"We're sorry," the girl mumbled. "We can't take coins from Cabalists. We didn't know yesterday. We'll give it back."

"Nonsense," snapped Ren. "Work done well must be rewarded. Pick it up, and spend it wisely. Or unwisely."

She tugged her reins hard, turning her horse to the right and heading toward the citadel. By her scowl and the sour, tart scent of her sweat, Tarrik guessed she was angry and upset, but he couldn't work out why.

On the corner where the blossom-lined street met a wider avenue, a scaffold had been constructed. Three bodies swung there, hanged by the neck: two women and a man, tongues lolling, bulging eyes partially devoured by birds. Next to them, two iron cages held a pile of rags and bones from which hung dried flesh. Tarrik couldn't discern if the bodies had been male or female.

"Wrongdoers," said Ren flatly. "The Tainted Cabal is strong here, unlike on the eastern continent across the Simorga Sea. Their thoughts have turned from mere survival to shaping an empire. Progress requires sacrifice, order."

Tarrik knew all too well what she meant. To build an empire required more than sacrifice. There needed to be laws, and warriors to enforce those laws. People would suffer, though many wouldn't know a better way. "Wrongdoers" were made an example of. What better way to deter criminals or potential rebels than showing them someone they knew dancing at the end of a hangman's rope, face purpling, defecating as they died.

On the other side of the scaffold stood a squad of soldiers wearing black enameled breastplates and vambraces, their wary eyes taking in everyone who passed. People averted their gazes and hurried their steps.

The soldiers wore open-faced helms, but their lower faces were covered with masks of black leather, leaving only the eyes clear, and their armor showed the same four squares as Ren's brooch, stenciled in gold paint. Stamped on both sides of their helms and shoulder pauldrons were a runic numeral and a bird. Since most of the soldiers bore the ancient Skanuric rune for "one," Tarrik assumed the marks were signs of rank.

They were armed with long spears, bucklers, and short swords. But from the way they handled the spears, he thought they probably knew how not to trip over them and not much more. His hands ached for the grip of a well-made spear rather than his pigsticker.

More soldiers filed past two by two, twenty-four of them in total, heads held high, eyes arrogant, faces masked. One of them noticed Ren and barked a command. As one, they raised their fists to strike their chest plates over the heart.

Ren inclined her head, then urged her horse forward, and soon she and Tarrik left the intersection behind. Curious glances followed them, and more than a few startled, fear-filled looks. Tarrik could smell the emotions of the people around them on the light breeze: fear and anger, distrust and envy. He surmised that the Tainted Cabal wasn't entirely welcome here in Ivrian.

The citadel grew until it blotted out the sky before them: a massive edifice built from seamed basalt. The blacks and grays of the stone seemed to draw in the sunlight, to suck the very heat from the day. Even here in the well-to-do section of the city, beggars and street rats hid in the narrow side alleys, reaching out importuning hands, croaking and moaning, then shrinking back into the shadows at the first sign of a black-masked soldier.

Two square towers stood on either side of a barbican, adorned with gold and crimson flags featuring four joined squares, much like Ren's brooch and the soldiers' armor. Above the barbican was a pennant showing a red eagle on white; the guards stationed beside the gate and on the tower battlements wore surcoats with the same symbol. Tarrik guessed it was the sign of the ruler of Ivrian, or the city itself.

Ren rode through the gate without stopping. The guards shuffled their feet uneasily, and one broke ranks for half a step before thinking better of it. Tarrik would have had them all flogged bloody if they were under his command. Letting a stranger through without challenge. Disgraceful.

Inside the gate was a vast area of basalt pavers. Soldiers drilled to the left, around fifty of them, their spear work sloppy. To the right, a procession of wagons and carts lined up at a wide doorway, and heavily muscled workers unloaded barrels and crates. Directly ahead was a pair of massive iron-banded timber doors, which stood open.

Ren rode straight for them, and this time two of eight guards stepped forward to intercept her. "Halt!" They and their companions eyed Tarrik and Ren uneasily, their white-knuckled hands clenching their spears.

Ren dismounted and beckoned to two stable hands—a brown-haired boy and a blonde girl, both with hay in their hair—waiting on the right. Tarrik saw behind them a corral that contained three saddled mounts and multiple doorways from which exuded the stench of horses and their excrement. Tarrik was only too glad to leave the foul-smelling beast and feel solid ground beneath him.

"I am Lady Branwen of the Nine," Ren said. "I am not expected. Send word to the commander here and whoever else requires notifying."

A guard stepped forward, wisps of sandy beard escaping the sides of his mask. "My lady, if you will wait outside, I'll send word to the commander. Is there anyone who can vouch for your identity?"

"There is not. And I prefer to wait inside. We will require refreshments."

"I am under orders to—"

Ren stamped a foot. Thunder cracked like a thousand whips, and dust swirled in a sudden gust of air that rustled their clothes. The guards shielded their eyes, blinking at the irritation. The wind died as abruptly as it had come, but a web of cracks emanated from Ren across the pavers.

"I will wait inside and will require refreshments," she repeated.

The bearded guard licked his lips and bowed. "Yes, my lady."

Another guard rushed off, presumably to take word to the commander, while three others led Ren and Tarrik inside. The two walked past paneled walls and elaborate doors set in metal frames and many wide, spiraling staircases. Servants bustled everywhere, some cleaning, some carrying linen. Many avoided the newest guests, stopping and retreating, or kept their heads lowered, eyes on the floor.

Sorcerer and demon entered a room furnished with velvet lounges and low tables. A girl dressed in a simple smock hurriedly set out trays of fruit and nuts and a crystal carafe of red wine before bowing her way out backward. The three guards remained, standing at attention by the only door. Tarrik noted there were no windows. Illumination was provided by alchemical globes set into iron sconces, which gave off a soft yellow light. Murals of hunting scenes covered the walls. Animals Tarrik barely recognized tore at each other with tooth and claw, while humans on horseback shot arrows into the fiercest-looking creatures and held up severed heads dripping gore as trophies.

He left Ren picking at the fruit and positioned himself between her and the guards, his back to a wall, hand resting on the pommel of his pigsticker. She seemed at ease, but that could be a facade.

All three guards looked professional enough, though from the way he'd seen the other soldiers handling the spears, they were probably incompetent. Armies focused on working together, not as individuals, which was a weakness in certain situations—like this one.

In his mind, he rehearsed his first moves against them if it came down to violence. Limbs severed, blood splashing across the—

He heard a firm knock on the door. A woman walked in dressed in a tight-fitting shirt and skirt of scarlet, with a Tainted Cabal brooch similar to Ren's pinned next to her heart, though hers was crafted from silver. Her artfully curled brown hair appeared artificial and dull next to Ren's long black braid.

She took a few steps toward Ren, then stopped and bowed as Tarrik moved to intercept her. The woman leaned to the left and smiled past him. "My lady, your presence is required."

"Where?" asked Ren.

"The commander's hall. Alone, my lady."

"My man follows where I go. No exceptions."

"I . . ." The woman frowned, looking from Ren to Tarrik and back again.

"Lead on," said Ren. She plucked an apricot from a bowl and strode toward the door. Tarrik moved to shadow her.

In the paneled hallway, the woman gave them a wan smile and led them farther into the citadel. Behind them, the three masked guards followed.

The stone floor underfoot was old, showing indentations from centuries of traffic. Some sections were carpeted with rugs, many of them faded and threadbare.

Ren slowed slightly to bite into her apricot and made to touch Tarrik's arm to gain his attention. He jerked aside.

Ren blinked, then whispered, "Guard your words, and make no rash actions unless I'm threatened."

He nodded, torn between wanting her threatened and the knowledge it would place him in danger.

They picked up their pace to close with the woman. As they passed a potted plant, Ren placed her apricot seed onto the soil at its base.

They ascended a wide marble staircase that wound from the first floor to the third without leading onto the second. At the end of another corridor, the woman led them into a hall. Floor-to-ceiling windows covered one wall, and Tarrik had to squint to allow his eyes to adjust to the bright light let in. The floor was white marble, and three massive chandeliers hung from chains, their oil lamps unlit.

Guards were stationed along the wall opposite the windows—at least a dozen. A few clutches of men and women milled about, all garbed in shining silks and brocaded velvets. Some elderly and frail-looking humans sat at tables along with clusters of what looked to be nobles and merchants and high-ranking officials. And in a chair on a crescent dais above them—more like a throne—was a man who could only be the commander.

His brown hair was cut short but still in need of tidying, and above lips like sausages, his watery eyes gazed at Tarrik and Ren with a predatory gleam. He could be younger than Ren, though Tarrik wasn't sure. His clothes were expensive, with gold trim on his boots, sleeves, and collar, though the patterned scarf around his neck was faded. A jeweled dagger and sword hung from his belt, the gaudy decorations impractical and pitiful. To Tarrik, he reeked of sour piss and wine. And fear.

To either side of him stood a plain-robed man with a short beard. Both had talismans hanging from their belts—focus and calculation aids that marked them as sorcerers.

The commander stood, one hand on the arm of his chair for support. "I am Commander Veljor, lord of Ivrian, warlord of the Sixth Army of the Tainted Cabal, conqueror of the Plains of Khisig-Utgall."

Ren stepped forward. "Heavy titles indeed. I am Lady Branwen of the Nine."

The words were softly spoken, but they caused the buzz of conversation to die. The two sorcerers clutched their talismans.

Veljor smiled faintly, an amused grin that puzzled Tarrik.

Two servants brought forward a padded chair and placed it ten paces from the dais, its wooden legs squeaking on the marble. The commander gestured to Ren to sit.

Ren released the hook that secured her orichalcum sword to her back and let the blade slide to her hip, then positioned it at her side as she perched on the edge of the chair. Veljor could not hide the covetous look he gave the weapon.

Tarrik felt Ren's bindings constrict, forcing him to protect her. He stepped to the left and slightly behind her, where he could draw easily and step in front to intercept an attack if need be. She needn't have bothered, for he was on high alert. This place felt like a den of marfesh. He loosened his shoulders.

"Your man makes no obeisance," said Veljor.

Ren tilted her head, regarding the commander. "He holds no allegiance, except to me."

Veljor wrinkled his nose, as if talking of servants was distasteful. "I am intrigued you are here, Lady Branwen. I must admit, when word was first brought to me, I was skeptical. Another of the Nine in our city. But my sorcerers confirmed it was you after your little display. If you'd sent word of your arrival, such disruptions would not be necessary."

Tarrik saw Ren stiffen for an instant before she affected disinterest. "I find I receive a more honest reception this way."

Veljor sat in his chair, leaned back a little, and frowned. "Word of the Nine is sketchy, if you'll forgive my honesty. We follow the Tainted Cabal. They have proven their worth as allies and instructors in many things. But the Nine . . . rumors of your power precede you, though little is known of what you actually do."

Veljor's sorcerers remained focused on Ren, nervously touching their talismans. They looked like dogs set to guard a lion.

"We are still a part of the Cabal," Ren said. "Have no fear. I am here to gather information and to locate and study artifacts from the ancient ruins. It is both my hobby and my calling. Ivrian seems a good place to start my exploration of the western continent."

"You don't find it interesting that another of the Nine is here?"

"We do not keep tabs on one another. Our purpose is clear, and each of us works toward the greater glory of Nysrog and the Tainted Cabal."

"All praise Nysrog, the Deliverer, Reaper of Men, First among Demons, and Unchainer of Souls," said Veljor.

"May he channel our desires," intoned Ren.

The words skittered up Tarrik's spine. The Cabalists apparently followed Nysrog because they wanted him to amplify and focus their atavistic urges. Such devotion was anathema in the demon realms and a sign of just how far Nysrog had descended into madness. It was a constant battle not to lose total control, to surrender to your emotions and lusts, and even the greatest of demons sometimes failed.

"You will join us for dinner tonight," Veljor said. His words weren't a request.

Ren smiled. "I am honored, Commander Veljor. My man and I will attend."

"It will be an intimate gathering. I don't think—"

"He will accompany me."

Her tone was like ice, and Veljor flinched. He coughed into his hand to cover his reaction before returning Ren's smile.

Tarrik smelled the hate emanating from him and suddenly feared for himself in this place where everyone and everything were unknown.

"You will tell me more of your purpose at dinner," said Veljor. "Until then you may have the run of the common areas of the citadel."

"We are still tired from our journey," Ren told him. "We will retire to the rooms you provide for us and join you this evening at any hour you require."

Veljor pouted, his sausage lips making the expression ludicrous. Tarrik noted the conversational din that had subsided earlier hadn't returned. He glanced to the sides of the room and saw that everyone was fixated on the dialogue between Ren and Veljor. Something was off.

"Very well," the commander said. "Is there anything else you need?"

"My man here wishes for a weapon. His broke when fighting off bandits, and he's had to make do with a commoner's sword since."

Veljor looked behind them to where the woman who'd led them from the reception room stood quietly. "Caterine will see to your needs—won't you, my dear?"

"Yes, my lord." She curtsied low.

Veljor stood and bowed to Ren. She rose and did the same.

Veljor's eyes flicked to Tarrik, who again made no obeisance. The commander's jaw clenched. A small man with no honor, enraged at not receiving what he perceived as his due.

It was only after they'd left the hall that Tarrik realized Veljor did not wear the symbol of the Tainted Cabal.

The servant, Caterine, led the pair along more paneled hallways and down wide spiraling staircases. Uneasy after their encounter with Veljor, Tarrik walked at a proper distance behind Ren, two paces. Close enough to barrel her out of danger or pull her behind him, and far enough to draw his knife without impediment.

They emerged into a courtyard of packed earth, dustier and dirtier than any place inside the citadel they'd seen so far. Fire-hardened ceramic pipes descended the walls to deposit their water into rain barrels and troughs, and wooden training dummies dotted the area. At intervals around the yard, stands held staves, spears, wooden practice swords, and a few steel weapons. A dozen or so soldiers trained with swords and spears, and these caught Tarrik's eye, along with the ferocious clatter of their weapons. They were stripped to the waist and moved more swiftly and precisely than the common guards, which betokened greater skill and long hours of training.

Caterine beckoned her guests through wide doors into a large room. Heat, fumes, and the clanging of metal came from forges to their left, where solid men wearing thick leather aprons and gloves pounded steel and stoked furnaces.

Caterine waited, hands clasped in front of her, until one man, shorter than the others, removed his gloves and approached. His face was covered with a bristly gray beard, his forearms scarred from cuts and burns, and a jagged, hair-free seam ran from his jaw up to an ear. He glanced at Tarrik, then at Ren, and finally at Caterine.

"Suppose you're here for a weapon?" he said in a deep voice.

Caterine nodded. "Commander Veljor would like a sword for—"

"No sword," Tarrik said, unbuckling his weapon belt. "A spear. A good one. This pigsticker can go to someone better suited to it than I." He tossed the sword aside, and it thudded onto the dirt.

The blacksmith's eyes narrowed, and a callused hand came up to stroke his beard. "An easy weapon to learn but a hard one to master. Right then. This way."

He led them deeper inside the room and unlocked one of five large iron-banded doors. Inside were long fighting weapons of all kinds, leaning against walls and stacked in barrels, with a few mounted to the wall. Most looked to be the same as the spears the soldiers outside used: heavy hafted with short tips. But there were also pole arms, lances, and javelins, and some elaborately bladed monstrosities.

Tarrik moved aside a forest of spears and shook his head. Nothing. Most were too heavy to be effective. He might as well go back to using the pigsticker.

Then a six-foot haft mounted above his head caught his eye. It was thinner than the others, easier to handle, and made of solid blackwood, smooth and polished, as if it had seen much use. The tip was a good foot and a half long, and flat metal wings jutted from where it joined the shaft—three fingers wide each, enough to deflect blades and useful for a myriad of other purposes. He wasn't likely to find a better spear unless he had one custom made, and that was improbable.

"This one," he said, and reached up to take the weapon down. The spear was heavier than he'd expected.

"You've a good eye," rumbled the blacksmith. "That's been gathering dust for years. The common soldiers prefer a heavier shaft, while the senior officers favor swords. The last man to use it was quite the legend. It's said he slew dead-eyes by the hundreds, ghouls by the score, and even a few wraithes."

"Not a soldier then?" said Ren.

The implication was that only a sorcerer, one of great power, could stand against a wraithe. Tarrik recalled Contian explaining they were one of the elder races of this world, possessing eldritch powers normal humans couldn't hope to match.

"No," the blacksmith agreed. He turned back to Tarrik. "If you've chosen, I'll get back to the forge. If I don't keep an eye on my workers, the swords will be crooked and the horseshoes straight."

Tarrik hefted the spear and transferred it from hand to hand, feeling the wood, the balance, the sheer brutality of the thing. It was a weapon made for an expert, hidden away under the dust in a storeroom. The cumbersome spears of the soldiers paled into insignificance by comparison. And the blackwood was as hard as steel, known to dampen sorcerous abilities and emanations.

That gave him pause. Would Ren allow him to keep it?

"You can use it," she said, as if reading his mind. Her message was clear: the blackwood wouldn't interfere with her arcane bindings of him. "Perhaps the story of the previous owner killing wraithes with the spear isn't so far-fetched."

The infantrymen were still practicing in the courtyard. An addition to the group drew Tarrik's attention: a lanky soldier lounging against one of the rain barrels. He was garbed like the others with black leather armor and vambraces and the same helm with a mask over his lower face, leaving his eyes clear. He sauntered toward Tarrik and Ren with a dangerous grace. He was a good head taller than the other soldiers, though still shorter than Tarrik.

Tarrik could have sworn he heard Caterine mutter "Shit" under her breath. She angled them toward a side door out of the courtyard, but the soldier intercepted them.

"I see we have some new arrivals," he bellowed, and Tarrik imagined the false smile beneath the mask.

The man's armor was polished and scuff-free, and a longer-than-usual sword swung from his hip. Tarrik smelled arrogance and violence emanating from him. He stepped between the soldier and Ren and saw her nod briefly in response. Commander Veljor had sent someone to test Tarrik and presumably injure him as payback for his failure to abase himself sufficiently.

Truly, humans were savages.

The soldier would be a blades man without peer and ordered to make a show of their fight before bringing it to an abrupt conclusion with a sliced hamstring for Tarrik, or perhaps a blade through his forearm or even his heart. Already, the other soldiers in the courtyard had stopped their sparring and gathered into small groups. Coins were exchanged along with urgent whispers.

Caterine held both hands out in front of her as if to push the soldier away. "Captain Albin, these are Commander Veljor's honored guests. They are weary and on their way to their rooms—"

"Come now," interrupted Albin. "It looks like this man has a new weapon he'd like to test. From the looks of it, it's been gathering dust with the other rejects for some time."

He glared at Tarrik, as if expecting an immediate reaction to his attempted insult. Tarrik remained silent and leaned on the shaft of his newly acquired spear. He glanced at Ren, and the sorcerer looked away.

Blood and fire. Fighting when there was no need was a waste of energy, but without Ren's intervention, he couldn't see another way out of the situation. She would want him to win, to teach Veljor a lesson. And she seemed curiously confident he wouldn't lose.

"Big fellow, aren't you?" Albin said. "Muscles slow you down, make you easy pickings. Then it's like carving a roast!" He laughed too loudly, and the soldiers around them joined in.

When Tarrik didn't respond, he added, "Don't speak much. Do you speak at all?"

"When words are required." An image of punching the pompous fool in the face and a flash of his uncontrolled empathy hit Tarrik: Albin crouched over the insensate form of a woman, one hand stealing her purse while the other groped under her skirt. "You have the soiled mind and heart of a thief and a molester. You are a broken man."

Albin's face darkened. "I take it you don't get your wick wet much, standing silent or speaking nonsense wherever you go. No wonder you're so uptight. Women are wooed with words, isn't that right, Caterine?"

"It depends which hole you're talking out of," the servant said curtly.

Albin's eyes bored into Caterine's, and she looked away, her hands gripping her dress.

Albin turned back to Tarrik. "What say you to a sparring match? Your spear against my sword. A little fun to keep us sharp and to impress the ladies."

"I agree," Tarrik said.

Albin blinked, clearly not having expected so ready a response. He turned to the gathering crowd, which now included servants who'd been passing by. Young men and women watched from windows around the courtyard. Word had spread quickly of Veljor's plan, it seemed.

"Clear a space!" shouted Albin. "You'll get to see why spears are for peasants and swords are for noble warriors!"

Cheers rose at his words. More coins changed hands among the soldiers and the servants.

Albin stripped off his armor, revealing a bronzed, chiseled torso that drew the eye of almost every woman and man there. He removed his helmet and face mask, showing a strong, clean-shaven chin and thin lips.

Tarrik looked around for somewhere to place his just-purchased coat and shirt. He didn't want them to get dirty.

"I'll hold your clothes," said Ren. "Make this quick."

She held his spear too while he unbuttoned and removed his coat and shirt. A murmur ran through the crowd when he turned to face them. His silver-gray skin, lined with sinew and striated muscle, was a stark contrast to Albin's brown skin and well-defined form.

A hand touched his arm, and he jerked away. Caterine. She swallowed, and her eyes flicked to Albin. "Beware of his speed," she whispered, and moved aside.

"You must be a savage from the far south," exclaimed Albin. "Or a filthy San-Kharr. Only they have gray skin." He raised his voice as he drew a thick leather glove over his left hand. "We have a wild man here, from the dangerous south. An animal not fit to be among us."

The hubbub rose in volume as the crowd finally realized what was happening. Albin had been sent to teach a lesson to the outsiders. Some cursed their initial wagers, and frantic negotiations of new ones ensued. Tarrik saw men indicating thighs and throats, betting where he would be injured first.

He stepped into a clear space, his spear in the crook of his arm. The crowd had spread into a loose circle around the edges of the courtyard, giving the two combatants ample room to fight.

"Aren't you going to use one of those wooden practice swords? And I'll swap for a blunt spear." He knew the answer already, but wanted to reinforce to those watching that this fight wasn't his idea.

"My good man, the time for negotiating the terms of our bout was when you agreed to it. It's too late now to wriggle out of it like the coward you are."

Tarrik stretched his neck to relax it. "What are the rules then?"

"No rules were stated. It is usual for the man who strikes first blood to be announced the winner."

Tarrik nodded. This whole thing was a farce, and the sooner it was over, the better.

Albin drew his sword, showing a polished blade a hand longer than usual. He waved it back and forth and squatted a few times to loosen up.

Tarrik remained still, his hands clenched around the black shaft of the spear. He hadn't taken a drink this morning to deaden his emotions, and now he was glad. His anger rose. This time he encouraged its hot caress. The swordsman was an arrogant fool, a tool to be used and discarded by his lord, though he knew it not.

The same, then, as Tarrik. The realization struck him to his core. His stomach felt leaden for a moment until his mounting rage scoured the sensation away.

"Are you ready?" said Albin. "I wouldn't want to be accused of having an unfair advantage."

Laughter erupted. The crowd thought the arrogant puppet already had the bout won.

Tarrik nodded and widened his stance. His heart pounded like the hammers in the forge. Blood coursed through his veins. This *human* dared to fight him, to appease his bloodthirsty jackal of a lord.

Albin rushed at Tarrik and leaped forward, his sword extending in the blink of an eye. Tarrik pivoted and struck the weapon aside, then again as Albin followed with another attack. The man's reach was extraordinary. Coupling that with the longer blade and his swiftness, he must have ended many a fight in the first few moments.

As Tarrik jumped backward, he slid his hands along the shaft and brought the spear swinging around. Albin sprang back to avoid the hissing blade and again as Tarrik made another circle with the spear. The weapon felt good in his hands. Far more natural to him than a sword.

He admonished himself for getting carried away. Showmanship wasn't for hardened warriors.

He thrust at Albin again and again, and each time the swordsman dodged or parried the spear. Tarrik kept at it, not giving the man any respite. Thrust. Thrust. Thrust.

Frustrated, Albin tried to beat the spear down and trap it under his sword so he could step inside Tarrik's reach. Tarrik twisted the haft and jerked the tip's wings, dragging Albin's blade to the side, and the swordsman almost lost his grip.

Albin leaped backward, waving his sword in a flourish as if all was going to his design. His face, however, was contorted with anger.

He backpedaled, and Tarrik let him. The swordsman remained out of range, breathing through his nose, then turned his back on Tarrik to address the crowd. Perhaps he was counting on them to warn him, and on his own speed, if Tarrik should launch an attack.

"Such a show you will see!" he shouted. "This barbarian faces the best Ivrian has to offer. And he will be found wanting!"

Savage roars and cheers followed the idiot's speech. Tarrik should have sliced his hamstring or stabbed him through the back. No rules meant no rules, though he was sure the crowd wouldn't see it that way.

Albin turned back to face Tarrik, who jumped forward and thrust his spear two-handed at the man. Albin smacked it away with his sword, once, twice, a third time. As he parried the last attack, he danced forward inside Tarrik's guard and grabbed his own blade with his gloved hand, driving it against the spear shaft. Tarrik spun to disengage, but Albin was too quick, his half-sword grip giving the blade a speed and weight it wouldn't normally have.

Albin shoved the spear aside and sliced his blade toward Tarrik's stomach. Tarrik planted the butt of the spear in the ground, twisted, and vaulted into the air, using the shaft as a pole to spin him away from Albin and his blade.

He released one hand and whirled the shaft in a wide loop to keep his opponent at bay. Albin grinned as he backed up a few steps, letting the spear whistle past harmlessly. His chest was sheened with sweat, and his smile wasn't as confident as before.

He turned to the crowd again, and Tarrik rolled his eyes. "Nobility against savagery!" crowed Albin. "He doesn't even fight with style! Poke, poke, poke, like he's in the bedroom!"

Tarrik looked at Ren. She raised a fist with an outstretched thumb and traced a line across her throat. *So be it.*

Tarrik focused his anger, using it to quash any misgivings about his next move.

"A blade master's weapon against a peasant's spear!" shouted Albin.

Tarrik hefted his spear and cast it with all his might. It hammered through Albin's back and penetrated up to the side wings of his blade.

The crowd cried out in horror as Albin staggered a few steps, his sword falling from nerveless fingers. He tipped forward and smacked face-first into the packed earth. One leg twitched as the last of his life left him. The spear stood straight up in his back like a flagpole, moving back and forth slightly.

Tarrik's heart swelled to bursting. Another of this slaver race dead! His blood roared like a pounding waterfall in his ears. He wanted to tear out the man's liver and eat it raw.

A moment's stunned silence erupted into anger and threats. Hands reached not for coins wagered but for weapons.

A boom of thunder ripped through the air, and a tumultuous wind sent dust swirling. Men and women covered their eyes and ducked their heads, their clothes flapping. A low hum vibrated Tarrik's eardrums, and a circular wall of crimson and violet sprang up around him.

"Enough!" shouted Ren, her voice amplified, resonating like a lion's roar. "There were no rules specified! Let this be a lesson for all. There is always someone more skilled, a better warrior. And never turn your back on an opponent."

She nodded to Tarrik, and he walked toward Albin through air made thick with hatred and disgust. With a jerk he tugged his spear free, then looked at the crowd, meeting as many eyes as he could. Did they think this was a game?

He thrust the spear downward. Albin's corpse shuddered as his spine was severed. Tarrik stabbed again, twisting the tip to horrified gasps. He yanked the blade out, and scarlet dripped across the dirt. He decided not to spit on Albin's corpse or wipe his spear tip on him, in case such gestures sent the crowd into an uncontrollable frenzy.

What would Ren do then? Would she char their flesh and bones to ash?

When the sorcerous shield dissipated, Tarrik moved back to stand with Ren and Caterine. Blood pounded in his ears, in his groin.

The servant's face was as white as bleached bone, her mouth twisted as if she'd swallowed something unpalatable.

"That was ill done," she said.

"He was a fool," replied Ren.

"He didn't deserve to die."

"And my man did? Albin would have killed him, and for what? Because Veljor felt slighted?"

Caterine schooled her expression into blankness, smoothed her skirt with her hands. "Commander Veljor would do no such thing. Captain Albin acted of his own accord."

"Of course. Let us go, before the situation becomes untenable."

Hisses and shouts followed the trio as Caterine took demon and sorcerer through an exit and along more paneled corridors and wide stairways. Eventually they came to a door with two guards stationed outside. Tarrik reckoned they'd circled back in the citadel and were somewhere close to Veljor's hall.

"Your rooms," said Caterine. "I hope they are satisfactory."

The suite comprised four rooms: a vast reception space with couches, padded armchairs, and side tables holding candles and a vase of dried flowers; a main bedroom; a smaller one with a single cot; and another bathing and "preparation" area. The furnishings were of high quality, and the thick pile rugs were pleasing to walk on.

Servants entered with the travelers' gear, and Caterine directed them to place the bags atop a low table in the reception room.

"I will leave you now and return when you are required for dinner," she told Ren, and hurried away on slippered feet.

Tarrik found a cloth in the preparation room and wiped the gore from his spear. The guards outside hadn't reacted when they'd seen the sign of slaughter, which spoke of firm discipline and restraint. No doubt by the time their shift ended, the story of Albin's demise would be widely circulated.

Ren was checking her gear. Before opening her saddlebags, she spoke words under her breath—a sorcerous cant. There were probably a few stable hands massaging their hands right now, like the street rat outside the tailor's shop.

Tarrik moved his own gear into what he presumed was his room, the one with the single cot. He grabbed the bottle of spirits from his saddlebag. The drink burned going down his throat, and he noticed his hands were shaking. How long had they been betraying him? He had to keep them out of Ren's view. He feared she was assessing his weaknesses as much as he was hers.

Another long swallow, and the bottle was empty. He tossed it onto the cot and strode back into the reception room. The alcohol had taken the edge off his emotions, but it would be some time before the blood-lust left him.

Ren was in her bedroom, unpacking her clothes. She must have heard him, as she came out straight away.

"Are you upset I ordered the man killed?" she asked.

Tarrik didn't know what the sorcerer was involved in or what her plans were. But the more he learned of her intentions, the more he could use that knowledge to plot against her and find a way to escape.

Although he couldn't act directly against Ren, he might be able to turn others against her or give her wrong information. And if she were killed, he'd be free.

What concerned him right now was that even nobles supposedly loyal to the Tainted Cabal thought they could get away with so blatant an insult to Ren. Was it because she was one of the Nine?

"Albin was dead the moment Veljor ordered him to maim or kill me. He was nothing. Prey. Meat. Why would Veljor affront you so? Are you not all part of the Cabal? Does this have something to do with the Nine?"

"The less you know, the better. All that matters to you is my protection. The spear is a decent weapon. Are you going to name it?"

Name it? A tool? Humans were strange. "No. It is a weapon, an extension of its wielder."

Ren nodded slowly. "I would not normally use you in such a way. When Albin appeared, I knew we had no choice. I find I have plenty of lives to spend, and I do not have the luxury of virtue."

"And yet you did use me." And he'd enjoyed it. The violence, the bloodlust, the release . . .

"I wish it didn't have to be this way—"

"It doesn't! Say the words, and unbind me. Return me to my realm." Tarrik wasn't strong enough to return himself yet.

"I cannot. You are here to protect me. I own you, body and soul. Do not forget it."

How could he?

"Why do you need me to protect you from mad commanders and arrogant minions? You could burn them to charcoal and scatter their remains with a few arcane words!"

"I preferred it when you were silent, insolent demon! Do not question me!"

Ren snarled a cant, and the Wracking Nerves pummeled him. Agony scorched Tarrik's skin, scoured his bones. He cried out, fell limply to the floor.

The punishment faded. Tarrik kept his eyes closed and fists clenched. *I'll see you dead! I'll gouge out your eyes and carve your skin to a bloody pulp.*

He hauled himself up, swallowing blood, and glared at Ren.

"Enough of your disrespect," she said. "I need to rest and plan. Speak no more of what happened."

Tarrik glowered at her but remained silent, as she wished. His legs felt weak, and he ground his teeth at his contemptible feebleness.

"You will accompany me to the dining hall tonight, but I have a task for you while everyone is eating. I do not know who of the Nine is also here, but I suspect they were the instigator of the assault upon me at the tower and during the days before."

She gnawed on her already-chewed knuckle, realized what she was doing, and ceased.

"This place is full of arrogant fools and vipers," Tarrik said. "I do not like it."

"Neither do I."

Tarrik wanted to keep his peace but could not stop himself. "One of the Nine attacking another of the Nine?"

"We all serve our savior, Samal Rak-shazza. But he has given us leave to fight for position among ourselves. Only the strong survive, as it should be."

"Apart from wanting you dead, does this sorcerer present a threat to your plans?"

"Leave my plans to me, demon. The less you know, the less you can reveal."

"I am bound to serve you."

"And yet in certain situations you are able to harm me. It follows that you may also be able to reveal more about me than I wish." Ren rubbed her eyes. "Get some rest. We'll wait here until we're called to dinner."

Chapter Five

The dregs of the bottle of spirits had dampened Tarrik's emotions for a short time, but the rage had returned with a vengeance. It burned in his veins, causing him to grind his teeth and his hands to shake uncontrollably.

If Ren noticed, she said nothing. She sat cross-legged on her bed, eyes open but unfocused, as if staring into a realm only sorcerers were aware of.

She remained that way the entire day, not reacting to Tarrik's impatient pacing around the reception room or the honing of his spear. He eventually settled himself and tried to calm his thoughts. But he needed a drink.

Tarrik faced the prospect of the commander's dinner at Ren's side with dread. Not because he was afraid of Veljor or what the deranged meat-bag might devise next, but because of the fever of wrath that still burned in his veins.

There was a knock at the door.

Ren blinked, turning her head toward the sound. Tarrik rolled to his feet and grasped his spear. He was over by the door in a heartbeat.

"Lady Branwen," came Caterine's muffled voice. "Commander Veljor would have your presence at dinner."

Ren rubbed her eyes and stretched her neck. "We will be out presently."

For a long moment there was no response; then Caterine said, "I will wait outside so I may escort you."

"Excellent. I will not be long."

Ren levered herself off the bed and knuckled the small of her back. Ignoring Tarrik, she brushed imaginary dust from her charcoal skirt, then tugged on her short coat. Only as she buckled her sword to her back and adjusted the chest strap to avoid her brooches did she deign to notice him.

"Come here," she said.

Tarrik obeyed, stopping a pace from her.

"Firstly, you need to blend in more. You're too . . . reptilian."

He had no idea what she meant, and frowned.

"Lizardlike," clarified Ren. "You're completely still for minutes at a time, and when you do move, it's quick and precise. And you hardly blink."

"I am a predator, not prey. I conserve my energy and strike when it's most opportune."

"Just . . . try to move more. Mimic humans."

Should I trip over my own feet and drool like a mindless idiot?

"I'll try."

His mind flashed to his wife, Jaquel, who had taught him to dance with her—a human activity she'd enjoyed. He'd done his best to accommodate her, though the endeavor had often ended with them laughing at each other. Tarrik's chest tightened with the memory and the pang of loss, and he averted his gaze from Ren. His beloved's face formed in his mind: delicate and gentle, just like her soul. He still missed Jaquel, even after so long. He would have done anything for her. Anything. No matter whether it went against his upbringing or broke the demon lords' rules. He *had* done anything and had paid the price willingly.

But he couldn't stop time.

Tarrik shook his head and ruthlessly thrust the image away.

"Good. I have a task for you while I'm at this dinner. I can handle Veljor and whatever he has planned. After today's display, it will not be anything subtle. Though perhaps seeing you missing will give him pause and stay his hand."

"As you wish." He was curious about this task, but she would have to tell him of her own accord. She would get no prompting from him. Then a thought to keep her safe occurred to him, her bindings forcing a question from his lips. "Will your arts protect you from poison or drugs?"

She eyed him warily. "No. However, I have many antidotes and a means of detecting such threats if I concentrate. I doubt Veljor would be so deceptive. He is a man of violence and must be seen to dominate rather than dispose of someone unobtrusively. He would want people to know it was he who did the deed."

"There are other Cabalists here. Would they not help you?"

Ren looked away, her teeth biting her lower lip. "If someone plans my downfall, they will be disappointed. Whatever happens, we will be leaving tomorrow. Now, to your task. An adviser from the Tainted Cabal is posted with each ruler or leader who pledges allegiance. Someone powerful—to protect them but also to remind them of the Tainted Cabal's might. The sorcerer assigned to Veljor is Roska Fridle. She will be at the dinner tonight to welcome another high-ranking Cabalist, which means her residence will be empty."

Tarrik grunted. "Except for her sorcerous wards, her guards, and whatever other protections she has."

"I can help you with the arcane wards—at least, to perceive them. Other than that, you're on your own. If anyone sees you in her residence or can infer it was you, they are to die. Is that understood?"

He nodded. "Am I to lie in wait for Roska Fridle?" A task he did not relish. Sorcerers were hard to surprise and harder to kill.

"No. You are to steal an artifact from her."

So she would make him a common thief. No surprise. Sorcerers had no shame.

"What does the artifact look like? Where is it?"

"Roska's rooms are in the northwest of the citadel, on the top floor, with access to a rooftop courtyard, so she can absorb the dawn- and dusk-tides in private. The courtyard allows entry to her rooms for someone who can reach it unobserved. My sources were quite clear on this, and they're paid well enough to discover such information."

"Am I to fly up to the rooftop? Perhaps climb like a monkey?"

Ren gave him a hard look. "Do not think I am unaware of your talents. It is a simple task for you to reach the roof and the courtyard. Once inside her rooms, you are to locate her study, which will be warded. Search for the artifact, and bring it back to me. I will keep Veljor and Roska occupied at dinner."

She knew far less than she thought about his talents. "And the artifact?"

Ren traced a small circle on her palm with a finger. "So big, maybe the size of a coin—I'm not entirely sure. A disc of orichalcum with a small, flat bloodstone at its center."

"You're not sure?"

"I saw a drawing, but there was no scale for reference."

"And what is its purpose? A catalyst to enable your incantations?"

She withdrew what looked to be a brass magnifying glass from her pocket and held it out. "This will allow you to see sorcerous wards. It's the best I can do, and you won't be able to disarm them. But you can pass through them if there are shadows on the other side."

He slipped the object inside his pocket. She knew about his shadow-step talent then, which wasn't surprising if she had Contian's notes. The old sorcerer had used Tarrik's talent to play many a joke on his colleagues.

"You'll require a weapon of some sort," she said, and gestured to a blade on her bedside table. "Take one of my knives, as your spear is too noticeable."

Tarrik nodded, though he didn't need it. "Anything else?"

"Yes. I'll leave here first. And be careful. I wouldn't want to see you injured or worse."

He didn't reply to the false claim of concern, just took the sheathed knife and buckled its slender belt around his waist. He looked at his spear with regret.

Ren adjusted her belt and her sword's chest strap before moving to the door and opening it. She smiled brightly at Caterine, who leaned against the opposite wall beside a guard.

Tarrik could see that Caterine and the guards feared Ren. It was in their eyes, the flare of their nostrils, the stench of cowardice around them, their expressions of caution and respect when she looked away. The sorcerer held a formidable power. She was deadlier and more evil than any of them. A killer. And a supreme beauty.

Tarrik squeezed that thought to a kernel and hid it in his deepest recesses. He could not afford to let his emotions affect his attitude toward the woman who'd made a slave of him.

"I'm ready," Ren said to Caterine. "Lead on."

Caterine glanced at Tarrik. "Your man isn't coming?"

"No," said Ren.

Caterine narrowed her eyes but led Ren away. The guards at their posts followed behind.

Tarrik waited a dozen heartbeats before checking the corridor. Clear. He slipped quietly along in the same direction they'd gone, but at a staircase he ascended to the next level. Then, as the steps continued up, he kept going.

They ended at a wooden landing with three corridors leading off it. The floors were scuffed and the varnish rubbed bare in places, so he assumed this was a less used section of the citadel or perhaps one mostly frequented by servants. The area was dark and dingy, with only a single lamp lighting the top of the stairs. Its feeble glow was rapidly overwhelmed by gloom a few paces down the corridors.

One corridor led northwest, presumably in the direction of Roska's rooms. Tarrik padded down it, keeping close to the wall to avoid squeaking floorboards. His form wasn't built for stealth, and although he had the demonic talent of remaining unnoticed, he lacked the trick of wrapping shadows around himself to aid concealment.

Footsteps sounded ahead, and he ducked into a side room. He left the door open a crack and stood behind it, next to sheet-covered furniture stacked higher than his head. A servant bearing a dim lamp hurried past. Tarrik waited until the footsteps had vanished, then slipped back out into the corridor and continued.

When the corridor ended at a window, he took out Ren's lens. The wide door to his left shone bright with crisscrossed wards of white and crimson. Roska's, presumably. With reluctance, Tarrik decided Ren was correct. The best way inside Roska's suite would be from the rooftop courtyard, which would probably be less secure due to its private location.

He shoved the lens into his pocket and stepped silently to the window, lifted the latch, and levered the window open. Poking his head out, he looked up. Stone gargoyles perched atop the crenellations: winged monkeys and lion-headed birds, one with a snake in its jaws. He stared at them, waiting for one to move—you could never be too careful—but they remained as lifeless as stone. He knew of a higher demon, Aira Phenue-Drovik, who'd been badly injured by an ensorcelled statue. The demon had become obsessed with a human princess of renowned beauty. Her desire had blinded her as she peered through a window at the sleeping princess, intending to overpower the woman and sate her lust, and she had failed to notice the stone gargoyle come to life beside her. It had massive pincers and snipped her left arm off. Aira had barely made it back to her summoner before passing out from blood loss. She was now ridiculed as a lack-limb. Tarrik chuckled at the memory. He wouldn't make the same mistake.

The granite window surround was carved and offered plenty of hand and feet grips. The parapet was three feet above. Tarrik eased himself onto the external ledge and closed and latched the window. Anything left disturbed offered a clue to a canny investigator. He just hoped he wouldn't have to come back this way.

In a few heartbeats he was pulling himself up onto the parapet next to a gargoyle carved in the shape of a stork with bat ears. There was a short drop on the other side to a small paved courtyard. He was in luck.

He clambered down and crouched low, hand on Ren's knife hilt even though he didn't need the metal blade. His shadow-blade catalyst was more potent than any sword, a weapon he wanted to keep from Ren and use only in emergencies, when it would remain a secret.

He waited for a dozen heartbeats, and when nothing attacked him, he moved to a door set into a short wall. He used the lens again and perceived the door was warded, but not nearly as heavily as the main entrance to Roska's suite. Tarrik knelt and peered through the keyhole, careful not to press his face close to the metal. He could just make out a shadowed wall opposite. Perfect.

He waited for a hundred count, ears pricked to any noise coming from inside. When he heard none, he again focused on the shadows through the keyhole and poured himself into the darkness. His essence dissolved into the void, re-forming against the wall on the other side of the door.

He froze, only his eyes moving as he searched for threats in the gloom. When none appeared, he allowed himself a sigh of relief.

Tarrik slowly made his way down a rickety set of narrow wooden stairs, hands to the walls on either side. He had many talents, but seeing in pitch-black wasn't one of them.

He came to another door and jerked his hand back when it touched a hinge. His heart hammered in his chest, but no sorcerous scourge appeared to flay the skin from his bones.

Through the lens he saw that only the handle and lock were warded. Again, he shadow-stepped past and into the room on the other side, where he instantly slid behind the curtains at a floor-to-ceiling window.

The room was carpeted and similar to the reception room in Ren's suite: couches, padded armchairs, and carved side tables holding numerous decanters of wine and bottles of spirits. It seemed Roska was fond of entertaining. Above the fireplace an alchemical globe emitted a soft glow.

Three other rooms led off this one. If the suites were all of a similar layout, the smallest should be the preparation room, the largest the bedroom—which left the middle one as the study.

The lens showed the door was free of wards, and why wouldn't it be? To get this far, an ordinary thief would have triggered one of the two entrance doors and be dead or in a whole lot of trouble. But Tarrik was no ordinary thief. He wasn't a thief at all, really, and to have his abilities abused like this was an indignity. He piled it atop all the other indignities Ren had forced upon him. A list that grew longer every day.

Inside the study, a walnut writing desk stood in front of a wall of bookshelves, only a third filled with leather-bound tomes and rolls of parchment. Against one wall sat a sturdy, iron-bound chest secured with a large padlock. Presumably where the artifact was secured.

He took a step toward it, and an eldritch tremor passed over his skin. He froze, eyes darting around for the cause. It had been sorcery, but . . .

The air crackled as the temperature plunged and cold caressed his hands and face. Then heat invaded with an orange glow, pushing the frigid air aside. A familiar scent of sulfur and rancid meat invaded Tarrik's nostrils.

There was no point concealing himself. He stood next to the chest, arms by his sides to appear as nonthreatening as possible.

The demon appeared as a scale-armored man wielding a burning long sword in his right hand and a wickedly curved dagger in his left.

Scorching cinders dropped from the sword to burn holes in the carpet; the metal scales of the armor were blackened and corroded, as if seared by immense heat. The demon's head was covered by a faded scarlet hood, which gave off red steam and concealed the face. But Tarrik knew who this was: Ananias Grimur-Sigvatux, demon of the Thirty-Ninth Order, and, to all intents and purposes, Tarrik's superior.

Blood and fire. He was dead.

Ananias's form solidified swiftly, and the floor creaked under his weight. The fact that the demon bore his own armor and weapons meant this was a summons of fiendish complexity performed so rapidly it boggled Tarrik's mind. The sorcerer had had to bring physical objects through the veil separately, then gift them to the demon without strings attached—which could only happen if the demon knew a summoning was imminent. And that could only mean one thing: Ananias had made a pact with the sorcerer Roska Fridle and willingly answered her summons.

Tarrik knew his triggering of that summons would have alerted the Tainted Cabal sorcerer, who would already be rushing back to her rooms.

"I smell you, Tarrik Nal-Valim. Bow to me, or suffer the consequences."

The demon's words were slow and heavy, breathed from lungs and a throat burned by constant flames.

Tarrik swallowed and glanced at the warded door behind him. To run was his first thought—but in a blink Ren's arcane binding held him fast. She had given him a task, and he was bound to see it through to the best of his ability. Fight it was, then. He cast any thought of fleeing from his mind, and the sorcerous chains binding his limbs and torso relented, leaving a prickling pain to remind him of their existence.

Being of a higher order, Ananias was faster and stronger and possessed more talents than Tarrik. The only way out of this was by guile and trickery. But Ananias would expect that.

"I cannot," Tarrik told the demon. "You know this."

The shadowy hood rose to regard him. Glowing ruby eyes shone from the darkness within. "How are you not dead yet, race traitor?"

Tarrik tried to shrug, found his shoulders bunching. The rebuke hadn't lost its sting after all this time, though he perceived his alleged crime of marrying a human woman in a different light.

"Why destroy a useful tool?" he countered.

"The last I heard, you were exiled to Shimrax, scavenging among the gray sand and rock with other criminals. Hardly a tool close to the hands of the demon lords."

"The Council of Lords declared I was to be branded and exiled, stripped of all wealth, but to remain alive."

"Anyone else would have killed themselves for shame. I guess the lower demon within never ceases to fight."

"I've survived this far and will not give in easily."

"There can be but one outcome here. Your death."

"I know."

"Then you are resigned to falling? Where is your fight? Where is your hope?"

"I abandoned hope long ago."

"Ah. A defeatist then."

"I am merely a slave. I do my master's bidding."

"Like the last time? That excuse never washed with me. We all see what you really are, Tarrik Nal-Valim. Weak. Foolish. An abomination."

"I see farther than you. When you let your desires rule you, you are a slave still."

"You are a fool."

Hardly.

A lone knife against the infernal sword and dagger held by a demon greater than he was. Tarrik knew there was only one chance to exit this room alive. One toss of the dice, which would probably see him dead and his essence subsumed by Ananias. Perhaps his opponent would then be powerful enough to ascend to the fortieth level and be recognized as a lord. Such was the main goal of all higher-level demons: kill and absorb the other's spirit to become greater, stronger.

Almost all. Tarrik had long ago lost the desire to become more powerful. What was the point?

He unbuckled the belt that held Ren's knife and tossed it to the floor beside him. "Let us fight then. But these human weapons bore me. Let us fight demon against demon. Weaponless and—"

"No."

The long sword's searing blade flashed at him, and Tarrik threw himself backward. Pain erupted along a scorching line across his torso. He crashed into a chair, which splintered under his weight, and a jagged chunk of wood pierced his left arm.

He scrambled to his feet, dripping purple blood from chest and limb. Ananias stood silently, regarding him with ember eyes.

Tarrik pressed a hand to the cut in an effort to staunch the blood. He made the wound look worse than it was, dropping to one knee, panting like cornered prey. He groped for his dark-tide power, creating a conduit to the shadow-blade catalyst embedded in his right forearm, and prepared a cant on his lips.

He forced a rictus of humiliation, made his words come out labored and reluctant. "You have . . . the advantage of me . . . I cannot flee . . ."

"My bargain with this filthy human sorcerer was well struck," cried Ananias gleefully. "Never could I have imagined such a reward. You are undone!" The ruby eyes shone brightly. "Bow your head! Submit to me!"

Tarrik lowered his head, his eyes remaining on Ananias. He let his blood flow freely and placed both hands on the floor, set to spring.

Ananias drew his curved dagger along his forearm, creating a trickle of indigo. Blood against blood, essence against essence. As Tarrik's life left him, Ananias would use his repository of dark-tide power to absorb it into himself.

With a final savage grin, Ananias swung his burning blade out wide, then overhead.

Tarrik leaped.

Faster than thought, Ananias dropped his knife, seized Tarrik by the throat, and shook him as if he were a child. Tarrik jerked wildly in the terrible grip, feet dangling above the floor. His throat ached as his breath was cut off. His fists battered at the stonelike claw holding him. After a fierce struggle, where Tarrik gained not an iota of release, he forced himself to go limp.

Ananias smiled, his grip relenting slightly to allow Tarrik to draw breath. "You are overmatched. I know your bindings forced you to attack, and I will make your death swift. I do not care to tarry in this repulsive world."

Tarrik sucked in air, then barked a cant. A yard of shimmering force sprang from his hand, formed from his catalyst. His shadow-blade, rarest of the rare talents. He swung the iridescent blade up and sliced through the arm holding him aloft. Blood spurted. Ananias howled.

As his feet hit the floor, Tarrik darted his blade toward his opponent's chest.

Despite the agony of amputation, Ananias wrenched his sword into a parry. Tarrik stuttered another cant, and his shadow-blade vanished, re-forming in the instant Ananias's sword passed through the expected point of impact without resistance. Ananias, overbalanced, tried to recover . . . too late. Tarrik's shadow-blade sank deep into the demon's chest.

Ananias's eyes widened, and he cried out in mortal agony. Deep-purple heart's blood erupted from his mouth, spilling like wine overflowing a glass.

With a vicious jerk, Tarrik yanked his blade to the side. It pulled free from Ananias's chest, trailing blood and ichor.

"You were greedy, Ananias, thinking about the reward before you won the fight."

The demon's hand, which could previously have torn Tarrik limb from limb, clutched desperately at him. But Ananias was already too weak. The fatal damage was done.

Tarrik smiled ferociously, uttering a cant he'd never thought he'd use again—one of domination, of the triumph of the strong over the weak.

He pressed his cut torso to Ananias's. A connection solidified between them, not physical but ethereal. Agony exploded in Tarrik's head: pain and pleasure combined. A scream tore from his throat, and his muscles and bones burned with infernal energy. Tears poured from his squeezed-shut eyes. His hands convulsed into tight claws. Burning. He was burning from the inside.

The pain lessened, then vanished as if it had never happened.

Tarrik opened his eyes and found himself lying in a pool of pinkish goo—what remained of Ananias. Strangely, it smelled of dirt and iron. To the side lay the demon's severed limb.

He tried to stand, slipped in the mess, and fell on his ass. He crawled to the clean carpet to the side of the puddle and doubled over panting, legs and arms shaking.

He had to pull himself together. There would be time to go over what had happened later. Roska Fridle would be here soon, and she would have felt the passing of her summons into oblivion. She would be prepared with her most virulent sorcery. His survival wasn't assured yet.

Tarrik felt for the wound across his torso, found it still open and leaking. He could barely move his left arm. When he tried, spikes of pain shot through him. The splinter of chair would have to be removed by someone else.

Focus, he told himself.

Ananias's weapons and armor had disappeared, rebounded back to the abyssal realm when the demon died.

Tarrik looked at the iron-bound chest and fumbled Ren's lens from his pocket. It had cracked in two. When he tried to view any arcane wards on the chest, he saw none but couldn't tell if the lens was working or broken.

There was no time.

Tarrik whispered a cant and brought his shadow-blade into being again. He struck at the chest's lock, averting his gaze in case sorcerous traps unleashed fatal energies. To his surprise, there was no overt sorcery, as his blade sliced through metal and wood. The lock clanked to the floor in two pieces.

He dissipated his blade and flipped the chest's lid. Inside were blackwood boxes of different sizes. He frantically opened them and in the fifth found the coin-size orichalcum disc inset with a bloodstone.

Rushed steps sounded in the hallway—at least a dozen guards—and a woman began speaking harsh cants.

Tarrik pocketed the disc and lurched to the reception room, where he grabbed a bottle of strong spirits. He shadow-stepped through the stairway door and dashed up to shadow-step outside to the rooftop courtyard.

With any luck Roska would be thrown by the puddle of pink goo and arm that remained of Ananias, and her undisturbed wards. She'd likely search her rooms first for the intruder, which would give Tarrik more time to escape. Hopefully he hadn't left a trail of blood . . .

He leaned on the low wall to catch his breath, a hand pressed to his side to stop the bleeding as best he could. He could feel a warm trickle from his upper-left-arm wound.

Pushing the pain aside, he focused on a patch of shadow under a large tree thirty paces from the citadel wall. An instant later he was standing on the ground under the tree's branches. Sweat dripped from his brow, and his clothes stuck to his skin. He glanced up to the courtyard. He couldn't see any sign of the sorcerer. But the next shadow-step had to take him much farther if he wanted to be confident of not getting caught.

He focused on the shadowed side of a stable wall, obvious from the water troughs and bales of hay and the corral outside. He gave himself to the shadows and was there.

A gasp came from a nearby shape in the darkness. Tarrik whirled and came face-to-face with a blonde-haired girl—one of the stable hands who'd taken his and Ren's horses. She sat behind a hay bale with a half-eaten apple in her hand. Her wide eyes stared into his, then dropped to his dripping wounds.

"Blood and fire!" uttered Tarrik, and the girl whimpered. His thoughts swirled as he grappled desperately for a solution, all the while knowing there wasn't one.

She stood, her bottom lip trembling, the unfinished apple falling from nerveless fingers to the dirt. "Don't . . . please . . ."

Tarrik had no choice. The command Ren had placed on him, her sorcerous bindings, compelled him to act. *If anyone sees you in her residence, or can infer it was you, they are to die. Is that understood?*

"I'm sorry," he said.

The girl hadn't moved, hadn't attempted to flee. Her shoulders slumped, and she dipped her head.

At least he could make it quick.

Tarrik spoke a cant, and his shadow-blade sprang to life. He pushed it into the girl's chest, through her heart. She gasped again, a soft whimper, then slumped to the dirt.

Tears leaked from his eyes as he withdrew his catalyst's blade. He wiped them away angrily, cursing his weakness. The children of humans were not like the lower demons, which knew only hunger and lust. There was an innocence to them at the beginning of their lives. He'd seen it, felt it, when Jaquel had given birth to their own daughter, who had died young. The feeling had torn at his very essence.

Why should he care about humans? His years in this world, away from the abyssal realms, had sapped his hardness, made him more human. He'd struggled—and failed—to overcome the cursed softness before. And that had been the cause of his disgrace and exile. That punishment, after all he'd come to care about had been ripped away from him—Jaquel, Contian—had sent him spiraling into almost madness.

He lifted the girl's body, shadow-stepped back to the tree, and placed her beneath it, gently arranging her into a restful pose, her back against the rough bark, hands clasped in her lap.

Chapter Six

There were no guards outside Ren's rooms. If there had been, Tarrik would have had to kill them. He wondered how Ren would have explained her way out of such slaughter.

He staggered inside and slammed the door shut. An attempt to lie on his cot ended in pain and cursing as the jagged splinter in his shoulder dug in deeper.

Tarrik ended up sitting, his unwounded shoulder leaning against the wall. Clenching the bottle of spirits between his thighs, he used his good hand to uncork it and swallowed half the contents. His left shoulder and arm tingled as they lost feeling. Ren would have to tend to his injuries, whenever she returned.

He didn't have to wait long. Three times, heavy feet stomped past the suite: no doubt guards rushing to reinforce Roska's security or perhaps Veljor's. Tarrik's purple blood in Roska's rooms would be obvious. She'd know another demon was responsible for the theft, for killing Ananias.

Tarrik heard a lighter step and sensed his master's presence as she came closer. He swallowed another mouthful of liquor, stoppered the bottle, and tossed it onto his cot.

Ren opened the door a crack and slipped through. She took one look at Tarrik and spoke a series of cants. He knew she must be warding the door.

"You're a mess," she said.

"I return successful, Master," he said flatly, and placed the disc on the cot.

She frowned at him and moved closer. "Your wounds . . . I don't know if—"

"I have resigned myself to your touch. I will be of more use once they're seen to."

If Ren thought anything of his formal tone and words, she made no response. Instead, she rummaged through her gear and came back with a thin leather kit. She opened it to reveal numerous vials, metal implements, spools of thread, different-size needles, and what looked like rolled-up bandages.

She grimaced as she probed around the wooden splinter in his shoulder. Her fingers came away covered with his blood. "This is going to hurt," she said, and removed a pair of pincers from her kit along with a pouch.

She placed a kerchief on the bed and poured a light-brown powder onto it from the pouch. Then she grasped the splinter with the pincers. Tarrik gasped involuntarily at the spike of pain.

"Do you want to bite down on something?" she asked.

"Your neck."

"At least you've retained your sense of humor."

"Get on with it," he growled.

Pain was familiar to Tarrik, as it was to all demons. You became accustomed to pain early on, or you died. If you were hurting, you knew you were still alive. There was a certain comfort to the sensation, which grounded him in reality.

Ren yanked the splinter out. The puncture wound ached like fire, but Tarrik only clenched his teeth. His chest heaved as he kept his eyes on Ren's. She scooped some of the powder onto his arm, which was now pouring blood, and he felt his skin tighten.

"The powder should stop the blood flow," she said. "Then I can sew it up. It will also help to sterilize the wound."

She cast more powder onto the wound in his side, then threaded a curved needle and, without hesitation, stabbed it into his flesh and began sewing up the slash from Ananias's blade. Tarrik had to force himself not to flinch from her touch on his skin.

"This looks burned slightly. What happened?"

"I made it inside Roska's rooms without incident, but moving toward the chest triggered a defense she'd prepared. A demon was summoned."

"A minor one?"

"I wouldn't be injured if so. It was Ananias Grimur-Sigvatux, demon of the Thirty-Ninth Order."

"I take it he's dead? Or did you merely escape?"

"He was stronger and more powerful than I. There was no way to escape."

"And yet here you are. Alive. How?"

"Just because an opponent is stronger doesn't mean they're smarter. I killed him."

Ren uttered an amused chuckle. "Roska won't be pleased." She inserted a final stitch and tied the thread off. "There. Now your arm."

Tarrik turned slightly so she had more room to move.

"Where's my knife?" she asked.

"I lost it. In Roska's rooms."

Ren huffed. "This has turned into a disaster. Luckily the blade was nondescript—they're unlikely to trace it back to me. Scrying won't work either. The Cabalists are always fighting among themselves. Roska will have too many suspects to choose from."

Tarrik still seethed with remorse and anger over the girl's death. The liquor had done nothing to stifle those feelings.

"You have the artifact you wanted. And a powerful demon under Roska's control has been slain, which will significantly weaken her. Now we can leave and go on to the next evil plan you have in mind."

Ren's eyes narrowed, and her jaw muscles clenched. "Evil? You have no idea. What I've seen . . . what I've endured . . ."

"Spare me your protestations. When I fled, I encountered a girl—the stable hand who took my horse. She was sitting outside the stables eating an apple."

Ren ceased sewing up his arm. He couldn't see her expression behind him. For a moment, he thought she might say something, but she resumed her stitching.

"*If anyone sees you in her residence, or can infer it was you, they are to die*," he parroted. "I placed her corpse under a tree nearby. She'll probably not be found until morning."

He grimaced at a particularly hard tug on the thread.

"I'm done," Ren said. "I'll bandage your shoulder, but not your chest. The latter is a shallow cut and shouldn't open unless you exert yourself."

She left him, and he could hear her washing her hands in the preparation room. She returned drying them on a towel, then busied herself repacking her kit. He didn't know what he'd expected when he'd told her of the girl's death, but it certainly wasn't this emotionless calm.

Tarrik picked up the artifact, the cause of all of this turmoil, and handed it to her. He hoped the orichalcum disc was worth the mayhem and pain. Ren smiled.

He took out the cracked lens next, and her smile slipped. "It broke when Ananias slashed my chest and I landed on the chair."

He lay down on the cot, his back to Ren, the bottle of spirits at his side.

She padded away, and he heard her getting ready for sleep. It wasn't until she was under her blankets and her breathing steadied that Tarrik let himself relax and consider what had happened in Roska's rooms.

He had absorbed a higher-level demon, and the consequences were numerous. The constraints a sorcerer placed on a demon were finely tuned to individual strength. When Tarrik changed—and he would once he could assimilate Ananias's power—Ren's bindings might no longer hold him. Even if they only weakened, Tarrik would surely gain some leeway, some freedom. Only time would tell.

He was sure Ren didn't know of the effects of him killing Ananias, or she would have strengthened her bindings at the very least.

He felt Ananias's essence in his mind like an egg waiting to be cracked.

And the egg had to be eaten slowly, or Tarrik risked losing himself.

Before dawn lit the sky outside, the soft shuffling of booted feet woke Tarrik. He made out at least four pairs, possibly five, but the guards didn't hammer down the door. He listened while they positioned themselves in the hallway outside and swapped a few hushed words. He decided it was guard duty as normal. And if the city's elite forces hadn't come by now to restrain him and Ren and haul them before Veljor to mete out justice—whatever that consisted of in this blasted place—they'd probably gotten away with the raid on Roska's rooms. The sorcerer herself might suspect them, but Tarrik reasoned she'd be powerless to act without hard evidence.

He dragged himself off the cot, wincing as his arm spiked with pain and his side burned. At least he'd managed a full night's sleep—no Samal-sent dreams to disturb Ren, no attack from another strange dead-eye—so his wounds were already healing. His hand searched for and found the bottle of spirits he'd snatched yesterday. He took a deep swallow. Today would no doubt be interesting, and he'd need to keep a tight lid on his emotions.

He heard rustling as Ren rose from her bed. She stood in his doorway dressed in her long-sleeved robe.

"If anyone comes, they're to wait outside. You will remain here to guard me."

She moved to the preparation room and closed the door. From inside he heard sounds of washing, clothes rustling, buckles clinking.

Tarrik tugged on his coat. His clothes would need a wash soon—they were starting to reek—but the smell helped to mask the musk of the humans that inflamed him.

Ren came out dressed in the worn and stained traveling leathers she'd been wearing when she'd summoned him. "We're leaving," she said, grabbing her sword and buckling it to her back. She touched its hilt as if for reassurance.

"Won't that look suspicious?"

"It's of no matter. I got what I came for, and Roska can't prove I had anything to do with what happened last night. Besides, I have someone planting rumors to misdirect her."

Unless she sees you have the artifact. But Tarrik couldn't see a way of alerting Roska while Ren's bindings still held him. Best to bide his time and seek another opportunity.

"Collect our gear, and follow me."

Tarrik did as ordered and shouldered their saddlebags, grasped his spear, and followed Ren to the door. His wounds twinged with discomfort, and he grimaced.

"We will escort you, my lady," a guard said when they exited the suite.

Ren smiled. "Of course."

The guards filed in behind Tarrik, except for one who hared off in the other direction. Tarrik developed an itch between his shoulder blades as Ren led them along corridors and down stairs.

When they reached the courtyard where they'd left their horses, she halted and turned to the guards. "Have our mounts saddled and brought out."

"You're leaving?" said one of them.

Not too bright, these humans.

Ren nodded. "Is there an order I cannot?"

"No, my lady."

The guard waited a moment before walking toward the stables at a deliberately slow pace. He obviously knew his commander wouldn't want Ren to leave but was too lowly to do anything about it. He probably hoped the guard he'd sent scurrying off would bring him new orders.

"Serenity Branwen!" barked a man's voice.

Tarrik whirled, bringing his spear up in front of an oddly dressed human.

He was as tall as Tarrik and considerably bulkier, dressed in dirt-stained, torn garments only fit for burning. He held an orichalcum staff, the top of which was formed into the face of an old man. A goatlike stench clung to him, which Tarrik recognized as madness.

Three steps behind him stood a young girl with brown hair and a greenish cast to her skin who was clad in a plain brown skirt and shirt.

"Puck Moonan," said Ren. She gestured at Tarrik to lower his spear.

Puck ignored Tarrik, but the girl sneered at him and laughed.

The scruffy sorcerer crossed his arms, placed his palms against his chest, and bowed. "Samal will rise."

Ren repeated the gesture. "Praise Samal, Lord of Life."

Tarrik felt sick to his stomach, horrified at their worship. Samal was a deceiver, a manipulator, yet they acted as if he were divine. Was this Samal's plan: to become lord of both humans and demons? If true, it was an abomination. The demon lords would not stand for such a travesty. They would fight—if they could. Many higher-level demons had died in the wars, but Tarrik didn't know if they'd fallen to the humans fighting Nysrog or to some scheme of Samal's to strengthen himself. How powerful was Samal now? Had he gained that power by betraying and subsuming his fellow demons? No one knew. No one had seen or sensed Samal since Nysrog had been banished from this world.

Puck spoke, his voice curiously breathless and soft for such a big man. "Lady Branwen, a pleasure to find you here. I was unaware you were in Ivrian."

"My work takes me to many places, some hospitable, some not."

"And chaos seems to follow you. Roska Fridle had an unwelcome visitor last night. A most curious encounter. An artifact was stolen, and a demon she'd chained was banished."

So, Roska preferred to keep secret the fact that her demon had been absorbed by another of its kind. Did Puck know the truth? Was he perpetuating her lies? At least this would prevent Ren suspecting Tarrik might have absorbed the demon. He glanced at her. She remained smiling.

"Demons are not my strength," she told Puck. "Or I'd stay and assist with the investigation."

Puck looked at the young woman behind him, who frowned, then wrinkled her nose.

This seemed to signal something to the sorcerer, as he turned back to Ren. "Your specialty is artifacts, is it not?"

"As well you know. They are easier to work with, more predictable."

"Yes . . . you could be a great power, Lady Branwen. Someone to be reckoned with. Yet you throw it all away by refusing to deal with demons."

"We each serve Samal in our own way. Do you question his choice in me? I do the Adversary's work, as do we all. You know it is impossible for me to act against his wishes."

"I do," Puck said. "Which is why I'll let this go . . . this time."

"There is nothing to let go. Now, if you'll excuse me, we are leaving."

"Of course. I will see you at the next meeting of the council?"

Ren paused, then nodded once. "It is an important one. I'll make sure I'm there."

"Good."

Puck turned on his heel, grabbed the young woman by the shoulder, and dragged her across the courtyard with him. She cast a spite-filled glance back at Ren and Tarrik.

As soon as they'd disappeared through a doorway, Ren gestured to the stable hands to bring their horses out. Tarrik noticed both were boys.

"Let's go," said Ren.

Tarrik settled their saddlebags on the appropriate animals and mounted his gray. He kept his spear to hand, lying across one thigh.

Ren led the way out of the citadel and along the streets of Ivrian. She kept her gaze straight ahead, not acknowledging salutes from any of the soldiers they passed or glancing at the hanged men and women at almost every intersection.

Once they were out of the city and a few miles along the north road, she slowed her horse and allowed Tarrik to come alongside her.

"I suppose you have questions about Puck."

Tarrik did but was wary of revealing more about himself. From the tension between Ren and her fellow member of the Nine, he guessed all was not well within their faction. It might be something he could use to his advantage, but how? Best to feign disinterest for now.

"No," he said.

Ren ignored his indifference. "The Nine are . . . troubled. We work for the glory of the Adversary and yet are given free rein to betray and even kill one another. We are constantly jockeying for position in preparation for when the Adversary is freed. This is something you demons do, is it not—kill each other for personal gain?"

"In this, at least, humans and demons are alike."

She gnawed on her knuckle. When she stopped, he saw it was bleeding again.

"Some of the Nine see reality differently now after the Adversary's . . . treatment of them."

He knew what he'd smelled on Puck Moonan. "They went insane?"

Ren looked away. She didn't answer.

Blood and fire. These insane sorcerers were attempting to free Samal Rak-shazza, a demon lord whose spiderlike manipulations and powers were second to none. And Tarrik was caught in the middle, actually helping to bring this about.

Had Ren also been driven crazy? He couldn't smell it on her, but her actions so far weren't reassuring.

"The Tainted Cabalists seek to assert control over every person on this continent and all lands under human sway," she said, her gaze fixed on the road ahead. "Then they will begin a push to liberate the wilderness from the creatures and monsters that make it their home. The inhumans. This would be a worthwhile goal."

Except these sorcerers also wanted the power of the demons for themselves and sought to bring back Nysrog. Didn't they realize the insane demon lord would destroy everything they were trying to create? Or were they blind?

"And Samal's goal?" asked Tarrik.

"Is not for the likes of you to know."

Ren urged her horse into a canter, and after a moment Tarrik did the same.

The fields and farms became sparser as the miles passed. They stopped for a brief midday meal, which consisted of Ren rummaging through her saddlebags and tossing Tarrik a packet of cured meat. While he gnawed on the tough fare, Ren ate an apple and an orange, followed by a wedge of cheese, and strolled around and stretched her legs.

After eating his fill, Tarrik stowed the remaining meat in his saddle-bags and drank some water, then a few swallows of spirits. He noted with disquiet that the new bottle was already running low.

Ren stood staring into the sun, eyes narrowed to slits, apparently dazzled. Tarrik wondered if she'd been beguiled by some malicious cant. *I can only hope.* He sensed both dawn- and dusk-tide emanations swirling around her.

He waited.

And waited.

Then, without warning, Ren cupped her hands in front of her. A chime rang, and a flash as bright as the sun erupted from the air between them. She gasped, and it disappeared. She shook her hands as if they pained her, and when she turned to Tarrik, her face was beaded with sweat. He could faintly smell triumph.

"You know about the dawn- and dusk-tides?" she said.

"A very little."

She examined him with narrowed eyes. "And how much do you know about the dark-tide?"

Careful. "As much as any demon."

"You absorb it and manipulate it. What control do you have over the process?"

Tarrik didn't want to speak of such things to a human, but her bindings forced him to. "Demon talents are both innate and learned. Some do not require cants; we can effect them unthinkingly. Others require a catalyst, calculations to design and control them, and cants to bring them into being, like your enchantments."

She glanced at his chest, then rubbed her fingers over her left breast. "I did not see a catalyst under the skin over your heart. Does that mean some of your cants do not require a catalyst to take effect?"

He knew all human sorcerers required a catalyst for their incantations. Contian had told him that its implantation under the skin over their heart was a requirement of the sorcery schools. He hesitated, considering a response that would both answer her question and misdirect.

"Some dark-tide sorcery I require a catalyst for, but . . ." He spread his hands in a gesture of helplessness.

Ren nodded. "A condition of your exile."

He looked away and shrugged, as if the loss of his sorcerous powers didn't trouble him. He knew she would see through the false bravado. "There were many conditions prescribed upon me." But relinquishing his catalyst wasn't one of them.

"Are you aware the dark-tide power isn't really from the dark?" she said.

He gave her a startled look. "What do you mean?"

That was impossible. Was she trying to confuse him? Everything was backward with these people, this world. Their mastery of some things, such as sorcery, was exceptional; but their understanding of many other things was flawed. She must be trying to lure him into her confidence. It would not work.

Ren tilted her head toward him. After a moment, she grunted. "Never mind. Do you know of anyone able to harness the sun's power?"

Tarrik allowed himself to smile. If that was what she was thinking of doing, she really was a fool. "In our history, a few have tried. Perhaps some were successful."

"Do not attempt to deceive me. None were able to. All who tried were consumed."

She was correct. They'd ended up a pile of ashes in a charred ring. "How do you know?"

"Because the sun would have scourged them, cleansed them. Changed them forever."

"How do you know?" he repeated.

Ren gave him a sidelong glance, then mounted her horse. "I read about it somewhere. It is of no matter. Let's get going."

He said nothing, wanting to keep his guard up. Like any sorcerer, she was dangerous. And these questions were no exception. But what had she meant about the dark-tide power?

Farther along, Ren turned off the road and led them along a livestock track until they came to an abandoned farm. Weeds grew over the paddocks and smothered the house and barn, which were falling apart. A dilapidated shed sheltered a stone trough and a pump. A bucket lay on its side, a plant growing from within.

"We'll stop here," said Ren.

Tarrik glanced at the sun, which would not set for a while. "Why?"

"Because I said so."

He grunted and dismounted, stiff and sore from his healing wounds. Movement caught his eye—large crabs clustered on the ground around tree trunks. Their bodies were bigger than his head, their shells a tawny brown with legs tinged blue.

"Beezle-crabs. They eat the yellow-green beezle-fruits," said Ren.

"Are they edible?" A couple of the creatures cooking on the fire later would do wonders for his mood.

She snorted in amusement and shook her head. "Always thinking of your stomach. Yes, they're considered a delicacy in some parts of the world." She lifted the bucket and dumped out the soil that had accumulated inside, along with the plant. "Gather some wood and start a fire. I'll see if the water in the well is palatable." She wandered off in the direction of a distant stream.

And what other mighty task would you have me undertake, Master? Cleaning your boots? Tarrik gathered the wood with ill grace, knowing he was in a temper and hardly caring. Outside of the city, he could let some of his self-control slip.

He piled two armfuls of fallen branches near the well. Soon after he'd returned with a bunch of twigs, he saw Ren pouring water from the bucket into the pump. She drove the squeaking handle up and down until water poured into the trough.

The sun was still a ways from setting. There must be a reason they'd stopped here. Perhaps she wanted another bath . . .

"Something amusing?" asked Ren.

Tarrik realized he was smiling and schooled his expression into blankness. "Are you intending to bathe again?"

"You should try it. You're getting a bit fragrant."

"Is that a command?"

She squinted at him. "Why not? Bathe yourself, demon, and wash your hair. You're beginning to stink. We need people to think you're human." She delved into her belongings and came out with a bar of soap. She tossed it to Tarrik. "Go to the stream now. I'll have a task for you when you return."

Tarrik left her to her pumping.

The stream was cold and frightening. There was a sandy bank and a shallow section, but just beyond it the water ran swift and deep. Deeper than anything in the infernal realms. Tarrik hoped their journey wouldn't involve crossing rivers—or worse still, having to swim to avoid pursuers. Perhaps he should tell Ren now that he couldn't swim. He winced at the thought of flailing around in dark water where his feet couldn't touch the bottom.

Swallowing his dread, he stripped, immersed himself up to his thighs, and washed. The soap smelled faintly of crab apple blossoms, though nowhere near as overpowering as the real thing. He washed his hair first, dunking his head rapidly to rinse it, then started on his body. His wounds smarted, but the cold water numbed them.

He was no stranger to this washing process; Jaquel had insisted regularly on the human ritual. His touch on his skin reminded him it had been weeks since he'd had congress with another. His thoughts wandered to Pris and her advances. He imagined her hands all over his body, her warm flesh in his grip, his lips on hers. His heart hammered in his chest, and his mouth became dry. Their flesh burned where they touched, sending delightful shivers through him. Her nails dug into his back.

He uttered a wordless groan as the pressure in his groin grew painful. He pictured the woman's face but saw Ren staring up at him with the same mischievous smile as Jaquel. Tarrik swore, and his dream evaporated. He fell back into the water with a splash.

For a while he lay there, letting the water cool his ardor and his anger. Had Ren ensorcelled him? Was that what she had been doing while staring into the sun—using her powers as a key to his soul?

"Having fun?"

Tarrik thrashed and spluttered while Ren stared at him with narrowed eyes.

"You've been gone for a while, so I thought to check on you," she said.

He rose, exited the water dripping, and collected his clothes. Hesitating, he decided not to get dressed. Ren's prudishness was a weakness he could exploit.

"By all the gods, demon—cover yourself!"

Tarrik affected a frown. "I am drying off." He had to obey, so chose to bring his clothes up to cover his chest.

Ren let out a breath and hurried back to their campsite. The sky was orange from the setting sun as he followed her, still naked. She'd started the fire, and it blazed with fierce abandon, its heat reminding him of his realms. When would he return?

Ren averted her eyes and waved a hand in his direction. "Get dressed."

He did as ordered. While he tugged on his clothes, she took from her saddlebag the same kit she'd used to sew up his wounds. She opened it and set the kit atop her saddle, then produced the artifact he'd stolen from Roska.

"Come here," she said, glowering as if he'd just tried to kill her.

Filled with trepidation, Tarrik complied.

Ren drew a thin knife from the kit and held it out to him. "I'm going to choose my words carefully here. Follow my directions assiduously. I'll be watching, and my bindings will restrain you. If you try to deviate even slightly, it will be the Wracking Nerves for you. And I won't be gentle this time."

Tarrik remembered the searing pain that had sent him tumbling to the ground and retching. That had been gentle? He examined the knife. It was as thin as a leaf and razor-sharp.

"What do you want me to do?" he said.

Ren's pink tongue darted out to lick her lips. She swallowed, then undid the top four buttons on her shirt. She tugged her right arm from the sleeve to bare her skin, then touched the back of her shoulder with her other hand. Her flesh was covered with scars, and Tarrik realized she'd never revealed herself before. Even when bathing in the river, she'd remained hidden, and every time they'd been together in her rooms, she'd been robed. Some of the scars were hair thin, others thick with hardened tissue. They covered every inch of her shoulder and continued under her shirt where he couldn't see.

Scars overlaid with scars.

Someone had tortured and tormented her.

"What happened?" he asked.

Ren busied herself with her kit, threading a curved needle and laying out a bandage. Just as Tarrik decided she wasn't going to answer, she spoke.

"When Samal . . . when he . . . takes you as one of the Nine, he breaks you. First the body, then the mind." She held up the artifact. "When I give you directions, you are to follow them precisely and act only when I give you permission to. Am I clear?"

Tarrik looked from the knife to the artifact in her hand and to her bared shoulder. Understanding dawned on him: she wanted him to implant the object under her skin, like a catalyst. Was it a catalyst? It didn't look or feel like any he'd seen.

"Yes," he replied.

Perhaps she'd thought to garner sympathy with the sight of her ruined skin. But he wasn't about to weep for her. He had a knife, and she was close and vulnerable. There was always a chance she'd slip up.

Ren took a deep breath. "Take the small bottle from my kit there. No, the other one. Now pour some over my skin and the knife."

She knelt in the dirt by the firelight, and he did as she asked. The clear liquid cooled his fingers rapidly as it dried, and the astringent scent of pure alcohol filled the air, though it wasn't enough to cover Ren's fear.

She reeked of the emotion, because she was asking him to cut her or because of something else? What was the artifact capable of?

"You are to make a single incision, a semicircle one inch in length, taking care to only penetrate my skin to a depth of . . . a quarter of an inch. Do you understand?"

"Yes." Tarrik tried to bring the knife close but found himself frozen by Ren's bindings. "I—"

"Good. I haven't given you permission yet. Now I do. Make the first cut."

Tarrik pricked her skin to the desired depth and traced a curve, which began to leak crimson. Ren hissed, and he realized she hadn't taken anything to dull the pain. She needed all her senses and awareness. If she messed up her instructions, she'd be meat in his hands.

She spoke through clenched teeth. "Now the powder to stop the bleeding. A light dusting."

Tarrik opened the pouch and sprinkled the wound. Immediately the blood flow stopped.

"Now, slice under the skin at the same depth to create a flap. Then insert the artifact and sew the flap up."

He placed the knife against the wound, then tried to drive it into her neck. His muscles strained against the iron grip of her bindings.

Ren looked over her shoulder at him. "You cannot overcome your baseness, can you?"

What did she know of him? Nothing! Blood and fire, he wanted to spill her blood and batter her senseless.

"Do as I command!" she barked.

Tarrik strained for a few more heartbeats, then gave up. He blinked sweat from his eyes, vowing to unlock Ananias's essence as soon as he could.

He made the second cut and shoved the disc under her skin. Ren winced and grimaced but held herself steady. Tarrik couldn't help thinking she'd taken the pain well, but from her scarred skin, he supposed she was used to it.

"Now sew up the incision," said Ren.

He did as he was told, unsure whether touching her skin repelled or aroused him.

"What does the artifact do?" he asked.

"It's . . . an augmentation. It can store a vast amount of all tidal powers, though it isn't itself a catalyst. If I'm compromised or cornered, and there are no other options, I can unleash the arcane energies within it. A last resort."

Tarrik had never heard of such a thing, nor could he come up with a reason anyone would want it under his or her skin. The release of such energies would mean Ren's death, along with anyone around her. She was probably lying.

"The world is incredibly complex, Tarrik. Can one person hope to stand against the might of a river?" Her voice grew tight, and she shook her head.

Tarrik had no idea what she was talking about and no desire to find out. Her goals were nothing to him.

"It will leave a scar," he said without thinking.

"One more doesn't matter. Have you finished?"

"Yes."

"Then take the bandage, and wrap my shoulder. Not too tightly, as I need to move my arm."

He unrolled the bandage and wrapped it underneath her arm and around her shoulder. Then he picked up the small bottle of alcohol and took a swig. It burned his throat and stomach, but the pain felt good and took his mind off killing her.

"That's all?" he said.

"Yes. You're finished."

"You should try trusting me more often. I have to obey your commands, and I cannot kill you. We're in this together."

Ren scoffed weakly. "Trust you? A demon."

"Better than being a slaver."

"I use what tools I have. If you knew what—" She broke off, shaking her head. "I trust my horse to take me where I want to go. You, I trust less than a rabid dog."

"I'm not an animal to be leashed and brought to heel whenever—"

"No, you're a blasted demon! A defiler of women and men and children! You exist only to bring chaos and to sate your own base lusts. Don't think I don't know this. Look at me! Look at my scars! Tell the hundreds of thousands of people killed by Nysrog and his followers that you're not an animal. You should be begging me for forgiveness for what your kind has done to mine."

"You're a fool! The demons had no choice. They were ripped from their world and forced to obey malicious masters like you. When you beat a dog so, it fears you. When you force it to fight in order to eat, of course it's reduced to animal urges. You brought the demons here and let their base instincts loose. Don't blame them. Blame your sorcerers."

"And the higher demons? Nysrog the Black, the Glutton of Souls?"

What was she saying? Did she abhor what Nysrog and the Tainted Cabal did? But wasn't she one of them? She had been subjugated by the Adversary and was bound to serve him. As Tarrik was bound to serve her . . . except her chains had started with torture, a tormenting of the flesh before the mind.

No. He cast such thoughts aside. She was still a slaver.

"Your kind brought this upon themselves. Slavers and seekers after power! Users of—"

"Cease talking before I punish you, foul demon!"

Tarrik clamped his mouth shut. A dose of the Wracking Nerves wouldn't serve any purpose. Silently, he cursed himself for his loss of control. He resolved to do better. He had to if he was to survive this accursed place. He must pander to Ren, get her to trust him, all the while working on absorbing Ananias and using his strength to break free of her bindings.

Ren moved to her saddlebags and pulled out a journal. She began writing. She didn't look to be in pain from the incision and implantation of the artifact.

Tarrik sat by the fire, trying not to think. A twig snapped over by the beezle-fruit trees, and he turned his head to investigate.

"It's just a crab. You're jumpy," said Ren.

"Jumpy?" Tarrik reached for his spear, vowing to keep it close while they were out in the wilderness. His hands tightened around the shaft, squeezing hard with the remnants of his anger.

"You're always alert. When you see something move, or there's a sudden sound, you move your head to investigate it, then freeze."

"My realms are not kind to the unaware. I am your bodyguard. It is my job to be vigilant. Would you rather I ceased to guard you?"

"No. I'd rather you tried to appear normal."

"So I am to protect you by not being alert? Your words make no sense."

"No . . . just minimize your sudden movements. Now, go and catch a few of the beezle-crabs, and throw them on the fire. They won't take long to cook. They move slowly, so it's easy to avoid their claws—but I should warn you, they can snap your fingers off."

By the time night fell, Tarrik had eaten two of the crabs, and Ren one. Their flesh was succulent and tasty, not as fishy as he'd expected. He supposed they did live on land.

Ren pumped water with her left arm, and they washed their hands and plates before she told Tarrik to rest and brought out a leather-bound book to read—the grimoire. Again she generated a sorcerous globe above her head to provide enough light.

Tarrik wasn't sure what to do with himself out here alone with his slaver, under the stars. He glanced at Ren, but her attention was consumed by her reading. Occasionally she frowned and mouthed words, as if familiarizing herself with their sounds. She seemed unconcerned that a sending from Samal might show up. Then again, she had said such a manifestation shouldn't happen again.

After another swallow of spirits, Tarrik tossed a few branches onto the fire and settled down beside it. The heat felt good on his face and hands, a reminder of home. He turned his attention to the churning mass inside him that was Ananias's essence.

His heart drummed in his chest as he realized there were both hope and terror here. Hope of returning to his realm of exile and somehow redeeming himself, thereby being granted permission to rejoin demon society. And terror that he might fall short of this goal and be forever outcast. He could have wept at the strength of emotions roiling within him.

He remembered the first higher demon he'd defeated and absorbed: Bergrunn Unnur-Valgerour, self-appointed brood mother of the aesheyak—minor demons similar to spiders, though as large as the beezle-crabs. A whirlwind had roared around him, through his mind, as her essence had invigorated and strengthened him. Afterward, his body had developed over months to become more. His mind had sharpened, expanded to another level of consciousness. And his command over the dark-tide had grown—so much so he'd thought he could sometimes feel it even when the moons shone in the night sky.

But Ananias was something else. His essence was a bottomless deep, a void Tarrik might drown in if he wasn't careful. It had happened to other higher demons: overconfidence led to rushed mistakes and then a descent into madness. Perhaps that was what had happened to Nysrog. And maybe the Adversary had succumbed as well.

Absorbing another's essence was always a test, Tarrik realized. Only the sane, the strong of will, and the careful passed. To fail was to lose yourself to the roiling energies and condemn your mind. He must proceed softly. Haste was the enemy here.

Besides, Ren would likely sense him accessing the dark-tide and react with violence. He must bide his time.

The next morning, Ren turned their horses loose, slapping their rumps until they cantered away. Though Tarrik wasn't sorry to see the beasts go, he thought they could have at least killed one and eaten its meat.

Ren watched them stop some distance away to crop the grass growing across fields long fallow. When she turned to Tarrik, her eyes were bright and wild.

She is mad, like others of the Nine.

"We were followed yesterday," she said. "They used sorcery to keep an eye on us during the night, to make sure we didn't sneak away under the cover of darkness."

Tarrik grunted. "Someone sent by Veljor? Or Puck Moonan?"

"I don't know. The incantations didn't have Puck's scent. Perhaps his apprentice or one of the sorcerers in Veljor's employ."

"The green-skinned waif?"

"She does have Illapa blood, which makes Puck's choice curious indeed."

He had no idea why and didn't care. "Shall I kill them?"

Ren squinted into the blazing sun, shading her eyes. "No. We will be gone from here soon. They won't hinder us."

Since she'd freed the horses, Tarrik decided she must have a sorcerous transport solution. Surely she couldn't be powerful enough to shadow-step them farther than their line of sight? Besides, she didn't have control over the dark-tide.

"Gather our gear, including the saddles, and put them over there in the sunlight." Without further explanation, she strode to the water pump and began cranking the rusted metal handle.

Tarrik suppressed a growl and set to his task, glancing with hunger toward the beezle-fruit trees and the horde of clacking crabs underneath.

When he was finished, Tarrik retrieved his spear and stood by their gear. Ren continued to pump water until the trough was full again. It had drained overnight through a crack in its side. She stepped gingerly over the mud surrounding the trough and filled the bucket with water.

She looked at him then, her eyes glowing with a golden light, and spoke a cant. Then another.

Heat rose from a circle of ground to Tarrik's left, smoking as though it were molten rock. Swaths of flame erupted and scoured the grass to fine ash. He glimpsed a twinkle in the air over the now-blackened circle.

Ren heaved the bucket of water over the sorcery-scarred earth. Steam erupted upon contact, but none of the vapor plumed into the sky. Instead, a haze hung suspended over the circle as if caught in an invisible net.

Another cant, this one shouted. Sweat poured from Ren's face.

Tarrik retreated a step. What was she doing? Waves of heat blasted his face, sent bugs leaping from the surviving grass around the circle. Strangely, he sensed only minimal dawn- and dusk-tide emanations. Perhaps she was testing her storage amulet.

Blue light erupted around the circle, filaments scribing the shape of a thin disc that hovered a foot above the scorched ground.

Ren poured more water from the bucket over the disc, and the liquid evaporated instantly. She dropped the bucket and strode to Tarrik's side. She smelled of arcane power and the parched cleanliness of clothes dried in bright sunlight. Above all, she smelled pleased with herself.

"The water is essential," she told him. "It both harnesses and reflects light. And light is power. All of the tides—the dawn, the dusk, and the dark—are born of light."

She was a fool. "Not the dark-tide."

Ren regarded him with amusement, which raised his hackles. "If you say so."

"And what is this you've wrought with your sorcery?"

"A conveyance. Place our gear on the platform. The heat won't penetrate the top from underneath. Be quick about it, though, or you might char your new boots."

Ren took a step up onto the shimmering disc, which stood suspended over the ground. "Come. We have a long way to travel." She stepped to the east side and knelt, bowing her head and whispering cants.

Tarrik swallowed his misgivings and piled their gear in the middle of the disc. Close to the platform he could feel the fierce heat from underneath penetrating his boot leather. He fetched his spear, then stood on the disc. He could see through its scintillating cobalt to the ash-strewn ground beneath.

He'd never heard of such an arcane contrivance. Even Contian had relied on mundane means of travel. Ren must be much more powerful than the old man had been, though he supposed the Nine had been chosen for their sorcerous potency—if what Ren said could be believed.

"Sit," she said.

Tarrik complied, placing his spear beside him. Fifty yards away, the horses grazed unperturbed, and the crabs searched for nourishment beneath the beezle-fruit trees.

Ren raised her arms, and crimson-violet lightning answered her call. She grasped its sparking tendrils in both hands. The disc lurched forward, then rose into the sky. Wind whipped about them, tugging their clothes and lashing their hair. Trees passed in a blur; then the pair were above the canopy, rising still higher. A fall from such a height would burst them open like ripe fruit, Tarrik thought uneasily.

Ren stood and cast her gaze behind Tarrik, searching the sky.

Tarrik turned to see black orbs trailing smoke scorching through the sky toward them. They originated from a single point on the ground, a mile from where they'd made camp. He clutched his spear and scrambled to his feet. There was nowhere to run.

Ren sang cant after cant, gathering more and more power unto herself. She laughed, as if being assailed were amusing.

She is insane.

The dark orbs hammered into Ren's ethereal wards and glanced off into the clouds above. The disc rocked, and Tarrik staggered, falling to his knees. Ren tottered but remained upright. She cried out as cracks appeared in her wards.

She snarled another cant, and eldritch power answered. Tarrik felt her wards repair.

Plumes of incandescence surged outward from her, following the dispersing trails of smoke back to their source. The air seemed to crack asunder as her incantations hit the earth in a fiery crush. Trees and boulders were immolated. A fissure opened up in the ground. Dust and embers swirled. Tarrik stared openmouthed at the destruction.

Ren placed her hands on her hips and gazed at the burning ground, waiting.

No further sorcery assaulted them.

She returned to the front of the disc. "Well, she won't try that again."

He gathered his wits. "Did Puck send her after you?"

She shook her head. "He may be insane, but he isn't stupid. His apprentice acted on her own. Like so many of the young, she thinks she knows everything, but she has much to learn. One day, someone will squash her like a bug. Today, I let her live. And she knows it."

Chapter Seven

Tarrik couldn't determine how fast they were flying, but miles and miles of lands passed quickly beneath them. The wind gusted occasionally around him, but Ren, sitting at the leading edge of the disc, must have constructed a shield of some sort in front of her. Her head was bowed, and in her hands she held lightning-struck clouds that glowed golden and sparked with brilliant white sorcery. Tendrils of the strange power straggled over her arms and face, trailing behind her like vaporous hair.

A light rain squall came upon them as they left sight of land and coasted over the Simorga Sea, but its droplets puffed into steam before they splattered Tarrik. He perceived that the heat from the enchantment that powered the disc must emanate in all directions while they were aloft.

The white-flecked field of blue stretched away underneath them, and the air was crisp and clean. A fleet of fishing ships heading back to the coast looked like toys. Tarrik experienced a rush of terror at the thought of all that water. If Ren's sorcery were to fail, they would plummet into those blue depths and never resurface. He'd seen drowned bodies before, and once the broken limbs and shattered skull of a woman who had thrown herself over a cliff into the waves below to escape ravening demons. He had been one of them, back before he'd advanced to a higher order.

He swallowed down the last of Roska Fridle's spirits and sighed. How far until they reached their destination he didn't know. With a sniff, he rolled the empty bottle across the platform and watched it drop over the side. The heat from the disc shattered the container, and glass whizzed behind them as if shot from a bow. He shuddered as the debris faded to a speck, then disappeared into the blue. There was no end to this sky or the ocean. It was as if they were the only living beings in existence.

Finally, a faint smudge ahead grew steadily into a landmass. Rugged cliffs spotted with dark beaches rose to windswept grasses and then to mountainous forests.

"Niyas," said Ren, and Tarrik thought there was relief in her tone.

An island country, Tarrik knew that much from past experience. Ruled by a queen. Or it had been before. Much could change in this world fairly quickly. A defect, he supposed, of the humans' short lives.

Behind them the sun brushed the edge of the ocean and began to paint the sky orange and red. The fiery colors reminded him of home, though he had come to find the sky's usual pale blue calming. Tarrik suddenly realized they had been descending slowly for some time. He could now discern individual foam-crested waves. Nearby a flock of seagulls alighted on the water, some diving to feed on a shoal of small fish that formed a shadow beneath the surface.

"Who will you have me steal from here?" he said.

Ren didn't answer. Instead, she stood and raised her arms above her head, stretching her back. Her orichalcum-hilted sword still hung down along her spine; she hadn't taken it off since they'd left Ivrian.

Even though they'd been flying the entire day, Ren didn't look the worse for wear. In fact, despite her incision, she seemed invigorated, which made Tarrik curious. The prolonged use of sorcery had to have exhausted her repositories; likely she'd want to reach land before dark in order to take advantage of the dusk-tide to build up her strength, then pass a quiet night until she could absorb the dawn-tide too.

He frowned when he saw a mass of buildings to the north with a smoky haze lingering above them. He gauged it to be a small city and wondered why Ren would risk alighting so close when she was weak. She would be an easy target for enemies in her depleted state, which meant he would become a target too.

They curved in low along the coast, and Tarrik realized Ren was heading for a narrow cove with a black-sand beach battered by waves higher than his head. To his surprise, as they approached, he noticed three horses, all shades of brown, tied to a large driftwood log, and a fire blazed on the sand. Only one of the horses was saddled, and there was someone waiting for them. A small man waved as they approached, as if unconcerned to see a sorcerer and a demon descending from the sky, then returned to tending the fire.

The disc skimmed a foot above the sand and slowed as they came within a few dozen paces of the man and then hovered over the sand, which hissed and steamed around them. The black sandy beach stank of rotting fruit and decay, a cloying, inescapable odor caused by what, Tarrik wasn't sure. Perhaps it came from the mounds of seaweed tangled around driftwood strewn along the tide line. Past the sand and cliffs, verdant mountains rose to dominate the sky, so green that Tarrik could imagine the thick, syrupy air beneath the canopy, an unwelcome contrast to the thin, dry air of his abyssal realms.

"Bring our gear," Ren said without looking at him, and she hopped down onto the sand and walked toward the fire and the man.

His injuries were rapidly healing, but he wasn't happy with her command. Tarrik gingerly shouldered both sets of saddlebags, picked up one saddle, and stepped off the platform. When he was far enough away from the disc's residual heat, he dropped his load onto the cool sand and went back for the other saddle, then made a final trip to retrieve his spear. As he lifted it, the disc sparkled beneath him and disappeared. He jumped a foot to the ground, landing with a crack on sand that had been turned to glass. He tottered as heat rose to caress him, and Ren turned.

"Quickly," she said over the gnashing waves and gusting wind. Ren had already taken a plate from the man and was perched on another log near the horses.

Tarrik trudged toward her and the stranger, leaving their bags where he'd dropped them. He wasn't going to lug everything over to the fire when they could walk the horses to the gear later.

"Who's this?" the man said to Ren as Tarrik approached. "You said bring an extra horse, but I thought it might be for equipment. You know I don't like surprises. Has his background been checked? Where's he from? Big bastard, isn't he—a bloody savage."

The man was barely taller than Ren and of a similar build. He had deep crimson skin, light-brown hair, and a forked beard. And, to go with the beard, the voluble man had hairs growing out of his nostrils. His eyes were brown, with almond-shaped pupils much like a cat's. Apart from his odd skin and eyes, his face was somehow nondescript, with no single defining feature.

"He's my new bodyguard," Ren said. "That's all you need to know. He isn't like others of his kind." She began eating a sizeable pink-scaled roasted fish along with toasted slices of bread.

"That remains to be seen," the man said, and narrowed his eyes at Tarrik.

Other than salt and sweat, no scent came from him, Tarrik realized, almost as if his body reflected his nondescript face. At least he wasn't a demon.

Tarrik jammed the butt of his spear into the sand so it stood upright and took the plate of food the man held out. Ignoring the pewter fork, he used his fingers to dig into the white flesh of the fish and sated his physical hunger. The bread he left untouched since it was hard to stomach.

The man watched him warily for a few moments. "Did she forget to feed you? She forgets to eat herself sometimes. Well, you do," he added when Ren rolled her eyes.

The two of them seemed at ease together—friends or colleagues, Tarrik thought. .

The fish was flavorsome, although lacking the animal delight of red meat. The meal would do for now until he could find something with warm blood running through its veins. Between this and the crabs, he felt he was missing some vital nutrient, and perhaps he'd lose strength if he kept up this unnatural diet.

"Who are you?" Tarrik asked around a mouthful.

The man glanced at Ren, and she nodded her permission.

"Veika Yunnik, employed by the Lady Branwen to oversee various matters in Niyas. And you are . . . ?"

"Tarrik."

"Just Tarrik? From the far south, I assume?" A shrewd look came to Veika's face. "Does Bidzil the Deathless still lead the Blood Shakar tribe?"

Tarrik knew a trap when he heard one. He had no idea who the tribe or its leader were and cared less. Tarrik shrugged and turned the fish over to get at the flesh on the other side.

"Cat got your tongue?" said Veika.

A cat again. What cat? "I have been exiled for some time. If Bidzil the Deathless still rules, I wouldn't know." Both true statements.

Veika opened his mouth again, but Ren hushed him. "Enough. Let me eat in peace. And I assume we're not camping on this beach tonight? The wind coming off the ocean will chill me to the bone."

"Ah, my lady, but you would look so lovely in the moonlight reflected off the waves, the tangerine flames of the fire highlighting your burnished skin and midnight hair. Why, such a sight would—"

"We're not at court now, Veika. And you know better than to try to impress me with flattering words."

"It is the truth, my lady, hardly flattery. Have you given any thought to my proposal that you approach the lord of Atya and propose a marriage of—"

"I have not. My studies do not allow time for such diversions."

"Hardly a diversion, my lady. You would become one of the most powerful—"

"We'll discuss this at a later time," snapped Ren.

She put her plate on the sand beside her, and Tarrik saw she'd barely touched the fish and bread. He didn't blame her for being put off her food by Veika's chatter. He talked far too much for such a small man. Tarrik already felt like punching him in the mouth to quiet him.

Veika bowed his head and grimaced, then busied himself cleaning up. He tossed the remains of Ren's meal into the fire, then did the same with the skin and bones and bread left on Tarrik's plate. He took the plates and forks and a griddle he'd used to roast the fish down to the water to wash them.

"Who is this runt?" Tarrik said.

"Don't call him that. He's one of my spymasters, a good one. He's been in my employ for over a decade."

"What hold do you have over him?"

She looked at him. "Is that what you think of me?"

"You must have something he wants, or you know some secret of his that he doesn't want known. Why else would he serve you? Or perhaps you've bound him as you have me."

"His wife and daughter were taken by slavers from the south. He went after them, but by the time he found them, they were almost unrecognizable. They'd been starved, beaten, and abused. They didn't survive the trip back to Niyas. Veika returned to his job as a trader, but his heart wasn't in it. When I met him, he'd lost something vital, something to keep him going, and he was close to losing the will to live. I saw he had gained other skills while searching for his loved ones and offered him employment and a cause greater than any other he'd known."

That explained Veika's barely concealed hostility, since he thought Tarrik was from beyond the Jargalan Desert. The man's life was a sob story, then. A weak man who had been unable to protect what he valued. And now he was a stray dog eating out of the first friendly hand. What if another master offered a tastier treat? Perhaps Tarrik could undermine his loyalty. Except the only things he had to offer were himself and his spear, both limited by Ren's bindings.

"He talks too much," he said.

"That has been remarked upon before," said Veika from behind him. He stacked the wet plates and utensils into a sack. "Watch your mouth, Tarrik. Rudeness will get you killed in some places."

"If you were a threat, you'd already be dead."

"Charming. I don't know where you find them, Lady Branwen."

"All sorts of places," said Ren. "Now, let us get a good night's sleep. I assume you've arranged a campsite?"

Veika nodded. "We'll saddle up and be there soon. It's not far."

He looked at Tarrik. Tarrik stared back.

"The saddles," Veika prompted.

"Tarrik doesn't know how to saddle a horse," interjected Ren. "They ride lizards where he's from, as you well know."

"Almost the same thing." Shaking his head, Veika scooped sand onto the fire to smother it, then collected the three horses' reins. He led them over to the pile of gear and soon had them saddled and the cinches tightened.

They rode up the beach and onto an ascending rocky path that took them along a crumbling rise to a flat area of wiry grass. Veika rode at the fore, and Tarrik remained at the rear. He needed a drink, some dripping red meat, and a woman to sate him. What he had was a spear and a reeking animal.

They'd gone barely fifty paces when Veika called a halt. A few twisted shrubs with interwoven branches bent by the constant wind formed the bones of a shelter. A covering of thick canvas was roped over the top and pegged to the ground to form a crude roof. Wood was already stacked inside a ring of stones, and two leather satchels were tucked under one of the bushes.

"It's not much, but it'll keep the wind out," said Veika as they dismounted.

"Thank you," said Ren. "It's far better than sleeping in the open out here. Tarrik, help Veika stow our gear. I'm going to sleep. I'm exhausted." She found a spot underneath the shelter, rolled herself in a blanket, and lay still.

Very odd, Tarrik decided. While directing her sorcerous contrivance, Ren had been full of energy, even at the end of their trip when daylight was fading. And now she was fatigued and hadn't even replenished her repository with the dusk-tide. Surely it was depleted. He was wise enough to know something strange had happened.

Veika ignored Ren's command, settled himself beside the ring of stones, and struck an alchemical fire stick to set the kindling ablaze.

Tarrik looked at his horse, which returned his stare. He propped his spear against the shelter and set to work. He felt Veika's gaze on him, as if the man wanted to catch his eye to gloat about not helping, but Tarrik ignored him. He packed their bags and saddles into a pile and tied the horses to the shrubs, where they could graze the windswept grass.

"Don't talk much, do you?" said Veika as Tarrik squatted on his haunches on the other side of the fire.

"I try to avoid it." The heat on his face felt comforting, and he closed his eyes, enjoying the orange light flickering on his lids.

"Better to have people think you're an idiot than have your words confirm it, I guess."

Tarrik allowed himself a small smile. This Veika was annoying, but his words were as wind. He almost responded with a jibe about failing to protect one's family but thought better of it. He didn't know how long they'd have to travel together, and the man might yet be useful to get to Ren. Such a ploy would be easier if the runt wasn't hostile.

"Most savages from the south would have drawn steel at that insult," said Veika.

"I'm not most savages," replied Tarrik, opening his eyes. "And I wouldn't need steel."

Veika had been running a whetstone along a dagger. Now he twirled the blade with a flourish, and it disappeared, probably inside his sleeve. "I don't like working with people I don't know. And even less with ignorant savages."

"Do you have any spirits?" Tarrik asked. The runt's chattering was annoying, and he seemed to want to irritate. Perhaps that was his plan, to needle until his opponent snapped.

"I have a bottle of rum, Black Widow's Barrel. Niyas is famed for it."

"Fetch it."

Veika's eyes bored into Tarrik's. "It's very expensive."

Tarrik grinned and held out a hand. "I'll owe you."

After a moment's hesitation, Veika rose and rummaged through his saddlebag. He produced a brown glass bottle with a black label and handed it to Tarrik, who uncorked the drink and took a long swig. The rum was too sweet for his taste, but it burned his throat and numbed his emotions, all that was required.

"By the gods, take it easy," snarled Veika.

Tarrik wiped the back of his hand across his lips and passed the bottle back to him. "It'll do."

"It'll do? This rum was aged in fired oak barrels for ten years! The finest sugarcane in Niyas was pressed for its juice—"

"It's a bit sweet. Do you have anything else?"

Veika's face turned red. "It's rum! Fermenting gets rid of the sugar." He cradled the bottle like it was a baby and sulked back to his side of the fire. He wiped its neck on his sleeve before taking a sip. "Too sweet!" he muttered, shaking his head.

A pile of flat cakes sat atop a stone, warming by the fire. Veika picked one up and munched on it. Tarrik assumed he was supposed to ask for his share but didn't. Even though the rum had left a disgusting sugariness in his mouth and he wanted to get rid of the lingering taste, asking this idiot for food was a step too far. Besides, the flat cake probably tasted like sawdust.

He went through their gear until he found Ren's healing kit and the bottle of pure alcohol. He swished it around in his mouth before swallowing. When he returned to the fire, Veika had a puzzled look on his face.

"You're disgusting," he said. "That's for cleaning wounds."

"We savages usually are disgusting. The southern lands are harsh and do not tolerate niceties."

"You're no gods-damned savage. And don't try to deny it. You could be one, but too much is off about you. Few would see it, but I'm paid to notice things others don't."

Tarrik remained silent. He grabbed his own blanket and settled down close to the fire, laying his spear beside him. He wasn't in a hurry to sleep but just wanted to get away from the runt's ceaseless prattling. He felt Veika's gaze on him but wasn't worried about the man trying to kill him. Veika was in Ren's employ and seemed both fearful of her and loyal.

He lay still, the warmth of the fire at his back, and eventually heard Veika take to his own makeshift bed. Seemingly only moments later, Tarrik jerked upright, his spear instantly in his hand, at the sound of an animal screeching.

The red and white crescent moons shed little light, and the night was dark, a band of stars stretching across the sky in a speckled ribbon. Something howled in the distance, and Tarrik clambered to his feet. Veika's blanket was empty, though Ren still slept, it appeared.

Tarrik found the small man a dozen yards away, his face turned to the eastern hills. He held out the bottle of Black Widow's Barrel as Tarrik approached. Tarrik shuddered and shook his head.

"More for me," said Veika. He took a sip and smacked his lips appreciatively.

"What's out there?" Tarrik asked.

"A manticarr. Sounds like it stumbled on a pack of wolves. It'll probably kill them all and spend the night feeding, so we should be safe. I don't like Lady Branwen being out in the wilderness like this; it's too risky. There's a wraithe here in the south too—I've seen her from a distance. I'm not sure even Ren could match such an ancient being. Anyway, we'll be in Dwemor Port tomorrow."

"What's a manticarr?"

"A gods-damned creature as big as a house. Don't you know anything?"

"I know how to kill people."

"I'll bet you do. Well, you'll find plenty of work with the Lady Branwen."

Chapter Eight

"Why would a single man need three saddles?" Veika said. "People notice such things. And when they do, they start to ask questions. I don't want people asking questions about me or about the people I work for."

Tarrik let the man's voice roll over him and disappear into the wind. Veika had talked all morning, through much of their midday meal, and into the afternoon. He was silent only when his mouth was full. Ren seemed to cope well enough, but already Tarrik wanted to throw him off a cliff. A high one.

Now, as they neared the city of Dwemor Port, Veika slowed his horse to ride alongside Ren and spoke in a low tone, clearly hoping Tarrik wouldn't hear.

"Are you sure you can trust him?"

"More than most," she said, and Tarrik knew she was referring to her sorcerous bindings.

"That doesn't alleviate my concerns. I will find someone more suitable for you. This—"

"This warrior is suitable."

"But I don't know him," said Veika.

"Neither does anyone else."

Veika glanced over his shoulder at Tarrik, pursing his lips and scratching his head. Perhaps he was worried he wouldn't be paid if Tarrik let Ren get killed. Or perhaps he lusted after his master.

"May I remind you that your last choice didn't work out," he said softly.

So Tarrik had had a predecessor. It had to have been a human warrior, since Tarrik was her first summoning. He racked his brain but couldn't recall any other higher demon having gone missing in mysterious circumstances recently. Despite his exile, he still kept in touch, as gossip traveled freely between realms.

"You may. But in this I stand resolute."

"I seldom question your wisdom, my lady—"

"You seldom don't!" said Ren, laughing. "But I am firm on this. I believe he is the best choice."

"He doesn't say much."

"He doesn't have to. It's not his job."

They crested a large hill, and the city wall came into view below: weathered stone held together with crumbling mortar and topped with a wooden palisade of sharpened stakes. Behind it huddled a sizeable city, its streets filled with the restless thrum of humanity, all unaware they lived in a cage of their own making. Buildings stretched as far as the eye could see, shrouded by smoke, and a deepwater harbor crowded with ships sat on the western edge. Canals flowed from the harbor to crisscross the relatively flat city. Tarrik could make out more walls inside the outer one; clearly the city had expanded as its inhabitants had swelled in number. The older walls were now festooned with wooden buildings that rose high above the rest.

The southern gate was unguarded. "Most of the traffic comes from the north and from the harbor," explained Veika.

A few crimson-skinned, bored-looking officials half-heartedly checked wagons and people for contraband as they entered and left: a poke of a pole into loose hay, a cursory glance at vegetables and livestock, a tap on sealed barrels to ensure they were full of liquid and not something else. One official's eyes widened as he saw Veika. He had the same almond-shaped pupils, Tarrik noted. The guard waved them into the city without inspection.

To Tarrik's eye, the city's residents were a stark contrast to those he'd seen in Ivrian. Most were crimson skinned of one shade or another with the same cat's eyes Veika had, though colors ranged from pale yellow, to brown, to orange and golden. Traits of the Niyandrian race, guessed Tarrik. They appeared more cheerful and also smelled happier. There was less fear and anger in the atmosphere. So far the trio had passed only one squad of soldiers, all busy helping a wagoner change a broken wheel. The occasional dog weaved through the crowd, and there wasn't a hanged corpse or gibbet in sight. Tarrik concluded that whoever ruled Niyas was more benevolent than those rulers on the western continent under the influence of the Tainted Cabal. But as he knew, the longer the leash, the more trouble a dog could get into.

They rode along streets crowded with two- and three-story buildings on either side and past canals crossed by stone and timber bridges and narrow timber walkways for foot traffic. Veika exchanged a few words with all different types: shopkeepers standing in doorways, old women sitting at windows, food vendors on street corners, and even a couple of street urchins. Each conversation usually ended with him handing over a coin or two; Ren seemed content not to hasten him along.

Finally Veika led them down a cobbled street and through an archway into the yard of a two-story, brown-brick building roofed with wooden shingles.

"I'll take care of the horses and your gear," he said to Ren. "You go inside. Jendra's expecting you."

Ren dismounted. "Tarrik will see to our bags. But I appreciate you looking after the horses."

Tarrik tossed both sets of saddlebags over one shoulder before taking up his spear. As he followed Ren, Veika called after him, "Watch your head."

142

A set of double doors led into a kitchen. Tarrik ducked beneath the low lintel. When he straightened, his head brushed a ceiling beam.

A severe-looking, sharp-nosed woman wearing plain gray trousers and a navy shirt dusted flour from her hands before she greeted Ren with a smile and hug. Tarrik noticed a loaded crossbow on the central workbench and a knife block with enough steel to satisfy an eight-armed idol.

"I came as quickly as I could," said Ren.

The woman—Jendra, Tarrik presumed—nodded. "I'm grateful. You know I wouldn't ask if it wasn't important."

"Hush now. If one of the Nine is out of line, I have to act."

Tarrik wondered what rules there were for the Nine. Surely they could do whatever they desired. If they were like Ren, then they had great power and could avoid any consequences.

Jendra returned to the task of kneading dough, pounding the mass as if it were the face of someone she wanted to punish. A greased loaf tin sat to her right, flanked by a cast-iron oven stoked with coals. "At first we were puzzled; then Veika found out that Lischen the Nightwhisperer is in Dwemor. She must have slipped into the city some months ago and kept a very low profile ever since." She paused in punching the dough to wipe away a tear. "We should have realized when we found out it was children with the spark. It's not right, and the Queen's Guard can't do anything . . . well, you know why."

"I'm here now," Ren said. "I'll sort this mess out, and everything will be back to normal."

Jendra snorted. "It won't be normal for those whose children were taken. What of them?"

Ren hesitated and bit her lower lip. "I don't know."

"They're as good as dead. You know it."

Ren stepped to the woman and held her shoulders. "I'll put a stop to this, Jendra. I promise."

Ren was making a lot of promises, and Tarrik thought there was a good chance she'd break some of them. Tarrik understood now. "With the spark" must mean the children who had been born with dawn- and dusk-tide repositories, and thus the ability to use sorcery. Tarrik surmised that someone was abusing the children's power or wanted it for themselves.

This member of the Nine, Lischen the Nightwhisperer, had been abducting children who had the potential to become sorcerers. And Ren pretended to care. Why? These people were fools to trust her.

"Where should I put our gear?" he said, sick of the farce.

Jendra seemed to notice him for the first time. She looked him up and down and gave him a disapproving glare. "Upstairs, third door on the right. You'll sleep in the stables."

"He'll sleep in my room," Ren said firmly.

Jendra's mouth dropped open, and she paled. "My lady, a savage! I cannot condone—"

Ren cut her off. "There have been several attempts on my life over the last few weeks. I need my bodyguard close. There will be no impropriety—I assure you."

With a final glare at Tarrik, Jendra turned back to her dough and began shaping it. "Well," she huffed, "it's not for me to tell you how to live your life. Once you're settled in and washed up, come back down, and we'll discuss what information we have over a light meal."

"As long as there's hot tea as well," said Ren with a smile.

"You know there will be. Hurry along, and we can get started."

Tarrik followed Ren up a set of creaking stairs and into a small room with only one bed. It would be large enough for two, just. Perhaps there was opportunity here . . . forced intimacy could play tricks on people, cause their animal instincts to override their conscious minds. Accidental touch had a way of awakening desire and lowering one's guard. If he was fortunate, he would find a chink in her armor to exploit. Ananias's powerful essence churned away inside him, and he touched against its surface briefly. The hardness of the barrier was almost reassuring, as if his salvation was nearly within his grasp.

Ren opened the curtains to let in light through a narrow window with an ornate iron grille in the shape of a vine. Expensive-looking bars, decided Tarrik. He noted that all the other windows in the building sported the same security. The bars would keep out thieves and intruders but also trapped inside those who might want to escape. Other exits must exist, then, maybe a rooftop door or an underground tunnel.

"Put our gear on the floor in the corner, and come down to the kitchen," Ren said. "It'll be dark soon, and we've no time to waste."

"We often seem to run into sorcerers of the Nine," Tarrik said. "A strange coincidence."

Ren gave him a flat stare. "This is the circle I operate in. It would be odd not to encounter them."

Tarrik didn't believe her. Ren had gone out of her way to bring them here, at considerable personal risk and expenditure of her power, to pretend to help people whom she'd gulled into trusting her. "Don't tell me you're helping these people out of the goodness of your heart. You're doing it because you want to sabotage one of your fellow sorcerers."

"I don't expect you to believe me," she said coldly. "Which is why I won't explain myself to you."

He changed direction, trying to push her off balance. "What happened to the bodyguard before me? Did he die in your service?"

Ren paused, and her lips drew into a thin line. "There are frequent assassination attempts on all Tainted Cabal members. I was somewhat incapacitated at the time and wasn't able to shield him."

"Dangerous enemies make you a dangerous woman."

"Some think so."

As did Tarrik. Ren was formidable, but even the hardest stone could be made to crack.

"In most instances your lack of curiosity is to your advantage," Ren added. "In others, it will be your undoing."

Tarrik inclined his head. "I am so advised."

"Do you think I don't know you're mocking me?"

"I care not either way."

"I would prefer your presence here to be bearable."

"For you or me?"

She scowled at him for a heartbeat, then turned her gaze to the room. "The bodyguard before you suffered an unfortunate cant which made a pincushion of his body. His blood covered the walls and floor. Can you, Tarrik Nal-Valim, demon of the Thirty-Seventh Order, protect yourself against such a cant?"

His hand tightened on his spear. "You know I cannot."

"Best remember that. Give me good reason to keep you alive." She turned her back on him and left the room.

Tarrik heard her footsteps fade as she descended the stairs. His jaw clenched, and he paced around the room, trying to work out his anger. Stay alive, then absorb Ananias. That was his plan. After that . . . he'd have to figure out another plan. Ren was not someone to take lightly.

Tarrik did as he was told and stored their bags, then went downstairs.

Jendra poured black tea into three blue-glazed mugs, all chipped and cracked. Veika was already sipping his tea, his eyes fixed on Tarrik.

Jendra picked up a jar and offered it around. "Honey?"

"Yes, please," said Ren.

When she'd added a spoonful and stirred, Jendra turned to Tarrik, who shook his head in disgust. He sipped the tea to try to fit in. The infusion was hot but tasted like leaf-strewn water left to stagnate and turn brown.

"He doesn't speak much," Jendra remarked.

"I didn't employ him for his conversation," said Ren.

Jendra chuckled softly.

"Are you sure you don't want to rest tonight?" Veika asked Ren. "We can gather more information tomorrow, and maybe you can scry for the Nightwhisperer too. We'll be in a better position to act then."

"You won't be acting," said Ren. "It'll be just Tarrik and myself. There will be too much sorcery, and you'll be in danger. Now, tell me what you know."

Veika's lips pursed, and he stroked his beard, obviously put out by Ren's refusal to include him. Eventually he grimaced and, voice tight with tension, said, "A young girl went missing a few months back. Her mother sent her out to buy bread and a few other things, and she never returned. There was the usual outcry, and the locals came together to search for her, but they couldn't find any trace. Most assumed the worst: a lunatic who prefers his women young, or she was taken by slavers. After a week most stopped searching, except for her family." He paused and coughed. "The girl had recently been tested for sorcerous aptitude, and a school had offered her an apprenticeship."

"Which school wanted her?" asked Ren.

"The Evokers."

She let out a low whistle. "A rare talent then. The Evokers are picky, so much so it's a wonder their school hasn't died out."

Tarrik glanced sidelong at Ren. Her father, Contian, had been the grandmaster of the Red Gate Covenant, who were one of the Evokers' main rivals. Did she also belong to an ancient school of sorcery? Did she have contacts there she could use? If so, he wouldn't have thought she would still be welcome there, not now that she was a member of the Tainted Cabal. But humans often kept the people they hated close, a peculiarity Tarrik found puzzling.

"The Evokers said they hadn't seen the girl since the testing," Jendra added, topping up everyone's mugs as she talked. "They were quite put out at losing her, as they thought they had a good one in the girl. Even attempted a scrying, which didn't work. From that, they assumed the girl was no longer inside the city."

Ren tapped her nails on her mug. "And then they found her body?"

Jendra dropped her gaze to the floor. "Yes. Floating in a canal. Not a mark on her, but that's common with drownings."

"And that's what caught your attention: the fact that she was still in the city but the Evokers hadn't been able to scry her."

"Yes," said Veika, placing his mug on the table. "We put the word out to see if there was a pattern—whether children with the talent were disappearing after being tested and accepted by one of the sorcerous schools. It seemed there weren't any others, but then I found out Lischen was here. Her reputation is, as you know, quite . . . nasty."

"What else do you have?" Ren asked.

"We discovered that other children had gone missing. With a little digging, we were able to confirm they were all tested and rejected. Each bore a black mark rather than a red one."

Tarrik glanced at Ren, wondering what the marks signified. She answered before he opened his mouth to ask.

"Each child tested for arcane aptitude is marked on their index finger with black or red ensorcelled ink. Black for the rejects, and red for those with a spark that could be fanned into flame. The schools select from among the red-marked children and often give their chosen a pin to wear denoting their school. However, sorcery isn't respected everywhere. In some parts of the world, children with sorcerous ability have their throats cut." She sipped her tea, frowning. "If the first missing girl had great potential, why bother taking rejected children?"

"We don't know," said Jendra. "We're not even sure the disappearances are related."

Tarrik had to stop himself from rolling his eyes. He supposed the simplest tricks worked for a reason. The first girl was too obvious, so her abductors had changed their tactics.

"We'll focus on the first girl then," Ren said. "What was her name?"

"Aleena. Her mother is a basket weaver, and her father harvests and dyes the reeds."

"No sorcerers in her immediate family?"

"There was a grandfather originally from a small settlement who was found to have talent late in his life. But at that age there's not much the schools can do with potential sorcerers. From what we could find out, he worked for sorcerers apparently but never passed any of the tests."

Ren grunted. "That must be where she got it from. I need to know exactly where her body was found. And then I'll go and talk to the Evokers."

"What do you think is happening to these children?" Jendra's voice cracked with emotion.

"Nothing good. Which is why I need to act tonight."

Tarrik cursed inwardly. He was loath to help these idiots, but in the long term the gesture would work to his advantage. If he offered information now, they would begin to trust him. And more importantly, Ren would value him, hopefully enough to keep him alive. If Ren sent them out chasing down false leads, then there was a greater chance this Lischen would know someone was on her trail. Would that be good or bad for Tarrik? On the whole, probably bad. If there was a brawl between Ren and this other sorcerer, he'd likely be obliterated by the backlash. Ren wouldn't waste her power shielding him if that meant putting herself at a disadvantage—she'd already said as much about her previous bodyguard. Better for her and Tarrik to remain in the shadows so they could strike at a time of their own choosing.

Tarrik cleared his throat, and all eyes turned to him. "The latest missing children, which finger was inked?"

Veika waved a hand in dismissal. "It's always the index finger."

"Which finger were they inked on?" repeated Tarrik.

Ren caught on first. "The family might not know which finger it should be. Just a black mark would be good enough for them." She regarded Tarrik thoughtfully. "You're suggesting these children could have passed the test and should have been marked with red ensorcelled ink but were marked with black to show they were rejected, but on a different finger so the abductor could identify them."

"It's a possibility," said Tarrik. "Easy to determine who's who for later."

Ren nodded. "And when they were taken, no one connected it with their potential sorcerous ability. It's possible. Highly possible. Veika, gather as much information as you can on those missing children and the schools that tested them. Someone's been bribed—it has to be one of the testers. And for something of this magnitude, it'll involve a lot of coin. Have your people ask around about any local sorcerer who's come into money recently. Someone buying expensive items perhaps, or carousing at upscale establishments. That will be the clue we need to investigate further. Tarrik and I will wait for you in the Sun, outside the Queen's Guard citadel. We can head off from there as soon as you find something." She flashed Tarrik a smile. "Thank you."

Veika drained his mug, nodded to Ren and Jendra, and left, ignoring Tarrik.

He inclined his head. Best to leave it there and not press too hard for an acknowledgment that he'd been extremely helpful.

"And the Nightwhisperer?" asked Jendra.

"I'll scry for her. We of the Nine have a bond that cannot be broken, although it may be disguised at times, at great cost. I'll find her."

"And my task?" asked Jendra.

"Stay here. You're too valuable to lose, and this could become dangerous very quickly."

Jendra looked put out. "I can wield a crossbow, and my knife work isn't too shabby."

"There will be no safe place once the sorcery starts flying," Ren said, "and that's the most likely scenario here. Even if Lischen isn't involved, a sorcerer of great power must be to make use . . ." She stopped. "Never mind. Stay here, please. We'll let you know if you're needed."

Tarrik could tell that Ren knew exactly what was happening to the children and was loath to reveal it to Jendra. He could think of a few ways to make use of fledgling human sorcerers, and he'd seen experiments conducted on a young boy once. He had no doubt the children would be dead or horribly abused. Why hold back that information? Was it due to weakness? Or did she want to keep Jendra and Veika from questioning whether Ren herself might be capable of such atrocities? She might even be involved in all of this already, her actions now a smoke screen.

Ren shrugged to settle her sword on her back, and Tarrik followed her outside to the courtyard. The stench of hay and horseshit emanated from the stable's open doors.

"We'll take a cab," she said. "It's swifter and can fit down the narrow streets."

Outside the building, she waved down the first empty single-horse cab they saw. The driver was a woman clad in oilskins and sporting a broad-brimmed hat in case the weather turned to rain. Judging by the clouds rolling in from the west, Tarrik considered it a likely occurrence.

As they clattered along the cobbled streets on iron-bound wheels, the setting sun painted the sky red and violet. Tarrik watched Ren, but she didn't react at all to the presence of the dusk-tide. He couldn't sense it himself, but surely she needed to replenish her repository after their flight across the sea? Still, there was no sign she even noticed it was sunset. *Interesting.* Either she had drawn on the artifact he'd implanted under her skin to power her incantations, or she had such a vast dusk-tide repository that their flight hadn't come close to draining it.

Tarrik mulled over the second possibility. Ren was in constant danger and had her own agenda, so he didn't believe she'd deliberately leave herself vulnerable. So why wasn't she replenishing her power when she could? He was missing something, and it didn't sit well with him. He'd only get one chance to escape. If he failed, she'd reinforce her sorcerous chains, and he'd face tighter restrictions.

"Do we need to stop somewhere so you can partake of the dusk-tide?" he asked, keeping his voice low so their driver wouldn't hear.

Ren glanced at him briefly before returning to stare at the passing street. "I am sufficiently replenished. Do not ask me again."

Something was definitely strange here. His thoughts returned to their conversation about the dawn- and dusk-tides and Ren's implication that they were two sides of the same coin. He remembered her assertion that the dark-tide the demons used wasn't actually dark. Was she toying with him? If the dark-tide wasn't dark energy, what was it?

Their cab halted, and he found they'd entered a massive paved square dominated on one side by an immense five-story building. The edifice was squarish and ugly, with only narrow windows breaking its bleak exterior. The single wide entry was guarded by a squad of soldiers who wore thick leather leggings, long cream-colored tunics over hauberks, and wide-brimmed iron helms. They carried short spears and round shields, and short swords as sidearms.

Ren handed the driver a few coppers and disembarked. The woman waited until Tarrik had also alighted before tugging the brim of her hat and driving off.

The two were outside a tavern, and the sound of laughter and singing came from inside. Tarrik noted quite a few taverns and inns among the shops and eating establishments that lined the other three sides of the square. Apparently Dwemor Port had a vibrant nightlife. In other circumstances, if he'd been allowed a little leeway, he might have been drawn to such a place to find a woman.

Ren led them farther along the row of buildings before stopping outside a nondescript tavern with oil lanterns burning on both sides of a red-lacquered door. A wooden sign painted with a spoked yellow sun hung from a wrought-iron bracket.

"We'll wait here for Veika," she said.

A burly man just inside the door gave Ren a short nod before eyeing Tarrik up and down and frowning at his spear. With a quick glance at Ren, he let Tarrik in despite his obvious discomfort.

The interior was dingy and sparsely populated. Two walls were lined with private booths and upholstered benches. At a separate heavy table near a polished granite-topped counter sat three men nursing tankards and conversing in hushed tones. They had the scarred look of veteran fighters or bodyguards, and Tarrik noted each was positioned to keep an eye on one of the occupied booths. Their employers, presumably.

A gray-bearded man wearing a brown apron hurried over. "Lady Zophia! Welcome back to the Sun. A pleasure to see you again." He gestured toward an empty booth. "Please, take a seat. Your man can—"

"He stays with me, Astrik."

"—can be seated with you. Of course."

The booth was cramped and uncomfortable for Tarrik. He tried a few positions before settling on sitting sideways with his legs sticking out into the general area. He leaned his spear on the partition separating their booth from the next. The proprietor's smile slipped a little, but he didn't say anything. Instead, he focused on Ren, who'd hung her sword on an iron hook set into the partition.

"We have some lovely candied horseradish served with stuffed red peppers, and an exquisite potato omelet with onions and green peppers," he said as he placed cloth napkins on the table in front of them.

"That will be sufficient, thank you," said Ren. "I'll have a glass of red wine. The good wine, mind you."

Astrik chuckled falsely. "We don't serve anything else."

"And you, Tarrik?" Ren asked.

"And me . . . what?"

"What would you like to drink?"

The proprietor waited eagerly, as if Tarrik were about to hand him a purse filled with gold.

"Something strong," Tarrik said. "Spirits. And some meat—whatever you have."

Astrik stroked his beard. "We have just received a few bottles of Widow's Malt, but it's quite expensive."

Tarrik nodded toward Ren. "She's paying."

Black Widow's Barrel rum, and now Widow's Malt—was every distillery in this place run by widows?

Astrik looked to Ren, who nodded. "Excellent," he said. "Now, if you'll excuse—"

Tarrik held up a hand. "Make that three measures of Widow's Malt."

Again, the proprietor looked to Ren, this time with raised eyebrows.

"There are two of us," she said.

"And you're having the wine."

She sniffed. "Bring him what he asks for."

With a studiously blank expression, Astrik hurried off. Tarrik surveyed the room again and the three men watching over their employers. This was obviously where the wealthy came to meet and work out ways of taking more coin from those less fortunate.

"He had no fear of you. Why is that?" Tarrik said. He folded his arms and waited.

"The Tainted Cabal keeps a low profile here in Niyas. And the Nine are virtually unknown, except to scholars of history and those with their hands on the reins of power. Niyas's queen is a respectable sorcerer in her own right. She doesn't want her subjects thinking she's fallen under another sorcerer's control."

No sorcerer was respectable in Tarrik's opinion. "But she has, hasn't she?" From what he'd learned of the Tainted Cabal, its members had their hooks in almost everyone.

Ren toyed with her cloth napkin. "Less than the Cabalists would like. Her position here is almost unassailable, and she has her own sorcerers by her side."

She fell silent as the proprietor bustled over bearing a wooden tray. He deposited a crystal glass of red wine in front of Ren and three small crystal tumblers filled with a greenish-tinged amber liquid in front of Tarrik.

"Your food will be out presently," he said before hurrying away.

In a mostly empty tavern, he certainly seemed busy, Tarrik thought. But perhaps that was part of his act as a diligent server.

"So, we're just waiting?" he said.

"Yes. Relax, if you can. I have a feeling we have a long night ahead of us."

Which meant she was confident of finding and dealing with this Lischen the Nightwhisperer tonight. But what did Ren care if another of the Nine was abducting children? It was an awful lot of trouble to go through just to maintain a disguise of goodness for Veika and Jendra. Surely if Ren and Lischen were involved in a sorcerous confrontation, there would be consequences.

Under Ren's watchful gaze, he downed one of the small tumblers of Widow's Malt and then another immediately after.

"Why are you drinking so much?" she said. "I've noticed your habit. Can you not control yourself?"

Tarrik met her eyes. She thought he was giving in to unsavory urges. It was time to hand over another piece of information that would cause her to trust him a fraction more.

"It's not a matter of control. Or rather, not in the way you think. My metabolism is dissimilar to yours; alcohol affects me in a different way. Drinking helps to dampen my emotions. It won't make me drunk or impair my effectiveness."

"I read you were partial to spirits, but there was no explanation of the reason."

Contian's notes again. If the old man were still alive, Tarrik would have killed him for revealing so much. Or at least threatened to. Contian hadn't been anything like his daughter.

"It deadens us," he said. "In a way, it makes us more human."

His remark brought a snort of derision from Ren, but she didn't comment further.

Because she was still staring at him, he drank the third tumbler more slowly. There was none of the sweetness he couldn't abide in the rum. Instead it was nutty and spicy and winey, and thick enough to linger on his tongue and in his throat. This was one of the finest spirits he'd ever tasted, and he'd tried many varieties during his time with Contian.

The tavern door opened, and Tarrik and the three guards at the table all turned their heads. A boy came inside, his head only reaching as high as the doorman's stomach. He was dressed in brown woolen pants and a similar coat with wooden buttons. The Sun's doorman waved him through. The boy peered around the room, spotted Ren, and scurried over to their booth. He placed a folded note on the table, and Ren slid a copper coin across to him. The boy snatched it and was out the door in a trice. The three bodyguards watched the exchange before going back to sipping their drinks.

Ren read the note, and a frown appeared on her face. She sipped her wine and slipped the paper into a pocket.

Tarrik was about to ask what the message said when Astrik appeared bearing his tray again, this time laden with dishes. One contained a thick yellow cake; another held shiny red vegetables stuffed with something brown; and a third was covered with what looked like stiff white worms coated with powdered sugar. The fourth and final plate he deposited in front of Tarrik: it held a thick steak sliced thinly, still raw in the center. Tarrik's mouth watered. Finally. Red meat.

"Seared venison," Astrik said. "Would you like some sauce?"

Tarrik shook his head. "I'd like another plate."

Astrik collected the three empty tumblers and hesitated. "Another drink?"

"Bring the bottle," said Tarrik.

Astrik opened his mouth and turned to Ren.

"The bottle will be fine," she said.

"I . . . of course, my lady. If there's anything else . . . ?"

"Nothing, thank you. It all looks delicious."

Astrik grinned broadly and scurried away.

Tarrik looked at the disgusting vegetable dishes, winced, then picked up the silver filigreed fork and stabbed at a strip of the succulent meat. He closed his eyes as he chewed. Bliss.

"The message was from Veika," said Ren.

Tarrik swallowed and placed another slice in his mouth. "And?"

"You were right. It seems the abducted children were inked on a different finger. He's trying to find out who tested them. He's good at his job, so I expect he'll have an answer soon."

"So we wait until he does?"

She nodded. "After we've eaten, I'll scry for where Lischen is holed up. It'll be somewhere out of the way, and if she's involved in this cruelty, then it'll also be somewhere hidden. Safe from prying eyes and any chance this sorcery might be traced to her. The Queen's Guard would not abide such an atrocity if they knew about it. The queen is very protective of her subjects."

Atrocity. What a joke, Tarrik thought. He wondered why she felt the need to keep up this pretense when only he was present.

Neither spoke while they ate. Ren took delicate bites of her dishes but put away a decent portion; her appetite seemed to have improved since their arrival on the beach. Astrik brought another plate of bloody meat for Tarrik along with a bottle of the Widow's Malt.

When both of his plates were empty, he uncorked the bottle and took a swig. Its label showed a coat of arms featuring two red-furred lions holding up a silver shield.

"They're meant to be manticarrs," said Ren. "Of course they look nothing like that. Only the color is close. The widow Rapace took over running her husband's distillery when he was killed by a manticarr."

Tarrik shrugged, uninterested.

One of the three guards left with a hooded and cloaked woman—Tarrik could smell her floral perfume across the room. Shortly after, Veika walked through the door and hurried over to their booth, slightly breathless. He stank of sweat and excitement.

"Good news," he said, leaning over the table. "The sorcerer who tested the missing youths is named Rikart. He's middle-aged and lowly ranked among the Evokers. Rumor is he hasn't lived up to his promise. Too fond of women and drink." His eyes flicked to the bottle of spirits, then to Tarrik.

Tarrik smirked. "There's nothing wrong with either. And to say there's something wrong with liking women in front of Lady Branwen!" He shook his head theatrically.

"That's not what I meant! You're an idiot if you think you can get a rise out of me."

"Find this Rikart," commanded Ren, ignoring their exchange. "Tonight. If we're lucky, he'll have some idea where the nascent sorcerers were taken. The Evokers wouldn't view his actions too kindly; they're the preeminent sorcerous school in the world and fiercely guard their reputation. This Rikart has taken quite a risk. He must have been paid well for it."

Veika nodded and made to leave.

"Oh, and Veika," said Ren. He turned back to her. "If this Rikart has any intelligence, he'll have a well-planned escape route. He had to know he might be caught and would plan for any eventuality. Make sure he doesn't get away."

"Yes, my lady."

After Veika had exited, Ren shuffled along her bench to lean against the wall. "Stop trying to rile him, Tarrik. I won't stand for it. And I'm sure you don't want another dose of the Wracking Nerves. Now make sure I'm not disturbed while I'm scrying."

She put her head back and closed her eyes, to all appearances asleep. Within moments Tarrik sensed a swirling of dusk-tide power around her. He'd seen Contian perform many scryings and knew the basics, but it was beyond his own abilities to use the dawn- and dusk-tides in this way. All he knew was that Ren was sending her queries into the currents of the night and gathering the responses she received into a coherent answer. A chill brushed across his face as the dusk-tide forces solidified.

Out of the corner of his eye, he saw Astrik approaching with an empty tray. Tarrik stood and held a hand up. "No chatter. Remove the dishes, and make yourself scarce."

Astrik's face flushed, and he frowned at Tarrik. His eyes flicked to Ren's apparently sleeping form, and his voice came as a low hiss. "Listen here, servant! You're in my establishment—"

Tarrik held a finger to his lips. "Shhh."

Astrik went even redder. "Just you—"

"Shhh," Tarrik said again, and waved the man away.

Jaw working as though chewing a particularly large piece of gristle, Astrik gently placed the tray on the table and, with exaggerated care, loaded it with dishes. He huffed away and disappeared through a doorway behind the counter.

Ren said something too soft to hear, and Tarrik turned. She shook her head, opened her eyes, and blinked repeatedly as if to clear them. Then she sat up and took a deep swallow of her wine.

"Lischen is beneath the Temple of Nanshey. An odd choice, considering she likes her comforts and the temple is all but deserted. Nanshey's worshipers have almost died out; the remaining few are elderly and serve to keep the temple clean and squatters out. The older gods and goddesses haven't fared well in recent centuries. There are more interesting goddesses to worship these days than one with dominion over water and fish."

What entities these humans worshiped couldn't interest Tarrik less. "A suspicious location then. Do we confront the sorcerer now, or wait?"

"Wait. Sit. You're drawing attention."

Tarrik seated himself with ill-concealed grace. He wasn't happy about being squeezed into the booth again, but at least the wait gave him time to consider their current situation and how he could use it to his advantage. If Lischen was behind these disappearances, then Ren intended to confront another of the Nine. How could he ensure Ren would fail and be slain? His action would have to be subtle, one that didn't trigger her bindings or go against her commands.

And there was a bigger problem. If Tarrik got in the way of a clash of sorcerers, he would be reduced to a smudge of grease.

Chapter Nine

Demon and sorcerer didn't have long to wait before the same messenger boy entered the tavern and made straight for their booth. He placed another folded piece of paper in front of Ren, waited for his copper coin, and scurried away. Ren read the note and was silent.

"What is it?" Tarrik asked.

She wriggled out from behind the table and buckled on her sword. "Let's go."

Tarrik rose too and grabbed his spear.

Astrik came rushing over, rubbing his hands together. "Lady Zophia, I trust everything was to your satisfaction?"

"Everything was excellent, Astrik, as usual." She slipped him a gold coin, and he beamed at her. "Our departure is no reflection on you or your establishment. We've had some urgent news."

A cold drizzle slicked the cobblestones. Passersby had thinned considerably, and those who were still out hurried along with their heads down and shoulders hunched. Ren stood pressed to the wall under the Sun's eaves, which provided a modicum of protection.

"A carriage, Tarrik."

He looked at her in disbelief. She wanted him to go into the street with this disgusting wetness falling from the sky? *Rain. Probably one of the most horrible aspects of this cesspit of a world.*

"Flag down a carriage for us," she repeated. "The cabs aren't covered; they're useless in this weather."

Tarrik suppressed a growl and looked around. He wondered if she assigned him menial tasks to annoy him. Well, she wouldn't get a rise out of him this time. There was a carriage on the other side of the square, its driver pacing alongside it, a pipe in his mouth and smoke billowing around his head. Tarrik stomped across the slippery pavers, hunching his shoulders against the water. The gloom-filled night sky pissed water onto his head, which then ran down his face and into his mouth and eyes and trickled down the back of his shirt.

The driver turned an eye on him from under his broad-brimmed hat.

"My master requires your services," Tarrik said bluntly, and waved in the direction of the Sun.

The driver squinted and looked up at him. "All right. Where to?"

"I don't know."

"That's a fair distance. It'll cost extra," the driver said with a smile.

Tarrik frowned. "She'll pay whatever the cost is."

The driver sighed. "It was a joke. What you lack in brains you obviously make up for in brawn. I'm guessing you're her guard and not her bookkeeper." The man tapped his pipe against his boot, sending ash and embers and unburned tobacco onto the ground.

"I have no choice. I do whatever she asks."

The driver's gaze raked him from head to toe. "I'll just bet you do. Hop in, then. No point getting wetter than you need to."

The carriage seats were upholstered with leather and the walls paneled with a dark, varnished wood. Tarrik had just seated himself, keeping the sharp blade of his spear from touching anything, when a small board opened at the front and the driver peeked through the opening.

"That's her over by the Sun?" he asked.

"Yes."

The hole closed with a clack, and they began moving. Tarrik shivered. The cold and wet had chilled him to the bone. "When will my torment end?" he muttered bitterly to himself.

They stopped near the Sun, and Tarrik saw Ren wave to the driver. He caught her words through the thin walls. "Towers district, please. The closest bridge to Herron Street."

"Yes, ma'am."

Ren sat across from Tarrik, her sword across her thighs. She had a few wet specks on her shoulders and droplets in her hair. As they clattered along the streets, she didn't speak, which suited Tarrik. He was content to watch the darkened buildings while he contemplated how to betray her. Or perhaps he'd do better to bide his time. He still had to crack open and absorb Ananias's essence, which would give him more power to fight Ren's bindings. He ground his teeth and suppressed a growl. Patience wasn't his strong suit, but without it he might ruin his chances.

They crossed three stone bridges, then the timbre of the wheels changed, and Tarrik knew they were clattering across a wooden bridge. The carriage halted a short while later, and the panel opened.

"Herron Street," the driver said.

"Thank you." Ren handed him a silver coin. "There's another for you if you wait. We shouldn't be long. There's a tavern over there, but I'd prefer it if you didn't drink. Perhaps a hot tea instead to keep the chill out? I'll add another copper for your expense."

"I'm happy to wait, ma'am."

"Excellent." More coins changed hands; then Ren jerked her head at the carriage door. "With me, Tarrik."

As soon as they'd disembarked, the driver hitched his two horses outside a brightly lit eatery, then disappeared inside.

The street was crowded, with most passersby escaping the rain by keeping to covered walkways along the building fronts. A few glanced at Tarrik's spear and Ren's sword and quickened their step.

"You seem a bit preoccupied," Ren said. "Is there something on your mind?"

Careful . . . don't give her any cause to watch you closer than she already is.

"It's the rain—dreadful stuff. I'm not used to it." He tried a smile and immediately regretted it. Ren was no fool. He returned to his usual impassive expression. "And there's no *durbal-iluk* here."

"What does that mean? I don't speak demon."

It's Nazgrese, you ignoramus. "It is difficult to translate, but a close approximation would be a place where you feel at home and draw strength from, where you are your most authentic self."

Ren stared at him for a moment. "Many people don't have a place like that. Including me." And she strode off toward a side street.

Surly bitch. If she wanted to take the lead, he'd let her and also let her bear the brunt of any attack.

There were men guarding the third house down the side street: ugly, mean-looking brutes with neatly trimmed beards, thick leather jerkins, and weapons just about everywhere Tarrik could see. Swords, knives, axes, crossbows, blades in their boots, garrotes disguised as chains around their necks. There was a hardness to their bodies and limbs and in their eyes that came only from a familiarity with violence.

When they noticed Tarrik and Ren, their hands moved to their weapons. But when Ren got nearer, they nodded, and the two positioned in front of the door stood aside. It seemed she and her servant were expected, which could only mean Veika was involved. He was no ordinary spy if he could call on professionals such as these men at short notice.

Tarrik noted that the doorjamb was splintered; someone before them had bashed open the lock to gain entry. Inside, the room was plain, holding only a faded lounge and an armchair, a low table between them.

A man and a woman stood there, and it was the woman who held Tarrik's attention. She examined Ren and nodded. Her eyes lingered on Tarrik as if assessing his threat level, and he met her gaze evenly. She was a few years older than the men outside but not yet middle-aged. Her black trousers and midnight-blue shirt were of decent quality and close-fitting enough to reveal an athletic figure. Her brown hair was tied back in a short ponytail.

"Veika's through there," she said, pointing toward a curtained doorway.

The next room was a cluttered study with book-laden tables and chairs and a well-used desk covered with leather-bound tomes, scribbles and diagrams on sheets of paper, and five glazed mugs. A pale, overweight man lay on his back in a corner, staring at the ceiling with sightless eyes. His throat had been cut, though the wound was curiously bloodless. A stain spread across his trousers from his groin.

Veika glanced up from the sheets of paper he was examining filled with tiny script. "That's Rikart, in case you hadn't guessed. The body was still warm when we found it, but no sign of what killed him. All of his notes are still here, so we must have surprised the killer. There's a back exit."

Ren's look grew troubled. "So whatever killed him made its escape that way? And presumably entered from there too?"

"I believe so."

"You didn't send someone to the rear as soon as you arrived?"

Veika grimaced. "The front team went in too early—it was a cock-up. I had four men making their way to the back of the building, but they weren't in position yet. It won't happen again."

"It had better not."

Tarrik moved to the window, which was closed and locked. He knew of three different minor demons that could have made such a wound but didn't find their scents in the air. There was something else underneath the stench of piss, a smell like damp earth with undertones of wet fur. He recognized the mustiness from one of his missions with Contian in the bleak Jargalan Mountains—a larmarsh, a cruel lifeblood-drinker hardly ever seen, even in the wilderness. Contian had said the creatures only revealed themselves to feed. Tarrik recalled clearly the larmarsh they'd killed: a humanoid woman with twisted horns and claws, a wide mouth filled with pointed teeth, and blue-gray skin that blended into stone. If such a creature was in a populated city, it had to be under a sorcerer's control. Likely Lischen's.

"Your thoughts on the wound?" Ren asked Veika.

"I've never seen its like, though there have been rumors recently of people being murdered and their corpses drained of blood. A couple of thieves disappeared while crossing the rooftops. It got the other thieves scared, and they're lying low. The Watch are nowhere near as busy as usual."

Ren moved around the room, her fingers brushing across books and papers. Her eyes constantly flicked to the corpse. "Anything useful in his papers?"

Veika grinned. "It seems Rikart liked to keep meticulous notes when testing sorcerer candidates. He gave one set to the Evokers, falsely showing that children with high ability had failed. And he gave a different set with the true results to whoever was bribing him. From the discrepancies between the two, we can work out which youths disappeared."

"So Tarrik was correct?"

"It seems so," Veika conceded reluctantly.

Ren gave Tarrik an approving nod. He allowed himself a brief smile in response.

"What do you think of the wound?" Ren asked him.

Tarrik hesitated. How much did Ren know of his time with Contian? Had the old man detailed all their dealings in his notes? Ren might be testing his honesty. He couldn't afford to expose himself as a liar now, not when he'd broken the ice of her regard.

"The wound and also the smell of the creature are known to me. It was a larmarsh."

Veika barked a disbelieving laugh. "A myth used to frighten children in the south. If you have nothing sensible to say—"

Ren held up a hand to stop him. "Go on," she said to Tarrik.

"Your stunted man is right to be disbelieving." She'd said not to use the word "runt," but Tarrik was rewarded with an annoyed look from Veika. "I've only ever seen one larmarsh, many years ago. It took the warriors in our party one by one at night until only a sorcerer and myself were left. We managed to find the creature's lair and corner it. The larmarsh had defenses against all but the most virulent sorcery and howled like the damned when we finally brought it down. If I hadn't been there, the sorcerer would have died."

He met Ren's eyes, making sure to drive his point home while not revealing to others his connection to Contian.

She pursed her lips and tapped her cheek with a finger. "I've heard of something similar. But I thought the wound would be less . . . precise."

"Its claws are sharp," Tarrik said. "If Rikart's sorcery wasn't very powerful, the larmarsh would have brushed off anything he threw at it. Thus, the sorcerer became terrified and pissed himself and froze with fear. The creature could have sliced his throat in the blink of an eye, then drunk its fill."

"Lischen brought the demon here," said Veika.

"That seems to be the obvious conclusion," replied Ren. "I concur with your assessment, Tarrik. Veika, your work here is done. You won't be joining us for the final stage. You're too valuable to lose."

What Ren really meant was the runt would be a liability when the going became rough and weapons were drawn. However, he seemed to buy her lies, simpering like a fool as he showed her a page in the journal he was holding.

"Rikart wrote that he was offered a thousand gold talents for every potential sorcerer he kept secret from the Evokers. Payment once his finds were verified, which I assume means after the children were taken. Five lots of gold coin were deposited in his name at the Monolith Holdings Bank."

"Five thousand in gold would keep him in luxury for the rest of his miserable life," remarked Ren. "But it seems whoever paid him didn't want to risk him talking. They're winding up their operation; we'll need to be swift."

She bent over Rikart's corpse and spoke a cant, then grunted and straightened. "There's no lingering sorcery here. I'm inclined to believe Tarrik's scenario."

Veika held up the journal again. "There are several pages about Rikart's misgivings and his anger at the way the Evokers treated him. He received payment once a week from a woman who always came hooded and cloaked. He never saw her face. They met at midnight in a park close to the Temple of Nanshey."

"Lischen," breathed Ren. "I scried her in the temple."

Veika closed the journal and tossed it onto the desk. "It has to be."

"Collect all of his books and papers," Ren ordered. "You and Jendra can go through them and see if anything else interesting turns up. The Evokers will also need to be informed that one of their own betrayed them. They will owe us then, and a favor from the Evokers is a valuable thing."

"Yes, my lady."

Ren looked at Tarrik. "We're going to the Temple of Nanshey. Are you ready?"

The larmarsh he could handle himself, if it was distracted. "I have a weapon, don't I? But we'll need a couple of Veika's men to guard our backs." And to act as bait. Veika opened his mouth to protest Tarrik's suggestion, then closed it quickly as he presumably realized an objection would suggest he wanted Ren to fail.

"Speak to Aimy in the next room," he said. "She'll choose a couple of her best people."

"Thank you, Veika," said Ren, and gestured for Tarrik to follow.

Aimy stood a little straighter when Ren appeared and touched her fingers to her forehead. Ren produced a bulging purse that jingled when she shook it.

"I need two of your people to accompany us tonight," she said. "It'll be dangerous work—make no mistake. I need the best you've got."

Aimy licked her lips, but her eyes didn't drop to the purse and instead stayed fixed on Ren and Tarrik. "Just how dangerous? If you're going up against sorcerers—"

"That's not what we require of you," Ren said. "There's something else that needs putting down."

"A larmarsh," added Tarrik.

Aimy snorted with derision. "A tale to frighten children."

Tarrik thumped the butt of his spear onto the floorboards. The sharp crack of wood on wood echoed around the room. Aimy's hand went to the hilt of her rapier, and her knuckles whitened around the hilt.

"Then prepare to relive your childhood," Tarrik said. "Maybe you'll piss yourself with terror like the dead man did. We need warriors, not pants pissers. Ask your best to join us and they'll be paid well." *If they come out of this alive.*

It was always best if your bait was unaware of its role.

"All right," said Aimy, nodding slowly. "We'll take Gaukur. He's my best axeman."

Tarrik recalled a man outside with axes slightly larger than hatchets tucked into his belt. "Axes will do, as will your rapier. Heavier weapons are too slow. The larmarsh will be quicker than a cat."

Aimy raised her eyebrows. "Fought them before, have you?"

"Just the one."

Ren cleared her throat, and they both turned to regard her.

"The larmarsh is your responsibility," she told Aimy. "Keep it from me while I go after bigger fish. Kill it, and you're done for the night. Understood?"

"Crystal clear," said Aimy. She took a quick look inside the purse to confirm the coins were gold. "If there's anything else you need after this, make sure you look me up."

"I'll keep that in mind. Now shall we go?"

"All business. I like that."

Outside, Aimy beckoned to the short axeman, Gaukur, and they had a whispered conversation. He nodded, and Aimy clapped him on the back. She handed the bulging purse to another of her men; then she and Gaukur joined Tarrik and Ren. The axeman was stocky, bald, and clean-shaven with a cleft chin.

"Our destination is the Temple of Nanshey," said Ren.

"That's in Skull-Bottom, the next district to the north. We walking?" said Aimy.

"Time is of the essence, and we have a carriage waiting. Tarrik, if you'd be so kind as to fetch our driver."

Another menial task. Tarrik strode off toward the eatery. He heard soft footsteps behind him and found Aimy following.

She smiled. "I've never seen a southerner like you before, and I've spent some time way down south beyond the Jargalan Desert. They're all big down there—don't get me wrong—but their skin's a different shade. Blacker."

That was just what he needed: someone familiar with the southern lands who wouldn't be fooled by his cover story. He'd better distract her before she thought to ask more questions.

"You handed the gold purse to one of your men. Are you afraid we'll kill you once this is over?"

Aimy shook her head and laughed. "No. My share will go to my daughter if I don't make it back."

"Not your husband?"

"He died."

"Of what?"

"Infidelity."

"I've heard that can be painful."

To his surprise, Aimy offered no response. He glanced down and saw her jaw was clenched, her mouth drawn into a thin line. Perhaps she'd killed the man recently, and the wounds were still raw.

Her eyes flicked to his and then away. "What's the situation with you and the sorcerer? Are you lovers?"

As soon as the question was out, Ren's bindings tightened around him, causing him to stumble. "Bloody cobbles," he muttered to cover himself. She wouldn't allow him to reveal the details of their relationship, but he could certainly deny that he warmed her bed.

"There is nothing physical between us," he said.

"Then perhaps after tonight you and I can get to know one another better."

Tarrik halted. His heart beat faster, and heat rose to his face and groin. A slight twitch of Aimy's lips showed her amusement.

"It is unlikely my employer will allow me time to myself," he said. "I wish it could be otherwise."

They were a dozen steps from the eatery now, and through the window he saw the driver notice them, drain his mug, and rise. He emerged holding a burning fire stick to his pipe and puffing heartily. "I'll fetch my carriage. Your boss not here?"

Tarrik gestured to the side street. "We'll pick her up over there."

Inside the carriage, he tried to push thoughts of lying with Aimy from his mind. She was only bait, after all, and the worst thing he could do was to become attached, though that was unlikely from a simple dalliance.

"Does she hold something over you?" Aimy asked him.

"In a manner of speaking. I have to see this through with her." *One way or another.*

"Well, if you need any help extricating yourself, let me know." She flashed him a smile, the tip of her pink tongue protruding between her teeth.

The carriage jerked to a halt, and Ren boarded, followed by Gaukur, who sat beside Aimy. Ren handed the driver another silver through the opening. "The Temple of Nanshey, please."

"Right you are, ma'am."

They sat in silence during the journey, Tarrik aware of Aimy's eyes on him and Ren's presence by his side.

A short time later, they disembarked onto a paved main street next to a high wall. Presumably the temple was on the other side. Gaukur, who hadn't said a word yet, shifted the axe handles in his belt to loosen them. Aimy went through what looked to be a prefight ritual, touching each of her weapons and also the small of her back, where she must have a concealed blade.

"Are we going in through the front?" she asked Ren. "Or through the catacombs? And what resistance do you expect?"

Ren narrowed her eyes at the woman. "Having you with us has paid off already. We'll take the underground entrance."

"There's a way into the catacombs from the graveyard at the rear," Aimy said. "We use it sometimes to hide from the Watch. It's locked, but it's a simple mechanism."

"Take us there," said Ren. "As for resistance, the larmarsh is the worst you'll have to deal with. Tarrik, do you agree?"

Their three pairs of eyes regarded him: two bait, one slaver.

"The larmarsh would kill any ordinary humans," he said. "So we're unlikely to face any other attackers."

"If we're here for the larmarsh, what are you here for?" Aimy asked Ren.

"Sorcery," said Gaukur gruffly. He turned his head to spit onto the cobbles.

Ren eyed him. "As I said: You deal with the larmarsh, and your task is done. You've been well paid. No more questions."

Aimy nodded to Ren, and without another word she strode off down a side alley. Ren waved at Gaukur to follow, and she and Tarrik trailed behind. Aimy led them along the high brick wall to an iron gate, which she pushed open. Tarrik was surprised the rusty-looking hinges didn't squeak, then realized the mercenaries probably kept them well-oiled. Inside was a graveyard stretching fifty yards to a side. Long grasses and weeds grew beside carved-stone tombs and headstones, and only a few had fresh flowers laid in front of them.

They followed Aimy and Gaukur to the back wall of the temple. Remnants of whitewashed plaster, now turned gray, stuck in small patches to the brick underneath. Most of it looked to have crumbled away years ago. The narrow windows were covered in dirt and impossible to see through.

They stopped at a thick timber door with an iron lock. Aimy removed a set of picks from beneath her shirt. "This won't take long."

Ren uttered a cant, and the lock clicked open. "Allow me."

Aimy stared at her, then put her picks away. "This way then. It's a bit of a maze down here, and we haven't explored the lower levels, so stay close to me. Especially you, Tarrik."

"He'll stay with me," said Ren curtly.

Aimy raised her eyebrows and led them through the door to a brick corridor. From her pocket she produced an egg-size globe attached to a metal rod and shook it to agitate the alchemicals within. A soft glow sprang forth and steadily grew until it was as bright as several candles.

Footprints scuffed the dirty floor, and a web hung above the door. A black spider peered balefully at their intrusion but didn't move.

"Wait," commanded Ren. She closed her eyes, lips moving in a cant, and Tarrik felt dusk-tide sorcery emanate from her. Her eyes snapped open. "We need to go down."

Aimy exchanged a nervous glance with Gaukur.

"Something wrong?" asked Tarrik.

"We lost a few people several years ago. Found their bodies torn apart at the bottom of the stairs a couple of levels down. It looked like ghouls from the teeth marks on their bones. It's why we never venture down there."

"I'll protect you," said Tarrik. A goad and a lie.

Gaukur chuckled, and Aimy shot him an annoyed look. "The stairs are this way," she said.

The dirt on the floor cleared up a short way along the corridor, but mortar crumbled from the brick walls, and every surface was covered in thick dust and cobwebs. The stale air was redolent with decay. Horizontal niches punctuated the walls, filled with wooden coffins that had disintegrated with dry rot to reveal yellowed bones, many of them gnawed at. Scraps of cloth and leather were scattered among the remains, but no jewelry or trinkets. Thieves would have long ago made off with whatever was valuable, surmised Tarrik. Broken bricks and dirt were piled against walls, creating a trail along the corridors. They reached a stone spiral staircase leading down. Someone had placed broken crates across the opening.

"No one's disturbed this," Aimy said. "Are you sure we should be going down?"

"Very sure. There'll be more than one way into the lower levels." Ren smiled at Aimy and Gaukur. "We'll go first if you're scared."

Aimy stepped back. "After you."

Tarrik suppressed his laugh with a cough. Aimy was no fool.

Gaukur tugged his axes from his belt. Aimy followed his lead and drew her rapier; she also held a slender dagger in her left hand.

Ren spoke a cant, and a globe of brilliance fizzed above her head, illuminating the murk that pooled farther down the steps. With whispered words, she sent the light ahead to banish the darkness.

"Won't the larmarsh see us coming?" asked Aimy.

"Yes," said Tarrik. "But they're creatures of darkness, and the light will be painful to its eyes. It'll want to stay away from illumination. Which means we'll need to leave the light's protection if we're to kill it."

"Great," muttered Aimy under her breath.

Tarrik angled the blade of his spear so it led him down the stairs after Ren's light. A corridor turned off the first landing.

"Go down farther," said Ren behind him.

Tarrik continued to descend, wondering how he'd ended up at the front instead of the two he'd brought as bait. The creature wouldn't come near with Ren's light bleaching the catacombs, so there was still time to send Aimy and Gaukur into its clutches. His innate talent for concealment should keep him safe until the larmarsh struck, after which it would be too busy feeding to pay attention to Tarrik. At least, that was the plan. As he knew all too well, in the heat of confrontation most plans disintegrated like smoke in a wind.

They reached another landing. The staircase continued to spiral downward, but when Tarrik jerked his head in its direction, Ren shook hers.

"It's on this level," she said. "I sense faint emanations of vitality. Farther down is only decay and deadness."

Tarrik had no idea what she was talking about, but he took a deep lungful of the air coming from the corridor. Damp soil and fur. This was the place, all right.

He led them along another crumbling corridor until they reached a square room. There wasn't much to it: a square eight yards wide with a gray stone plinth in its center that supported a man's carved stone torso and head. His face was chipped and scarred where most of his facial features had been hammered off, along with his fingers. Three more corridors exited the space, one from each wall. Ren's arcane light floated up to brush the ceiling and revealed bones piled in one corner and covered with a gray-green mold. The remains smelled wet and earthy. Tarrik probed the debris beneath the plinth and found one of the man's fingers.

He dredged up almost-forgotten cants, sending dark-tide scrying tendrils out in front of him. One returned almost immediately, bringing the information he needed: the larmarsh was to their right, fifty paces distant. With a slice of luck he could avoid the creature until it attacked Aimy or Gaukur.

"Is Lischen on this level too?" Tarrik asked, leaning close to Ren and pitching his voice low.

Ren glanced back at Aimy and Gaukur, who were only just entering the room. "I'm not sure."

Tarrik nodded. "One thing at a time then." He turned to Aimy and Gaukur, their faces half-lit by Ren's globe. "Here's where you earn those gold coins. Gaukur, you take that corridor. Aimy, that one. I'll take the third."

Aimy frowned but didn't seem suspicious, which was good. "We're separating? Wouldn't it be best to stay together?"

"Then the larmarsh will never come for us. We need to lure it into attacking. Once a feeding frenzy comes over it, it'll pay little heed to anything else. If it comes at you, run—lead it back to this room and the sorcerous light. That's the only thing that'll make the beast hesitate. When one of us encounters the creature, you'll know it. It'll wail something terrible. Try not to piss yourself when it does—you don't want to meet the same fate as the sorcerer you found earlier. Don't worry about anyone else; just look after yourself. Once we've lured the thing back here, we'll kill it together."

Gaukur snorted. "If we ain't killed first."

Tarrik looked at Aimy. "I thought you said no pants pissers?"

Polished steel sparkled as Gaukur brandished an axe in Tarrik's direction. "I ain't no pants pisser."

"Then shut your hole."

"Settle down, both of you," snapped Aimy. "Gaukur, this job's paying enough to keep you for years. Let's just get it done and let this sorcerer do her sorcerizing. Tarrik's buying the drinks all night after we're done, aren't you?"

Tarrik knew that Aimy wanted a lot more than just drinks. And if he weren't bound by Ren, he might have taken her up on her offer. That is, if she was still alive after they'd taken care of the larmarsh.

Aimy's attempt to lessen the tension seemed to work. Gaukur stopped glaring at Tarrik and moved to assess the other three corridors.

"Watch out," Ren told Aimy. "He'll drink you both under the table."

If he weren't sure she was heartless, Tarrik would have thought Ren was trying to be funny. And if Aimy was amused, she didn't show it.

"We'll see," she said.

Tarrik had had enough of this. Humans might joke to keep their fear at bay, but a demon faced trouble head-on.

"You all know the plan," he said. "Aimy, you take the left passage, Gaukur the middle, and I'll take the right." There was more of a chance the larmarsh would take out the two mercenaries if they were closer together. "Enough talking. It's time we put this creature down."

He readied his spear and entered the right-hand passage. His boots shuffled across decades of detritus fallen from the funerary niches. As he moved aside a skull, he heard Aimy and Gaukur cautiously creeping along their tunnels. Idiots. Thirty paces along, he stopped before an intersection and pressed his back into a shallow alcove. The larmarsh wouldn't come for Ren while her eldritch light shone brightly, but the smell of the other humans would draw it like iron to a lodestone. All he had to do was stay out of its way for the time being.

He calmed his breathing and concentrated on disappearing into the crumbling brick wall. The shadows wouldn't obey him, as much as he'd tried over the centuries, but at least he could become unnoticeable. Unless he made any sudden moves, his innate talent of concealment would serve him well. He'd only just settled himself when he sensed something moving through the intersection nearby. He heard cloth rustle and saw a patch of deeper blackness, but it was gone before he could blink. A draft washed over him, redolent with the stench of wet fur and earth.

Tarrik gave the creature a head start before following. Around the corner, away from the harsh glare of Ren's globe, darkness enfolded him. He welcomed it, had an affinity with it, as did all higher demons. He could sense the walls to either side without seeing or touching them—another inborn talent that served demons well during the moonless nights in the abyssal realms, when prey tried to remain hidden and the predators roamed.

The larmarsh was between Tarrik and Gaukur now. He moved along the passage, careful not to lift his feet too high and crunch on bone. A low keening moan came from the blackness ten yards in front of him.

"Gaukur!" It was Aimy's urgent voice. Tarrik was unable to pinpoint her location.

"I'm alive," came the axeman's gruff reply. "I think it came from . . . wait . . . feck!"

The larmarsh's screeching wail drowned out anything else Gaukur shouted.

Tarrik raced toward the commotion, all attempts at secrecy abandoned. He paused at another intersection, then ran to the sounds of a scuffle. Gaukur screamed in defiance. Thuds sounded from his axes' heavy blows. Sparks skittered in the pitch-black as metal hit stone.

Midnight brightened as Ren's sorcerous globe neared. Tarrik could see Gaukur's huddled form lying in the dust, splashed with gore. His arms and back were a mess of shredded cloth and flesh. One hand was pressed to his ravaged neck, and scarlet leaked from between his fingers. His axes were a few feet away, both their blades covered with crimson.

He looked up at Tarrik accusingly before falling limp. Gaukur was no use to them now.

Aimy bolted out of a side passage and rushed to Gaukur's side. She dropped her weapons and placed one hand on his shoulder, the other on his head. Her jaw clenched, lips drawing into a grim line.

Tarrik kept his spear up, searching the darkness for signs of movement. Ren's eldritch globe faded to a lesser illumination. Good. He needed the larmarsh in a feeding frenzy, not scared away.

"We have to get Gaukur out of here," Aimy said. "A healer can save him."

"None of us will make it out if we don't kill the larmarsh first."

"Damn the creature to the abyss! I'll not let one of my own die here in this old tomb." She grabbed her blades and stood, glaring at Tarrik. He saw a tear roll down her cheek. "You killed him. You and your sorcerer," she spat. Her rapier blade trembled with suppressed rage.

A shadow rose behind her, almost touching the ceiling. Eyes of cobalt glowed in Ren's reflected sorcerous light.

Keep her talking.

"He killed himself by not being skilled enough," Tarrik told Aimy.

"You fecking bastard," she sobbed.

The black form that was the larmarsh remained still, as if assessing the situation. Tarrik retreated a step to present less of a threat. From the look of Gaukur, the beast had begun to feed but had left him when it heard Tarrik approach. The creature had a taste for blood now and wouldn't want to leave without finishing its meal. All that was left to do was kill the other human blocking its prey. Then the larmarsh would have two bodies to feast upon.

Tarrik flicked a glance behind him, as if checking the creature wasn't sneaking up on him. "Stick with the plan," he said to Aimy.

"Don't you fecking back away from me. You can carry Gaukur. Shit, look at him."

Mitchell Hogan

Aimy dropped her rapier and used her dagger to cut strips from her shirt hem to use as bandages. While she busied herself, Tarrik retreated a few more steps.

Darkness exploded as the larmarsh struck, turning into razor claws and a wailing fanged mouth, twisted horns, and a cobalt mane. Aimy only had time to gasp as it fell upon her. Scarlet sprayed from her flesh, and she flew through the air and slammed into the wall. Dust and fragments of brick rained down as she slumped to the floor, a bloodied wreck of torn flesh.

The larmarsh let out an eerie wail that assaulted Tarrik's ears. He lunged with his spear. The larmarsh spun away, and he missed its heart, slicing instead along the blue-gray skin over its ribs. The creature hissed and batted the shaft into the wall with such force it vibrated in Tarrik's hands. He leaped backward and brandished his spear again, keeping the tip aimed at the larmarsh's chest. It was female, with humanlike breasts that were small and flat. Aimy's and Gaukur's blood flecked its face and dripped from its lips.

Tarrik thrust at it again and again to keep its clawed hands away. The beast managed to grasp the shaft of his spear and yanked him forward, but he twisted with all his might and wrenched his weapon free.

Blood and fire! Is Ren expecting me to kill it alone?

He realized he'd retreated a good ten or so paces from where he'd been standing when Aimy was attacked. The larmarsh was too quick, too strong for him to do much more than keep it at bay. Again his thrusts were turned aside or dodged, the larmarsh striking the spear with such strength Tarrik feared the blade would shatter or the shaft splinter.

Where is Ren?

A terrible thought came to him: Perhaps he was also bait. Had she left him to die while she scurried away to deal with Lischen?

A sharp jerk pulled him forward, and he cursed his inattention. The larmarsh now held his spear in both its clawed hands. Tarrik twisted and jerked with all his strength but couldn't loosen the creature's grip. Its fanged mouth widened in a grin.

When it tugged at the spear again, Tarrik let go, and the creature stumbled backward. He thought about bringing forth his shadow-blade, but if Ren saw the weapon, his secret would be exposed. Besides, he had more than one trick. The fight wasn't over yet.

Wood clattered on stone as the larmarsh cast his spear to the ground. It advanced steadily, confident it had him, forcing Tarrik to retreat. He tripped over a skull, which broke into fragments under his weight. Darkness surrounded him as he moved farther and farther from the gloom Ren's distant globe provided. He glanced back at his spear, discarded in the dust, then at Aimy's rapier and dagger and Gaukur's axes. Which should he go for? The spear hadn't worked very well in these narrow passages.

A hiss escaped the larmarsh's mouth, and a plum-colored tongue flicked out to lick blood from its lips. As fast as lightning, it lunged for Tarrik.

He focused on the blackness behind it and poured himself into the shadows. His essence dissolved into the void just as the larmarsh reached for him. He almost felt its talons slashing through the space he'd left.

He re-formed behind the creature and sprinted for Gaukur's axes, sliding on his knees through the dust as he scrambled for their leather-bound handles.

A blow to his back scored burning lines into his skin and sent him slamming into a wall. His vision blurred. Wetness trickled down his spine.

He twisted and lashed out with a fist, hitting something with a solid thump. An iron grip latched on to his arm. Talons bit deep into his muscle, and he hissed with pain. He knew that trying to free his arm would result in shredded tissue, but if a lacerated limb was his only injury when this was finished, he'd count himself lucky.

Ignoring the agony, Tarrik threw himself into the larmarsh's clutches. The creature was strong, but as he'd found out when hunting with Contian, it was used to killing weak humans and therefore lacked finesse. He grabbed the larmarsh's arm with his free hand, yanked it toward him, and as quick as a snake, twisted the limb behind the creature's back. At the same time he stamped on the back of its knee. As its leg bent under the sudden pressure of body weight, the creature stumbled.

Tarrik grabbed a fistful of the larmarsh's hair and used momentum to hammer its head into the wall. Chips broke from the bricks, and he thought he heard bone crack. The larmarsh wailed, a sound filled with pain and rage.

Before the creature could recover, he wrapped his arms around it and grasped his wrists to lock his hold. The move wasn't ideal but all he had time for. The thing's rank hair pressed against his face, and he had to push his cheek hard against the back of the creature's head to prevent it from twisting around and sinking fangs into his flesh.

Screeching and gnashing teeth, the larmarsh writhed, trying to shake him off. Tarrik jerked back and forth, holding on for life. The larmarsh threw itself backward into the wall. Tarrik's head cracked against the brick, and his spine erupted in pain. His grip slipped for an instant, and a sudden surge of strength from the larmarsh almost caused him to lose his hold. *This was a bad idea.*

He slammed into the wall again, and spots swam before his eyes. *Blood and fire! Where's Ren?*

He tangled his leg with the larmarsh's and threw his weight onto it, bearing the twisting creature to the ground, where they thrashed among the dirt and splinters of bone. He had no choice now but to bring forth his shadow-blade, but his position was tricky. If he let go, the larmarsh would be on him in a blink, wreaking untold damage before he could kill it. Likely his wounds would be fatal.

Dust filled his eyes and mouth, and he coughed and blinked. When he could see beyond the blur of tears, Ren stood above them, Tarrik's spear in her hands. She was in danger now too, and her bindings forced him to protect her. The enchantment locked his arms and legs in place before his strength failed. She looked down on him struggling in the dirt with the larmarsh, muscles burning with exertion, sweat and tears trickling down his face, breath aching in his chest.

"Stay away!" he snarled at her. "Dawn- and dusk-tide won't do much against it."

A flicker of amusement crossed Ren's face, so brief Tarrik thought he'd imagined it.

"Some sorcery is effective only in the right hands," she said with a faint smile, then spoke a cant.

A light as bright as the sun erupted overhead. Spots swam before Tarrik's eyes, and he squeezed them shut against the painful white glare. Still, it penetrated his eyelids. He turned his head away.

The larmarsh keened and thrashed wildly, struggling against Tarrik's sinewy muscles and iron grasp. The tantalizing aroma of burned flesh filled his nostrils. All of a sudden, the larmarsh stilled. He opened his eyes to see the creature's skin had blackened and cracked, as if scorched by intense heat. His own skin was unharmed.

The larmarsh twisted and screamed, and Tarrik almost lost his grip. Flakes of charred skin fell from the monster, and its mouth opened wide, tongue writhing like a snake.

Ren thrust down with the spear and drove its blade through the larmarsh's skull. The creature shuddered, then went limp. Tarrik held tight still, fearing the beast might come alive for one final surge, even though the spear had surely taken its life.

More words spilled from Ren's lips, cant after fluid cant. She yanked the spear out, and the blade dripped gore onto the dust. A faint crackling sound came from the desiccated, burnt corpse, and its skin and muscle crumbled in Tarrik's grip to reveal blackened bones.

He pushed the skeleton away, and it clattered to the ground, leaving charcoal smears on his shirt and trousers. He stood and brushed down his clothes, trying to find something to say, wrestling for an explanation of what he'd just witnessed.

The last time he'd fought a larmarsh, Contian's sorcery had been all but useless—and he had been a grandmaster of one of the eminent schools. Afterward, the old sorcerer had expounded at length about the creature's innate resistance to the dawn- and dusk-tide forces. Yet Ren had used those same powers to kill the larmarsh. The spear through its skull hadn't been needed. Her incantations, almost effortlessly, had already pierced the creature's protections.

What was she? What powers did she have that other sorcerers didn't?

Ren clicked her fingers to catch Tarrik's attention and held his spear out to him. "You used them as bait."

She meant Aimy and Gaukur. "Yes. Are you upset?"

She glanced away, lips drawn into a tight line, then shook her head. "Many more will die before we're through. You do what you must to get the job done. Now, if you've finished prettying yourself, we still have work to do. Now that her creature is dead, Lischen will know we're here."

No somber words for the unfortunate Gaukur and Aimy from this heartless woman, even after they'd died to give her the advantage of surprise. Still, it was Tarrik who'd decided to use them as bait. He wouldn't shed a tear over the deaths of two more of this slaver race.

Tarrik took his spear and cast one final look at the remains of the larmarsh. "I take it you think you can best her one-on-one?"

Ren's mouth curled into a sad smile. "We tested one another long ago. We were evenly matched. Lischen will not run from me today, but she will fight with all the tricks she has learned over the centuries. I have disrupted her plans, and she will be angry. She will believe this is all part of my maneuvering for the return of the Adversary."

"So you two will fight each other to a standstill and then give up and both go your merry ways?" It sounded like a waste of energy to Tarrik, for no gain.

"I said we were equal long ago, not that we still are."

"Why is she called the Nightwhisperer?"

Ren stared at Tarrik, expressionless. "She went mad after . . . after what Samal did to her. As did we all."

Interesting. Ren admits her madness. But surely if she is mad, she wouldn't know it?

"Apart from you," he said, humoring her.

"Oh no, I went mad too. It was a bleak time for many years . . . anyway, Lischen believes there are creatures living in the darkness. There aren't, of course, but it's one of her symptoms. She sees them, talks to them." Ren turned her back and gestured for Tarrik to follow. "Come. Let's get this over with."

They passed the shredded corpses of Aimy and Gaukur. The axeman had a gaping slash across his belly, and his red-purple guts glistened wetly. Aimy's hair was slathered with congealed blood. He hoped her child would receive the coin Ren had paid for her mother's death. All young deserved a fighting chance.

Tarrik could only hope he would soon be done with this madwoman who'd bound him. If she'd been driven insane by Samal, there was no telling what she was capable of. And that meant danger for him. He could feel his chances of survival slipping away. He touched on the essence of Ananias in his mind, yearning for time.

Chapter Ten

Ren's footsteps quickened as she led Tarrik along more disused passage-ways. Her sorcerous globe traveled a dozen paces ahead, illuminating their path. She showed no hesitation at the intersections, not even paus-ing slightly to consider which path to take. Eventually they emerged into a sizeable passage with a ten-foot-wide stream of sludge flowing down the middle. The surface bubbled and emitted a foul-smelling stench. Tarrik gagged and brought an arm up to cover his nose and mouth.

"Sewage," said Ren, her fingers pinching her nose. "We'll be past it soon, I think. Lischen wouldn't live with this smell." She strode along-side the oozing channel for a hundred paces until they reached another side passage. "Here."

Rusty iron bars blocked the opening. Two had been pried apart wide enough to squeeze through, and recently, judging from the rust scraped off to reveal uncorroded metal beneath.

Ren whispered a cant, and her globe winked out, shrouding them in blackness. As his eyes adjusted, Tarrik saw a faint glow coming from along the passage. It looked like the yellow flickering of a candle.

"I'll go first," said Ren.

That was fine by Tarrik. He was out of his depth here and would try to keep his distance once the two sorcerers went at each other unless Ren's bindings forced him to intervene, which would mean her confidence in overpowering Lischen had been misplaced and Tarrik would have to face the other's sorcery without any of his own arcane defenses. Not an enticing prospect.

Ren squeezed easily through the gap between the bars and stood waiting for him. Tarrik led with his spear, sliding the tip up toward the ceiling, then felt a mild surge of panic as his shoulders became wedged. He grunted and pushed with his legs, and the bars scraped across his skin. Once through, he wondered if he should have feigned getting stuck so as to stay behind, but Ren knew of his shadow-step ability.

The passage was short, and they emerged into a small room with a narrow table and a single chair. Broken, scorched furniture stood piled in a corner. A lit lamp hung from a hook on one brick wall, with another opening opposite them. An inkwell had spilled its contents across the table, the ink still glistening wet, though no pen or papers or books were to be seen. Another smaller table contained dusty plates and vermin-chewed scraps of food covered in black-green mold. One plate held relatively fresh bread and a wedge of cheese. *The room must have easier access to get the furniture through*, Tarrik thought. *The bars in the grate must have been widened for the larmarsh to come and go.*

He tightened his grip on his spear and loosened his shoulders. Judging from the lamp, uneaten food, and still-wet ink, someone had clearly been here recently.

"She's in the next room," said Ren. She unbuckled her chest strap, letting her sword swing to her left hip.

Tarrik nodded. He wasn't sure he was ready for this confrontation. He felt as powerless as a leaf blowing in a storm.

They crossed the room and entered the opening in the opposite wall, which led them into a larger chamber. A woman—Lischen, Tarrik assumed—sat cross-legged on the floor, cradling a young girl in her arms. The sorcerer's long blonde hair hung forward, concealing her features. The girl's eyes stared sightlessly from a strangely sunken face, with skin so dry it had cracked but hadn't bled. Lischen stank strongly of goat. Wet goat.

Positioned around the room were old wooden relics, waist-high sculptures with only a few fragments of gold leaf remaining. One had tooth marks, and there were faint scratches on the brick walls. A cracked alembic, broken mortar, and various shattered vials and bottles littered a bench. Three cots stood against one wall, blankets covering the inert shapes that lay in them. Tarrik guessed they were the missing youths. From the look of the girl, there was no vitality left in any of them. Was that what happened when a sorcerer stole another's arcane spark? For that was what was happening here; Tarrik couldn't think of any other reason the youths had been taken.

He edged away from Ren a little, in case Lischen attacked without warning. To his surprise, Ren's bindings didn't restrict him in any way.

"Serenity Branwen," hissed Lischen. "You are far from your usual haunts. Why aren't you delving into another dusty old ruin to plumb its secrets?"

"What are you doing here?" Ren asked.

Lischen's head remained lowered, and her hand stroked the corpse's brown hair, which came out in clumps and fell to the floor. Tarrik saw that the back of the sorcerer's hand was crisscrossed with scars, like Ren's back.

"I was concerned about what I heard was happening here," Ren continued when Lischen didn't answer.

"And what did you hear? A few young sorcerers went missing? Who cares? Their loyalties would be to others, and that wouldn't serve me or our master, would it?"

Ren's voice grew hard. "You have gone too far. Your actions would turn the populace against us."

"Why would I care about them? Stupid worms. They are nothing! Our master has shown us the way. Take power for yourself, if you can. He took us, and we can take others. I have found a way, you see. The night whispers showed it to me. Oh, I know you think me insane, but they are real and have proven themselves."

Tarrik stepped to his right and turned his spear blade toward Lischen in case there was an opportunity to strike. His eyes flicked left and right, searching for a trap.

Lischen pointed at him, and he froze. "Leash your dog, Serenity, or I'll do it for you."

Ren held her hand up. Tarrik nodded and backed away a step, then brought up his spear so it was no longer pointed at Lischen. He reversed his grip in case he needed to throw the weapon.

"You killed my pet," Lischen accused Ren. "Should I repay your deed with the death of your bodyguard? Blood for blood, a life for a life?"

A chill swept over Tarrik's skin, and his heart pulsed faster. If she attacked him with sorcery, he was as good as dead.

"Its presence was disruptive," said Ren. "It should not have been taken from the wilderness."

"You are in no position to order me to do anything."

"What you are doing is an abomination," said Ren. "To augment your own power with the essence of others—"

"You always believed you were better than the rest of us," Lischen sneered. "While we came to our master willingly, you had to be dragged screaming."

Tarrik saw that Ren stiffened at the words, but she didn't reply.

"How we laughed at you when the bright knives went to work," Lischen continued. "When our master broke your body, it was just the beginning of your anguish. When he broke your mind, it was ecstasy. You were reduced to nothing, the same as us. And now you do his bidding willingly."

"You must stop what you are doing with these youths."

"I will not."

"Then I will be forced to stop you."

At that, Lischen brushed her hair from her face and looked at Ren for the first time. Tarrik was surprised to find her alluring. Burning blue eyes, full red lips, cheeks flushed pink, and the rest of her all pale-white skin. Then her face twisted with rage and the beauty became ugliness.

"It will be a pleasure to kill you, Serenity Branwen. You were never truly one of us. An outsider."

And if Lischen succeeded and Ren's bindings were broken? Dared Tarrik hope? It was unlikely she'd let Tarrik live after killing Ren, but could he offer Lischen something in exchange for his life? Her pet, the larmarsh, would need to be replaced, and she would need more youths for her experiments. He wouldn't undertake such action, of course, but offering to would buy him enough time to get away and return to the abyss.

"We are evenly matched," Ren said.

"Do you think I am truly mad? You are a fool! I am now so much more!"

Lischen snarled a cant, and a sphere of sky-blue crackling energy surrounded her.

Ren responded in kind, except her shield was composed of swirling golden sparkles.

Tarrik moved away until his back was against the wall. He could tip over the bench to his left to gain some protection, but he knew it wouldn't stand up to a sorcerous assault.

Lischen's eyes narrowed when she saw Ren's shield. "What is this? Did you find a warding artifact while you were grubbing underground among the remnants of your betters? It will not save you. The fledgling sorcerers' powers are now mine, and you will not stand against me. Even Ekthras, the greatest of the Nine, will fall to me."

She shrieked a cant, and violet and sapphire incandescent lines scissored and sliced over Ren's ward, crackling and spitting like water spattering on hot oil. Ren cried out and threw an arm up to protect her eyes from the glittering assault.

Yes! crowed Tarrik to himself, at the same time crouching low to avoid being scorched.

Lischen's mouth twisted into a sneer. She barked cant after cant. The air itself keened and shattered as all heat was leached from their surroundings. Tarrik's breath steamed, and his skin prickled as frost crystals spread across the floor, ascended the walls, and covered the furniture.

A fresh onslaught of indigo sparkles hammered Ren, and she fell to her knees. Her hands clenched into fists, knuckles white, and she grimaced in pain. Tarrik could see the tendons in her neck bulging. But still her shield held under the arcane assault. The air smoldered with fiery embers that scattered and danced in an eldritch wind, and the white frost evaporated, sending mist swirling around the room.

Lischen screeched with rage, her pale face red, eyes bulging. She spat more cants, fingers curled into claws, as if she would tear the flesh from Ren's bones. Her sorcerous lines battered Ren's spherical wards, which writhed and trembled.

Lischen's fury and Ren's impotence inflamed Tarrik. He found himself grinning, even as he shielded his face from the conflagration. He moaned with the yearning to be free, to see Ren's wards crack, for her flesh to be carved by sorcerous knives, her blood to boil. It was a fitting end for her, to be scourged by one of her own kind.

Ren's voice boomed above the cacophony. A brilliance erupted in the room, as glaring as the noon sun. Lischen cried out in pain and terror. Tarrik risked a glance and found Ren standing, a smile of triumph on her face.

No!

She raised her arms above her head, and her wards expanded around her. She spoke a cant, and white and golden lights answered her call. She gathered the sparkling emanations between her hands, then sent them whirling at Lischen.

Thunder cracked, and a sudden wind buffeted Tarrik. Lischen's wards tore like tissue, knocking her to the ground, where she trembled and spat blood. Her clothes smoldered, and smoke wafted from her form. Her hair burned and twisted into clumps. She wiped the back of a hand across her lips, leaving a crimson smear across her cheek.

She spoke a cant, and her shield surrounded her again, though even to Tarrik's eyes it was a weaker, paler version of the original. Ren called more eldritch lights to her grasp and pounded them into Lischen. The other sorcerer's shield shattered into motes.

No! Blood and fire!

Lischen struggled to her feet, her face sheened with sweat, pink and blistered as if sunburned. She stared at Ren, her mouth working soundlessly. Then her gaze dropped to the floor, and her shoulders slumped.

No! Fight, damn you to the abyss!

"I submit," croaked Lischen. "I see now what you have achieved."

Ren drew her sword. White incandescence shone from the blade, like intense moonlight, and despite the coolness of the color, heat poured from it in waves. Hot air blasted across Tarrik's skin, and sweat broke out on his forehead.

Lischen held a hand up, her voice pleading. "We can work together, Serenity. Your name will be revered, and Samal will raise you above us all! The dawn- and dusk-tides . . . who would think anyone could harness the—"

Ren struck faster than Tarrik thought she could move. Her blade passed through Lischen's torso as if she were made of smoke.

Lischen gasped, looking down in surprise. Her back arched, and an unholy screech tore from the depths of her soul. A blue-violet light erupted from her mouth and eyes, and her skin blackened and charred, cracking open to emit the same intense light coming from Ren's sword.

With one swift movement, Ren sheathed her blade, plunging the room into darkness. The only light now came from Lischen's glowing body, her jaws working in a silent scream.

"*Gith-ruthos!*" shouted Ren.

A glaring wave of the blue-white light erupted from her open palms in a flat plane and flashed over Lischen. The sorcerer's flesh spat embers, then broke into brittle chunks that fell to the floor and puffed to clouds of dust. Her incinerated muscles and organs followed, leaving only a skeleton scorched to obsidian. It clattered to the ground, the skull's eyeless sockets and blackened teeth a testament to the intensity of Ren's incantations.

She turned to Tarrik. "Don't just cower there, demon. We still have work to do."

Tarrik rose to his feet. What he'd just seen was like nothing he'd ever experienced before, not even with Contian, who had been an unmatched sorcerer in his prime. Ren had overpowered a sorcerer who was her equal and who had also been augmented by the power of several other sorcerers. Which meant that Ren herself had augmented her power, possibly in the same way.

A fleeting thought came to Tarrik: If the Nine were successful in freeing Samal Rak-shazza, the demon lord would once again permit, even encourage, humans to torture and enslave demons. What, if anything, could the demons do about it? When Tarrik returned to his realm, who could he tell? Who would believe him?

Ren moved to the cots and turned down the blankets to reveal burned and twisted carcasses. "I'll send Veika down here with a few men to clear the place out. The families deserve to know what happened to their children and bury their remains."

"I thought you were going to stop her," Tarrik said. "Not kill her. She was one of the Nine. You're one of them too."

"No. I'm something different."

Chapter Eleven

Back at the house, Ren created another flying disc out of water, steam, and sorcery as they prepared to leave Dwemor Port. It was still the middle of the night, but the rain had stopped, and the clouds had been mostly cleared by a fresh wind. Tarrik was grateful; the thought of flying on Ren's disc in a downpour made him tremble with disgust. He would be glad to leave this human city and the two people Ren had conned into believing she stood for something other than herself. He guessed that was why she hadn't wanted Veika to accompany them when they confronted Lischen, because he would have seen who she truly was. The stupid only stayed gulled if they were kept in the dark.

Slivers of both moons were high in the sky by the time Ren made it outside to where Tarrik had been waiting for what seemed like ages. Veika stood close by, silent for once. At Ren's order, Tarrik piled their gear on the platform—no saddles this time—then sat on it, his spear cradled across his arms. He half expected attacking soldiers to appear or a sorcerous assault—Ren had killed one of the Nine, after all. Surely there would be retribution from the others. But to his surprise nothing materialized.

He cast a sidelong glance at Ren as she ceased shouting cants, hopped onto the disc, and moved to what he assumed was the front. Did it have a front? Again, he could only sense a minimal draw of dawn- and dusk-tide emanations by Ren, which set his mind to wondering afresh. She was more powerful than Lischen, who had augmented herself with the powers of more than a few fledgling sorcerers. So where did Ren's power come from? Was its source the artifact Tarrik had stolen for her? He was no fool, especially when it came to sorcerers. He wouldn't put all his coin on one explanation. Sorcerers were never what they seemed.

"Do you have to go so soon?" asked Jendra, emerging from the kitchen.

"I'm sorry—I must," replied Ren.

"When will you be back?"

"I . . . I don't know."

Jendra opened her mouth to speak again, but Veika's hand on her arm stopped her. She frowned at him, then sighed in resignation.

They aren't sure whether they'll ever see her again. Tarrik found the thought calming and sat up a little straighter. The life of a sorcerer was risky, and the path Ren had chosen was more dangerous than most. The way she was going, she'd be certain to make a mistake, and that would be the end of her. He only had to stay alive until it happened.

Jendra approached the disc and handed Tarrik a small burlap sack. "Provisions," she said, and backed away quickly.

With a final brief wave at Veika and Jendra, Ren knelt and began to whisper cants. Crimson-violet lightning gathered between her hands, and she grasped its glittering strands. The shimmering disc rose into the air as heat waves cracked the stone pavers of the courtyard. Veika and Jendra scurried to a safe distance to prevent themselves from being scalded. Again, Ren smelled of arcane power—and of something that reminded Tarrik of sunlight, along with a tinge of reluctance.

They quickly ascended and were soon so high Tarrik lost sight of Veika and Jendra. With a lurch, the disc surged forward. Wind whipped across his face and ruffled his clothes.

"Get some sleep, if you can," shouted Ren above the rushing sound. "But first pass me one of whatever provisions Jendra gave us. I'm hungry, and it'll help keep me awake."

Tarrik hesitated as he reached for the small sack. What would happen if Ren fell asleep while they were in the sky?

Inside the sack were small parcels wrapped in waxed paper. Tarrik opened one to reveal a rounded loaf dotted with dried fruit. He grimaced, then noticed a bottle as well. He took it out and smiled when he saw the label: Widow's Malt. It also pictured a crow rather than stalks of cane from which rum was made. Veika must have included it. No doubt he thought Tarrik would get drunk and make a mistake, and Ren would get rid of him.

He wormed his way on his knees to Ren, not trusting himself to stand.

She gave him a look of amusement and took the small loaf. "I see you found Veika's present to you. He thought you'd enjoy it more than rum. He would never say it out loud, but he's glad you were able to keep me safe in the temple."

"Aimy and Gaukur died, though. I wouldn't imagine he was too pleased about that."

And Ren had scarcely required Tarrik's help to defend herself. He still believed he'd been intended as bait, just as he'd used Aimy and Gaukur to distract the larmarsh.

A determined smile came across his face as he considered what he'd survived so far: a demon of a higher order, a larmarsh, and one of the Nine. Let Ren think he was there to be used; he was stronger than she realized.

He looked up to see her frowning at him and schooled his expression into one of meekness. "Where are we going now?"

"Northwest until we reach the coast, then follow it north to Atya."

"Atya?"

"A city. I have business there."

"Why were you not concerned about creating this platform in possible sight of others in Dwemor Port but so secretive in Ivrian? We rode some distance from the city before you created it there."

Ren took a bite from the fruit loaf and gave him a thoughtful look. "We have a long way to travel. Get some sleep," she said, then turned her back on him.

He moved to the middle of the platform and tried to get comfortable. Clearly he'd asked too many questions, and Ren was suspicious.

The cork slid easily from the bottle, and he took a swig. The spirit burned his tongue and throat, but after a few moments he felt less on edge and more in control of himself. He returned the bottle to the sack and scoured his memory for any information about absorbing a higher-order demon. His previous absorptions had all been demons of a lower order and many years ago. The process had been difficult, but in the end, with patience and skill, he'd been rewarded. All he was certain of this time was that it was tricky and a process best done slowly. He didn't want to lose his mind. However, patience might be his downfall. The longer he waited, the more chance that Ren would get him killed.

Tarrik closed his eyes and found the hardened mass in his mind that was the remains of Ananias. It had a smooth surface that undulated slightly, as if something moved inside. When he pushed against the shell, it hardened and resisted his probe. He shook his head. Trying things he'd tried before wouldn't get him anywhere. He had to be smarter. He thought back to Ananias and what sort of a demon he'd been: cruel and cunning; partial to melodrama, as shown by the scarlet steam he had generated to conceal his face and the use of his dark-tide power to create fire. A waste of energy for little gain. Ananias was no genius.

Perhaps heat would corrode the shell around his essence? Generating heat inside one's own mind was dangerous, but Tarrik was confident he could shield himself using shadows.

A tiny part of his consciousness exulted at the thought of subsuming Ananias. A feral, desperate part.

He set to work.

Tarrik opened his eyes to find Ren staring at him. She was munching on another fruit loaf, which meant she'd taken one from the sack without him being aware of the movement.

He looked over the edge of the disc. Below, lit by moonlight, sheer cliffs rose from the ocean, a hundred yards high. The disc skimmed above them, heading in a northerly direction. If they'd reached the coast already, they were making better time than their first trip. Ren was in a hurry.

"What are you doing?" she asked.

"Thinking."

"About killing me, no doubt."

"No. Something else."

She sniffed and bit into the loaf. After a few moments of chewing, she said, "You should try to feel the stars. They're especially bright tonight, now that we're away from the city."

Feel the stars? What use was that? Both moons had sunk toward the horizon, and dawn couldn't be too far off.

Humor her. "I'll . . . try," he said.

Ren looked away as if the suggestion was of no importance to her. Why then had she suggested it?

"We'll stop soon and rest during the day," she said. "There are winged creatures that inhabit the cliffs along this coast. They're very territorial and might attack us. I can't keep us aloft and fight one off at the same time."

Good to know. His body had healed well, but a day of rest would do wonders.

"I'll find a relatively safe spot to land, and you can guard me while I sleep. I'll also place some wards in case we encounter anything you can't handle."

Tarrik's stomach rose as they began to descend, reminding him that he hadn't eaten since the tavern. The fruit loaves Ren seemed to enjoy so much turned his innards.

Ren flew them inland over stunted trees and windswept grasses until she found a rocky outcrop. The sun peeked over the horizon, casting an orange glow that reminded Tarrik of home.

He couldn't see many signs of life on the surrounding terrain: a few rabbits, a herd of wild goats, a bird of prey soaring high above. The presence of the animals eased Tarrik's mind, since it meant this area was clear of creatures such as larmarsh and manticarrs. Dead-eyes, on the other hand, hunted at night, as did a few other predators. But from what Ren had said, they would be long gone before the night dwellers came out.

"Off," said Ren as the disc hit the ground with a jarring thud.

Tarrik shouldered their saddlebags and grabbed Jendra's sack along with his spear. He leaped off the platform and hurried away from the surrounding heat. Wind buffeted him, cold from the sea. Without waiting for Ren, he strode over to the outcrop, which stood up from the grasslands like a wart. A small group of trees sat on the sheltered western side. He dumped the gear and sack, and, after a moment's hesitation, his spear as well, then set about gathering firewood. He was already shivering from the gusts, and the thought of an entire day guarding Ren while she slept set his teeth on edge.

He carried his pile of sticks and branches to the sheltered side of the rock. Ren was already relaxing, having found a comfortable slab of stone to lean her back against. She had her journal out and leafed through its pages. Beside her sat a tiny ink bottle and an ivory pen with a steel nib.

She looked up in annoyance as he dropped the wood at her feet with a clatter. "Go and catch a rabbit or two for a meal."

Tarrik gave her a short bow, grabbed his spear, and strode away. He found it a simple task to catch rabbits, even though they were quite swift when fleeing. He simply shadow-stepped to their burrows and grabbed them when they froze in surprise.

As he twisted the second rabbit's neck until it cracked, Tarrik's skin tingled. He felt three surges of arcane power from Ren. He stopped, the dead rabbit forgotten in his hands, but couldn't sense anything further. Had she wanted him gone while she performed sorcery? Or did she actually want rabbit to eat? Perhaps both, he decided.

He raised the corpse to his mouth, intending to taste its blood, but thoughts of the larmarsh killing Aimy and Gaukur stopped him. Tarrik had long since lost his squeamishness around slaughter and using others to ensure his own survival. Prey was prey, and humans were slavers, and worse. But a niggling discomfort kept returning. Aimy hadn't known he was a demon and had been attracted to him. She'd had her own hopes and desires, and a daughter. And he'd left her dead in a decrepit catacomb, her daughter without a mother.

But that was the way of the world—of all worlds—wasn't it? The strong and intelligent survived to fight another day. Still, he couldn't get Aimy out of his head. He'd never cared about such things before his time with Jaquel. She'd changed him more than he'd thought possible.

Flashes of memory swamped his thoughts until he could hardly breathe. He saw the boys and girls she'd taught running around her, smiling after their lessons had finished for the day, and her delight in their joy. He saw Jaquel chasing after the chickens when they'd gotten loose, eventually giving up and throwing herself onto the grass in surrender—the endearing way she would lift her hand to her throat when she laughed. He saw her sweat-streaked face as he taught her to fight with weapons and without, saw her eyes piercing his as they loved one another. Demon relationships were usually brief and fiery, but he'd always wanted more. In Jaquel he'd found a mate who made him better than he was without her; and because of his devotion, his deep, immortal love for her, giving up his freedom hadn't felt like compromise. And ultimately, he'd betrayed his own kind to keep her.

He sighed and returned to Ren.

She was writing in her journal, though beside the campfire there was now a square hole with precise edges and a mound of dirt beside it.

She placed her journal and her pen aside, drew a skinning blade, and set to work on the rabbits with a practiced hand, stripping their hides and gutting them. Their innards she deposited into the hole in the ground. They didn't have a spade, so Tarrik guessed that was the surge of power he'd felt. Or one of them.

What else had she done with sorcery? He glanced around but couldn't see any other changes.

As with the birds Ren had prepared before, once the rabbits were ready for cooking, it struck Tarrik again how like miniature demons they looked. He would have preferred the meat raw and watched with regret as Ren placed the carcasses into her cast-iron pot, added water and dried herbs, then put the lid on and placed the pot into the coals.

"Fill our canteens," she said. "There's a stream a few hundred yards north."

Tarrik walked off, leaving Ren staring into the flames. His shoulders and neck felt tight, and he shrugged to loosen the muscles. He paused when he felt another two surges of sorcery and looked back toward their camp. From this distance all he could see was the fire glowing in the morning light.

At the stream, he knelt on a rock and filled their canteens, then returned to the camp. Ren was now relaxing on a blanket on the ground, her journal and writing implements stowed back in her saddlebags. The pot was still in the coals, and Tarrik's stomach grumbled loud enough to be heard over the fire.

Ren laughed. "They'll be ready soon."

The orange glow lit her face and hair, and for an instant Tarrik thought she looked like Jaquel. He blinked and placed the full canteens beside their gear, then with shaking hands rummaged for the bottle Veika had given him. He swallowed a measure, then another, aware of Ren's eyes on him. When he returned the bottle to his saddlebag, he felt more in control.

Ren had said they would be staying here for the day while she recuperated from the exertions of their flight. But perhaps they were here so she could work her enchantments. Either way, the day promised to be boring, with Tarrik standing guard while she slept.

Ren pronounced the rabbits done. After the meat had cooled a little, they ate in silence. She ate more than she normally did, and from the set of her shoulders and her relaxed expression, Tarrik judged she preferred the outdoors to the city. She certainly knew how to skin and gut a variety of animals. He almost asked where she'd acquired such skills before stopping himself. It was a known strategy for summoners to create a bond between themselves and the demons so their slaves became accustomed to their bindings and even came to care for their captors. Tarrik wouldn't make that mistake.

He picked the bones clean, then threw them into the disturbingly precise hole. Ren waved a hand to indicate he should fill the cavity, and he used his booted foot to return and pack down the dirt. Then he busied himself inspecting his spear and honing the blade. He found a cloth and worked some oil into the shaft, which had suffered from years of neglect.

Ren stared into the rapidly diminishing coals, content to ignore him.

Finally, she said, "I know you felt my sorcery. Are you not intrigued as to what I was doing?"

"No."

Something nefarious, no doubt. The wards she usually put up didn't require the power he'd felt.

"Is lack of curiosity a Tarrik trait or a demon trait?"

"It's a survival trait."

"Ah."

Tarrik had had enough of talking to her. He rose, spear in hand. "I'm going to scout the area."

"As you wish. I will sleep before long, so return soon."

He walked increasingly wide circles around their campsite, stopping occasionally to practice forms, becoming more familiar with his weapon. The spear felt good in his hands, and he was glad he'd found it. Those fools could keep their swords and fancy footwork and ineffective techniques.

A snort of amusement escaped him when he remembered Albin's words just before Tarrik had killed him: "Spears are for peasants, and swords are for noble warriors!" Humans thought life was a game and that arrogance and posturing somehow gave you an advantage. Well, now that Albin had crossed the veil into death, he could contemplate his failings for all eternity.

When Tarrik returned to their camp, he found Ren wrapped in another blanket and the fire almost dead. He decided against adding more wood. Though a blaze would bring welcome heat, it might wake Ren, and he didn't want to talk to her.

He settled himself into a comfortable cross-legged position and turned his mind to breaking open Ananias's essence. He had a full day to work on the task and didn't intend to waste the time.

Chapter Twelve

Sometime after midday, Ren cried out in her sleep. Tarrik pulled back from scraping at the shell around Ananias's essence and leaped to his feet. He saw that her knuckle was between her teeth, and she'd worried it until it bled. Something stirred within him. She was doing herself damage, and he could use it as an opportunity to show her he could be relied on for care. Another step toward gaining her trust.

He found a strip of clean cloth in their saddlebags, and gently, so as not to rouse her, took her hand and bound the bleeding knuckle. As he worked, a sob escaped her, and she stirred but didn't wake. Something was tearing her up from the inside, and Tarrik didn't think it was her murder of another of the Nine.

He returned to his blanket and continued to work on breaking through to Ananias's essence. The process took hours of scraping and probing, but this wasn't a task to be rushed. He'd come too far over the centuries, fought through too much, to become careless and fail now.

Finally, he managed to coax a tiny trickle of essence from the roiling mass. It came to him reluctantly, but also hopefully, as if seeking a new home now that Ananias was gone. As the concentrated kernel expanded inside Tarrik he shuddered with pleasure, then quickly tore the scrap apart. He dispersed it through his mind before the essence could do any damage.

A milestone: the first fragment of essence to be absorbed. Others should come more quickly now.

He sealed the breach he'd created and quickly checked his work to ensure the shell was now whole. If it shattered and released all of its essence at once, Tarrik would lose his mind.

"Wake up."

Something prodded Tarrik. He opened his eyes to see it was Ren's boot. He groaned and levered himself to a sitting position. It was getting dark, and Ren had stirred the fire to life.

"You're supposed to be keeping watch," she said.

Tarrik's head ached, and his mouth was parched. He made it to his feet and drained half a canteen of water. Worrying away the layers of shell around the demon's essence had been exhausting, and the last thing he remembered was deciding to rest his eyes for a few moments.

"There were no threats," he said. "I made sure of it. Besides, your wards would have warned us."

"That's no cause for slackness. Do you need a taste of the Wracking Nerves to remind you of your duties?"

The hardness of her voice made him bow his head. She was angry, more so than his falling asleep warranted.

"I'm sorry," he said. "It won't happen again."

"It had better not."

He looked up to find her glaring at him. Her face was flushed, and both hands were clenched into fists. Her right hand was still bound with the cloth, now patched red.

She brandished her fist at him. "You did this while I slept? You touched me?"

Tarrik cursed inwardly. He'd miscalculated. Of course she wouldn't want someone touching her without permission. She was damaged and broken from Samal's violation of her body and mind.

"I . . . yes. Your hand was bleeding and—"

"What else did you do?"

"Nothing. If I overstepped, I—"

Ren barked a cant, and agony racked his bones and muscles. His skin felt as if it were being both scorched and flayed. He screamed and fell rigid to the ground. The Wracking Nerves continued without respite, and Tarrik found his mind collapsing into a smaller and smaller ball. Eventually the torture diminished until he could draw breath without pain. He remained curled up, face pressed to the dirt. When the agony faded to nothing, he crawled to his knees, then staggered to his feet. She'd castigated him more than was warranted; perhaps he was a surrogate for her anger against Samal. Ren couldn't express rage against her master but could punish her slave.

Despair filled him, but he clenched his jaw and steeled himself. Succumbing to a sorcerer's chastisement and becoming a meek slave was something that happened to other demons. But not him. Not Tarrik Nal-Valim, demon of the Thirty-Seventh Order. He had survived the stone walls of old Kargax when the invaders had torn them down and fed on the demons within. He'd fought his way through the breach at Ulrionaz when even demon lords had fallen to terrible sorceries and star-metal blades. And he would survive this. He would absorb Ananias fully and break Ren's bindings.

Tarrik took a deep breath and glowered at the source of his misery.

She regarded him with a sneer. "I see I have not broken you. Good. I was worried for a moment."

Tarrik swallowed his pride along with a mouthful of blood and saliva. "I meant no disrespect."

"Nevertheless, you gave it."

"It won't happen again."

Ren's eyes narrowed. "I dare say it will. Now, gather our gear. We have a long way to travel tonight, and I assume you'll want us to stop early."

Tarrik frowned. "Why?"

"Tonight is the full dark. You'll want to replenish your dark-tide powers."

Oh. Maybe it was because he was still recovering from the dose of Wracking Nerves, but he couldn't bring himself to dissemble.

"It will happen whether I focus on it or not. We demons do not need all the rigmarole you sorcerers go through with the dawn- and dusk-tides."

"Rigmarole? Is that how you see sorcerers—focused on unimportant rituals, as though playing some kind of game?"

He shook his head. "You humans can play with sorcery however you want. It doesn't matter to me. Demon abilities are innate." Mostly. "We don't use cants." Except sometimes.

Ren seemed to accept his explanation. She retrieved one of the full canteens and busied herself voicing cants to create another disc.

Tarrik made sure their gear was secure and stowed the cooking pot he hadn't yet washed.

Soon the disc was complete, and they were speeding into the coming dark. Tarrik rubbed his sore neck, wishing he could do something about his headache.

With the moons Chandra and Jagonath remaining beneath the horizon and full dark upon them, he saw the yellow lights of the city in the distance before he smelled its stench.

"Atya," Ren said as they descended, the wind whipping about them. Dawn cast a gray light across the landscape, lending it a washed-out look. "We're still on the coast, but this close to the Wastes, the people are tougher. They're used to hardship."

Tarrik recalled Contian speaking about the Wastes but couldn't remember any of the details. Something about battles and lingering fiendish emanations that harmed the land.

They flew over the city, Ren peering down as if searching for a landmark, brilliant white threads of sorcery streaming over her face and hair. She focused on something below, and the disc dropped like a stone. Tarrik's stomach rose to his throat, and he swallowed. It was an unpleasant sensation, one he didn't care to repeat.

They jerked to the left as Ren corrected her aim. He saw an imposing granite building rearing up from a deserted park surrounded by a wall. The building was cube shaped, with no windows or doors, unless they were set into one of the sides out of sight. Faint seams could be discerned in the granite, and the whole thing looked like it had been carved from one giant piece of rock. The shape reminded him of the sharp-edged hole Ren had dug with sorcery. Was there a connection?

They alighted on the flat roof, which consisted of the same murky gray granite as the walls. There were no railings to prevent a fall from such a height. Tarrik could see the ocean to the east and the city spreading out around them in all other directions, covered in a smoky haze.

A cube of stone stood out from the center of the roof, with a blackwood door on the side facing them. Tarrik's skin prickled, and his arm hairs stood on end. Powerful sorcery was present, and he sensed undertones of dark-tide beneath the human arcane emanations. Whatever this place was, he wanted nothing to do with it. He hoped Ren would get her business over with and get them away as quickly as possible.

The misty threads trailing over and behind her dissipated, and she stood and stretched, her arms above her head. Even though they'd been flying the entire night, she again seemed invigorated and showed no signs of needing to replenish her dawn-tide repository. This seemed a perfect place to Tarrik for such an activity: quiet and private, raised high above the city.

Ren adjusted her orichalcum sword and shifted the baldric across her chest slightly. She shaded her eyes from the morning sun, and Tarrik became aware of her gracefulness and lithe form. His mouth went dry, and heat surged to his face and groin. He allowed his eyes to roam over her with a feral shamelessness, then tore them away, fumbled with the sack, and took a deep swallow of spirits.

There was danger here—he knew all too well. For as demons' emotions ran deep, so could their lusts transform to love if left unguarded. That was what had happened with Jaquel, which had then led to his exile.

Consorting with humans always led to trouble.

"Bring our gear, and be quick about it," Ren said. "Sheelahn will make me pay if we tarry here overlong."

Sheelahn? Another sorcerer probably. Tarrik wiped his mouth and replaced the bottle. His hands shook, and he hid them from Ren's sight.

She hopped down from the platform into the haze of heat emanating from the granite beneath them. Tarrik noted with alarm that the stone had begun to glow a dim orange. He thought he could hear it cracking faintly. He shouldered their saddlebags, picked up the sack that still contained a few waxed paper–wrapped fruit loaves, and grabbed his spear. At least he didn't have to lug saddles around anymore.

Ren strode to the door, and Tarrik followed. The portal opened before she reached it to reveal a man wearing a mask of polished blackwood with no features except two eyeholes. He was skinny and almost as tall as Tarrik and wore a thick coat the color of gloomy rainclouds. His long black hair was twisted into multiple braids with no pattern that meant anything to Tarrik.

"Enter," the man said. "You are expected."

He stood inside an elaborate iron cage, which Tarrik decided must be a lifting device of some sort rather than stairs. A luxury afforded by the weak.

Ren entered the cage, and Tarrik squeezed in between her and the man, the saddlebags brushing against them both. There was a metallic groan and a clunk from above; then the floor lurched, and they began to descend.

"The Ethereal Sorceress will see you," the man said to Ren.

"We are honored," she replied.

"The demon is not invited."

Tarrik gave the man a sharp glance, then looked at Ren. She gave no indication she was perturbed that Tarrik's true nature had been recognized.

"He remains with me," she said.

The man paused, then nodded slightly. "As you wish."

He'd changed his mind quickly, and Tarrik wondered if the pause denoted a sorcerous communication with this Sheelahn.

They passed two doors; then the cage stopped, facing another. The masked face turned toward Tarrik but said nothing.

Ren poked Tarrik in the ribs. "You're blocking the way. Open the door."

Tarrik pushed the portal, and it swung open on silent hinges. He stepped out and to the side to let Ren and the masked man exit. Ahead lay a corridor with a forest-green carpet and alchemical globes in wall sconces.

Twenty paces along the corridor, at its end, stood another strange-looking figure. If this was Sheelahn the Ethereal Sorceress, she was the oddest sorcerer Tarrik had ever seen. Her face was covered by an orichalcum mask with a single cross-shaped opening. Behind it, he could see only impenetrable blackness. She wore long robes so thick it was impossible to discern what lay underneath. Each fold and twist of fabric stood out stiffly and precisely, as if pressed and starched. On her hands she wore black silk gloves.

Ren walked toward the sorceress but stopped a dozen paces short.

"You have a demon with you." Sheelahn's voice was oddly musical, reminiscent of birdsong.

"He is not to be harmed," said Ren firmly.

The mask tilted forward slightly, then returned to its original position. A nod. "I will buy it from you."

"He is not for sale."

"Everything is for sale or barter."

"That is where you are wrong."

"I am seldom wrong. But I admit people can form unnatural attachments to certain things."

Ren's fists clenched, and for a long moment she didn't move or speak. Tarrik could see the tendons in her neck straining. Had Sheelahn made an oblique reference to the Nine's, and therefore Ren's, ties to Samal? Was that what had rubbed her the wrong way? But why should it if she was bound to serve the demon?

"Why have you summoned me?" Ren asked through clenched teeth.

"There are Cabalist plans afoot here in Atya."

"There always are. It is none of my concern."

"And yet here you are."

"I have business in Atya."

"You owe me a favor," Sheelahn said.

"I . . . do," admitted Ren.

"It is agreed, then. You will find out what the Cabalists' designs are and disrupt them."

"I will do what I am able to, but not at the expense of my own plans or if it would diminish my position with the Cabalists."

"Agreed," Sheelahn said. "They are using demons. Your pet may lend you an advantage."

Tarrik suppressed a growl, and his hands tightened on the shaft of his spear.

Ren held up a hand. "Not a word from you, demon." She turned back to Sheelahn. "Is there anything else you can tell me?"

"The demons are tricky things, able to mimic humans. I would not have them in this city."

"I will do my best to ferret them out."

"That is sufficient. Your best is quite good, as I know, Sun-Child."

Ren nodded once, then turned on her heel. "Let's go," she said to Tarrik.

Sheelahn remained still and silent as they reentered the iron cage. There was another metallic clunk far above, and they began to ascend.

Ren had again agreed to interfere in the business of the Tainted Cabal or the Nine, Tarrik thought. The demons Sheelahn spoke about had to be jikin-nakar, who could shape-shift to resemble anything of a similar size and were able to absorb some of a human's memories in order to pass as one. They would fool humans but not a higher-order demon. Tarrik reminded himself to keep a watch for any of the jikin-nakar; their lack of scent should give them away.

The lift stopped at the first door, and Ren led Tarrik into a massive room with a checkered floor of shiny white and green marble tiles lit by five chandeliers of alchemical globes. The masked man was waiting for them and gestured to one of a dozen blackwood doors dotted around the walls. He let them outside to a manicured garden surrounding the building and closed the door as he departed.

Ren stopped on the pebbled path twenty paces from the building. "This is annoying. I didn't think Sheelahn would ask me to repay her so soon. But it may work to my advantage. I hadn't thought to . . ." She shook her head and muttered to herself under her breath.

"She called you Sun-Child," Tarrik said. "What does she mean?"

"A joke between us. It isn't important. What is important is that this might actually work out well for me. I hadn't dared hope, but . . ." She pursed her lips and glanced at Tarrik. "We'll hail a cab and go straight to the palace. I'm expected there too."

The path led them to the garden wall and a double gate fashioned from wrought iron. Outside, they signaled a single-horse open cab and were soon on their way. Not many people looked at the cab or its occupants as it bumped along the cobbled streets.

Compared to the inhabitants of Ivrian and Dwemor Port, these people were skinnier, dirtier, and more haggard. Tarrik spotted the occasional well-dressed man or woman, but overall he decided Atya was not a prosperous city. As they'd approached on Ren's disc, he'd noticed the surrounding lands were drier and far less vegetated than those surrounding Ivrian and Niyas—presumably the Wastes Ren had mentioned earlier. But Tarrik thought the people here looked more downtrodden than tough.

Ren stared at nothing, lost in thought. Her right hand was at her lips, and her teeth worried the strip of cloth around her knuckle.

Their driver stopped at a brick wall topped with arm-length iron spikes. The barrier had a single wide opening through which a crowd thronged both ways.

"Can't go no farther," he said. "Cabs aren't allowed through."

"I know—thank you," said Ren as she handed him a coin.

She alighted, and Tarrik followed. Through the opening he could see a massive building dominating a paved square. The palace was a jumble of ancient and newer architecture: spires and turrets, stained-glass windows, squat defensive towers, and multiple walls layered for defense. It looked both sprawling and formidable. Flags and pennants of many colors and designs flew atop the towers.

Ren placed her hands on her hips and sighed at the mass of people around the palace entrance.

Tarrik waved toward them. "Maybe you should just blast them to charcoal and give us easy access."

"You'd like that, wouldn't you?"

If they were human sorcerers and demon slavers, yes. But these common folk were mere ants.

Before Tarrik could reply, two wagons filled with soldiers barreled down the street toward them. The soldiers wore leather armor covered with heat-darkened metal scales and carried short swords and clubs.

Tarrik felt Ren's bindings tighten around him, urging him to protect her. He pulled her into a recessed doorway, putting himself between her and the soldiers.

The wagons clattered past and stopped thirty paces along the street. A carriage of black and scarlet lacquered wood with bright steel trims and fittings followed behind. Tarrik leaned out and saw the soldiers drag a man and a woman from a shop and into the carriage.

A young woman shouted imprecations and tussled with two of the soldiers. A basket lay where she'd dropped it, apples spilling on the ground. The soldiers shoved the woman to the ground and waved their clubs menacingly. She covered her head, and they hurried back to the wagons.

By the time the woman raised her head to reveal a tear-streaked face, the wagons and carriage had vanished down a side street. She cursed and picked up an apple but then just sat there dejectedly. Passersby scurried around, ignoring her.

Ren gave the woman a brief look, then beckoned Tarrik to follow her.

"Those weren't regular soldiers," he said. "Why did they take those people?"

"For spreading rumors, for subversion, for sabotage—any number of reasons. These people have their own history and ties to other ideals. The soldiers were Guardians."

"What do they guard?"

"Ideas. A concept of empire that is bigger than one person."

"And to guard this concept, they imprison anyone who disagrees?"

"Yes."

Ren reached the woman and bent to pick up the apples. When the basket was full, she held it out, but the woman didn't seem to see her. Ren placed the basket at her feet and turned away toward the crowded gate. Tarrik followed close behind.

"Ideas are everywhere," he said. "To imprison someone for history and ideas would mean imprisoning all. And yet many people walk these streets."

"They are the faithful. The rulers of this land have a vision that they have made possible by joining with the Tainted Cabal and the Nine."

Perhaps the Tainted Cabal and the Nine would create an empire of slaves, Tarrik thought. Turn the countryside into a wasteland and the humans into cattle, though few would realize the shackles placed upon them. Scarcity and hunger changed what you thought about, made the need for survival overriding.

Tarrik cared not. The humans could do as they wished with their world. But still a small part of him objected to this line of thinking. If he were somehow able to prevent the return of the Adversary and the untold damage he would cause but chose not to, wouldn't that make him just like the humans?

Ren muttered cants under her breath, and the crowd moved as if parted by invisible walls. She strode into the gap she'd created, ignoring the startled looks and ominous glances of fear, loathing, and jealousy.

Guards tried to calm the riled throng while at the same time acting respectfully toward Ren, standing at attention or saluting with a fist to the chest. Trying to do all things at once gave them a comical awkwardness, and Tarrik almost felt sorry for them.

"Isn't there an easier way in?" he asked.

"It helps to create an impression, and I'm fond of unsettling people. They think I'm thousands of miles away."

"I've noticed," he said. *Unsettling them and then killing them.*

Inside the wall was almost as chaotic as outside. Soldiers and servants scurried around, all acting as if they were on important business. Tarrik noticed another gate far to their left with a long line of wagons and carts. Their drivers and teamsters sat around chatting and smoking pipes, playing cards or dice. They were more barbaric than the drivers in Ivrian, and most wore stained and patched leathers. Their broad-brimmed hats sported feathers and the teeth of various animals.

Tarrik followed Ren across the paved square to another queue of people. She walked right past them, and when guards moved to intercept her, she sent a brief burst of multicolored tendrils into the air. They scurried back, bowing obsequiously. Tarrik was about to remark that they weren't much use as guards, then realized they knew they'd be slaughtered if it came to a fight with a sorcerer, and there were plenty of Cabalists and other sorcerers inside the palace who could deal with Ren if she was a threat.

They passed through an elaborate door wrought from brass and a brown wood and into a white-marbled foyer. The queue of people snaked in from outside, ending at a large desk, behind which sat three clerks taking petitioners' details before sending them down various corridors.

Ahead, a large opening offered passage into another marbled room flanked by two spiraling staircases that ended at iron-grilled doors leading to the floor above.

An official in a navy tunic scurried over to Ren, a pen and a wood-backed notebook in his hands. He was short and reedy with a lusterless complexion. "Lady Branwen," he said with perfunctory courtesy and wrote a brief note in his book. "I'll inform your colleagues that you have arrived and assign you a suite of rooms."

"Thank you," Ren said. "Have some refreshments brought as well. It has been a long journey."

"As you wish. I believe a meeting of the Cabal is scheduled for this morning. Will you be attending?"

"I will."

"Excellent. I'll let them know."

The official raised his pen in the air, and a young girl scurried over, also dressed in navy. She was pale skinned and a head shorter than Ren, her reddish hair in tight braids. She gave Tarrik and Ren furtive glances.

"Take Lady Branwen to the Green Elk Suite, Linriel," the official told the girl. "Then provide refreshments. Return to me as quickly as you can. We have a great number of visitors, and I don't want you shirking your duties."

"Yes, sir."

The man turned to Ren. "Follow Linriel, please. And if she doesn't meet your wishes or talks too much, report her to me. The servants are lacking in discipline these days, and it makes everyone's job harder."

Tarrik caught the girl rolling her eyes before she lowered her head.

"I'm sure she'll be fine," said Ren. "Lead away."

Linriel hurried toward the staircase on the right, and Ren and Tarrik followed. At the top were stationed two guards, who opened the iron grille while giving Ren and Tarrik suspicious stares. Once the trio was through the grille and into a mosaic-tiled chamber, Linriel slowed her pace, looked back, and smiled.

"It's a big palace, so you need to conserve your energy. Old Randin just stands around all day; he forgets how hard it is on the servants. If you want, I can bring some cakes and sweets to your rooms, but maybe I'd better taste them first, as there might be poison. Where are you from? Are you a sorcerer? Your man is scary. Where's he from? Somewhere terrible, I bet."

"You'd be correct," said Ren with a smile. "No cakes or sweets for us, but a pastry or two wouldn't go astray. I am a sorcerer, and I'm from far away."

"Call me Lin. Everyone does, apart from stuffy Randin."

Ren dealt with the chatty girl far better than Tarrik would have. He focused on the palace and its occupants. As they walked down a corridor, blue-clad servants moved to the side and bowed their heads. Guards were stationed at every junction, though some looked less disciplined than others. Tarrik noticed some spots of rust on weapons and helmets, and eyes flicking left and right when they should have been straight ahead, at attention. He guessed a few locals had been conscripted to bulk out the guards' numbers while the Cabal was in the palace. Whoever ruled in this city was obviously under their sway—a puppet. Tarrik would do better to concentrate on the Cabalists themselves and whatever they were up to. If there was a chance to disrupt their plans and put the blame on Ren, he would take it.

"Far away where?" Lin asked. "Can you teach me some sorcery? Are you rich?"

"Across the Simorga Sea," Ren replied. "Maybe, if you have the talent. And no."

They ascended another staircase, this one of polished wood, and found themselves outside a wide door painted with green antlers. The girl tugged on the brass handle and pulled the door open with a groan of exertion.

"I'll fetch your pastries now!" she said, and rushed off.

"Bring some meat," called Tarrik after her, not sure if she heard.

The rooms were much like the other suites they'd stayed in. Bedroom, preparation room, a smaller room for a servant, and a reception room. A few cream-colored woolen rugs were scattered about the floor. Ren closed the door while Tarrik placed their bags on the floor and leaned his spear against a wall.

"There is danger here," Ren said. "Do not let your guard down."

"As you command."

Ren looked at her bloodied knuckle and frowned. She dug through her saddlebags and came up with a pair of calfskin gloves and tugged them on.

"You have three tasks here, Tarrik. Protect me, survive any treachery, and keep a watch for the demons Sheelahn warned us about."

If there was any treachery, it was more likely to come from Ren. With any luck she would be kept busy with Cabal business, leaving him to his own devices. And he'd continue to worry at Ananias's essence.

Ren picked up a brush from the bedside table and ran it over her clothes. "The . . . favor I owe Sheelahn must be repaid. Her regard is too valuable to lose. The demons would be jikin-nakar—would they not?"

He was surprised at her knowledge. "I believe so. Rare, and supreme infiltrators and hunters. No match for higher-order demons, but humans would be easy prey."

"That is what disturbs me. A Cabalist has summoned them for an unknown purpose. I would have to find out more even if Sheelahn hadn't asked me to. My own plans—" She broke off and busied herself brushing her clothes.

Her own plans what? What exactly was Ren's end goal? Presumably to position herself as the preeminent of the Nine before the return of the Adversary. But that would be foolish to assume. And something about Ren was off.

"You haven't yet told me your goal," he said. "If I know more, I can assist. And as you told Veika, I'm more trustworthy than anyone else—since I'm bound."

She returned the brush to the side table, adjusting her sword across her back and the scabbard's belt over her chest. "I seek the return of Samal. All the Nine do. It is no secret."

"And yet you killed Lischen the Nightwhisperer, one of the Nine. And not by stealth but by direct confrontation. When Samal returns, surely he will know this? You won't be able to shield your thoughts from him."

"Let me worry about that. You're here to protect me, not cluck over me like a mother hen."

The door opened, and Lin came in bearing a tray loaded with dishes. She struggled under its weight, and Tarrik moved to take the tray from her before she dropped his meat all over the floor.

"Thank you," she said. There was a red mark on her cheek where someone had slapped her.

Tarrik placed the tray on a table between a lounge and an armchair. His mouth watered at the smell of cooked meat from one of the covered plates.

Ren bent to the girl's side so their eyes were level. "Who hit you?"

"It's nothing. I was too slow, and the kitchen girls are mean. I've had worse. When the cooks get angry, they spank you with a wooden spoon. It really hurts."

Ren rose and patted her on the shoulder. "And what does Old Randin say about that?"

"That it builds character. But I don't want to grow up to be like him. I'd rather be like you."

"I don't think that's something you should wish for. Perhaps you have a kinder life waiting for you."

Lin scowled at Ren, as if unsure whether she was joking. She turned to Tarrik. "You're not like anyone else I've met. You're big, but that's not it. You're quiet and still, but I don't think that's it either."

"He is a warrior, and a good one," Ren said.

Lin shivered and rubbed her arms. "He's dark, but there's a darkness inside him too, like at night." She lowered her eyes. "I'm sorry. I talk too much. That's why I'm always being punished."

Ren frowned thoughtfully. "It's all right," she told the girl. "There's a darkness inside all of us. It's how you deal with it that matters."

"If you say so. There are pastries on the tray." Lin bounced on the tips of her toes and eyed the food with eagerness.

Ren uncovered the dishes to reveal slices of beef, pickled eggs, candied crickets, and three pastries with a flaky, golden crust.

"Have you been tested for the mark?" she asked Lin.

"Not yet. But my grandmother was a sorcerer, and her mother too. Mine doesn't have the mark, but I'm hopeful. My da says I should forget about it and train to work in the library here. But it's too dusty and boring and full of old men."

"If I let you have a pastry," Ren said, "will you let me test you?"

Lin's eyes widened. She pursed her lips, then nodded. "It won't hurt, will it?"

"Not at all. I don't have ink to stain your finger, though, so you'll have to keep the result to yourself. And if you fail, you'll have more time to decide what you want to do with your life."

"And if I pass? Will you take me on as an apprentice?"

"I cannot. But I'll find someone who will. The Cabalists are . . . harsh. You wouldn't want to train with them."

"Some of them make my skin crawl. Like your man here, but worse."

"Did you hear that, Tarrik—you're unsettling to little girls."

"I unsettle many humans."

Lin looked sideways at him. "Is he not human?" she asked Ren.

Ren met Tarrik's eye and shook her head slightly. "Yes, he is, dear. He was just making a joke. A poor one. Now, let's get started with your testing."

Ren knelt on one of the cream woolen rugs in front of the girl and tilted her sword to the side. She took both Lin's hands in hers.

"What are you going to do to me?" the girl asked.

"I'll just close my eyes for a few moments. When I open them, the test will be done. It's that simple. I'll measure your dawn- and dusk-tide repositories and send a trickle of power to see if a catalyst will work on you."

"A catalyst?"

"A crystal imbued with sorcery; it makes all cants possible."

"Cants?"

Ren smiled. "Calculations and foci spoken in ancient Skanuric that draw forth and guide arcane power. Anyhow, save your questions for later. Don't be nervous. You'll be fine, and it won't hurt."

Ren closed her eyes.

Lin's lip trembled, and she looked to Tarrik.

He shrugged and ate another slice of meat. As he chewed, he felt a faint emanation from Ren, too small for him to determine whether it was dawn- or dusk-tide. He kept his eye on the women, in case something went wrong. With human sorcery you could never tell.

Lin watched him watching them, and after a few heartbeats her eyes narrowed. "You are funny. Odd, I mean."

Tarrik shrugged again and continued eating.

Soon Ren opened her eyes, smiling. "Well, that was a surprise."

"Am I a sorcerer?" Lin asked.

"Not yet, but you could be. Your repositories are significant." Ren glanced at Tarrik. "And you seem to have a talent for discernment as well."

Lin beamed and bounced on her tiptoes with excitement, her hands still clasping Ren's. "Oh, this is great! Wait till I tell the others! They'll be so jealous. And my ma will be happy!"

Ren stood and drew Lin over to the food. She chose the largest pastry and gave it to her. Lin couldn't take her eyes off Ren, gazing up at her in adoration. *Another pawn in Ren's game*, thought Tarrik. He felt sorry for the girl.

Suddenly Lin's breath quickened, and her expression turned to dismay. "I've been gone too long. I have to go." She twisted her hands free and rushed for the door.

Ren raised her voice after her. "Tell them what happened. And also tell them I've reserved you for the Red Gate Covenant."

Lin paused to give Ren a fleeting smile, uneaten pastry clutched in her hand. Then she was gone. Ren latched the door behind her and uttered a cant.

Ren's father, Contian, had been grandmaster of the Red Gate Covenant. Was Ren still affiliated with them in some way? Did they know she was one of the Nine? Surely they had to. Or perhaps she was no longer part of that school but still felt a certain loyalty.

Thinking about sorcerers and their convoluted designs gave him a headache. "She has potential, then?" he asked.

Ren's gaze remained on the door, a frown on her face. He didn't like the way she'd taken control of the young girl. He knew all too well how little mercy she had for others, how deadly she was to those who opposed her or merely got in her way. Fury rose in him, hatred of all the slaver-sorcerer stood for and of all humans and their terrible ways. Contian and Jaquel had been exceptions, gems among rocks.

As he thought about his dead wife, grief almost overwhelmed him. Tarrik found the bottle of spirits in his hands without realizing it and drew long and deep of its contents, uncaring of the burn in his throat and stomach.

"I have not seen you affected by drinking," Ren said. "But it is unnerving. Restrain yourself when we are in company."

Tarrik's reply strangled in his throat. He simply nodded his agreement.

As his rage subsided, he wondered why Ren taking control of Lin had caused such a reaction in him. His thoughts returned to the stable hand he'd had to kill at her command. He replaced the bottle in his saddlebag, suddenly weary of Ren and this world.

"Lin has a vast potential," Ren said, finally answering his question. "I dislike the thought of her training under the Tainted Cabal. I'll let the Red Gate know about her as soon as I can and arrange for her to be trained." She went to the tray of food and nibbled on a pastry. "I'm going to wash while you finish your meal. Watching you eat so much meat makes my stomach churn. Some of the Tainted Cabal are flesh eaters."

"We all are."

"I meant of humankind."

"Meat is meat."

"No, it isn't." She closed the door to the preparation room behind her.

Tarrik thought he understood now why Ren hid herself when washing or dressing and had shied away when Veika had suggested an advantageous marriage to the lord of Atya. Anyone who undressed the sorcerer to lie with her would see her scars and know she was damaged. For who could escape with a sound mind after his or her body had been scribed with knives as hers had?

Chapter Thirteen

Tarrik finished the final slice of meat and wiped his hands on one of the cloths provided, then swallowed more of the spirit. He felt much better than he had for a while. While Ren refreshed herself, he sat on a lounge, stretched his legs out, and relaxed.

When Ren emerged a short time later, she looked exactly the same to Tarrik.

"Let's go," she said. "The meeting will begin soon, and I don't want to be late."

"Important, is it?"

"Very much so."

Tarrik grabbed his spear and followed Ren out of the apartment. She walked along corridors and stairways as if she knew the palace well. Servants hurried out of their path, and the guards they periodically passed saluted Ren with fists on their chests. She ignored them all.

Eventually they entered a sizeable chamber teeming with well-dressed men and women of different races and colors. He noted a few gray San-Kharr, dusky-skinned Inkan-Andil, and a smattering of green-brown Illapa, who Tarrik recalled mostly lived in forests. Two pale-skinned Soreshi spoke in hushed tones with their heads together, their braids tied with colored cords that denoted their clan. But what stood out to Tarrik was the ostentatious display of wealth in the form of cloth and jewelry: silks and tightly woven wools, flax linen, and velvet. One woman wore a knee-length coat of pure white fur despite the heat. And all were adorned with gaudy rings and brooches and necklaces that glittered with an array of red, blue, and green gemstones.

Tarrik snorted in contempt. Such a crass display of riches was considered an appalling breach of etiquette in the abyssal realms. Power and skill were what really mattered, and there were other ways to demonstrate beauty and sophistication. Ostentatious shows of wealth made you a target and could restrict your movements. Survival mattered, whether in the wilderness or amid the demon lords' social circles.

A few of the chamber's inhabitants had bodyguards positioned behind them or to the side—the majority of the wealthy guests were sorcerers of some ilk or another, judging by their arrogant expressions and the talismans they had close to hand. A dozen soldiers were positioned around the walls of the room.

A large, round table sat in its center with a floral arrangement in the middle and plates of food—mostly dried fruits, nuts, skewered chunks of roasted meat and mushrooms, and pastries and cheeses—along with crystal decanters of red and white wine and scores of empty glasses. Everyone held a drink, mostly wine, but Tarrik spotted a trolley in a corner that held bottles of spirits.

"Stay close to me," murmured Ren. She made her way to the food table, ignoring the curious glances cast at her, and busied herself filling a small porcelain plate with a little from all the offerings.

When she turned around, a mustached man dressed in gray trousers and coat with gold piping approached her but was rebuffed by Ren's upheld hand before he could open his mouth. His face turned red, and he backed away.

Ren moved to an empty spot by a wall and concentrated on her plate. Tarrik positioned himself beside her and kept his eyes on the gathering while Ren took dainty bites of her food.

Even though everyone had noted Ren's rejection of the first man to approach her, that didn't stop the next. His skin had a faint bluish cast, and he was statuesque and broad shouldered. His emerald-green coat was festooned with medals and decorations, most of them engraved with a blockish, ugly script. His eyes were small, and his nose was big and slightly crooked from a break. He held two glasses of red wine and offered one to Ren as he approached. He gave off the same goatlike stench as Puck Moonan, signifying madness. Most likely one of the Nine.

Tarrik thought he shouldn't really be surprised they'd encountered another of the sorcerers, although they should probably now be called the Eight. He suppressed a smile. Would the Eight have less success in freeing Samal than the Nine? Possibly. He didn't know enough about sorcery to make a determination. He resolved to try to find out more from Ren later.

She shook her head. "No thank you, Indriol. I must keep my wits about me. As should you."

Indriol grinned and took a large swallow of wine, then followed it with the glass he'd brought for Ren. Tarrik noted a copper talisman in the shape of a fish at his belt, which also bore the blockish script in red enamel. At his side he carried an ornate orichalcum dagger with a moonstone pommel.

"My dearest Lady Branwen, we weren't expecting you. You always manage to surprise. I'd heard you were hundreds of miles away, digging up old ruins or such."

His voice was smooth and buttery. That combined with the man's ostentatious display of self-importance and his conceited air made Tarrik dislike him immediately.

Ren placed her plate on a side table. She crossed her arms, palms against her chest, and bowed. "Samal will rise."

"Of course," said Indriol, half-heartedly copying the gesture—a difficult task with a glass in each hand. "Praise Samal, Lord of Life." His eyes flicked to Tarrik before returning to Ren. "You are of course aware of the development with Lischen."

Tarrik kept a watch on Ren, but she merely frowned before picking up her plate again. "I sense an absence, but that could be many things," she said.

"I have some trusted people checking on her just in case. We are too close to our goal to let a small bump upset our success, but if Lischen has"—Indriol glanced around to make sure no one was nearby—"been rendered unavailable, we need to find out who is responsible and punish them appropriately." He took a sip of wine, studying Ren's face.

So the Nine were close to freeing Samal; that must be why Ren was making her play now, why she had killed Lischen. The others would be positioning themselves similarly, though would murdering one of their brethren be tolerated by Samal? Tarrik wondered again how Ren would avoid the demon lord's wrath.

Ren popped a cube of white cheese into her mouth. "I don't know where Lischen is—or was when we lost contact with her essence. She was always the most volatile of us, though, and her madness was uncontrollable."

Indriol chuckled. "Come now. You know we are not mad, merely . . . altered. We are Samal's now, and always will be."

As Ren opened her mouth to reply, someone rang a bell by a door at the far end of the chamber. The general murmur rose in volume as various men and women disengaged from their companions and made their way to the meeting of the Tainted Cabal.

Indriol placed his empty glass on the side table, next to Ren's plate. He gestured at the doorway. "Shall we?"

Ren inclined her head and walked side by side with Indriol to the meeting room. Tarrik followed. Already the crowd in the chamber had thinned considerably. As they approached the door, a guard stepped in front of Tarrik. He was a big man, and muscled.

"Not you," he growled, hand moving to the hilt of his sword.

Tarrik's rage was already bubbling close to the surface. His hand moved without thought, and he grabbed the guard by the throat, lifted him up, and slammed him against the wall. The other guards shouted in alarm, and swords hissed from sheaths.

"Tarrik!" said Ren.

The man tried to break Tarrik's grip and couldn't. His face grew red, and he dropped a hand to draw a dagger. Tarrik swiftly jerked him forward, then stepped behind him and wrapped his arm around his throat, pulling him in so the man's back was pressed against his chest. He leveled his spear at an approaching trio of guards and moved so the helpless guard was between him and them.

"Tarrik, enough!" said Ren. Her bindings tightened around him. "Let him go. You are not required at this meeting. I'll be all right without you."

"It seems your bodyguard is a bit jumpy," said a red-haired woman standing next to Ren. She wore a bronze-colored dress that left her shoulders bare, and Tarrik didn't need to see the circular talisman attached to her wide leather belt to realize she was a sorcerer. The corners of her mouth twitched in an arrogant smile, and she showed no sign of fear at the bared blades and sudden violence.

Ren flicked her an annoyed glance. "Yes, I have warned him about his behavior. But better him jumpy than me dead, don't you think?"

"Oh, certainly. You should endeavor to keep him out of mischief, though. The people of the south are no better than dogs until they're trained properly."

The guard struggled in Tarrik's grip, and he shoved the man away. He spun around immediately, rubbing his neck, then backed away toward his companions.

Tarrik's pulse still pounded in his veins, drumming in his ears. He knew he shouldn't have reacted so strongly, but his passions had overridden his common sense. With an effort of will no human could match, he forced himself to calm. Jaw clenched, fist tight around his spear, he managed a short bow to Ren and a second to the red-haired sorcerer.

"I will leave you then," he said, and pushed past the people behind him. He went straight to the spirits trolley and poured himself a double measure of a honey-colored liquid. By the time he'd downed it, Ren had disappeared, and the door to the meeting room was closed.

Two guards stood on either side of the door; one was the man Tarrik had tussled with. He stared at Tarrik with unconcealed hatred. Tarrik poured himself another measure and raised his glass to the guard before taking a sip. The man frowned and looked away. He said something to his companion, who laughed.

"Where did she find you?"

The red-haired woman had approached from Tarrik's other side. Her skin was pale, almost white, and colored strings were woven into her hair: black, blue, and brown. Tarrik wasn't knowledgeable enough to determine her exact kin from the strings, but he knew she was a Soreshi clanswoman from the plains of the eastern continent of Wiraya. The fact that she wasn't at the meeting meant she was either independent of the Tainted Cabal or so low in its hierarchy she hadn't been invited.

"The south," he replied.

"The south is a big place. Where?"

Tarrik wrinkled his nose at her pungent floral perfume; maybe she'd spilled the bottle over herself. He poured her a measure of the honey-colored spirit, and she took the offered glass with a nod of thanks. Her nails were painted a tawny gold to match her hair and dress.

"The Blood Shakar tribe, under Bidzil the Deathless," he told her. "Though I've been exiled for years." That should be sufficient, unless Veika had made it all up.

She held out a hand. "I'm Moushumi. Very pleased to meet you."

Tarrik took her hand, then found he wasn't sure whether to hang on or not. He let it go and ignored her raised eyebrows. "Tarrik, as you would have heard."

"I did. Lady Branwen is a personage of note, and all eyes were on her, so I couldn't miss your . . . encounter with the guard. You are quite protective of her."

"It's my job."

"It is a fine thing to command such loyalty. Still, there is more to life. The Orgols from beyond the tribes have made numerous incursions northward lately. It has been a warm spring and looks to be a hot summer. If so, they'll penetrate far into the north."

Tarrik sipped his drink. The Orgols were a nonhuman species from beyond the savage south: heavily muscled, midnight skinned, aggressive, generally malevolent, and possessing unsurpassed speed and ferocity. They also built surprisingly advanced and beautiful cities that few humans had ever seen. Tarrik had learned a little of their complex tongue and society on one of Contian's expeditions. If the Orgols killed some humans, it didn't matter to him.

"If you have family back there, or anyone you care about, I'd consider returning to help protect them," Moushumi added.

So that was her game: get rid of Ren's bodyguard and leave her unprotected. Whoever wanted Ren dead knew sorcery wouldn't succeed.

Tarrik nodded, as if considering her suggestion. She smiled at him, then turned to survey what remained of the crowd. Presumably, like her, they were unimportant.

She flicked her hair over her shoulder, and Tarrik caught a whiff of an animal stink underneath her heavy perfume.

Goat. She's one of the Nine.

He stared into his tumbler as if considering whether to refill it. His heartbeat increased, and his shoulders tightened. He shrugged to loosen them and couldn't help glancing at her bare shoulders and upper chest. Scar-free. Whatever Samal had done to break her, he hadn't needed to go as far as he had with Ren.

"And you are paid well?" she asked him.

"Well enough."

"Can I tell you a secret?"

"I wouldn't advise it."

Moushumi uttered a tinkling laugh. "Oh, you're precious. I can see why she chose you. But be careful with your mistress."

"She is my employer."

"Just don't get too close to her. It's dangerous."

"Danger is part of my job."

"Then I hope she is paying you well. Sorcerers are lodestones for trouble—you'll earn your coin and more, I dare say. You have to be very brave to do this job. If you're observant, you might even earn more. Enough to retire on. To leave this dangerous life behind." She reached up to toy with her earring, a red star sapphire dangling from a short gold chain.

Tarrik only nodded. He was in danger here, as was Ren. Did Moushumi want him to leave Ren or to spy on her? As if he could. Her bindings wouldn't allow him to betray her or even speak innocently of her business. If he did, it would lead to his ending. He itched to be gone from this place of vipers.

"I guard the Lady Branwen as best I'm able," he said. The words sounded weak even to his ear, and he cursed himself for responding at all.

"But she's inside, and you are . . . not."

He didn't reply. Whatever this woman wanted, he was tired of her.

"So you're not really guarding her at all, are you?" Moushumi continued.

"She is a sorcerer and can defend herself."

"Then why are you needed? Do you have other skills to offer a woman such as her? Perhaps at night? There are rumors about what some sorcerers get up to when in the throes of absorbing the dusk-tide. The process enervates them, it is said. Sharpens their appetites. But I forget: Serenity rarely bends to a man's touch."

Tarrik would wager she never forgot anything. He turned his gaze to Moushumi, who met it unflinchingly. He considered toying with her for his amusement. There was something feral about the woman; she smelled hungry. But whatever her skills, she couldn't untangle Tarrik from this mess except by killing Ren.

"Lady Branwen does not involve me in her sorcery."

"A shame. Well, I have to rush. Think about what I said. I'm sure we'll meet again soon." Moushumi finished her drink and handed him the empty glass. She sauntered away, and Tarrik caught a glimpse of a thin scar poking above the back of her dress.

Not entirely untouched.

He left her used glass on the trolley, refilled his own, then made his way over to the food table. Juggling his drink and spear and three meat skewers, he found a wall to lean against so he could eat, drink, and think.

He was still wondering what Moushumi had really wanted when the door to the meeting room opened and the guards scurried out of the way. Ren was first out. She looked around, spotted Tarrik, and walked over. Her mouth was drawn into a thin line, and she was flushed.

The meeting didn't go well for her then.

"Let's go," she snapped.

Tarrik divested himself of the skewers and glass and followed Ren out of the chamber. The heels of her boots clicked on the tiles as she practically stomped all the way back to their room.

Inside, she spoke a cant to seal the door and activate her wards. She whirled around and almost bumped into Tarrik. She uttered a curse and quickly moved around him. "Can't you stay out of the way?"

He leaned his spear against the wall and settled into an armchair. The seat was too small, and its sides pressed against him. Someone had lit the kindling in the fireplace and set two logs burning.

"What happened?" he asked.

"They are fools! They are going ahead with their plan, despite my reasoned arguments against it."

"What plan?"

"To free Samal, of course—what else? I suppose I can't blame them. They are bound to him. As am I."

Tarrik blinked. If Ren was one of the Nine, she was compelled to follow Samal's will. Why then would she argue against his release? And why did the others of the Nine not consider her a traitor?

"Why are you against it?" he asked.

"It's . . . not the right time. Too much could go wrong."

Tarrik was certain she was leaving out her real reason, but he was in no position to pry the truth from her. Perhaps her own position wasn't assured yet, and she wanted to dispose of a few more rivals first.

Another thought wormed its way into his mind: should he try to stop the Nine, who in their insanity didn't realize what they were doing would likely destroy their civilization? Though what the miserable humans had created wasn't impressive. But if he made the slightest move against such an outcome and Ren found out, she would unravel his eternal essence, and he would meet a true death for one of his kind.

Ren poked among the pastries Lin had brought, making disparaging noises. Tarrik shifted to make himself more comfortable, causing her to turn and glare at him.

There was a knock at the door. Ren disarmed her wards and nodded for Tarrik to open it.

A blue-clad boy held out an envelope with a wax seal. "For the Lady Branwen."

Tarrik took the message and closed the door. Ren almost snatched the envelope from his hands and sliced it open with her thumbnail. As she scanned the letter's contents, her expression turned to irritation and then anger. He saw her hands tremble as she let the paper and envelope fall to the floor. She stomped to a sideboard, poured herself a glass of strong spirits, and downed it in a gulp.

Tarrik kept his eyes off the letter, hoping she would forget it was there and he could read it later.

Ren poured herself more spirits, but after a single sip, she hurled the glass into the fireplace. It shattered, shards of glass scattering across the floor. Blue flames erupted as the liquor burned. She uttered harsh-sounding curses in Skanuric, followed by a long chant. Not for the first time, Tarrik wished he could speak the ancient language.

She grasped the edge of the sideboard and hunched her shoulders, her face turned away from Tarrik. Perhaps he should find out more.

"Ren . . . ," he began.

"Gods be damned, leave me! Go out and drink tonight—I give you leave. I need to think, and I can't do it with you looming above me." She slammed a plate down on the sideboard with such force it broke, sending nuts tumbling onto the floor rug. "Go, I said! And leave your spear. I don't want any more incidents with guards. I'll call when I need you."

Through her binding of him, presumably.

Tarrik was reluctant to go out weaponless, but if necessary he could probably disarm an attacker and take theirs. Or, if he could do so unobserved, use his shadow-blade. And he was excited at the prospect of some time to himself, with no directives from Ren. Before she could change her mind, he rose. He would leave the palace and head into the city.

When he was halfway to the door, Ren spoke a cant to disarm her wards. Tarrik left quickly and roamed down a couple of corridors and a staircase.

A man in an emerald-green coat approached from the opposite direction. Indriol. Tarrik wondered what all the medals on his coat signified. He looked for a side corridor or open door to escape into, but there was none. As Indriol neared, the stink of his madness became stronger. Tarrik lowered his gaze and hoped the man wouldn't bother him.

He was out of luck.

"Ah, you are Lady Branwen's bodyguard, are you not?"

Tarrik nodded and tried to pass, but Indriol blocked his way. He didn't think the sorcerer would kill him merely for giving offense, but Tarrik decided to put on a show of subservience. The sooner he was away from the man, the better.

Indriol reached for the copper fish talisman at his belt and uttered a cant. Tarrik froze as sorcerous chains tightened around him.

Chains designed to hold a demon.

Indriol knew what Tarrik was and had overridden Ren's bindings.

Chapter Fourteen

Indriol unlocked a door into a suite of rooms filled with sheet-covered furniture. He turned to a wall and opened a concealed panel.

"Thought you'd go unnoticed, did you?" he said to Tarrik. "You would have if I wasn't so adept at sensing demons."

Indriol stepped through the opening into a dusty corridor with a creaky wooden floor and a sorcerous globe floating above for illumination. Tarrik was compelled to follow, no matter how hard he tried to resist. Tendons bulged in his neck, and sweat dripped from his brow.

Tarrik thought he'd been so clever to avoid Ren's complete domination. He'd thought he'd tricked her into allowing him some minimal freedom, but all he had done was to leave room for another sorcerer to step in and bind him instead.

Indriol unlocked another dusty door, and they descended a steep, narrow wooden staircase that turned back on itself multiple times. Tarrik guessed they were deep underground when it stopped. They traversed another empty hallway and entered a room that stank of old blood and piss.

The metallic odor set Tarrik's heart pumping faster. Someone, or something, had spilled a great deal of blood here. He tried to snort the stench from his nostrils but could only manage a slight movement. He was starting to regret leaving his spear behind. But what could he have done with it anyway? How could he stab Indriol and free himself when he couldn't even walk or talk on his own?

Indriol spoke a cant, and the sorcerous globe wafted to a corner and remained there, shedding a yellow glow over the space. A broad oak table dominated the center of the room. Against the walls lay a number of workbenches and vats and a couple of chairs.

"Get on the table," Indriol said.

Tarrik obeyed.

"Lie down. Shift up a bit. That's better."

Indriol spoke cants. Something wrapped itself around Tarrik's wrists and ankles. He could move his eyes sufficiently to see lurid violet ropes binding him. Another snaked around his neck, constricting his throat, making it hard to breathe.

Indriol's control lessened slightly, and Tarrik immediately strained against the physical and mental bonds. He jerked his arms and legs, and the sorcerous ropes cut into his flesh. He clenched his teeth against the pain and redoubled his efforts. The bonds became slick with his blood, and eventually he ceased his struggles, taking harsh breaths of the rank air.

Bloody humans. He would torture Indriol in the abyss alongside Ren when he was free.

"That's better," Indriol said. "You cannot escape, and after I'm done with you, you won't want to."

Tarrik found he could speak now, but even if he summoned his shadow-blade, he would still be bound. "What do you want with me?"

"Blood and fluids, along with some essential tasks. You are mine now, and you will serve me well. Serenity was careless, the foolish girl. Fancy allowing a higher-order demon to just stroll the palace corridors! I almost couldn't believe it when I sensed you. A talent I have, which I keep to myself. Serenity's ignorance is my gain."

Tarrik tried to shadow-step into a dark corner. His innate ability failed him.

"I'll kill you and eat your heart!" he raged. "After I've flayed you alive."

Indriol smiled, but it faded quickly. "Oh, come now. We both know you're helpless. I could command you to cut your own throat, and you'd do it. But that would be a waste. I have much more interesting things in mind for you. Someone I know will pay handsomely for your blood and other fluids. Then I think you'll die a gory death that will disrupt Serenity's plans. Everyone saw you belong to her, so it will be delightfully ironic to use you against her."

Tarrik heard a scuff of boots in the corridor and turned his head to the doorway, the sorcerous rope abrading his neck. The woman who entered had long chestnut hair and tanned skin and was wearing a plain blue skirt with a charcoal shirt.

Indriol pointed to one of the chairs, and she sat without a word. A smell came from her, a discordant mix of herbs and cheap perfume. Tarrik sniffed again, trying to catch more of her scent amid the goat stench of Indriol's madness. The herbs were so strong she must have rubbed them on her skin, but why?

To give herself a scent.

He examined her again, certain now she was one of the shape-changing jikin-nakar demons Sheelahn had wanted Ren to dispose of. She wasn't dressed as a noble or wealthy merchant, though—more like a servant or handmaid.

"*Ishi krimp-atal, snagur ul Indriol,*" Tarrik said. Free my bonds, slave of Indriol.

The woman met his eyes and smiled, still not speaking.

"I see you recognize her," said Indriol. "Hardly surprising. She wouldn't have discovered you on her own, but now I can tell her and the others to keep a watch for any other demons concealed in our midst. It was very naughty of Serenity. And unexpected. She'll know by now her bindings have been usurped and likely scurry away and hide. She always does, you know. Her place in the Nine should have been given to another. Someone worthier."

Ren hadn't hidden from confronting Lischen, Tarrik thought, and she'd certainly proved herself more powerful. Something told him that Indriol's assessment of Ren was artfully guided by Ren herself.

Would she flee, as Indriol expected? Or would she come for him? Try as he might, Tarrik couldn't think of any reason Ren would put herself in danger for a demon slave she'd summoned. His fate now lay with another insane sorcerer, here in this room.

He returned his gaze to Indriol, who busied himself with a glass cylinder to which was attached a steel needle. The sorcerer found an empty vial on a workbench and wrinkled his nose at the cork stopper. "It'll have to do." He turned to Tarrik. "You, demon, are in a bit of trouble. I don't think you'll survive."

"I've seen trouble all my days," said Tarrik. "And I'm still here."

He couldn't rely on Ren. He'd have to extricate himself. Somehow. Indriol spoke a cant, and Tarrik's vision went black.

Tarrik's arm hurt. His wrists and ankles ached. And his mouth was as dry as the desert of Ceedur in the realm of Sharrak, where nothing living survived. His skin itched and burned as though it had been scorched by fire. He remembered wisps of dreams . . . hot blood in his mouth, frenzied couplings, Ren's face purpling as he squeezed her neck, her nails digging into his arms.

Something soft and rasping stroked the skin of his forearm. Tarrik cracked an eyelid and blinked at the sorcerous globe hanging from a chain attached to a beam above him. It seemed as bright as a sun.

A shadowed figure knelt beside him, licking his skin. He jerked his arm away, and the jikin-nakar jumped back, then scurried to a corner to crouch in the shadows. The jikin-nakar clutched a small knife in one hand. Smears of purple blood spread across her mouth and cheeks. Tarrik's blood.

He blinked again and looked down to see a dozen oozing cuts along his arm. His chest was also covered with finger-length incisions, and his pants were tugged down to his knees. *What have they done to me?* He checked, but everything seemed intact. He licked his lips, tasting his own salty sweat.

A gaunt man standing by the doorway turned and disappeared into the corridor. Tarrik tried to commit him to memory: short brown hair, alabaster skin, cream shirt with puffy sleeves, boots with blackened buckles.

The remaining jikin-nakar moved a step closer to Tarrik. Her eyes roamed across his body, and he saw hunger in them. The blood of a higher-order demon would be a rare treat for one of her kind.

"What is your name?" he croaked. "Bring me some water."

He'd gone thirsty before, for days on end when hunting. But he felt more than parched; he'd been . . . drained of vitality.

The jikin-nakar stared at him, and Tarrik wondered if she'd heard him. Then she moved to a workbench and exchanged the knife for a waterskin.

She squirted water into his mouth, and Tarrik swallowed greedily. He frowned when the demon returned the skin to the bench. He laid his head back and took a few deep breaths. He was alive. For now. Indriol had left. For now. He hadn't been maimed too badly. For now.

"What is your name?" he asked again.

"Aeshma."

"And which human form have you taken?"

"I am Myrian, a servant of Lord Ehren's. He is a senile old fool but tolerated at court, so I go where I please. Do what I want."

"Where is the real Myrian?"

"Dead, of course."

Of course. "What are Indriol's plans?" The sorcerer's arcane bonds felt as tight as when they'd first materialized.

Aeshma picked up the knife again, twisting it this way and that to catch the light, then watching the reflection scurry across the wall. Indriol had to have known the jikin-nakar would feed from Tarrik. Perhaps he'd counted on it.

"Do you know how to release me?" he asked.

"I can give you a swift release."

Tarrik licked his parched lips again and thought of a dozen different offers he could make the demon, knowing only one would tempt her.

"How close are you to transforming?"

Aeshma grinned. "Close. A few kills only. Absorbing you would make me strong."

"You wouldn't be able to absorb my essence," he warned. "You know it will be too strong for you. Do not fall into that trap. Think."

"It is worth the risk."

"No, it isn't. You've seen others succumb and be lost. You've heard the stories of how even the strongest lose their minds and wander forever or take their own life. You would be killing yourself."

"Maybe you lie."

"You know I don't. And I know you're not stupid or ignorant. Don't give in to temptation. Trust me. I made it to the Thirty-Seventh Order, and I've been in your situation many times before."

"With a higher-order demon helpless before you and a knife in your hand?"

"Well, not exactly. How many jikin-nakar has Indriol summoned?"

Aeshma crept closer. "Two." Her eyes moved to the cuts in his skin, following the trails of blood.

If she was answering truthfully, he knew she was sure he had no chance of escaping. Tarrik felt panic rise inside him. He tried to quell the emotion and was only partially successful. Aeshma would not be able to process his essence, especially combined with Ananias's. But he understood all too well the temptation to try.

Faint footsteps reached Tarrik's ears. Someone was descending the staircase at the end of the narrow hallway.

Aeshma hissed, then leaped forward and plunged her blade into the meat of Tarrik's thigh. He screamed at the pain, then forced his throat closed.

Aeshma returned to her chair, knees together, hands clasped in front of her. If not for the blood smeared across her face, she would have been a study of innocence. The blade remained stuck in Tarrik's thigh. Warm blood trickled from the wound onto the table.

The shadowed hallway was illuminated, and Indriol entered the room, another globe floating above his shoulder.

He glanced at Tarrik, who did his best to grin. *I'm still alive.*

Indriol's mouth twisted in distaste. "I see you had your way with him."

"Yes, Master. Thank you, Master," said Aeshma.

"He will be dead soon, so make good use of your opportunity."

"Yes, Master."

Indriol rubbed his chin and frowned at Tarrik. "There's something strange here. Serenity's bindings weren't quite complete, but I don't think it was because of a lack of skill. And why summon you at all? We all thought she didn't care for summoning, even though demons are useful tools."

Tarrik snarled and spat—or tried to. His mouth was too dry. He felt hope slipping away. Indriol's madness was less overt than Puck's or Lischen's, which made him far more dangerous.

"Serenity is a fool," the sorcerer continued. "It is dangerous not to fully restrain a demon. A mistake due to inexperience."

Tarrik tried to tell Indriol he was on borrowed time. That Serenity Branwen would come for her bodyguard and kill the sorcerer for this affront. A bluff, of course, but it was all he had. But his mouth wouldn't open. His tongue wouldn't move. Indriol was asserting more control over him than Ren ever had.

"Serenity won't be a problem once I'm powerful enough to gather my own sorcerers. Samal's bonds upon me have shown me the way. Soon I'll be able to dominate others just as my lord has the Nine. For now, I see my slave has let her base urges overwhelm her sense. Remain still." Indriol paused and chuckled. "As if you could do any different." He picked up a roll of cloth and a folded paper packet from a table and approached Tarrik. Without warning he yanked the dagger from Tarrik's thigh.

Tarrik clenched his teeth, and as the searing pain traveled up his body, he moaned. Indriol poured powder from the packet onto the wound. As it hit Tarrik's flesh, the pain and flow of purple blood lessened. Indriol used the cloth to bind the wound tightly. Some blood still flowed, staining the bandage, but soon stopped.

"You have to be of some use before I dispose of you," said Indriol. "I've patched the wound as best I can under the circumstances. It'll be enough to have you perform a task for me. Now, get up."

Tarrik levered himself into a sitting position. The sorcerous restraining ropes were gone.

Aeshma met his eyes, and her lips curled into a smile. He ignored her. She wasn't the danger here. Only Indriol could hand him over to her, if he didn't kill Tarrik first.

Moving his tongue and mouth, Tarrik worked up enough saliva to speak. "What is your will, Master?"

Indriol held a different dagger in his hand. Its thin blade was forged from steel, and rather plain, but the pommel resembled a wolf.

"Take it," he said, holding it out.

Tarrik grasped the hilt and tried with all his might to plunge the blade into Indriol's heart. He found himself frozen in place, as expected. He growled, muscles straining to no use. He almost barked a cant to bring forth his shadow-blade, before ruthlessly suppressing the urge. It wouldn't do to waste his only advantage, and what could he do now anyway?

Indriol gave him a wry smile. "This dagger was procured for me on the eastern continent, from Sansor in Kaile. The rulers of Kaile have been intruding in Atya's affairs for quite some time. They think their promises of trade and wealth will loosen the Cabal's hold here. You're going to prevent that from happening."

"How?"

He knew all too well what purpose most enslaved demons were put to: murder and desecration.

"The rulers of Kaile have sent diplomats here in secret. However, they are not your target. You're going to kill some of the Cabal's apprentice sorcerers. Their deaths will weaken the Cabal, and in this way I kill two birds with the one stone. Or five sorcerers with the one knife. When you leave this dagger behind, it will fan a spark of suspicion into a flame."

Humans and their wars. A decrepit race of short-lived imbeciles. So Indriol wanted to start a war, did he? Or perhaps divert attention from the Nine's attempt to free Samal?

"Get dressed," Indriol ordered.

Tarrik slid off the table and tugged his pants up. Aeshma handed him his shirt, and he shrugged it on, ignoring his stinging chest and arms, aching thigh, and the dried blood pinching his skin.

Indriol straightened Tarrik's collar. Tarrik tried to jerk away from his touch but couldn't move.

"There," Indriol said. "Almost presentable. I've set the apprentices a reading task that will take them several hours. Paliax is guarding the door so they don't get it into their heads to shirk their duty. Go up the stairs and through the concealed panel into the suite. Turn right outside, then take the second-left hallway. Do not speak to anyone on your way. You'll see a man dressed in charcoal pants and a puffy linen shirt standing outside the third door on the right. That's Paliax. He'll let you inside. Kill them all, and make it bloody. Leave the dagger. Paliax will shout for help, and when the guards come, make sure they see you. Then return here to me, making sure you're not followed, of course. You have my permission to kill anyone who tries to impede you."

"Yes, Master," said Tarrik. He had no choice.

He realized Indriol wanted him to be seen so the apprentices' deaths would be linked to Ren. How that tied in with Kaile he didn't know and didn't care.

Tarrik glanced one last time at Aeshma before leaving both of them in their hideaway.

"I'll see you soon," she said to his back.

Chapter Fifteen

The stairs creaked as Tarrik ascended, wincing at the pain of the knife wound in his thigh. The latch on the concealed panel was easily found, and once in the empty suite with its sheet-covered furniture, Tarrik slipped the dagger up his sleeve. Soon he was walking along the hallway. It was night outside, and the passages were mostly deserted and lit only by the occasional lamp. Three servants dressed in navy and carrying baskets of linen passed him, and Tarrik heard them giggling afterward.

He turned right and spotted the gaunt man from earlier standing outside a door: Paliax.

The jikin-nakar sneered at Tarrik as he approached, but Tarrik couldn't summon a response. He'd been sent to kill, and it was best to get the task done as quickly as possible to show Indriol what a good slave he was. Then maybe he'd keep Tarrik alive awhile longer. Unless there was a way to mess up Indriol's plans . . . Tarrik had never been one to avoid conflict, especially when it came to the human slavers.

"Has Aeshma touched you?"

Ah, they were a pair. Tarrik couldn't resist a jab. "How could she not? I am far above her, and you."

"She is mine. I will be pleased when our master disposes of you."

"As he will you, once you're of no use to him."

"Be about your assigned task."

Tarrik slipped the dagger from his sleeve and gripped the hilt. The oak door was right in front of him, with the apprentices on the other side.

He took a few breaths, then paused as a female servant rushed along the hallway toward them, carrying a tray laden with fruit. He reached his free hand for the door handle and found Paliax's grip on his upper arm.

"Not yet," the jikin-nakar said, voice pitched low.

Tarrik looked down at his hand. "Are you . . . impeding me?"

"You'll get to your task soon enough. Make sure you are seen on the way out after I raise the alarm."

"I think you're impeding me."

"Shut your mouth, or—"

Tarrik drove the dagger into Paliax's chest. The demon's mouth opened and closed, and both hands tried to push Tarrik away.

The serving woman screamed, dropped her tray, and ran.

Tarrik twisted the blade into the jikin-nakar's heart, then yanked it out and plunged it into the second heart. Purple blood spurted from both wounds, splashing Tarrik's hand as he jerked the dagger out. He let Paliax slump to the ground. The Cabalists couldn't miss such evidence that demons were somehow involved.

Raised voices and hurried footsteps approached the other side of the door. Of the serving woman there was no sign, but he could hear her screams getting fainter, and then shouts joining her hysterics. He waited for the apprentices to gather enough courage to open the door, except they didn't.

He heard hushed whispers, then a woman shrieked when she saw Paliax's blood seeping under the door. "That's blood! And it's purple!"

"Feck!" said a male voice.

Tarrik turned the handle, and the door opened on to five young faces—three men, two women. None had thought to shield themselves.

"I'm sorry," Tarrik said, and leaped at the closest man, blade flashing.

The deed was done in a few heartbeats before any of the young sorcerers had gathered their wits to defend themselves. The last one, a girl, Tarrik slaughtered midcant.

He dropped the dagger and surveyed the carnage. The five sorcerers lay akimbo around the sparsely furnished room lit by two alchemical globes. Their blood splashed across the walls, ceiling, and lounges from where Tarrik had whipped the dagger around. Their books, still open from their studies, were streaked with red.

Rage overcame Tarrik. Again he'd been ordered to slaughter, for no reason other than the machinations of a mad sorcerer. When humans summoned demons, they only wanted one thing: to kill in the furtherance of their own power. It was an atrocity to be used like this and a worse abomination to be forced to do someone else's bidding against your will.

Perhaps this is how Ren feels.

The thought stopped him as he turned to leave the carnage. Did some part of Ren know she had lost her will? Was that why she sometimes gave him leeway?

No, by her own actions she had shown she was a ruthless killer. Exactly the kind of creature Samal would value.

He expected Ren to abandon him to his fate with Indriol—which wouldn't be pleasant once the sorcerer learned Tarrik had killed Paliax and left evidence that demons were involved. Still, Indriol's madness seemed less overt, less emotional than Lischen's, so perhaps he could be reasoned with.

He ducked out of the room and stepped over the corpse. The demon hadn't reverted to his own shiny gray skin in death, but the strange-colored blood would be enough. And perhaps the humans would dissect the body.

Tarrik wanted to run, to leave the scene of slaughter behind. But he had commands to obey. He had to be seen leaving the murder site. He waited, listening to the approaching, excited voices, and allowed himself a grim smile. Indriol had been lax with the wording of his command. He wouldn't make the same mistake again.

When the first human appeared and noticed him, Tarrik broke into a sprint and bolted around the first corner. He shadow-stepped twice and easily lost his pursuers.

"What happened?" shouted Indriol, droplets of spit flying, his head shaking like wobbling aspic.

Not the best response, thought Tarrik. He drew a deep breath. "The demon impeded me. Your command was quite clear: kill anyone who impedes you. I had no choice."

Aeshma hissed at Tarrik. Her hands pulled at her hair, and she collapsed into a corner, sobbing.

"You idiot!" snarled Indriol. "Do you know how long it took me to find this pair? And the resources I used to summon them?"

"No. But if you made a mistake with me, you might have done something similar with this one." Tarrik pointed to Aeshma. "I can show you a few tricks to make sure—"

Indriol snarled a cant, and the Wracking Nerves slammed into Tarrik. His nerves burned with searing pain, and he screamed and collapsed to the floor. Indriol's punishment was similar to Ren's, though with a sharper, malicious edge. His heart pounded in his ears, and he tried to focus on its beat, to partition his mind against the torment.

His awareness brushed against Ananias's essence, and the barrier between it and Tarrik trembled, almost dissolved. Tarrik was so surprised he forgot about the pain for an instant—until he heard Indriol voicing another cant and the Wracking Nerves redoubled. He only knew burning torment and wailing then until the punishment ceased.

Tarrik lay on the floor, blood in his mouth, nails digging into his palms, marking his skin. His cheek ached where he'd bitten it. He groaned and spat purple onto the floor and rolled onto his back. After a few panting breaths, he struggled upright and leaned on the table in the center of the room.

Indriol sat in an armchair, affecting relaxation. But the goat stench surrounding him had amplified, and his hands gripped the arms of the chair so hard that veins stood out.

Aeshma glared at Tarrik from the corner. Her eyes were red from weeping, filled with grief.

"You sorcerers are too quick to punish," Tarrik said, repeating what he'd told Ren after she'd summoned him.

His mind roiled with the implication of what he'd sensed. Ananias's essence had also felt the agony of the Wracking Nerves. And its shell had almost broken open. There was great danger here, Tarrik knew. If the shell had cracked, the essence would have poured into him like a surge of water after a dam failed. But there was also opportunity, for if he could siphon enough of the essence into himself first, a final shattering of the shell should be easily weathered. And Tarrik's mind wouldn't be washed away in the flood.

Focus, he told himself. He couldn't afford another dose of the Wracking Nerves right now, not until he was ready for the shell to be fractured.

"What power does she use?" asked Indriol abruptly.

Tarrik hesitated and felt the sorcerer's arcane bindings tighten around his limbs and clamp his throat. Indriol spoke a cant, and Tarrik was forced to respond.

"I don't understand what you are asking. Dawn- and dusk-tide, like any other sorcerer."

Indriol's lips tightened. "You've traveled with her. What can she do? She was hundreds of miles away a few days ago—I know it! And yet now she is here."

"We flew," Tarrik said. "On a disc made from water and heat."

"Oh, come now, I'm not so stupid as you think. We all have ways of traveling, but that's absurd. She has a pact with Sheelahn, doesn't she?"

Why would that matter?

"Sheelahn asked her to repay a favor—that is all. You know I speak the truth. I cannot do otherwise because of your bindings."

"Bah! I trust nothing. Not demons, not the Nine, not the Cabal, and sometimes not even myself. What is Serenity's purpose?"

Indriol's questions jumped from topic to topic like a grasshopper. "I do not know."

"She would have killed you when you were no longer useful to her."

Perhaps. The fate of a summoned demon was always uncertain. And Ren had made no secret of the fact that he was only a tool.

"She is mad, you see," continued Indriol. "Samal was too strong for her weak mind. The others broke like twigs, but not I. *I* was too strong. I'll ask again: what power does she use? And no lies this time."

Tarrik glanced at Aeshma, who sneered at him. She had to know Indriol was insane. If she could help Tarrik escape . . . but how could he convince her after he'd killed her mate?

"I am unable to lie to you," Tarrik said again. "She created a disc of water and heat—"

"Lies! Are my bindings not enough to force you to tell the truth? What use are you if you lie? You have been intimate with her. You know her plans, what she seeks. You've seen her use whatever strange power she holds, and I'd wager you know exactly what it is. You are of demon blood; you have no loyalty to a human other than what is forced upon you. Tell me her secrets."

The barrage of questions threw Tarrik for a moment. He hesitated. "I have only guesses."

"What use are you then? A broken tool!"

Perhaps he could use Indriol's madness and arrogance against him. If Indriol died, would he be free? Or had the sorcerer simply usurped some of Ren's bindings and left the rest intact?

"Her power is her own, and I know nothing of it," Tarrik said. "But do not go against her. I swear she will end you."

Indriol laughed. "She has you wrapped around her finger still, like a dog sniffing after a bitch. She wasn't as strong as I was when Samal took us. We eight forged our own path to Samal, while she was chosen. An example of his power. Even the most powerful of Samal's enemies could not withstand his will. And she will fall to my power now, once I'm done with you here."

Time for a roll of the dice.

"She killed Lischen," Tarrik said. "With sorcery."

Indriol's amusement fled as quickly as it had come. He tilted his head and stared at Tarrik. "That is not possible. Lischen was bolstering her own power."

"Nevertheless, it happened."

"What of her sword?"

"I know she keeps it sheathed, and I'm not allowed to touch it. She keeps the weapon near her always."

Indriol chewed a thumbnail. "What are her secrets?"

"I do not know."

The sorcerer stood. "You are lying. Again! You are her creature still; I see that now. My bindings are not enough to control you. How she has done this is a mystery, but she won't be alive much longer."

His words held the sound of finality. Tarrik had to assume he would be killed too. Or perhaps Indriol would let Aeshma amuse herself with him first, which would mean more blood and pain. Two things he was used to.

"You are going to kill her?" he asked Indriol.

"When I find her. She has disappeared, like the coward she is."

"But I'm right here," said Ren, stepping out of the gloomy corridor.

Chapter Sixteen

White-hot hooks of sorcery jabbed into Tarrik's body and mind. Indriol's bindings were ripped away, and the familiar feel of Ren's reasserted themselves. He had no time to prepare and experienced the full brunt of the bindings anew. Pain seared through him, scouring his nerves and consciousness. His vision swam, and blackness closed in again. With a snarl he pushed it away.

Indriol barked a cant, and a shield of violet surrounded him. Ren's shield was the sphere of swirling golden sparkles Tarrik had seen before. He leaped to the side, not wanting to be flayed by stray arcane energy.

Aeshma bounded toward him, her knife clutched in one hand. She crouched low in a fighting stance.

Indriol yelled at Ren in a language Tarrik didn't understand. Ren shook her head and drew her sword, which was already at her hip. A furious white light painted the room, and waves of heat rolled over Tarrik.

Aeshma turned to look, and Tarrik pounced. He managed to grip the arm wielding the knife. She snarled and twisted but was no match for him now that he was in close.

Indriol shouted a cant, and sapphire lines scourged the surface of Ren's shield. Sharp cracks sounded as the eldritch threads skittered away from her wards and etched black lines into the stone walls. Either Ren or Indriol would likely die in the next few heartbeats, and for some inexplicable reason Tarrik found himself wishing it would be Indriol.

He clamped his other hand on Aeshma's arm and dragged her away from the sorcerers.

"I'll kill you!" she spat.

"I'm trying to save us both! Get down!"

Tarrik kicked her legs from beneath her, and they tumbled to the floor together. He squeezed Aeshma's wrist until she cried out in pain and dropped the knife, which he batted away. Then he wrapped his arms around her so she couldn't move. He grimaced as her teeth sank into his bicep.

Cants flowed from Ren and Indriol like discordant songs. Ice crystals formed across the ceiling and walls, vaporized to steam an instant later by a surge of roiling heat. The very air keened at the violence, and the armchairs and table in the room charred and smoked.

An indigo web materialized above Ren and fell onto her shield. She cried out and stumbled. Golden motes rushed to wherever the web touched her wards, attaching like dewdrops.

Ren waved her sword. Its shining blade passed through her shield and pierced Indriol's web, severing the taut strands. They thrummed as if plucked, then twisted and curled before evaporating into smoke.

Another web appeared and dropped onto Ren, its strands filtering through her shield. She fell to one knee, ducking her head to avoid them. Her shield held under the assault, and again her searing sword sliced the web to vapor.

Indriol roared, his face red, his arms outstretched toward his foe. He barked more cants, and a barrage of glittering tendrils skittered across Ren's wards, which sparked and began to fade.

She had been strong enough to put Lischen down, but Tarrik thought Indriol seemed more powerful and far more cunning. A look of fear crossed Ren's face, and Tarrik found himself pitying her, an emotion he hadn't felt for a long time.

Her mouth twisted in agony, and she lowered her sword until its tip touched the floor, sending white lightning skittering across the stone. Stray glints of sorcery floated in the air, writhing amid a white mist swirled by eldritch winds. Tarrik wanted Ren to die—but if she did, Indriol would be his new master, and he'd already revealed Tarrik's eventual fate under his will.

Tarrik looked down at Aeshma, who had stopped biting and now stared at him with naked fury. He relaxed his grip slightly and wormed one arm free, grabbed her hair, and pounded her head into the floor. Her eyes rolled back, and she went limp.

Ren had regained her feet, and her cants boomed like thunder. Incandescence erupted from nowhere with the intensity of a noonday sun. Indriol cried out in pain and backed away a step. Perhaps Ren had recovered, perhaps not. But Tarrik had to do something to alter the worst outcome for himself.

A quick glance confirmed the sorcerers only had eyes for each other, focused entirely on their arcane skirmish. He looked for Aeshma's knife, but that wouldn't do anything against a warded sorcerer. Instead, Tarrik lunged at the thick wooden table, now charred and smoking. With a grunt of exertion, his muscles bulging, he lifted the table off the floor and hurled it at Indriol.

The projectile hammered into the violet shield. Indriol was knocked off his feet midcant, his words stuttering as he flung his arms out.

Ren shouted a cant, and silver and golden emanations gathered in her hand. She sent them whirling at Indriol. There was an earsplitting crack, and a wave of force buffeted Tarrik, knocking him to the ground. Indriol's wards dissipated like burning mist. Ren's discharges latched on to him, and he screamed. His clothes smoldered and caught fire. Blood dribbled from blistered spots on his face and hands, staining his coat and pants.

Ren spoke another cant, calling more power to her hand, where it roiled silver and golden.

Indriol tried to speak, but only a moan escaped his lips. Smoke poured from his eyes, which burned with an intense golden light. He made it to his knees, despite the wounds he suffered, and crawled toward Ren, head lowered.

Some sorcerous vitality must be driving him, Tarrik thought.

Ren stepped forward, and her searing-white sword blade severed Indriol's neck. He slumped to the floor, the cut pumping his lifeblood. Blue-violet light erupted from his wounds and detached head, from his eyes and mouth, as if he burned from the inside. His skin immediately charred, then cracked and oozed crimson.

"*Gith-ruthos!*" shouted Ren. Tarrik remembered the words from when she had killed Lischen.

Blue-white light radiated from Ren and washed over Indriol's corpse. His flesh crackled and spat, its fats sizzling, dissolving into pieces that tumbled to the floor. In a few heartbeats, all that remained was a skeleton blackened to obsidian.

Ren staggered and steadied herself with one hand on the wall. She sheathed her blade, and the room plunged into semigloom, lit only by the single alchemical globe hanging from the ceiling beam. Overcome with exhaustion, she slumped to the ground, back resting against the wall.

Tarrik's thoughts skittered this way and that. Why had Ren rescued him? There could be no doubt: she had risked herself to find and free him when he'd expected her to cut her losses and run. He stood still, unsure of what to think, what to do.

Then his mind settled. He had cast his lot with Ren over Indriol. Now that she had defeated another of the Nine with his help, he hoped she'd trust him more.

He went to Ren and held his hand out. She looked up, then nodded and took his grip. As soon as she'd hauled herself to her feet, she let go.

"Another of the Nine destroyed," said Tarrik. "Your plan is working well. Whatever it is."

Ren rubbed her eyes. "This wasn't my plan. But it'll do. Come, we must flee. Bring the jikin-nakar—carry her if you must."

They hurried along corridors, passing guards scurrying in all directions. Of the usually innumerable servants there was no sign.

She came for me. She risked her life.

Tarrik shook his head to clear it of the treacherous thoughts. There had to be another explanation. Perhaps Ren had wanted to kill Indriol anyway. But she'd said it wasn't part of her plan.

Lies. You cannot trust a human sorcerer.

But Ren had killed another of the Nine. Her actions were inconsistent with her avowed aim to return the dreaded Adversary to the world.

Tarrik was so preoccupied that he didn't notice how far they'd come until they passed through an iron-grilled door, then down the spiral staircase to the white marbled foyer below. Standing by the brass-and-wood entry doors were ten armed and armored guards, along with Lin, who was trying to hold Tarrik's spear upright with her small hands.

She gave a nervous smile of relief when she saw them. She was dressed in shirt, sturdy traveling pants, and boots and wore a leather backpack and a belt holding a small knife. Their saddlebags were at her feet. Ren had obviously decided to take the girl with them. Well, she could babysit her.

Two guards approached Ren and Tarrik. "No one is to leave," one of them snapped. "By order of—"

"There is a demon loose," said Ren calmly, and the guards' expressions changed from stern to horrified. "The Cabalists are taking care of it, but I have been given another urgent task. Open the doors."

The guards frowned and looked suspiciously at the jikin-nakar Tarrik carried. "Who is the woman? Why is she unconscious?"

"She is ill," replied Ren. "I'm taking her to be cured. Open the doors."

"We cannot, my lady. Our orders are—"

"I know what your orders are. And I have my own. Open the doors, or I'll scorch your flesh from your bones, and you'll die writhing in agony."

The two guards looked at each other, uncertain whether they should obey.

"Open the doors now!" shouted Ren.

She extended her hands. Lightning arced from splayed fingers, spreading in a web of brilliant white. Energy slicked over the guards, who recoiled and yelped. A sudden gust of air swirled dust around them, and the air stank with a burned, somehow sweet, alchemical aroma. All of the guards shielded their eyes, and two fell to their knees in terror. When the wind died, the lightning had dissipated.

The guards backed away, eyes wide and mouths open. Lin's gaze was fixed on Ren in awe.

"Open. The. Doors," said Ren.

Half a dozen guards lifted the heavy wooden beam securing the doors and pushed one side open. Tarrik shouldered the saddlebags on the opposite side to Aeshma, and Ren bade him and Lin follow her outside.

They hurried across the paved square toward the gates in the wall, darkness shrouding them. There were only a few torches burning atop the wall at guard posts.

"Can I do that trick?" Lin asked. "Or maybe something smaller first. Do you think I'll—"

"Later, Lin," said Ren firmly. "Please save your questions. Tarrik, I must lean on you. I find myself somewhat depleted."

Without waiting for a response, she clutched Tarrik's arm, and he felt her trembling. She leaned her weight on him and stumbled. Though it was awkward since he was carrying both Aeshma and their bags, he slipped an arm around Ren's back to prop her up.

She slumped against him, her feet dragging as they made their way to the gate. Lin struggled to manage Tarrik's spear before settling the shaft on her shoulder like she'd seen the guards do.

The girl giggled, and Tarrik gave her a sharp look.

"No wonder you're so big," she said, "if you have to carry everything and everyone like a mule."

Tarrik growled at her and heard Ren chuckle softly.

The guards at the gate knew something was amiss inside the palace but clearly hadn't had any orders yet to lock down their post. They waved the small group through.

"A carriage," muttered Ren. "Or a cab. It doesn't matter."

Tarrik waved at a cab driver across the street, and the woman nodded back, touching the brim of her hat. She drove over and leaped down to assist.

Tarrik made to help Ren into the cab, but she squeezed his arm. "No. The girl and the . . . woman."

She touched Aeshma's forehead and whispered a cant. The driver's lips thinned, and she took a step back.

"Put the woman inside, Tarrik, and our gear. She'll remain as she is for a while now. Lin, could you please give Tarrik his spear and also get in the cab?"

Tarrik rolled Aeshma off his shoulder and onto a wooden seat. She thumped onto the hard surface, and Ren, Lin, and the driver all turned to stare at him, their eyes narrowing.

"She's hardier than she looks," he muttered as he deposited the saddlebags and returned to the street. He took his spear from Lin and felt relief as he grasped the blackwood shaft.

As soon as Lin had hauled herself into the cab, Ren handed the driver a silver talent. "Drive them to the Ethereal Sorceress's building, and ensure they make it inside. The doorman will help with the woman."

"Yes, my lady," the woman said, leaping up to her perch and driving off.

Ren clamped on to Tarrik's arm again. She pointed to a spot by the wall surrounding the palace, and he half carried her over. It was almost pitch-black, and his boot slipped when he trod in something squishy. He cursed.

"Farther along the wall," said Ren, gasping in pain as Tarrik moved them a hundred paces. "Enough."

A well-lit tavern appeared across the street, and the boisterous sounds coming from inside indicated the place was busy. The lamps outside shed enough light that Tarrik could make out Ren's twisted mouth.

"Are you injured?" he asked.

"Indriol was powerful. He was almost my undoing. How ironic that would have been, eh, Tarrik—if I'd died rescuing you?"

Tarrik couldn't help himself. "Why did you come for me?"

"I couldn't leave you in Indriol's hands. You're my responsibility."

Was she lying? If so, what was her endgame? And if she wasn't, what did that mean? Did it mean she wasn't evil? But how was that possible, given her loyalty to Samal?

His mind jumped from theory to theory but always circled back to the uncomfortable idea that Ren had as many layers as an onion. Beneath her cold exterior beat a heart that could be swayed.

His skittering thoughts were interrupted by Ren's voice. "I have another task for you." She withdrew an object from a pocket. A silver statuette of a bull, crudely molded and engraved with Skanuric script. "You can take someone with you when you shadow-step, correct?"

Tarrik thought about lying but knew that Ren was probably testing him. "Yes."

"I have to get to Indriol's rooms unseen. There were too many guards rushing around before, and we needed to get out before they locked the palace down."

Tarrik shook his head. "We need to get you to a healer."

"This is more important."

"More important than not dying?"

"Yes."

"Do you know where his rooms are?"

"As a matter of fact, they're on the third floor, directly opposite if we happened to be atop this wall."

Tarrik had to smile. Ren rarely left anything to chance, and that, at least, he could admire.

"I presume you're coming to get past his wards. Do I have your permission to touch you? I need to draw you in close."

Ren's eyes flicked away, and she folded her arms across her stomach. "You have my permission."

Tarrik clasped his arms around her and held her to his chest, felt her trembling at his touch. He looked up into the darkness and poured himself into it. His essence, and Ren's, dissolved into the void and re-formed atop the wall.

"Ugh, gods!" cursed Ren softly. "That was awful. I feel like I've been turned inside out."

"You get used to it. Now, which window?"

She pointed. "To the left of the double windows, covered with a hood. There's a balcony—"

"I see it."

Again, Tarrik shadow-stepped. Ren immediately pushed him away, her eyes wild, lips drawn back into a snarl. She stared at him for a moment before composing herself.

"I'm sorry . . . I . . . never mind."

Tarrik just nodded.

Samal had been harsh when he'd broken her, leaving her sensitive to all touch. Perhaps because he hated humans or because it was in his nature.

In a flash of insight Tarrik realized Ren was as much a product of slavery as he was. Could he really hate her for hating all demons?

Ren turned to the balcony doors and spoke a cant. A minute flash of violet light materialized, and the lock clicked open. She turned the handle, and Tarrik followed her inside.

"Stay here," she commanded.

Three alchemical globes cast a stark yellow light over Indriol's bedroom, judging by the four-poster bed. Ren moved gingerly to a side table upon which sat a number of artifacts on a velvet cloth. One of them was an exact replica of the silver bull. She muttered another cant, swapped the two statuettes, and returned to Tarrik.

"We're done," she said, and placed a hand on his arm to steady herself.

Her face was drawn and blanched, and she leaned a considerable amount of her weight on him. He smelled blood. Indriol had injured Ren more than she was letting on. Surely Tarrik wouldn't get another chance like this?

His heart beat faster, and he almost spoke the cant to bring forth his shadow-blade and strike her down. But something stayed his hand—and then he couldn't anyway, as Ren's bindings stole his will and stopped him. Injured though she might be and depleted from her fight with Indriol, she still had mastery over him.

Tarrik trembled, shaken to his core. What had stayed him?

Chapter Seventeen

Tarrik picked her up and shadow-stepped to the wall, then down to the street. "You are wounded," he said.

"I'll be all right with some rest. Hail a carriage, not a cab. If I'm seen in this state, there might be rumors. Take us to Sheelahn."

Tarrik did as commanded, and soon they were rumbling down a main street toward the Ethereal Sorceress's building. Apparently in Atya no one raised an eyebrow at a man carrying a woman into a carriage. He sat back in the leather upholstered seat and felt something sticky on his thigh. His hand came away smeared with Ren's blood.

He looked at her, wedged into the corner of her seat, eyes closed, breathing shallow, damp patches on her shirt.

Ren had risked her life to rescue him from Indriol and in the process had been severely injured. Again, why had she come for him? She could have easily swapped the statuettes herself while Indriol was busy with Tarrik and his own schemes.

Ren had enslaved him. She had forced him to kill. She deserved death, and worse.

"Tarrik."

He looked up to find her staring at him. He was struck by how exhausted she looked, how fearful and alone. Just like when he'd first seen her in the deserted tower.

"What is it?" he said.

"You swore an oath to Contian many years ago . . ."

Not this again.

"And you should honor it now. Serve me of your own free will."

Never.

"Why?" he asked.

"What hope does one person have against the might of the world? Is it possible to shift the course of a river?"

She wasn't making much sense. Maybe her injuries were worse than he'd thought. Her eyes flickered yellow orbs of reflected lantern light.

"I am one person," she went on. "I am attempting to change the course of a river. I think Contian would be proud of me. Or perhaps not. Perhaps he would argue against what I do, bid me flee far from here. As if I wouldn't be found and flayed, and probably worse.

"We fought, he and I. I was . . . difficult. But all children fight with their parents. I see him, parts of him, in some men. He had hardened himself against the world. I even see something of him in you. I understand why you became friends. Serve me without bindings. No, *help* me."

Her words touched Tarrik, delivered as they were in a moment of vulnerability. But perhaps that was what she had planned.

"I cannot," he said.

She turned her face away, disappointed with his response. "So be it," she said with finality.

Ren paid their driver and leaned on Tarrik as they approached Sheelahn's building. The immense, windowless structure, an enormous darkness against the night sky, disturbed Tarrik in a visceral way. The place felt like a prison.

"Rumor has it this building was built in one night by spirits," Ren said as they neared the blackwood doors bound with cold iron. "As were all of Sheelahn's buildings in the major cities."

She grimaced and stumbled. Tarrik lifted her and threw her over his shoulder. He couldn't see any other way to carry her while he held his spear. Her sword was close to his ear, and he could feel its power like a faint buzzing.

Ren grunted. "This isn't the most comfortable position."

"I do not like this place. Nor do I trust Sheelahn."

"That is wise."

Tarrik felt the heat of her body against his. He took a deep breath through his nose. Strange . . . there was none of the goat stench of madness the others of the Nine exuded. This close, all he could discern was a scent like clothes that had recently dried in full sun.

"Did you just smell me?" Ren asked.

"No."

Tarrik ascended the wide stone steps, and the door opened before he could knock. The same masked doorman, or attendant, or whatever he was, stood there waiting for them.

"Enter," he said. "You are expected."

Tarrik carried Ren inside, then stopped on the white-and-green checkered marble floor, not sure where to go. A dozen blackwood doors led off the entrance hall.

"The Ethereal Sorceress will see you alone," said the man. "The demon is not invited."

"Put me down, please, Tarrik."

He did so and sneered at the servant. Why did he think Ren would leave him behind if she hadn't last time?

"Agreed," said Ren.

Tarrik gave her a sharp glance. What was she going to discuss with Sheelahn that she didn't want him to hear? And where were Lin and Aeshma?

Ren hunched over, one hand pressed to her side. Under the alchemical-globe chandeliers lighting the entrance hall, he saw blackened veins under her skin where Indriol's incantations had wounded her.

She held her hand out to the servant, who hesitated before taking it. They disappeared through one of the doors, and Tarrik looked around for a comfortable spot to wait. There wasn't one. Just tiles and doors. He settled for leaning against a wall, his spear grasped in both hands. And waited.

And waited.

And waited.

He was about to start on spear forms when a door opened and Ren came out, struggling under the weight of their saddlebags. For his amusement, he took his time approaching to help.

Ren looked a lot better. The blackened veins had disappeared, and if she'd tried to carry their gear earlier, she would have collapsed. Whatever had happened between Ren and Sheelahn, part of the encounter had involved healing. He saw that her eyes were still shadowed, though, and she still wore her bloodstained clothes.

"Where are Lin and Aeshma?" he asked.

Ren frowned. "Was that the jikin-nakar's name?"

"Yes."

"Lin is safe. Sheelahn will make arrangements for her with the Red Gate Covenant."

"And Aeshma?"

"Forget about her. You will not see her again."

Tarrik recalled Sheelahn offering to buy him from Ren. Had Ren sold Aeshma to the sorcerer instead?

"Did you give her to Sheelahn as payment?"

"I said forget about the demon. Do not ask me about her again."

Tarrik's hands tightened about the shaft of his spear, but he managed to clamp down on his anger. A drink would help. He glanced toward his saddlebags.

"Bring them," said Ren. "We're going to the roof."

Another journey through the night. "Where to this time?"

"Ruruc, a city northwest of here. It's where the Nine will be gathering."

For their attempt to free Samal? They would regret bringing the Adversary back to their world. But perhaps they couldn't help themselves. Their minds had been corrupted, taken from them, and molded to Samal's designs. In some ways he felt sorry for them, for were they not as he was? Enslaved? An uncomfortable thought that wouldn't go away.

He returned his thoughts to the most important matter for himself: how to break free of Ren's bindings. The easiest way was by Ren's death. That had to be his focus. Everything else was a distraction.

He briefly touched Ananias's essence in his mind, remembering how the shell protecting it had almost crumbled when Indriol hit him with the Wracking Nerves. Was he ready to absorb the remaining power without going insane? He felt he was close; perhaps another few trickles of essence and he'd be bolstered enough. Then he would needle Ren into using the Wracking Nerves on him. And if he was successful and could control the flood of demon essence and hold on to sanity, what then? He knew he should kill Ren and be done with this wretched world, but what was really happening between her and the Tainted Cabal and the Nine? Could he leave them to release Samal into this world and risk his malicious reach extending into the abyssal realms?

But Tarrik was only one demon, without significant power. What could he do?

"Sheelahn could transport us there quickly," Ren was saying, "but the cost is too high. I'll have to do it myself."

"Another disc?" he asked. His planning would have to wait.

"Another disc." Ren passed a hand across her weary face, then tugged at her soiled shirt. "I'll change first. Come."

Tarrik shouldered their saddlebags. He wished he had Veika's bottle of spirits in his hand, but they'd soon be aloft, and he'd have time for a drink then. Ren led him to a door that opened onto one of the iron cages. Soon they emerged onto the flat roof. The door closed behind them, and Tarrik could hear the cage creaking as it descended.

"Do you have any of Veika's whiskey left?" she asked.

"I do."

"Fetch it, please. I'll need a fortifying drink before I start."

Tarrik rummaged around in his saddlebag for the bottle. The man-ticarrs on the label seemed to glower at him.

Ren swallowed a mouthful, then another, and handed the bottle back. Tarrik took the opportunity to drink from it himself but stopped when he found Ren gazing upon him.

"What is it?" he asked.

"Contian was right about you."

Meddling old fool. If I'd known he lied about destroying his notes on me, I'd have wrung his scrawny neck.

"In what way?" he said.

"That you aren't like other demons."

"I'm exactly like other demons," he said before he could stop himself. *Blood and fire!* He was supposed to be meek and trustworthy. "What I mean is, you already know that minor demons are ruled by their passions. Once enslaved by humans, they're put to evil deeds. We higher-order demons have more self-control."

"So you've said."

"It is the truth."

Ren sniffed. She went through her saddlebags and pulled out a crimson shirt and charcoal skirt and another short coat. All black except for the shirt.

"Turn around," she said curtly.

Tarrik obliged and heard buckles click and cloth rustle as Ren changed.

"All right, I'm done," she said.

Dressed in clean clothes, with her silver-buckled boots and studded belt, she might have stepped from a preparation room ready for her day—apart from her darkened eyes and the stray hairs that escaped her braids. One strand stuck out, and Tarrik resisted the urge to tuck it back in. He turned away, aching to be gone from here.

Ren created another flying disc out of water and steam and sorcery. Again, Tarrik could only sense a minimal draw of dawn- and dusk-tide emanations. Where did her power come from?

"Tarrik!" snapped Ren. "I've asked you twice. Get on. We have to leave."

Tarrik hurriedly climbed onto the platform, dropped their saddlebags, and sat, cradling his spear in his arms. Heat waves cracked the stone roof as the shimmering blue disc rose swiftly into the air. He settled in for a long flight to whatever awaited them in Ruruc.

They spent the next three nights flying over a sandblasted, rocky wasteland. During daylight hours they rested under flimsy makeshift tents fashioned from their blankets. On the first night, when they reached a river, Ren directed them west to follow it; then the water veered to the north, and they continued along its reverse course. On the third night they came to hills, which rose to become mountains that climbed like jagged teeth on the horizon to the west.

Ruruc was nestled among the hills, a human city much like any other: buildings crammed together, too much smoke, and the stench of humans permeating the air. Tarrik had seen many of their cities by now and wasn't impressed. They were all the same, apart from superficial differences. None were carved from rock faces or dug deep within the earth for protection like most demon cities, and he found himself longing for the enclosed spaces he was used to. When you hunted at night and the darkness surrounded you like a blanket, you didn't feel so exposed.

Ren began their descent into a walled compound a few hundred yards north of the city's walls. A well-worn road connected the two, though its only traveler was a man towing a mule toward Ruruc. The disc landed on a packed-earth courtyard, barely attracting a glimpse of interest from another man forking hay from a wagon in a corralled area and three children running around and whacking at each other with sticks.

Perhaps a sorcerer descending from the sky was commonplace here, Tarrik thought.

Ren voiced a cant, and her crimson-violet tendrils dissipated. "Get off," she snapped at him, and he gathered their gear and hurried onto the scorching-hot earth around the disc. His boots began to smoke, and he ran a dozen or so steps to escape the heat.

A bald man in an ocher robe cinched at the waist with a thin leather belt exited one of the buildings to their left and approached at a hurried pace. He glanced at Tarrik, his eyes instantly sliding off and dismissing him. They came to rest on Ren, and he smiled toothily.

He stank of goat. Another of the mad Nine, then. Or just an insane sorcerer.

"Lady Branwen! You're here in good time," said the bald man. He didn't even have the grace to cover his head, devoid of hair that he could braid into a semblance of respectability.

Ren walked slowly toward him, seemingly unaware that the soles of her boots were smoking on the heated dirt. "Marren. I hadn't thought to see you yet."

He squinted up at the blazing sun, then shaded his eyes with a hand. "Well, here I am." He crossed his arms, palms against his chest, and bowed. "Samal will rise."

Ren repeated the gesture. "Praise Samal, Lord of Life."

Definitely one of the Nine.

"Let's get inside. It's already warm, and the day will only become hotter. Come, please."

He gestured for them to follow him into the building he'd emerged from, which was much cooler than outside. They passed through an entrance hallway and into a square chamber with divans and numerous cushions situated around a low table covered with plates of edibles: nuts and dates, sliced bread and cheeses, and hardboiled eggs.

Four muscular men were stationed around the walls, each wearing just a linen loincloth and armed with a pair of sheathed long daggers. All four waved giant fans to generate a breeze in the chamber, though from their chiseled torsos, callused hands, and scar-covered arms, Tarrik could see they were proficient warriors.

Next to the doorway stood a short-haired woman in a white robe. She kept her head lowered and eyes on the floor.

Marren gestured to one of the divans, which was upholstered with fabric patterned with pink flowers of some sort. "Sit, please. Help yourself to refreshments. I'll have someone fetch wine."

He clicked his fingers at the woman by the door, and she nodded without looking up and scurried away.

Ren unbuckled her chest strap and swung her sword to her hip. Tarrik tensed. For an instant he thought she would draw it and do away with Marren right then and there. But she moved to the divan and sat.

Tarrik positioned himself behind her and placed their saddlebags on the floor. Marren's eyes never moved from Ren.

The woman hurried back into the room bearing a tray with three brass goblets. She slid the tray onto the low table and carried a goblet to each of them in turn, holding the cups carefully with both hands as if she'd be beheaded for spilling a drop.

Marren was served first; he grabbed the goblet and slurped noisily. Ren received hers with a nod of thanks to the woman and took a delicate sip.

Tarrik eyed the liquid, a red wine that looked watered down. He drained the goblet. The drink was weak and insipid but better than nothing.

"Do you have it?" Marren said suddenly. He placed his goblet on the table and clasped his hands in front of him.

"You never could control your impulses," said Ren. She reached across and picked up a date.

"Well, do you?"

"Yes. As promised. One for you and another for Lera."

Ren nibbled daintily on the date, but Tarrik could tell she was focused on the conversation. Her shoulders were tense, her movements too studied. What was so important here? Ren played her own game, of that he was certain, but what was that game? Did she want all of the Nine dead—for herself to be Samal's only chosen?

"Where is it?" Marren wriggled to the edge of the divan, his face shiny with perspiration.

Ren finished the date, took another sip of wine, then placed her goblet on the table. "Tarrik, my saddlebag, please, if you will."

He had no idea why she was being so polite. He lifted Ren's bag and placed it beside her on the divan. She unbuckled the flap and drew out two black-velvet-wrapped items Tarrik had never seen before.

Marren leaned forward, licking his lips. Ren half stood and held one out to him, and he practically snatched it from her. He sat back, hands trembling, and unwrapped the object to reveal a silver statuette of a man covered with Skanuric script. The figure was blocky and crude, topped by a square hat, with his arms by his sides.

Tarrik felt a trickle of power from Marren. His hands tightened around his spear, but Ren didn't react.

"Is this a joke?" said Marren. "Oh, it has an orichalcum core."

"Correct," said Ren. "The ancients saw fit to disguise the metal. Or perhaps they thought the silver looked better. One never knows with them; their thoughts don't usually follow our logic."

A slow smile spread across Marren's face, and both of his slender hands stroked the statuette. The black velvet cloth lay discarded beside him. "You have outdone yourself, Lady Branwen. With these, we are sure to succeed. This world is ours. And soon the vermin and leeches will know our true power."

"Indeed. My man will deliver the twin to Lera. She is here, isn't she?"

"Oh yes, in the city at her residence." Marren gazed at the silver man as if it were his lover.

Ren held the second wrapped statuette out to Tarrik. "Take this to Silver Spears Avenue, to the residence of Lera the Betrayer of Shadows. Take a cab—the driver will know where to go. Tell Lera you've been sent by me, hand her the statuette, then return."

How do you betray a shadow? Tarrik decided not to ask. He took the artifact from Ren.

"Do not tarry," she said, meeting his eye.

Marren frowned at Tarrik. "Hurry up, man! You're dealing with things you cannot understand. Do as she bids!"

Tarrik shoved the statuette into a pocket and left the room.

"We have much to discuss," he heard Marren say. "Did you hear what happened to Lischen? I've only just received word. And now Indriol has gone silent. Someone is moving against us."

That would be Ren.

Chapter Eighteen

Outside was already hotter, or at least it seemed so to Tarrik. Or perhaps the weather only felt so after the cool interior. The children had abandoned their rough game and were sitting under a veranda, eating large pieces of a reddish fruit. No one else was about. Security was lax here, but maybe the population feared the Nine and the Cabal so much they remained cowed. The worms.

Would he return to find Ren had killed Marren? Another of the Nine added to her tally? Tarrik grinned at the thought of another of the sorcerous slavers dead. But somehow he doubted that would hinder the remaining Nine's plans to free Samal.

He left the walled compound and walked south toward the city along the well-worn road. The sun beat down relentlessly, and a searing wind blew gritty dirt that pattered against his boots. For a few moments Tarrik allowed himself to enjoy the sounds and sensations that were so much like home. All that was missing was the sun setting and the faint cries of prey as they hunkered down to wait out the perilous night.

He shouldered his spear as he reluctantly trudged the last few hundred yards to the city gate. He squinted. There wasn't even a gate, just an opening. And as he entered the city, he couldn't see any guards.

Weeds and grasses sprouted from the pavers, surviving despite the heat and dryness, giving the place a desolate look.

On the other side of the entranceway stood a collection of stalls, all shaded by sheets of cloth tied over wooden frames. One sold huge rounds of cheese stacked atop crates; another, fruits and vegetables; and at another, a woman stood behind a sturdy table cluttered with bunches of dried herbs and numerous bottles and vials. As Tarrik wandered through the market, the vendors barely stirred from their chairs, too busy cooling themselves with colorful fans. Everyone wore a head covering of some sort to shield them from the midday heat: broad-brimmed hats, head scarves, hoods. A young boy carrying a basket filled with bundles of dried leaves meandered among them. Most of the vendors exchanged a coin for a bundle, then peeled off a leaf and began to chew.

"Cheeses fresh from the farm!" shouted a man. "Cow's milk, goat's milk, and sheep's milk cheeses!"

Tarrik turned up his nose. No demon would eat such a disgusting creation.

"Potions and remedies!" cried the woman at the cluttered table, loudly but without enthusiasm. "Herbs and medicines to cure any ill and inject you with vigor!"

Tarrik ignored all their calls. Thirty yards up the almost deserted street stood a sorry-looking nag attached to an even sorrier-looking open-topped cab. The horse was mangy and thin, and the cab's paint was peeled and cracked. The driver lay along her seat, a broad-brimmed hat covering her face. As Tarrik approached, he could hear her snoring.

He thumped a fist on the side of the cab, and she jerked awake and sat up. She rubbed her eyes and glared at Tarrik; then her expression softened. "Where to?" she said, patting down her wild blonde hair and putting on her hat.

Tarrik climbed up to a dirty passenger seat. "Silver Spears Avenue. The residence of Lera the Betrayer of Shadows."

The driver stopped fiddling with the reins and glanced over her shoulder at him. "That'll be extra."

Tarrik sniffed, unconcerned. Money was just another human conceit. Barter was sufficient, arranged by your household and the demons subservient to you, and when you lived for as long as demons did, wealth wasn't a focus. Ren hadn't given him any coin, but he had his own, taken from the sorcerer he'd killed after being summoned.

They clattered off, the nag moving slower than Tarrik could have walked.

"That's a fine, long spear you have," the driver said.

Tarrik blinked. "Yes." He watched the streets passing by and wondered why the woman shot him an annoyed look.

To the east, a massive stone tower reared above all the other buildings of the city. It was almost as wide as Sheelahn's structure and at least three times as high.

"What's that place?" Tarrik asked the driver, pointing.

"You're not from around here, are you? The Demon Tower was raised by the Cabalists hundreds of years ago, and they've protected Ruruc ever since." She raised her curled fingers to her lips and mumbled something.

"Why is it named the Demon Tower?" Tarrik said.

"You must have grown up under a rock. The Cabalists protect this land from the demons sent against them by the people in the eastern continent, who've succumbed to debauchery and lust for unholy power. They summon demons to do their bidding, and the Cabalists are in a constant war against them."

Tarrik grunted and held back from asking more questions. What the woman had told him was the opposite of reality, but people only knew what they'd been taught or had figured out themselves. The Cabal had obviously been deceiving the population here for centuries. No good would come of him questioning their methods. He sat back and let the driver do her job.

The people they passed looked tired and listless, and many wore patched and stained clothes. He observed dark-gray-skinned San-Kharr,

276

reddish-tinged Traguh-raj, greenish Illapa, and a multitude of other races and mixes. Tarrik even saw an almost-obsidian-skinned man who towered above everyone else and whose clothes bulged like a bag of melons—probably of Orgol blood from the far south. Everyone had narrowed eyes against the bright sun and heat, which made them look suspicious.

Tarrik and the driver passed another cab that was drawn by an even mangier horse whose head drooped so low it could lick the ground. He caught a glimpse of muscled skin, and for an instant thought it was one of Marren's fan-waving guards. But when he stood to peer over the crowd, the man had disappeared. Perhaps Marren was checking to make sure he delivered the artifact. Tarrik sat back down and vowed to remain alert.

His driver pulled up beside a half-open gate barely attached to its rusted hinges. "This is it. Ugly place, isn't it?"

Lera's residence was a squat building behind a dilapidated wooden fence. Weeds choked the grounds, and wild vines seemed to be all that was holding the fence together. Tarrik had expected something grander, or at least in better condition.

"How much do I owe you?" he asked.

"Four silvers."

Tarrik wasn't sure what the usual rate was, but four silvers seemed a lot for such a short ride. He fished out four coins and handed them to the driver. It was only money.

She looked at them, then back at Tarrik. "You're not bargaining?"

"No."

She laughed, shaking her head. "These are talents, from the south. They weigh more than the nobles we use here. Must be nice not to have to worry about coin."

"If I need more, I'll take it."

"Not here you won't—not with the Cabal running the city. Thieves are punished by flogging and amputation. Worse criminals are drowned without trial."

"Where I'm from, thieves are staked out for a day under the hot sun, then left for the animals of the night to devour. There's nothing left in the morning."

"Sounds gruesome," she said.

"Only if you watch."

"You don't say." She looked at the coins in her palm, then handed two back to him. "I'll be on my way—unless you need a ride back?"

Tarrik shook his head. He knew the way now, and it was faster to walk.

The cab drove off, and he strode along a weed-covered path to Lera's lair. Flakes of blue paint from the decaying front door littered the wooden veranda, which had flecks of crimson too. He narrowed his eyes and examined the red spots closely, then scraped one off with his thumbnail. Blood. Someone, or something, had been messily killed in front of this door fairly recently.

He looked upon an iron door knocker shaped like a lion's head. Tarrik knocked three times. *Twice for enmity, thrice for friendship* was the custom in his realm. Not that anyone here would care.

After a short while he heard footsteps approaching—hard heels on tile. The door opened to reveal a short woman with cascading golden hair. She wore a thin white dress upon which had been sewn dozens of rubies in silver settings. Each seemed to sparkle with an inner glow and threw out crimson streaks of light.

"What do you want?" the woman snapped. She and her dress were tidy and clean, in stark contrast to the outside of the building.

"I am here at the behest of the Lady Branwen, to see Lera the Betrayer of Shadows."

The woman waved a hand. "Bah. That's an old name. It's Lera of the Fireflies now. That's why I had this dress made."

So this was Lera. Tarrik inhaled and caught a faint stench of goat. Despite her innocuous yet strange appearance, he'd do well to get his task over with quickly.

He withdrew the velvet-wrapped statuette from his pocket and held it out.

Lera stared at the object and blinked. "What's this?"

"I think it's a statuette."

"From Lady Branwen?"

"Yes." When Lera didn't take it, Tarrik felt the need to offer more information. "Marren seemed pleased with his."

She sniffed, then stepped aside and waved at Tarrik to enter the house.

He hesitated, wanting to be on his way, but offending one of the Nine probably wasn't wise. He crossed the threshold and stopped one pace inside. He held out the statuette again, and again Lera ignored it.

"Come with me," she said and closed the door.

She walked across the entrance hall and ascended a wooden staircase. There wasn't anything he could do except follow.

He noticed dirt and dry leaves across the floor. The woodwork was dusty, and the painted walls had patches of mildew. On the next floor, she led him into what he thought was a cozy meeting room until he realized the chairs were grimy and the refreshments were covered with green and yellow mold.

"I'll take the statuette now," said Lera. "You can wait here until I return." She left the room, closing the door behind her.

Tarrik leaned his spear against the wall and decided not to sit. He caught movement at the corner of his eye and saw a cockroach crawling over a plate of dust-covered fruits. Judging from the wrinkled and shrunken appearance, the food must have been sitting there for weeks, if not longer.

After some time, Tarrik sensed a tug at his awareness. It was gone in an instant but left him feeling uneasy. He didn't think Lera had been examining him—his first fear after what had happened with Indriol. The sensation had Ren's flavor, but he couldn't say how he knew that. He checked her bindings around him; they were unchanged.

He waited, but there was no further disturbance.

The room's single window was dirty, and he used a cloth napkin from the table to wipe a pane clean enough to see out of. Tarrik looked over the street and noticed the cab and driver who'd brought him were still nearby. She was asleep again, hat over her face. He might have done the same if there was a clean space to lie down.

Tarrik paced the room as the wait grew longer. Perhaps Lera was testing the artifact, or maybe she'd simply forgotten about him. He wouldn't be surprised. Ren had told him not to tarry, but he needed a drink and red meat. The cab driver would know of somewhere he could find food.

He was about to gather his spear and leave when he heard Lera approaching. She entered the room and gave him a brief smile, then tossed him a coin-filled purse. Tarrik caught it reflexively.

"Go on—open it," she said.

Tarrik did so and found the bag brimming with a mixture of silver and gold coins.

"Lady Branwen doesn't require your employment any longer. She asked me to give you this as compensation."

Tarrik raised his eyebrows. "Did she?"

Lera was acting like he was a mercenary bodyguard, not a summoned demon. His mind worked furiously as he realized she had no idea what he was. And she was trying to get rid of him, much as Moushumi had.

Lera opened the door and gestured to Tarrik to leave. "Lady Branwen has pressing business to attend to. She thanks you for your service and hopes the coin is adequate compensation for cutting your employment short."

Tarrik clasped his spear and gave Lera a shallow bow. "It is indeed. Such generosity. Truly Lady Branwen is a pearl among sorcerers." Lera's false smile turned to a frown, and Tarrik thought he might be overdoing it. "Ah, well, I'll be going, then."

He sidled through the door and hurried down the stairs, with Lera trailing behind. He resisted the urge to run, but his shoulders itched as he half expected her to stab him or use sorcery. He reminded himself that an attack was unlikely with Lera trying to get rid of him with such a large payment. Besides, as one of the Nine, if she wanted him dead, he would be a cooling corpse already.

Ren's bindings were urging him to return to her. The sense of danger was palpable and increased as Tarrik exited the front door and walked to the street. What was the tug he'd felt earlier? Had Ren tried to summon him and been silenced?

Lera had to know he could easily return to Ren and discover she hadn't let him go. So what was her plan? *If she's as insane as the rest of the Nine, maybe she doesn't have one.*

For an instant Tarrik debated whether to take the cab but dismissed the notion. He needed to return to Ren as quickly as possible. He waited until he'd turned a corner and was out of sight of Lera's house, then broke into a run.

Tarrik drew curious looks as he barreled down the streets. One man bellowed at him, something about a race, and when Tarrik dodged around a slow-moving wagon loaded with barrels, he almost speared a woman standing to the side. She screeched as his spear blade passed within inches of her face and shouted curses at his receding back.

Sweat dripped from him as he took a shortcut down the stairs and found himself on the main avenue leading to Ruruc's northern gate. The tug of Ren's bindings had grown stronger, and he had to resist them to move in directions not arrow straight toward her. Then suddenly, their driving urge disappeared. He stumbled in confusion, but found his balance and managed not to fall.

By the time he reached the gate, his chest burned, and his mouth and throat were dry. His head pounded with the surging beat of his pulse and rattling breath. He slowed his pace and wiped sweat from his brow with his sleeve.

It seemed to take twice as long to cover the worn road to the walled compound, even though he jogged. Inside, the packed-earth courtyard was deserted.

Tarrik made his way to Marren's building. When he barged into the room where he'd left Ren, a wall of muscled guards met him, their long daggers pointed at him.

Marren was still sitting on his divan. Of Ren and her sword, no sign.

"I didn't think to see you again," said Marren.

Tarrik glanced at the divan where Ren had sat and noted both their saddlebags were missing. But the room still looked as it had earlier, with not a cushion or plate out of place. If Ren had been assaulted, either she'd been overpowered instantly or given in without a fight.

Tarrik ground his teeth, then crossed his arms, his palms against his chest, and bowed. "Samal will rise."

Marren frowned and did the same. "Praise Samal, Lord of Life."

"Where is Lady Branwen?"

"I'm surprised you're still on your feet."

"I'm used to running. Where is Lady Branwen?"

Marren chuckled and picked up his goblet of wine. He sipped it and smacked his lips. "I meant from the drugged wine. Branwen felt the effects soon after you left. I bear her no ill will myself, but this was a long time coming. She should have anticipated it."

Perhaps she did, which is why she's killing you one by one.

It explained the tug on his bindings that he'd felt, an instant when Ren knew she was betrayed and attempted to summon Tarrik before the drugs had taken hold of her. But she wasn't dead, or her binding on him would have dissipated.

Tarrik doubled up suddenly as if he'd been kicked in the stomach. He reeled, groaning, feeling cold despite the heat. *It's the bindings,* he told himself. There was no imperative pulling him in a certain direction, but he still felt the compulsion to protect Ren.

She came for me.

Tarrik shook his head to dismiss the traitorous thought.

"Where is she?" he asked Marren.

"I had no part in this, apart from the wine," said the sorcerer. "I hold no particular malice toward Lady Branwen, unlike my colleagues. Lera, Puck, and Moushumi decided Serenity was unworthy of the honor Samal bestowed upon her. And with our lord's return imminent, she must be disposed of." He sighed. "I have no time for such distractions. Lord Samal's release is at hand, and the others insist on playing stupid games to position themselves. It's best if you take the coin that Lera gave you and disappear. Live a good life somewhere—just not here. If you make a fuss and look for Branwen, you'll be killed."

Fear rose within Tarrik. Fear for himself, when Ren told the Nine of his existence. And fear for her—what she would suffer at the hands of her colleagues.

Why should he fear for her? He tried to smother the feeling and forced himself to stand straight, staring at Marren, his chest hard and aching.

Ren's fate with the Nine was already sealed. They would soon discover that she'd killed two of their number, and she would be punished. Would they kill her quickly or torment her? Torment was good; he wanted Ren to suffer.

She came for me.

No, she came to kill Indriol. Freeing Tarrik was a side benefit for her.

She came for me.

When he didn't move or speak, Marren said, "Answer me, man! Cat got your tongue?"

The phrase brought a smile to Tarrik's lips as he remembered Ren saying such to him. "What cat?" he asked softly.

Marren frowned. "It's a figure of speech. It means you're silent when you're expected to speak."

So that was the meaning.

Tarrik's grip tightened on his spear. Four guards of unknown skill, all wielding daggers. And one of the Nine. To fight them was madness. Moving slowly, he shouldered his spear and backed up a step.

"Samal will know of the Nine's treachery," he said. "There will be no hiding it from him."

"Which is why Branwen has been taken by the Cabal. The Nine's hands are clean."

The Tainted Cabal. Demon slavers and the cause of countless demon deaths. They would wring Ren until her secrets spilled from her like her blood.

"How long will they torture her?"

"Days probably. Are you squeamish? Branwen will have much knowledge to share, and she's no stranger to pain."

Ren would reveal that Tarrik was a demon. The Cabal would hunt him down and take over Ren's bindings. Unless she died to protect him. Unlikely.

She came for me.

"Where have they taken her?"

"Nowhere you can get to." Marren stood, still holding his goblet. "Go. Forget Branwen. Whatever contract you had with her is void. Take the coin, and spend it on whatever you want. We aren't without mercy. Well, I'm not. If you linger much longer, you'll regret it."

Tarrik bowed once more. "You are wise. I have had many masters, and Lady Branwen was merely another. I'll join a trading caravan heading to the coast."

"You do that." Marren watched Tarrik as he backed away.

Tarrik kept his eyes on the sorcerer too until he was out in the hallway. Then he turned and left the building.

Chapter Nineteen

The sun beat down as hot as a forge. Tarrik left the compound but stopped fifty paces up the road. He leaned on his spear and considered his options. The deep blue cloudless sky sent a shiver of unease through him. It was so . . . empty. High above, a tiny speck moved in circles. A bird of prey.

Marren would likely send a guard to keep an eye on him and make sure he left Ruruc, probably the same man Tarrik had spotted following him before. If he even looked like he was going after Ren, they'd kill him.

Her bindings commanded him to protect her, to do her no harm, but right now, in this situation, he could walk away. Or at least delay until she was killed. He had no idea where she was or how to get to her.

She came for me.

Blood and fire! She'd enslaved him! And then saved him from Indriol.

Fool! She's nothing like Contian or Jaquel.

Tarrik stormed toward the city. He needed a drink to dampen his emotions; then he'd be able to see sense.

He strode through the unguarded gate and past the lethargic market vendors.

"You there!" Tarrik said to a tall woman wearing colored silks. Her face was mostly covered with a head scarf, leaving only her brown eyes visible. "Where's the nearest place I can get a drink?"

"The Severed Head is a few streets that way." She pointed along a side street. "It's a rough establishment, though—"

"That's fine." Tarrik left her gaping.

He found the tavern easily enough. The severed head on the sign was greenish black, lumpy, and misshapen, and its neck oozed drips of orange. Some type of wilderness creature, he thought, though he couldn't figure out which one.

Inside, worn floorboards were covered with a thin layer of sawdust—a sure sign they expected spilled ale or blood. Tarrik moved to the bar along one wall where a scrawny man with a straggly gray beard nursed a tankard.

The tavern keeper wore a leather apron and swatted at flies with a woven cane implement. He glanced at Tarrik, slapped the swatter at something on the bar, then put on a false grin. "Welcome, wanderer! We have ale to quench the mightiest—"

"Something stronger," growled Tarrik. "From the Widow's Distillery. Nothing sweet like rum." He tossed a gold coin onto the bar. "I'll need the bottle."

The tavern keeper scooped up the coin in a flash. "Of course, of course! We cater to all types here."

He ducked under the bar and rummaged around, coming up after a few moments with a dust-covered bottle of green glass. He gave it a cursory wipe with his sleeve and placed it on the counter. Tarrik took the bottle and looked around for a quiet corner. A few other patrons sat about, though all seemed interested in their drinks rather than conversation.

He uncorked the bottle and took a long swig. The spirit went down burning and spread a welcome warmth through his empty stomach.

"Ah, go easy," said the tavern keeper nervously. "I'll not have you throwing up and passing out. The scavengers here will pick you clean, and I don't want you blaming me."

"Food," said Tarrik. "Meat."

He made his way to an empty table and leaned his spear against the wall next to it. The chair gave a creak of protest when he sat down but seemed sturdy enough.

Bloody sorcerers. He took another swallow. Time was he'd been content to live out his life in exile, one of the outcasts who had no involvement in the goings-on of the higher demons. Always thinking only a day ahead to where his next meal would come from or how the day's card games might play out. And now here he was, sitting in a strange tavern, drinking among pathetic humans, waiting to see whether the sorcerers would figure out that Ren had bound a demon and who his new master would be. Puck? Moushumi? Lera? Or even Marren?

The funny thing was, he thought, they'd all be worse than Ren.

A woman entered the tavern scantily clad in tight silks, her lips painted red. She handed the tavern keeper a coin, then eyed the customers. Tarrik took another swallow and ignored her.

She sauntered between the tables until she ended up at his. "Buy a girl a drink?" she said throatily, fixing her eyes on him.

"Piss off," he said. As worked up as he was right now, he wasn't in the mood for a woman.

She blinked and drew her shoulders back.

"I said get lost!"

She sneered at him and walked away, finding an elderly man in a side booth to pester. Good. She wasn't a patch on Jaquel.

Or Ren.

Tarrik coughed, spraying spirits across the table. He coughed again and wiped his mouth with the back of his hand. Blood and fire, what was wrong with him?

He sniffed and swallowed more of the liquor and cursed when he found the bottle almost empty.

A server emerged from a doorway beside the counter, carrying a plate piled high with slices of meat. He deposited it on Tarrik's table. "That'll be a silver."

Tarrik handed over another gold coin and waved the empty bottle at him. "More of the same. And quickly."

Ren and the Nine could die burning in a bonfire, and he wouldn't care. She'd enslaved him! And then come to save him. Blood and fire!

He rubbed his aching eyes and tried to ignore the insistent ache of Ren's bindings. He felt sorrow, for an unfathomable reason. Leaving her to be tortured and killed would be justice, wouldn't it?

The second bottle came. He took a swig, then set to eating the meat. It was overcooked, but the pinkness in the center was almost palatable. He devoured the fare anyway, using his fingers to eat. When he was done, he licked them clean, then sat back, legs stretched out in front of him, nursing the now half-empty bottle.

Ren's bindings still pulled at him, but they were weak. Weaker than earlier? Difficult to determine.

For a long time Tarrik sat there, wondering about his future and past. And about Ren. Who was she really? Killing Lischen and Indriol had to have weakened the Nine and was a trespass that Samal surely wouldn't forgive. Ren had argued that the Nine should not go ahead with their attempt to free Samal. Or so she'd told him. But she was Samal's creature just as much as the rest of them.

Tarrik took another swig and found the bottle empty again. He slammed it onto the table, and the Widow's container tipped over and rolled over the edge, shattering on the floor. Every head turned to stare at him.

Lost in his thoughts, he hadn't seen the place fill up, but a score or more people were drinking there now—mostly laborers, judging from their thick builds, worn clothes, and tired eyes. He didn't care for their disparaging stares, the uncouth remarks they didn't bother to hide. He was Tarrik Nal-Valim, demon of the Thirty-Seventh Order! And they were mere animals, fit only to serve him or die by his blade!

Despite the two bottles of spirits, his anger sprang to life, going instantly from banked coals to a raging bonfire. Red swamped his vision. He realized he was on his feet, his hands clamped into fists, glaring at an empty spot in front of him.

Someone stepped into his line of sight. "Calm down, friend," rumbled a deep voice.

The first thing Tarrik took in was the man's midnight skin. Next was his height and bulging muscles, the arms roped with sinew. Orgol blood ran thick in this man's veins. He would be quick too. A heavy sword hung from his hip.

"Calm down?" said Tarrik incredulously. This lump of meat had no right to command him. He didn't know what Tarrik had lost. Freedom. His home. Self-respect. Ren.

"Blood and fire!" he shouted, and the man backed away a step and drew his blade. The thick sword moved as easily as a stick despite its weight. The man's eyes held no fear.

Tarrik sneered at him. His every muscle itched to fight this half-breed and pound him into the dirt. He would break his arms and legs and spill his guts on the sawdust. But his rage was best focused elsewhere.

He kept his voice low, managed to speak through clenched teeth. "I'm leaving."

The man nodded, but his sword didn't move a hair.

Tarrik grabbed his spear, then made a wide circle around the man. Disappointed murmurs followed him all the way outside. No doubt wagers had been made on who would win a fight.

On another day, Tarrik would have made an example of the muscled patron, as he had with Albin in Ivrian. But not today. Not now.

He was going to do something stupid. He was going to find Ren.

Chapter Twenty

Tarrik hefted his spear and set off at a jog. Across the city, the Demon Tower loomed. Ren would be there—he was sure. At the thought, her bindings grew stronger, tugging at him. He still felt he could ignore them if he wanted to, but his own feelings were more of a compulsion now than her sorcery. The Tainted Cabalists thought they could use demons for their own ends. Today, they would find out what an unfettered demon was capable of. Tarrik let the rage inside him come to life. His head swam; his arms and chest ached for violence.

He reached the paved square in front of the tower and looked up at it rearing into the sky. The edifice's stone blocks were gigantic, and the seams between blocks were barely visible. The only door was wide open, and four leather-armored guards were stationed there, two to either side.

This close, Tarrik felt he could sense Ren inside the tower. But whether this was the result of her bindings calling to him or his imagination, he couldn't tell.

If the Cabalists intended to keep Ren a prisoner for any length of time, they would have to prevent her from using sorcery. This could be done a number of ways, but the easiest was to keep sorcerers unconscious and deep underground, unable to replenish their repositories with the dawn- and dusk-tides. Eventually their power would leak away, and they'd be helpless.

His stomach clenched at the thought of what the Cabalists would be doing to Ren. He had to get inside, then make his way to the lower levels.

He mentally assessed his repository of dark-tide power. He hadn't used much, and as always, his store leaked far less than that of other demons. It was a talent that was barely understood, or so he'd been told. By his judgment he had enough for a dozen or so shadow-steps and a few bursts of his shadow-blade before he was drained to the dregs. That would have to be enough.

He hefted his spear and walked slowly toward the tower. As he did, he stoked his anger—held it tight, nursed it.

The guards saw him coming. They stood up straighter and loosened their swords in their sheaths.

Tarrik loosened his shoulders and stretched his neck to either side. His hands quivered with all the suppressed rage the spirits hadn't been able to dampen. Blood surged through his veins, drummed in his head. He grinned, relishing the violence to come. Finally, he was free to take out his anger on these human slavers.

"Halt!" shouted a guard. "What business do you have here?"

"Move aside!" snarled Tarrik.

The guards' swords rang from their sheaths. Their blades swung up to point at Tarrik.

So be it.

Tarrik allowed his fury to fill him with its heat and strength. He swapped his spear to his left hand and uttered a cant. His dark-tide power connected to the conduit he'd created, and his shadow-blade materialized in his right hand.

The guard in front of Tarrik only had time to widen his eyes in surprise before a shimmering sword of pure force sliced through his neck. Blood sprayed from the wound, splashing the pavers.

As the guard's body crumpled lifelessly, Tarrik leaped for another, darting his shadow-blade toward the man's chest. He jerked backward, and Tarrik thrust with his spear, puncturing his leather armor. The man cried out in pain, one hand grabbing the spear shaft, its blade deep inside his stomach. With a savage grin and a twist, Tarrik yanked the spear free, and the guard fell to the ground, spurting blood and screaming.

Tarrik shouted another cant, and his shadow-blade vanished. He gripped his spear with both hands as the remaining two guards came for him. One leaped forward and lunged, trying to get inside Tarrik's guard. Tarrik batted the sword aside with the spear's shaft, jumped forward, and hammered its butt into the man's face. Bone cracked, and the guard reeled.

Tarrik dodged to the side, and the second guard's blade passed through the space he'd vacated. Whipping his spear around, he swept the man's feet from under him. The guard fell with a thump and rolled away.

Tarrik ignored him and returned to the other. One hand clutched his face, which dripped crimson, while the other held his shaking sword. His eyes darted, as if he were searching for someone to help him. Tarrik thrust once, twice, both deliberate feints, then jabbed his spear tip into the guard's thigh. The man screeched and staggered away, dropping his sword as he fell.

Tarrik spun, spear blade cutting through the air, causing the last guard to fall back. The man circled Tarrik warily and danced backward out of reach when Tarrik moved to close the distance between them. Stalling for time.

Tarrik faked a thrust, sending the man leaping aside, then turned and darted toward the third guard. He plunged his spear into the man's side, twisted, then jerked it free.

"No!" the remaining guard exclaimed with horror. "You fecking pig! You're a dead man!"

Tarrik spoke a cant, and his shadow-blade sprang into existence again. He thrust with his spear, then tossed it into the guard's legs while simultaneously charging at him. The guard tried to dodge but tripped on the spear shaft tangling his legs. He stumbled, and Tarrik drove his shadow-blade into his chest. The man moaned and gurgled as blood spilled from his lips.

"I'm not a man," said Tarrik. "And mercy is for the weak."

He slashed his shadow-blade across the man's throat, then sprinted through the now-undefended door into the Demon Tower.

The entrance foyer was massive and meant to impress, with polished marble tiles and gilded chairs and tables. Far above hung chandeliers with dozens of alchemical globes. *Good*, Tarrik thought. *That means the shadows will be stable.*

Men and women rushed toward him, having heard the commotion outside. When they saw his gore-spattered appearance, they turned and fled.

He ignored them, searching for those who stood their ground and whose lips moved with cants of sorcery. Two women and a man. Shimmering spheres of emerald power sprang up around them. Tainted Cabal sorcerers.

"Where is she?" roared Tarrik.

Let them know why he'd come. Let them know that their foolish actions had brought forth a demon's wrath. Violence and death and ruin.

One of the female sorcerers glanced at the man. She wore a blue silken dress, and long metal needles held up her abundant brown hair.

The man held out a hand to stop the woman and stepped toward Tarrik himself. He boasted a graying beard and dismissive sneer.

"Surrender now, and your death will be swift," he said.

The third sorcerer sidled slowly to the man's right in an attempt to move out of Tarrik's line of sight.

"Where is she?" repeated Tarrik.

The man affected a puzzled frown. "Who?"

Enough of this farce. Tarrik might not be able to penetrate occult wards, but there was more than one way to kill or render sorcerers ineffective. The easiest way to negate their power, of course, was not to be in their view. He stepped back, feigning uncertainty, and took in the shadowed areas of the entry foyer. They were few and not dark enough. To his right, though, was an inky corridor.

Tarrik snarled and ran at the male sorcerer. His mouth opened in shock.

Midstride, Tarrik fixed his sight inside the corridor and poured himself into the darkness. His essence dissolved into the void, and he re-formed thirty paces away, against the wall in the shadows. Out of the sorcerers' vision.

He ran along the tiled passageway, searching for a way down. He barely had any thoughts other than to find Ren and kill anyone who tried to stop him.

Crackling sorcery sounded behind him, and the corridor was lit with brilliant blue light—the sorcerers reacting to his disappearance. He hoped they might believe him invisible or concealed somewhere in the chamber with them. Their confusion and their attempt to find him would buy him valuable time as they scoured the room with incantations.

Tarrik skidded around a corner and met the eyes of a surprised woman. She fumbled for the talisman at her belt, but his spear caught her in the stomach. She screamed and doubled over, her hands clutching the shaft. He jerked the spear to the side and landed a boot in her ribs, kicking her free. She tumbled against the wall, curled into a ball.

He ignored her cries and ran past. Her wailing would alert the other sorcerers of his location. Even more so than before, speed was urgent.

He spoke his seldom-used scrying cants, sending dark-tide tendrils out in front of him. Almost immediately one rebounded, bringing information with it: a staircase down.

Tarrik took a corridor to the right, heading toward the stairs. Two guards appeared before him, moving slowly. Too slowly. One died in a spray of blood as Tarrik's spear blade opened his throat. The second only had time to fumble for his sword before he too collapsed from a double thrust to his chest.

Elation filled Tarrik. He laughed and bellowed in his native Nazgrese—words of jubilation, rage, and challenge. He barely saw whoever it was he killed next. Servant, guard, or sorcerer, they all fell to his spear when he came upon them from the darkness.

A guard stationed at the top of the stairs managed to draw his short sword just as Tarrik threw his spear. The guard twisted, and the spear blade opened a gash in his side before it thudded into the wall. He grunted but stood his ground.

Tarrik charged, spoke a cant. His shadow-blade materialized. It blocked the guard's feeble thrust, shoving it to the side, then ripped across the man's stomach. Tarrik leaped over the crumpling guard, yanked his spear free, and raced down the stairs.

His boot slipped, and he almost fell, and then he slowed his pace. As Tarrik descended, the stone walls darkened, shining with dampness and salt encrustations. He sent out another scrying wave and found Ren. Somewhere ahead, maybe fifty paces.

He came to an iron-bound door with a massive lock. A torch burned in a sconce, sending flickering orange light across the walls. Tarrik turned the door handle, and the lock clicked open. When he wasn't seared by wards, he grinned ferally. He was still alive and had almost reached Ren.

By now the sorcerers would know his goal. They would be gathering, readying themselves to kill him, fearful of what would happen if Ren were freed.

He thrust the door open and came face-to-face with four guards. They wore mismatched boiled leather and armor that looked to have been scavenged from a full set. Each held only a short sword.

The guardroom floor was covered with straw, and a dozen crates and barrels were stacked against the walls. One barrel was surrounded by four stools and topped with cards and dice, a handful of copper coins, and a waterskin. Beyond the room, he saw cell doors of solid timber with iron-barred windows.

The guards pointed their blades at Tarrik, their wide eyes taking in his dripping spear and blood-spattered appearance.

"Surrender!" one shouted.

Tarrik leaped forward, his first spear thrust piercing a guard's eye into his brain. He parried another guard's sword with the spear's shaft, then kicked the man in the knee. Bone cracked, and the man collapsed to the floor before being finished off with a quick stab in his side.

Tarrik moved on to the final two guards. One had backed away a few paces and looked ready to run. The other came at Tarrik in a wild rush. He was the tallest of the four, well-built, and his thrusts and slashes were guided by an expert hand. His blade came in a blur, straight as an arrow, and Tarrik barely managed to twist and turn it aside. The edge cut through his shirt and drew a burning slice across his skin.

He hissed and used his momentum to bring himself around to slash with his shadow-blade at the man's thigh. It was met with steel and turned aside.

Tarrik aimed for the guard's neck and again was blocked.

Running out of time. Kill him.

A counter came at Tarrik, quick and placed well—a stab to the chest that would have killed him. Using his spear shaft, he forced the blade down and to the side, leaving the man wide open. His shadow-blade skewered throat, tongue, and bone to pierce the brain. He jerked his blade free, and the guard slumped to the floor.

The fourth guard looked frantically over his shoulder before facing Tarrik again. Maybe he thought to barricade himself in a cell.

"I surrender," the guard said, licking his lips and lowering his blade.

Tarrik launched his spear. It flew straight and true and punctured the guard's chest. He cried out and fell backward, scrabbling hands grabbing the spear. He tugged it free, screaming and crying at the same time, and scrunched into a ball on the straw, as if trying to contain his life before it ebbed away.

Tarrik locked the door, then dragged the crates and barrels over and stacked them against it. The barrier wouldn't stop a sorcerer for long but would hinder guards. He fetched his spear and strode to the cells, his blood coursing through his veins, pounding in his head.

The first cell held a spindly woman clad in filthy rags. She sat unmoving on a pile of straw in a corner, her eyes fixed on Tarrik. He moved to the next, which was empty.

Across the corridor, an old man rushed to his cell door, his hands latching on to the window bars. He had a soiled beard and hair and cackled maniacally. "Wine!" he shouted with rotten breath through brown teeth. "Bring me wine!"

Tarrik left him to his screaming. The next cell was empty; then there was only one left at the end. Another iron-bound and locked door. With a key in the lock.

The door opened to a sizeable room. A man stood before Tarrik surrounded by a spherical shield of shimmering blue. The sorcerer grinned and raised a hand to point at Tarrik. He snarled a cant.

Tarrik dissolved into the shadows and re-formed behind the sorcerer.

Sheets of sorcerous flame erupted into the space where Tarrik had been standing, through the door, and into the cellblock. Straw ignited, and the crates and barrels charred. Smoke filled the air.

Screams came from the cells, abruptly ceasing after a moment. The sorcerer turned his head away from the intense heat, no doubt assuming Tarrik had been caught in the blast and killed.

Tarrik ran a few steps and slammed his shoulder into the sorcerer's shield. The man flew toward the door and his own flames. His shield winked out as he lost concentration and tumbled into the conflagration. He rolled across the floor, his clothes bursting into flame, his hands sizzling on the blistering stone. He screeched in agony, and Tarrik stopped his cries with a well-timed thrust of his spear.

"Tarrik," croaked Ren from behind him.

Chapter Twenty-One

Tarrik whirled to see Ren sitting on the ground behind floor-to-ceiling bars. She was naked, and her hair was damp and plastered to her skin. For the first time Tarrik saw the results of Samal's torment on her flesh. Newly incised lines crusted with dried blood covered old mutilations.

She struggled to rise, failed. Whatever they had done to her in such a short time had seriously weakened her. She had the same scared look he'd seen when she'd summoned him, though this time it was more intense. A trembling hand came up to cover her face, and he saw that her knuckle was raw and covered with fresh blood from where she'd worried at it.

He averted his eyes from her nakedness and stalked closer. He drew a breath laden with smoke, which caused him to cough and lower his head. The straw had been reduced to ash, and the wood ignited by sorcery was now only smoldering.

Something tugged at him. *Free her*, it urged.

"Do not touch the bars," said Ren. "They are warded, and you will die. You should not have come for me. I have gambled and lost."

"I am your slave. I could do nothing else."

A weak laugh escaped Ren's lips and transformed into a cough. "Untrue. I don't know why you've come, but it was a mistake. I am close to death. They have poisoned me, along with everything else. Leave now, while you can. Maybe you have a chance to escape."

Her words confused Tarrik. Her bindings had urged him to her, hadn't they?

Ren lowered her head, and her frame shook with sobs. She wiped her eyes with the back of her hands and slowly raised her head. Tears streamed down her cheeks, but her mouth twisted into a smile. She wasn't crying; she was laughing.

She gave him a look filled with pity and lifted a hand to touch a bloody patch above her breast, over her heart. They had cut her catalyst from her.

All of a sudden her words made sense. He was free of her accursed bindings! He was free!

Then what had urged him to come for her?

Tarrik's heart lurched as he realized—his own feelings had brought him here. No . . . it wasn't possible. His eyes widened in shock, and he clasped his hands over his head. He could feel his arms shaking. She was a human, an enslaver of demons. But he had come to free her even after her bindings upon him had dissolved. His deep rage, his twisted emotions . . . the confusion . . . the truth was, he cared.

The room spun around him, and he sank to the stone floor, horrified. *Not again.* His attachment to Jaquel had brought only suffering.

"What have you done to me?" he said.

"Nothing. You came here of your own volition. But you should go now."

"Is that a command?" he said automatically.

"Yes. No. I don't know. Tarrik, I am bone weary. I am alone, and I'm afraid. I have no more honor to lose. You should flee. At least one of us will survive."

Tarrik's thoughts swirled in a maelstrom. He couldn't focus. What was he supposed to do?

"I could help you escape," he said. "But why should I?"

"Do you think I would take this path for no reason? I will never win this fight without shedding blood—and there's little chance to survive what I'm doing. But I cannot do it without someone to help. Without you."

Ren glared at him, angry at her fate, and yet there was a determination about her. A fierceness of spirit. Her similarity to Jaquel sent him reeling, and the room spun. He steadied himself, hands on the solid stone floor, and took a deep breath.

Ren bit her bottom lip, her hands gripped tightly in her lap. "I'm sorry I had to involve you in this. Flee now, Tarrik. Run. And when I . . . when I die . . . you'll be truly free. If you're not strong enough to return yourself, seek out the masters from the Red Gate Covenant. Tell them you served me. They'll find a way to send you back to your realm. But I implore you . . . there is the slimmest chance I might live. My life is in your hands."

He was a shadow-blade. Of course he was strong enough. Tarrik said nothing, but his anger boiled anew. Ren had chosen to enslave him. If he was truly free, he should carve her heart from her chest. But would he?

She came for me.

He clenched his hands into fists, suppressed his rage. For long moments he stared at Ren, his master, beaten and alone in her cell. With a start he saw there was no fresh incision where he'd implanted the artifact for her.

"Could you not have used the artifact to destroy your captors?" he asked. And herself with them. Suicide by sorcery—a fitting end.

"I'm saving it for when things get truly desperate." She laughed softly.

Tarrik wondered if this was how her madness manifested: an inability to see how dire her situation was.

"That was a poor joke," Ren continued. "The truth is, I was too afraid to use it. I find that despite my resolve, despite the efforts I've made to harden myself, I cling desperately to life. Is that strange? I don't think so." She shifted her weight and winced. "I wish . . ."

"For what?" snarled Tarrik. "What is it that you wish for?"

"Another way. Something . . ." She sniffed and wiped her eyes. "Enough. There's no point crying about it."

She drew her shoulders back and sat up straight, staring deep into his eyes. Once again Tarrik was struck by how she reminded him of Jaquel. They shared the same strength and intensity, a spirit of unbridled purpose wedded to intellect.

"You didn't happen to see any water out there, did you?" asked Ren.

"The guards had a waterskin."

"Fetch it."

Tarrik did so and tossed the skin between the bars to her. She raised it in trembling hands and gulped greedily.

"The Cabal sorcerers will be here soon," he said. "And they've removed your catalyst."

"Yes."

"So you still have power but no way to harness it?"

"Yes. They'll leave me here until my repositories drain away to nothing first, just to be sure. It's over."

Tarrik reached through the bars, careful not to touch them, and placed his hand on the cold stone floor. "Not yet."

He withdrew his hand, leaving behind the catalyst he had taken from the sorcerer he'd killed shortly after being summoned by Ren. To his surprise, she didn't immediately seize the crystal. Instead she stared at it, long and hard.

"Take it," he said.

She reached out, but at the last moment snatched her hand back.

"Take it," he repeated. "Why do you hesitate?"

"Because I'm afraid."

"You've lasted this long. You've killed two of the Nine that I know of. Free yourself, and fight them!"

"Why did you come?" she said.

Because you came for me.

"I don't know."

Ren appraised him, her eyes narrowing. Then she nodded. "That'll have to do."

She grasped the catalyst and was consumed by a blinding iridescence.

Tarrik shielded his eyes until the light dimmed and he could look at her. Ren stood and met his gaze, a slight smile on her lips. She touched three of the steel bars with a finger. Each one turned a reddish brown, then crumbled into a pile of rust. The fine powder billowed around her feet, and she stepped through it.

Free.

She held out a hand to Tarrik. He stared at her palm for a heartbeat before ignoring it, grabbing his spear, and rising to his feet.

Shouts came from the other side of the locked and barricaded door at the end of the cellblock.

"I'm aware of them," said Ren in response to his unasked question. "Avert your eyes. I must get dressed."

Her clothes and their saddlebags were on a bench against the wall. The bags had been emptied, their contents examined. Her sword was there as well, still sheathed. His eyes alighted on a table covered with a linen cloth that held various sharp implements. A few were smeared with blood—Ren's, he presumed.

"Why did they leave your sword here?" asked Tarrik. Such carelessness seemed odd for the Cabalists.

"They were trying to torture its secret from me and needed it close."

Tarrik grunted. "There might be more than a few sorcerers out there,"

"It doesn't matter. Unless I'm incapacitated, they're no match for me." Ren frowned at him and said again, "Turn your back, please."

Tarrik did so, smiling at her display of modesty when he'd already seen all there was to see. There was a rustle of cloth, and buckles clinked as Ren dressed herself.

"You can turn around now," she said.

She was wearing her usual charcoal outfit, though it was wrinkled. Her face was wan and drawn, and one hand clutched the bench in support. The other held the waterskin.

Tarrik saw that her sword was once again strapped to her back. He frowned. "Your sword . . . will you not need to use it?"

Ren shook her head. "I am too weak."

She had lied to him. Again.

"You said you had power."

"I do. Nothing these fools would recognize. But I need to get to the roof, and quickly. Gather our gear—we might need it. And there are a few things there I'd hate to lose."

Tarrik shoved everything back into the saddlebags, including Ren's journal and personal effects. He shouldered both. "We're flying out of here?"

"Soon, yes. First I have to replenish myself."

She took a step toward the door, staggered, and fell to her hands and knees. Tarrik rushed to her, pulled her upright by her arm, and felt her quake beneath his touch. She clung to him, the catalyst still clutched in one hand, and he supported her entire weight. It seemed they might not escape after all.

"I'm afraid you'll have to carry me," she said, her voice wavering.

Tarrik shifted his spear to his other shoulder and scooped her up. He could feel warm dampness leaking through her clothes—blood. She stank of it, and sweat and grime. Ren seemed so slight in his arms. So tragically beautiful, both helpless and strong, a jewel men would die to possess. But Tarrik knew she would never let herself become another's possession.

The noises from behind the locked door grew louder. A deep voice shouted a cant, and the door shuddered under the impact of something heavy.

Despite her weakened condition, Ren snorted softly. "They haven't sent their best sorcerers. Just whoever was close, I guess. They'll be in here soon, though. It's best if we get going."

"To the roof?"

"Yes. If you please, Tarrik."

"The door is blocked and locked," he pointed out.

"I'll take care of it."

Tarrik strode toward the door, still carrying Ren, and stopped when she squeezed his arm. "Close enough," she said.

She whispered cants, haltingly at first, then with more confidence. Tarrik sensed the same lack of dawn- and dusk-tide power to her sorcery as on previous occasions. And then her voice boomed with sorcerous amplification. A light appeared between them and the door, faint and rosy. A hum filled the air, vibrating deep in Tarrik's bones.

The sorcerous light waxed, blasting the room with illumination. Tarrik had to close his eyes and turn his head from the glare. After a brief moment it lessened, and he opened them again. The room was afire with tiny motes that sparkled and danced in heated currents. Dust, he realized.

She had set the very air aflame.

The crates and barrels he'd stacked against the door smoked and blackened. The heads of the doornails glowed orange, and the iron bands creaked with sudden expansion as Ren's sorcery scorched metal. It became difficult to breathe in the hot air.

"You want to chain me?" said Ren. "I will teach you about power." She chanted a phrase: "*Kelbrul-azur.*"

A heartbeat passed. Then a spherical ward encased Tarrik and Ren in a golden glare.

Blinding lines of light incised the air, straight and precise, as blistering and destructive as white-hot steel. The barrels and crates exploded into splinters that swirled in a vortex and burned to ash. Iron cracked, and the door twisted and split.

On the other side, two sorcerers shouted cants into the crackling thunder. Behind them, soldiers cried out in terror and raised their arms against the fiery onslaught.

Stone crumbled and blew in jagged chunks across the sorcerers' arcane shields and hammered into the soldiers' bodies. Ren's blinding lines followed, hissing through dust and debris, dissecting wards and flesh, destroying everything in their path. The sorcerers fell to the stone floor, sodden with their own blood.

Ren continued her cants, and the brilliant lines sawed and severed. Dead and wounded soldiers lay in ragged heaps, screeching and wailing. Sorcery silenced their despair.

"*Milhil ewa-seng,*" gasped Ren, letting forth a strange cackle.

Tarrik tore his eyes from the destruction to look at her. Her teeth were bared and streaked with crimson. A cough racked her frame, and she turned and spat a stream of blood onto the ash-strewn floor. She wiped a trembling hand across her mouth. "We must hurry. Go now, and do not stop."

Tarrik carried Ren through the blasted and smoking remains of those who had come against her. Golden light followed the duo, illuminating their path. He couldn't see where the glow came from.

He ascended the steps, shoulders itching, expecting sorcery and steel at any moment. Shouts came from above them, and he hesitated.

"Keep moving," Ren urged. "Run, Tarrik!"

And so he did. His legs took the steps three at a time, and they barreled into a hallway full of surprised soldiers and talisman-clutching sorcerers.

Ren's hand tightened on his arm, fingers and nails digging into his skin. She spoke a cant, and more of her golden lines appeared. Straight and true, they sliced through steel and leather, muscle and bone. Crimson whipped across the walls. Human meat collapsed into writhing heaps, bawling and shrieking or forever silent. Fat rendered and burst into smoky flame.

Tarrik spoke his own cant, drawing on his dark-tide power, and sent out shadow tendrils. The scrying found a way up: a long spiral staircase.

He turned from the carnage and raced along another hallway. Something hammered into him, and he lurched into the wall. Unearthly lights battered the shield around them, thrashing and smoking, scraping sparks.

"Keep going!" screamed Ren.

Tarrik regained his footing and heard sorcerous cants from behind. Coruscating fire enveloped them, blinding him. He stumbled again, and Ren cried out at the jolt to her injured flesh.

Scorching heat flayed across Tarrik's back. Ren's shield was weakening. He pushed forward, struggling to see, blinking furiously. Where were the stairs? Ahead . . . somewhere.

He forced himself to move, though blinding lights cascaded around him, burning his eyes.

Blood and fire, where are those stairs?

There.

He darted through a wide opening, and the assault on them lessened. Ren's heaving breaths sounded loudly in his ears.

He glanced up, saw the wide stone stairs winding around the inside of a massive cylinder, only a thin iron balustrade between them and the edge. He searched for the darkest patch in the gloom above.

"What are you doing?" said Ren.

"Trust me," he replied, and poured himself into the darkness.

Their essence dissolved and re-formed a hundred yards up the staircase. Ren coughed and spat again, splashing red across the stone.

Tarrik blinked away sweat and grimaced at the tiredness in his muscles. The stairs were greased with dingy light. The two stood just to the side of a column, in its shadow.

Ren's hand pulled at his arm. "Keep moving, you lummox."

Tarrik leaped up the stairs. A fleeting glance behind showed soldiers pouring through a doorway, along with several unarmed men and women. Cabal sorcerers.

"They are coming," he gasped, trying to increase his pace without tripping on the unfamiliarly spaced steps. He managed a half jog, which drew gasps of pain from Ren. He glanced at her and saw that her red-rimmed eyes were half-lidded.

They heard shouted cants from below. Glittering lights soared up the staircase toward them, their radiance painting the walls and stairs with a sapphire glow.

Ren bared her teeth and responded. Her cants emerged as a sparkling fury, plummeting toward their foes with a wailing screech, weaving curved trails before detonating with thunderous cracks.

The stone trembled under Tarrik's feet. He ran on, casting a frantic glance downward. The soldiers and sorcerers were rent into pieces by Ren's shimmering lights. The air seemed to shriek under the assault. Blood slicked the stairs, and the survivors slipped and skidded.

Tumultuous roars sounded as Ren's eldritch sorcery battered their pursuers. Hammer after hammer. Crack after crack. Stone chipped and shattered. Stairs broke and crumbled, graven with white and golden emanations, barring the way to those who pursued them. Tarrik tightened his grip on Ren and ran. She had given them a chance.

Up and up he raced, his booted feet slapping stone until his lungs and throat burned. No sorcery followed their wild dash. All he could hear of the sorcerers and soldiers below was the wailing of the injured. Ren's head lolled against him, her eyes closed, mouth slightly open. She looked haggard, her skin ashen and streaked with dust.

He looked up and saw an opening high above, and a light. The golden light of the sun.

"I see the sun," he said, his voice croaking in his dry throat.

Ren groaned and opened her eyes. She blinked, then moaned. "Hurry," she said in the barest whisper.

Tarrik urged his burning muscles forward. Step by aching step he ascended, and eventually the sunlit doorway appeared before him. He lurched through it and felt heat and light envelop him.

Ren panted and shuddered in his arms. "Put me down," she gasped.

Tarrik lowered her to the stone, and she immediately pushed away from him, staggering a few steps into the bright light. Blood and dust streaked her back.

Ren sobbed. She turned to face Tarrik, then fell to her knees. Tears rolled down her cheeks. "Thank you," she said. "I will not forget."

"We still have to get out of here," he reminded her. "And in your condition, that's unlikely."

She was too weak, too wounded. The sorceries she'd used to get them here had to have drained her. And they needed water . . .

"Water!" Tarrik spat the word. Ren couldn't create her platform without it. In the commotion, he'd forgotten.

"I have some," she said, and held up the waterskin she'd brought from the cellblock. She placed it carefully on the ground next to her, then unbuckled her sword and set that down too. "But first, I need to replenish myself."

Tarrik glanced at the yellow sun high in the sky. "It's too late for the dawn-tide and too early for the dusk. We're stuck here until evening. Do you have enough power to see off hours of assault from the Cabalists?"

"That will not be necessary."

Ren lay on her back and stretched out her arms and legs until she was sprawled on the roof of the tower.

She is insane.

Tarrik licked his lips and decided he'd made a mistake. He should have left her to rot. His blood boiled, and anger surged through him—at himself most of all. That was what this world did to you. It took your hardness, honed over years and orders ascended, and diminished you. Contian had softened him, as had Jaquel. And now Ren was doing the same.

He needed a drink.

Ren lay unmoving, bathing in the sun's light. For a dozen heartbeats nothing happened; then she began to glow.

Tarrik backed up a step and shook his head, not believing his eyes. He found himself struggling for breath.

Ren moaned, then cried out. Her hands curled into claws, fingernails scraping across stone. Golden waves rolled over her, painting her clothes and face—an eldritch power Tarrik knew nothing of. She wore a rapturous smile.

Blood and fire, she is exquisite.

He was instantly gripped with horror. Not again. He couldn't care for another human. But here he was, bound not by Ren's sorcery, but by his own emotions and loyalty. He couldn't look away.

For a dozen heartbeats the light traversed Ren's form. Tarrik dared not approach to see if she was all right. Then the light scattered and disappeared, leaving only a few yellow motes that twinkled into nothing. Ren lay there, her chest heaving, the smile still plastered on her face. Her skin streamed sweat, and there were scarlet patches on the stone where she'd smeared her own blood.

She cracked an eye open, and her expression changed to one of relief. She sat up and dusted her hands, then stood. She seemed surprisingly strong for someone who had moments ago been close to death.

Tarrik frowned. Sheelahn had called Ren "Sun-Child." Was this the power that Indriol thought she had drawn on—something different from the dawn- and dusk-tides? He recalled the scent that had come off her when she had created her disc—of sunlight. And what Ren had said of herself: *I'm something different.*

For a few moments he stood, confused, then found his voice. "What are you? Where does your power come from?"

"There is more power than just the dawn-, dusk-, and dark-tides, Tarrik. There is the sun. All other tides have their roots in the sun—and the stars."

"Not the dark-tide."

"Yes. Even the dark-tide. It is misnamed." She glanced toward the staircase. "We don't have time to discuss such affairs now. I am restored. I will not punish the Cabalists, though they deserve it and more. I will be done with them soon, one way or another."

Ren had succeeded where all others had failed, Tarrik thought. She had learned the secret of containing the sun's power. With its potency she might be greater than any other sorcerer before her. It was no wonder she'd been able to kill Lischen and Indriol. And she would hand that knowledge over to Samal when he was free. Except her own actions suggested she was standing up to the Nine. More than suggested . . . after all, she'd killed two of them already. And if the Nine were stopped, then Samal would remain imprisoned.

Ren gazed at him, her sheathed sword held casually in both hands. "You know my secret now. You have seen it with your own eyes. I've been able to keep it from the Nine, my cleansing. I should kill you."

"Then do it."

She wouldn't kill him. He knew it in his bones. And he didn't want her to. She needed him. She had come to save him, and he'd done the same for her.

He could send himself back to the abyssal realms now. But would she let him go—or try to stop him?

He wanted to hate her for what she'd done to him. He wanted to have her start the process of return . . . but something held him back. There were too many inconsistencies, too many questions. Was Ren trying to save the rest of humankind—and perhaps also much of demonkind?

She shook her head. "I still need you. I'll ask one more thing of you: come with me, and I'll tell you all I can. Then you can decide whether to stay or return to your exile. Do you agree?"

"Yes," said Tarrik, and hoped he wouldn't regret his decision.

Chapter Twenty-Two

They passed a few hours of flight with hardly a word said between them. Ren's face was drawn and her movements jerky—no doubt a side effect of the physical and mental torture she'd endured.

A storm loomed ahead: churning clouds shot through with forked tongues of lightning. Thunder blasted them as they skirted its edge, blustery wind whipping at their clothes and hair. Just when Tarrik was about to suggest they seek cover, he felt his stomach rise as the disc descended.

Ren landed them at the bottom of a cliff, the ground shrouded in the deep sable of night. Only a few scraggly grasses and stunted bushes grew in the cliff's shelter, and there was no fresh water that Tarrik could see or hear. Only a stagnant pond with yellow edges was nearby, filled with green scum.

"I need to rest," said Ren quietly.

"Aren't we supposed to be having a discussion?"

She passed a trembling hand across her brow. "Yes. When I wake. Please, bear with me. I fear I will collapse if I stay awake any longer."

She stumbled to where Tarrik had dropped their gear and, after a few moments of fumbling, came up with a hooded lantern and a curious object she struck to light it. The glow caught something white moving toward them.

Tarrik hissed and brandished his spear. "Watch out!"

He glimpsed an emaciated figure with long limbs and white eyes. The being gave a faint moan, then scurried into the darkness. Tarrik peered after it. A dead-eye. And where there was one, there was usually a pack, and in rarer cases a tribe. He hoped it wouldn't return with others.

"You're on guard for the rest of the night," said Ren. "I'm unable to set wards yet. You can doze during daylight tomorrow."

Tarrik grunted. She was still giving him orders. But he had agreed to hear her out. "Hurry up and get some sleep. I want to return to my realm as soon as possible."

"You're so sure you will return?"

Tarrik snorted. He'd learned that nothing was certain. "Sleep. I'll keep an eye out."

And continue to work on absorbing Ananias's essence.

Tarrik woke in a shaking horror, as if he'd been caught with his mind wandering in the middle of a hunt to realize his prey had turned upon him and he was no longer the hunter, but the hunted. The makeshift campsite reeled around Tarrik, and everything looked out of place.

Where was he? What was he doing here?

He sat up and drew in a ragged breath. He'd fallen asleep in his exhaustion.

On the other side of their saddlebags, Ren lay on her blanket, one-half twisted around her body as if she'd writhed in her sleep. Her eyes were closed, stray locks of hair she hadn't braided falling across her face.

She groaned and whimpered. Her breath came in short, sharp gasps. There was a red stain on her blanket near her mouth, and Tarrik saw she'd worried her knuckle again in her sleep. Her lips moved, speaking words so softly he couldn't quite catch them, but they had the ring of Skanuric.

Tarrik considered moving to her, wrapping her finger so she did no more damage to it tonight. But he stopped himself before he was half out of his own blanket. Ren would not want him to touch her without permission. She had made that abundantly clear.

He settled back and tried to calm his breathing, but just then she cried out in her sleep. Ren thrashed so violently that she woke herself. She scrambled from her blanket and stood staring into the night, a savage snarl on her face, breathing heavily. She saw Tarrik, on his feet too now, spear in hand, and her expression changed to one of relief before she schooled it into blankness.

She wiped sweat from her face and glanced at the lantern Tarrik had left alight beside her makeshift bed. "I take it no dead-eyes have attacked?"

"No. You never seem to sleep well," he added.

She looked around again, then sat on her blanket cross-legged, rubbed both palms into her eyes, and yawned. "I suppose now is as good a time as any to explain." She looked Tarrik in the eye. "I would like you to serve me willingly."

This again. "I will serve no one unless forced to."

"You served Contian."

"Do not speak of him! You don't have the right!"

"He was my father! Though I barely saw him. You knew him far better than I did . . . than I ever will!" Her hands clenched into fists, and she pounded one against her knee with an audible smack. Then she cleared her throat. "Please . . . tell me about him."

Her reaction rocked Tarrik back on his heels. He narrowed his eyes and considered her for a moment.

He had to admit to himself that Ren touched him. This woman who was so powerful herself but still longed to know about the father she looked up to. Tarrik trembled, his throat tight, as he remembered his own child who'd died young, whom he'd never gotten the chance to know.

Contian—the only human Tarrik had ever trusted apart from Jaquel. Even Delfina, Contian's wife, had looked upon Tarrik as an abomination, and he had been the cause of grief between the two of them. Perhaps that was where he should start.

He spoke slowly, softly. "I was with Contian when he rescued the woman who would become his first apprentice and later his wife."

"Delfina? My mother."

"Yes."

"Tell me."

Memories flooded back to Tarrik. He did his best to describe them. "We were out 'treasure hunting,' as Contian liked to call it—walking over ancient battlefields on the off chance looters had missed sorcerous artifacts. Contian liked to smoke his pipe and ponder history and how it made corpses of all men." Tarrik laughed. "That pipe! Its smoke brought more than a few dead-eyes to us, but he never seemed to care. An entire tribe of the creatures wasn't enough to trouble him.

"Anyhow, one night we heard the baying of a pack of ghouls that had cornered a young woman. She was out gathering a certain tiny fungus that glows in moonlight. Exhausted from fleeing the creatures, she had unwittingly scrambled down a dead-end gully. Contian rained fire down upon them, but as usual he was overzealous, and the conflagration was in danger of burning the girl to charcoal too. So he went down there to save her. He walked right into the inferno, atop rock glowing orange from the heat, his wards surrounding him, and came out cradling a black-haired girl in his arms. As I recall, she wasn't very appreciative when she woke. Called him an idiot and a fool."

Ren had stood while he spoke and closed the distance between them. She stopped an arm's length from him. "My mother told me that story. She said Contian was always overenthusiastic with his cants. That sorcery was continually a wonder for him."

"Isn't it for you?" Tarrik asked. "Such power you wield. Most humans would be jealous."

Ren folded her arms around her waist and looked away. "What has that power brought me? Nothing but torment and misery. I would gladly be rid of it, but I cannot. Not when there's one last thing for me to do."

"Destroy the Nine and keep Samal imprisoned?" Tarrik said. He'd figured out that much at least. The demon lord's release would plunge this world into nightmare. But wasn't that humans' lot? To know misery and disappointment. To live with the knowledge that no matter what the perversity or injury, whatever indignity or horror, there was nothing else. They were what they were and could not evolve, as demons did.

But although he couldn't care less about the humans, he knew freeing Samal was a mistake. One that the world would come to regret.

Ren looked at him in surprise. "Yes. How did you know?"

"Give me some credit. You have already killed Lischen and Indriol. My guess is more of the Nine are on your list when we reach Samal's prison. Do you have a chance of succeeding?"

Ren hesitated. "I think so. A slim one. The consequences, though, would be dire."

"Worse than Samal entering this world again?"

She gave him a wan smile. "No. You are right, Tarrik. What is the weight of a few deaths when so many could be prevented? It would be foolish of me not to try. I know, more than anyone, how malevolent Samal is. I used to fight against him and Nysrog, as you know, until I came to Samal's attention, and he added me to his disciples. I was bound to him as human sorcerers do with demons. I was tormented, tortured, broken, and then reassembled into a sorcerer whose only purpose was to serve Samal. Once I was taken, I was forever changed. I did such things that would give you nightmares, and I enjoyed them. I was his creature, body and soul. There is no coming back from what I've done. Even after I inadvertently broke his bindings upon me, I could not return.

"Samal must remain imprisoned. The world cannot afford to let him walk free again with the Nine behind him. I cannot let that happen. I *will* not. Will you help me? I find I require an ally when I thought

I had hardened myself not to need anyone. I have been alone for so long, against impossible odds and almost certain death, that I forget what it's like to be otherwise."

Had she forgotten what she'd done to him, Tarrik wondered. Or did she view it as insignificant? Or necessary?

"Why should I help you, sorcerer, demon slaver?"

Ren ignored his question. Instead, she looked away and toyed with one of the silver buttons on her shirt. "Delfina told me of Jaquel."

Tarrik froze, his heart hammering in his chest, his throat tight.

Ren continued as if she hadn't noticed his distress. "At first I was incredulous. A demon and a human in love—who would credit such a happening? With what I knew of demonkind at the time, it seemed . . . impossible. But I have to admit, now that I know you, I have seen another side to the higher-order demons. Or to you at least."

Tarrik found words tumbling from his throat. "Jaquel was a wonder among humans. Fierce. Intelligent. Caring. To Contian, Delfina was the finest treasure he found on his wanderings. For me, that treasure was Jaquel."

Ren reached for his hand but withdrew before touching him. "I can see the qualities Jaquel would admire in you, demon though you are. You are formidable and fearsome and sometimes recklessly brave. You have what many demons, even many humans, lack: a sense of honor."

Tarrik shook his head. "I only do what I have to, to survive."

"When many others would have given up. Is that not a virtue? I know you are capable of loyalty, and of love too. Myself, I have no time for such things. There's always a price, Tarrik. Whatever you want to achieve, it is never without a cost. Some things are bigger than any individual, and they're worth dying for. It is likely I will be dead in the next few days. But I will gladly give my life to keep Samal interned." Ren looked Tarrik in the eyes again. "Will you help me willingly, without being bound or compelled?"

Ren obviously thought spending her life in an attempt to keep Samal imprisoned was worthwhile. The question was, should Tarrik risk his own?

He thought of the pain and misery he'd experienced when the demon lords had banished him to Shimrax, the Guttering Wastes. Remembered the agony of the sorcerous brand seared into his skin, marking him an exile. He had been abused and mistreated, but it wasn't in his nature to wish subjugation, slavery, and a true death on the higher-order demons who had punished him. If he did help Ren, he wouldn't only be helping to save humankind; for if Samal was to turn his gaze toward the abyssal realms, then Tarrik might just be saving demonkind too. Something larger than himself and his honor was at stake now.

He looked at Ren. Like Tarrik, she had been a slave. She'd been a slave for decades. Until one day she'd learned to harness the sun's power, and it had cleansed her. She was free of Samal's taint.

A bond had grown between them—that much was true. But he was also unbound now. Free. He could leave this horrid world and its wretched humans forever.

He laughed softly. He couldn't walk away. The Nine had to be stopped. Samal must remain imprisoned. And if Ren required his help to achieve those things, so be it.

And perhaps there was the slimmest chance of redemption for Tarrik. It was only with valorous, altruistic deeds that a demon could be cleansed of the taint of exile. But here, on this wretched human world, who would know or care?

Days of flying followed, north and east into the Wastes. Just as on their previous flights, they traveled by night and rested by day. As the miles passed, Tarrik fell into a stupor. How Ren could handle their boring trip while she controlled her potent sorcery was beyond him. She was stronger than he had given her credit for. He'd never seen Contian endure such a display of power combined with single-minded focus.

The Wastes consisted of dry earth and rocks, some sand, and more rocks. As they left Ruruc far behind, the air became thinner and colder, and far to the north he could just make out a white band on the horizon. Snow. Tarrik shuddered with dread. Water so cold it had frozen solid. Worse than the hated rain of this world. If he found himself in a frigid, northern, snow-blasted land, he just might lose all courage and try to kill Ren and hope she put him out of his misery.

Tarrik was left to mostly sit behind her and think. Now that he was looking for it, Tarrik could tell when Ren replenished herself using the sun's power. No wonder he hadn't sensed her using the dawn- or dusk-tides when creating and flying her platforms. The very idea of what Ren had accomplished was something he had trouble grasping. And the fact of it stunned him. Tarrik's knowledge of the dawn- and dusk-tides was minimal, and he couldn't imagine just what was possible using the sun's power.

He was quieter than normal, which led to Ren stating he had reverted to an even more lizardlike manner. His mind was so absorbed with the ramifications of what he'd witnessed that he forgot to work on absorbing more of Ananias's essence. And when he tried, his thoughts were hard to corral. Concentrating was almost impossible.

On the fourth day of their journey, as dawn broke slowly, Tarrik saw in the distance an earthen pyramid rising from the rocky landscape. Samal's tomb. He quashed the nauseous feeling that accompanied the descent of the disc and wrapped his arms around himself against the chill.

As they moved closer, he saw that the pyramid stood on a square base with stunted grayish-green bushes upon its slopes and a thicket of what looked like white branches spread around its perimeter. Haphazard mounds of rocks were piled around the pyramid, smaller ones often surrounding a larger heap, and a few of the largest stacks standing alone. On the south side, rocks had been stacked to form two walls that led like a promenade to a squat, square tower that must be the tomb's entrance. On the northern side of the pyramid were fallen walls and roofless buildings. Someone had tried to build a permanent settlement there at some stage, and it had failed.

On the western side, which stood in shade, there were many more signs of activity: rows of tents, their pegs pounded into the hard earth; half a dozen pavilions flying pennants; baggage and provision wagons standing in long trains. The giant lizards that pulled the wagons were foraging on hardy plants farther to the south of the pyramid. Smoke from scores of cooking fires hazed the air, and standards of a dozen colors and symbols fluttered limply in the faint breeze. Forces loyal to the Nine had been here for quite some time, surmised Tarrik.

His gaze returned to the earthen pyramid. Within lay Samal Rakshazza, the Adversary—one of the most powerful demon lords, a manipulator and deceiver. His had been the mind behind Nysrog's attempted devastation of this world, the real danger the humans remained unaware of. When Samal was freed from his prison, the denizens of Wiraya would know suffering such as they had never before experienced.

Ren's platform descended from its lofty heights, and more details came into view. Men and women moved about the encampment, their breath steaming in the frigid morning air. What few horses and oxen there were stamped and complained in the frosty gloom. Campfires dotted around the area sent thin plumes of smoke into the breezeless sky.

Close to the passageway leading to the entrance to the tomb stood a massive wain, its frame painted garish reds and oranges. The great bed of the vehicle held a score of cattle and horses: some lying down, obviously distraught; others hanging their heads over the low sides of the wain, hooves clashing against the timbers in an effort to escape. Tarrik couldn't determine a use for the animals other than food.

The white branches stacked around the base of the pyramid turned out to be bones, bleached by the sun. Most were too big to be human, and Tarrik had the uneasy feeling that they were demon bones. Perhaps this was the place where Samal had made his last stand. Tarrik wouldn't put it past him to have sacrificed all the demons under him to delay the inevitable.

Ren landed the disc on a bare patch of earth midway between two pavilions. The queues of humans waiting to collect their morning rations gawked at the arrival.

Ren spoke a cant, and her unearthly power tendrils dissipated. "Well," she said, "this is it." Her eyes were bloodshot, and stray hairs stuck out from her usually tight braid.

Tarrik gathered their bags and his spear, stepped down, and hurried across the steaming, sizzling earth around the disc. Ren followed, crossing the heated ground slowly, her eyes hooded and wary, glancing all around.

Puck Moonan emerged from one of the pavilions, trailed by his young apprentice. The sorcerer hadn't changed since Tarrik had seen him last; he was still wearing the same stained and torn garments, and even from a distance his goatlike reek was evident.

Puck stopped, leaning on his orichalcum staff topped with the old man's head, and glared at Ren. His apprentice stood behind him and to one side, her greenish skin looking washed out in the gray light of dawn. She kept glancing at Ren, then away, no doubt remembering how her superior could have blasted her out of existence but had stayed her hand. Tarrik wouldn't have offered such a mercy, given she'd attacked them without provocation.

"Ignore them," Ren told him and walked away from the sorcerers toward the second pavilion.

Tarrik glanced at the piles of bones that surrounded the massive tomb. There were no grasses, lichens, or desert-hardy plants growing around them. The first signs of life were the patches of yellow grass a hundred yards away, which could have sprouted months or years ago.

"I'm afraid they're mostly demon bones," Ren said. "Though there are plenty of human bones there as well. For centuries, thieves have been drawn to this place by rumors of riches within the tomb. They never make it past the perimeter."

"Sorcery?"

She nodded. "To keep out those that don't die getting here. Most die out in the Wastes, at the mercy of creatures as old as time and as vicious as any created."

Four fully armored guards stood at the entrance to the second pavilion, a sword in each hand, their tips resting on the ground. They turned their helmeted heads to regard Ren and Tarrik, and he was shocked to see their eyes were blank orichalcum orbs. The orange metal was also chased into their armor and swords.

"Tarrik!" snapped Ren, and he hurried after her.

The pavilion was dark inside, and Tarrik squinted until his eyes adjusted. High poles supported the roof, which was made of tanned leather with sections of crimson and scarlet tassels. The floor was covered with lush carpets upon which sat chairs and lounges and tables of all sizes. The central pole, as thick as a tree, was carved to resemble twining vines with budding flowers. Light filtered down through open flaps in the roof, illuminating the center of the pavilion and leaving the sides in shadow.

A black-skinned woman leaned against a sturdy table laden with food. She possibly had Orgol blood in her veins, Tarrik thought, considering her skin color, height, and musculature. Her spiked hair was a slightly browner shade of black and cut short. The scent of goat emanating from her wasn't as powerful as Puck's but had a sharp, sour tinge.

She turned to appraise Ren with a wry smile, then used the hand that wasn't holding a goblet to tap her opposite shoulder perfunctorily. "Samal will rise," she said.

It seemed not all of the Nine were fervent in their worship of Samal. Interesting.

Ren returned the woman's smile. "Praise Samal, Lord of Life."

"Now that that's over," said the woman, "I'm sure you're dying for something to eat and drink. Who's the new bodyguard?" She looked Tarrik up and down with a mischievous smile.

"Just someone I picked up in Ivrian. He's performed adequately so far." Ren glanced at Tarrik. "Tarrik, this is Jawo-linger. She is one of the Nine. And . . . a friend."

Jawo-linger continued to eye Tarrik and gestured to the table of food. "I'm sure you're famished as well. Go ahead and eat. Serenity and I have a lot to catch up on. Marren hasn't arrived yet, in case you weren't aware. I'm looking forward to chatting with him as well, as long as his half-naked servants aren't anywhere in sight."

She poured red wine into another goblet and held it out to Ren, who took it with murmured thanks.

Tarrik dumped their saddlebags and his spear next to a long couch and moved to the table. There were a few plates of cured animal flesh and a couple of bottles of spirits along with the wine, so he was satisfied he wouldn't remain hungry for long. As he piled a plate with meat, Ren and Jawo-linger spoke in low tones.

"The Tainted Cabalists have been preparing the way, and the others of the Nine are trickling in," said Jawo-linger. "They don't have the same method of transport you have—I still can't figure out how you do it—but they'll all be here on time."

"That's good," Ren replied. "With two of us dead, it will be touch and go, even with the artifacts I've procured to assist us. We'll be walking a fine line, using all of our power. There's no room for error."

Jawo-linger seemed to bounce on her toes, a smile on her face. "Did you manage to procure one for me?"

"Yes. I'll hand it over to you soon, once I've tested it further."

Jawo's eyes had a faraway look as she said, "After all this time. We're so close." Her expression swiftly changed to one of consternation. "But someone seeks to hinder us. Do you have any information about what happened to Lischen and Indriol?"

Ren shook her head. "You're more sensitive to our shared bond than I am. What did you sense?"

Tarrik shoved a thick slice of meat into his mouth, pretending not to be interested. The flesh was salty and chewy and flavored with unfamiliar herbs.

If the other sorcerers discovered that Ren was responsible for killing two of their Nine, her fate would be sealed.

"Each underwent a sorcerous battle before their bond was shattered," Jawo-linger said. "That's all I could sense. I fear the worst—that they were targeted by the same murderer and there's a plot afoot to weaken us. My coin is on the Cabal's enemies on the eastern continent—perhaps the Order of the Blazing Sun. They're on the decline, but it wouldn't surprise me if they were determined to strike a blow before their power wanes." She sighed and shook her head. "But it could be any number of organizations, really. Until we know more about how Lischen and Indriol died, I can only speculate."

She laughed briefly. "I initially thought it could be one of us, but everyone's location is accounted for. No one was near Lischen and Indriol when they were slain. Although, as usual, I cannot account for you."

Ren shrugged. "My bond to Samal and the Nine has always been inconsistent—you know this. Besides, Lischen and Indriol were much more powerful than I. Especially Indriol. If I'd moved against him, I'd be the one missing from this gathering."

Jawo-linger nodded. "I know. But the others would like to blame you if they could. I fear their dislike blinds them."

"Who have you sent to investigate the deaths? We can't spare many sorcerers, surely, not this close to realizing our goal?"

"My apprentice, Rokkvi, along with Moushumi's man. And that brings me to another subject. When are you taking on an apprentice? We need to increase our numbers and pass on our knowledge. If what I fear about Lischen and Indriol is true, all the more reason to strengthen ourselves and destroy our enemies. And there are many of those who'd happily see us all dead."

"I have someone in mind," said Ren. "But she's young."

"Really? Who?"

"No one you know. Have Rokkvi and Ursael reported anything of note?"

"Only that Ekthras found a valuable artifact among Indriol's possessions. A silver bull that Indriol must have been keeping secret from us. Ekthras claims it is powerful and will assist with our final cants."

Ren sipped her wine. "We must wait to see if Rokkvi and Ursael find out anything else. For now, my focus is on the task ahead of us. The Cabalists claim to be helping us, but there is an internal faction that would be happy to see us fail and leave Samal interned forever."

"I haven't heard any whispers that they'll do anything to disrupt proceedings," said Jawo-linger. "They fear our power, the worms, but they also covet it. We should be on our guard."

"When am I not?"

"Then I don't need to tell you to be wary of Ekthras. He claims to be able to summon a score of demons at once, with proper preparation," said Jawo-linger.

"That would require a great deal of power. But most would be uncontrollable—you know that. A higher-order demon could command them, if they were willing," said Ren dryly.

"I gather that's something he's working on."

Ren drained her goblet and returned it to the table, then placed a hand on Jawo-linger's shoulder. "I need to rest before the final surge. Until then, I'll help with the lesser wards and traps as best I can."

"Don't tire yourself out. With our numbers diminished, we'll all need to contribute more to break Samal's bonds."

"Don't worry. My artifacts will protect us and augment the final cants. We're so close. It will all be over soon."

"Yes. And it will be glorious! Thank you, Serenity, for everything. I've had a tent set up for you and assigned you a servant. She's old and doesn't talk much. I thought you'd like her."

Ren thanked Jawo-linger as well, then turned to Tarrik and jerked her head toward the exit. He shoved a final handful of meat into his mouth and dropped his plate onto a side table, then gathered their gear. On the way out, he grabbed a bottle of spirits.

Outside, they had to stop to let a train of laden mules trudge past. Tarrik found his gaze again drawn to the pyramid as he swallowed the meat and took a swig. The liquid was bright orange and tasted strange but had the familiar burn and accompanying numbness.

Ren looked sidelong at him. "How are you enjoying the salted rat?"

Rat? He'd eaten worse, and would again. "Meat is meat."

"I can't argue with that." She looked disappointed he hadn't reacted differently.

Tarrik swallowed another mouthful of vermin, then noticed Ren was holding out her hand for the bottle.

She took a sip. "Urgh. Jawo has no taste. This is made from carrots."

Tarrik shrugged. It didn't matter what the spirits were made from, as long as drinking the liquor dulled his emotions. He shifted their saddlebags on his shoulder. The mule train was almost past.

"You're quieter than usual," said Ren.

"In a few days I might be dead. Or bound again. Or subsumed into Samal if he decides to take my essence to make himself stronger."

Tarrik's felt his knees weaken and sneered at his own softness. His hand tightened around his spear, and he clenched his teeth. What would he do when the demon lord fixed his cruel gaze upon him? Would he bend his knee, overshadowed by Samal's power? Or would he try to flee, having no desire to be chained to another master? His thoughts briefly touched on the hard shell around Ananias's essence for reassurance. If he could find a way to take it into himself, his powers would multiply. The absorption might be his only chance for survival.

"I won't let that happen," Ren said.

You will have no choice. "Samal will be weak after his long imprisonment. He'll need nourishment. You were bound to him, Ren; if he gets so much as a toehold in this world, you will have to obey whatever he demands of you."

She waved a hand in dismissal and skirted behind the last mule in the train. He was distracted by the sway of her hips as he followed.

Ren stopped in front of a single-poled pavilion smaller than Jawo-linger's, its roof and walls made of thick canvas rather than leather. Two armored, orichalcum-eyed guards stood at the entrance, their hands on massive swords. Their helmeted heads turned to regard Ren and Tarrik, but after a heartbeat they returned to gazing straight ahead.

Ren pushed through the entrance flap, and Tarrik followed. Inside, the only illumination came from two lamps hanging from a rope suspended below the ceiling and a brazier filled with glowing coals that gave out meager heat. There wasn't much in the way of furniture or comforts: a few scattered chairs and stools on thin rugs, and a mound of blankets and cushions in a corner that looked like an unmade bed. A lone table held a few bottles and one crystal goblet.

A crone shambled out of the gloom. She had a balding pate with a few scraggly gray hairs and wore a shapeless robe of plain wool.

"Jawo-linger didn't tell me your name," said Ren.

The old woman stared at her with rheumy eyes. "Elisa," she croaked, and pulled a tattered rag from a pocket to wipe the table.

"Elisa, I'm expecting a chest to be delivered," Ren said. "Have them leave it here. It is not to be tampered with."

Elisa ceased her dusting, turned to Ren, and nodded once, then returned to wiping the table. She'd gone over the entire surface at least twice, Tarrik thought.

The armored guards were a concern. Who were they, and who controlled them? If their eyes had been replaced with orichalcum, sorcery was at work.

"Are the guards human?" he asked Ren in a low voice.

"Mostly. Ekthras created them. He calls them dreadlords—he was ever prone to vanity and poor taste. Each is a prisoner sentenced to hanging. They are made of flesh but altered by incantations." She glanced at Elisa. "Leave us, please."

The old woman ceased her dusting, bobbed her head in a nod, and hurried away.

Ren watched her until she exited the tent, then continued. "Ekthras was the first of the Nine that Samal created. Or should I say enslaved. Ekthras's intelligence and sorcerous knowledge are without peer; he is the greatest practitioner of the dawn- and dusk-tides ever to have lived."

"And what of the sun's power?"

Ren gave him a brief smile. "He knows not that secret. A good thing too, for Ekthras is consumed by inhuman desires. During the demon war he terrorized nations and butchered hundreds of thousands. He was feared and hated, and rightly so. He is a tyrant and in another age would no doubt have risen to command an empire built on despair—a dark lord unconstrained by morality, ruling by strength and terror. I suppose that's one thing Samal did for this world: he stopped the rise of such a madman. But Ekthras is not your concern. Keep your mind on the dreadlords. They are augmented to make them faster and stronger than normal. And if you should end up fighting one, don't let it hit you with its great sword."

"Do they have a weakness I can exploit?"

She thought for a moment. "Not really. Blood loss or decapitation are the only things that will stop them. But with their armor, neither is likely. Best to avoid them if you can. Now, we'd better get to work. Leave our saddlebags here, and come with me. Bring your bottle."

"Don't you need to rest?"

"I can't. This place stirs too many memories within me. The atrocities on both sides during the war were horrific. And then Samal . . . in my sleep I see the horrors still—the blood streaming in rivers, men and women burning, horses and cattle blasted to shredded meat and cracked bones. Babies screaming." She met his eyes. "People killed their children rather than let the demons capture them. Can you imagine?"

Tarrik could imagine. He'd seen those things too. Nothing he could say would lessen the nightmares.

Chapter Twenty-Three

He dropped their gear beside the mound of blankets and followed Ren back outside. As soon as they emerged into the daylight, Tarrik felt himself drawn to the pyramid. The immense effort required to raise such a thing staggered him. Had it been built by those who had imprisoned Samal or by his worshipers afterward?

Puck's apprentice stood a dozen paces away, glaring at them.

Ren shouted at her, "Begone! Return to your master."

The woman frowned, half turned as if to leave, before turning back to face them. She opened her mouth to speak, then closed it and departed at an almost run. She too left the stench of goat in her wake.

"She is mad," remarked Tarrik.

"Yes, but not from Samal's touch. She was already like that when Puck took her on as an apprentice. He is far gone himself and becoming more unstable." She shaded her eyes from the rising sun. "Come."

Ren walked quickly along a worn path that joined a wide road that spread out ahead of them all the way to the pyramid. Flat rocks in the dirt underfoot told Tarrik they trod the ruins of an ancient road. Once this place must have gleamed as brightly as a newly built city. Now it was almost forgotten by all except the Cabal and the Nine—and the thieves who tried to break into the tomb.

They passed a cook fire with three soldiers sitting around it, chatting in hushed tones. Flames flickered over a meager pile of sticks, as if they'd had difficulty scrounging for fuel. Oats bubbled in a pot, and bacon sizzled in a fry pan. Ren stopped for a portion of both, which the soldiers handed over without speaking. As she and Tarrik continued along the road toward the tomb, she spooned the food into her mouth as if it were her last meal.

They came to a line designated by red flags flying on long poles driven into the ground. More orichalcum-eyed guards were stationed in front of the markers, their backs to the pyramid, gazes fixed firmly ahead. Off to both sides stood two groups of men and women, each studying a large parchment and engaged in intense discussion. From the talismans at their belts, Tarrik reckoned they were sorcerers.

A wagon filled with wooden coffins was stationed close by. Two teamsters stood by it, smoking pipes and watching the sorcerers. A few dozen yards beyond them were several empty graves with piles of earth beside them and eleven metallic markers showing the already-filled plots.

"It's dangerous work," said Ren, nodding toward the wagon and makeshift cemetery. "The Cabal's ancient foes set traps around the pyramid, and these Cabal sorcerers are here to learn how to bypass them. Those who fail are injured, or worse. And all those who fall while undertaking such a momentous task are honored."

"I'd imagine unearthing a demon lord interned in an arcane prison would be hazardous. The corpses get a nice shiny gravestone," Tarrik said.

A woman sorcerer with short blonde hair shouted at her colleagues and stamped her foot. She waved a hand toward a flag, then pointed at the parchment and shook her head vigorously. A male sorcerer sat on the ground nearby, arms clasped around his knees, staring at the flags.

"There's trouble brewing between the Cabal and the Nine," said Ren. "They've never worked well together."

The closest group of sorcerers had stopped their deliberations to stare at Ren. With a glance at her companions, one woman approached.

She wore a red silk dress split at the sides to reveal black leggings, and her brown hair was cut short. She had high cheekbones and friendly eyes and a smile Tarrik had often seen on women who weren't afraid to kill.

Ten paces away she stopped and bowed to Ren, then spoke quickly. At first Tarrik couldn't understand what she said, so thick was her accent, but his ears quickly adjusted to the tumble of long vowels and strangled pronunciations.

"And then Rusina stuttered on a cant when a demon emerged, and her shield wasn't solid in time. It took three of us to get the foul creature off her, and by then we were too late. We're trying our best, but the dangers are tremendous. We're working day and night. We need more rest."

"I understand," said Ren. "But the Cabal sent you here to learn, to test yourselves. You can run back to Ruruc in disgrace, if you dare, or you can stretch your abilities now and return to acclaim. It's your choice. An opportunity like this only comes once in a lifetime."

"I . . . I mean, we . . ." The woman glanced over her shoulder at her companions. "We could really use some help with the more intricate calculations and cants."

"The Nine are all busy preparing for the final breakthrough. The traps and imprisoned beings outside the pyramid are far lesser than those we will be facing once the real work begins," Ren told her. "This is a test of your abilities, and it seems you're failing. If you're unhappy with your task, I suggest you return to Ruruc. The same goes for your colleagues."

The woman bowed a few times, then backed away before hurrying across the dusty ground to return to her group.

Ren ignored the Cabalists' renewed stares and walked toward two barrels that seemed to designate an entrance of sorts to the row of flags that led to the tomb's base. Tarrik saw that stacks of bleached bones were piled to either side of the entrance tower and along the pyramid's base.

Ren strode past the orichalcum-eyed dreadlords that flanked both sides of the barrels and came to a stop in front of a group of flags arranged in a rough circle. She removed a cloth from her pocket and stretched it between both hands. Tarrik saw she held a map of the pyramid and the surrounding land, with numerous minute notations and symbols mostly congregated around the entrance tower.

A hundred yards away stood the tower itself. Writing ringed its sinister opening, angular and primitive. Tarrik recognized it as ancient Skanuric. For the letters to be visible from this distance, they must be huge.

His eyes were drawn to the pitch-black maw beneath the writing. As he gazed at it, the darkness swam. There seemed to be something more than darkness there, and at the same time something less. He became light-headed and swayed on his feet, then stumbled to his hands and knees, his head spinning, his stomach twisting. Bile spilled from his mouth as he heaved onto the dirt.

Ren touched a hand to his shoulder, seeming to ground him somehow. He spat to remove the sour taste from his mouth, found his spear, and stood slowly, brushing dust from his pants.

"What is it?" he asked, keeping his gaze from the gaping opening.

"Samal is imprisoned in another dimension. The pyramid covers a stone structure laced with orichalcum, but it isn't a physical prison. It's a conduit. The opening you can see is composed of the very fabric of reality, twisted to suit a particular purpose. No one can look at it for very long, as you found out—the gate bends the eye and the mind. You stood up to it better than most, though. Probably your demonic nature, or the fact you're used to traveling from one world to another." She looked thoughtful. "I should investigate this further." Then her eyes narrowed, and she smiled wryly. "Here I am, thinking there might be a future for me beyond Samal's release. Anyhow, the Nine have spent many years attempting to unravel the sorcerous wards and have more or less succeeded."

"More or less?"

"You have to be careful, as the gate remains mesmerizing—it pulls you in. One of the Cabalists' apprentices lost his mind and dashed into the void."

"Where did he end up? With Samal?"

"No one knows."

For the first time Tarrik grasped the scale of what the Nine had undertaken to attempt to free Samal. This prison had been created by armies of warriors and sorcerers with a combined power never again seen in this world. Scores of sorcerers must have worked upon the cell, and only because they could not kill Samal. The Adversary had lived up to the name given him by the other demon lords. And now the Nine—depleted to seven—believed they were powerful enough to break Samal free. If they succeeded, they would be unstoppable.

My fate is bound up with the fate of this world. If Samal returns, I will cease to exist.

Tarrik's eyes flicked to the blackness again, and he tore them away, focusing instead on the bones along the base of the pyramid.

"Who piled the bones there?" he asked.

"We don't know."

"Haven't you been here before to try to free the Adversary?"

"No. The Nine were scattered, our powers suppressed, voluntarily and involuntarily. We were hunted by those who opposed Nysrog and his armies. It's a miracle that all Nine of us made it this far without anyone being killed."

"Until you came along."

"I have always been part of the Nine."

"But not in the beginning? Indriol told me the others gave themselves willingly to Samal. You had to be corrupted."

Ren stared at the prison, her mouth twisted in revulsion. "It doesn't matter now. My previous life is a distant memory. It's impossible to return there. All I can do is . . . well, do my best."

"Were you one of those imprisoned after Nysrog's defeat?"

She shook her head. "I ran. Scared out of my mind and always looking over my shoulder—with good reason. I ended up in the far south, a
thousand miles from the Jargalan Desert. After my first encounter with
the Orgols, they left me pretty much alone. I traded basic sorceries for
food and essentials and learned their tongue over a few months. I'd
been living out there for years before I stumbled on the curious story
of a shaman who could bend light. She could do much more than that,
as I found out."

Ah. So that was where Ren had stumbled onto the secret of her sun
power. "What happened to the shaman?"

"I killed her. Samal's bindings are strong, even from within his
prison. They permit no mercy. I have killed many in Samal's name over
the decades. It wearies me. I have become too accustomed to the sight
of corpses."

"Your actions are not yours, not really. Samal is your master. You
are his slave."

"Samal is the fist that pounds us, the claws that tear. The hand
that molds us. Just as humans found a way to control demons, Samal
reversed the process. The Nine are his slaves. He is powerful, Tarrik,
and he cannot be stopped. Some thought to try, long ago. I was one
of them."

"You're going to try again."

Ren laughed softly. "I am a fool."

Tarrik didn't reply. He was frightened to realize that Ren reminded
him more and more of Contian, who had treated him with respect and
as a friend. Tarrik was wary of the similarity, knowing that demon emotions ran deep, and succumbing to them could cause him great misery
and pain. His passions were not easily diminished.

What was she like before Samal corrupted her?

"Blood and fire," he muttered to himself.

Ren glanced at him. A mischievous glint came into her eyes, and she smiled at him. A moment later it was gone. She swung her sword to the side and crouched on her heels. She plucked a stem of grass, dried to straw, and wrapped it around a finger, then stared unflinchingly at the portal to Samal's prison.

Tarrik couldn't look at it for more than a heartbeat before he had to tear his gaze free or risk another display of weakness. He moved a few paces away and leaned on his spear. Ren looked like she didn't want to be disturbed, and he had much to think about. What would the return of the Adversary mean for this world, especially if Samal gained access to Ren's sun power? Once Samal was free and turned his gaze to Tarrik, he wouldn't see a fellow demon, just a source of power to be absorbed and exploited. And Ren, under his command, would simply hand Tarrik over.

Unless . . . if Tarrik could absorb the essence of Ananias before then, he might have enough power to flee if Ren died.

He scratched at the shell around the essence. He could feel it pulsing within, almost like a heartbeat. Warmth emanated from the surface, welcoming rather than dangerous. For the moment.

He pushed against a section that felt softer than its surrounds and was rewarded with a short burst of energy. He scooped the morsel up and corralled it with dark-tide tethers so he could absorb the energy gradually instead of all at once.

Heat spread through his mind, filling him with vigor. He almost felt his dark-tide abilities growing stronger. Blood surged through his body, coursed along his arms and legs, his torso, creating delicious shivers. Such delight! He wanted more. Needed more.

He reached for the shell again but regained his senses and pulled back. To lose control now would be to lose himself entirely. But how much time did he have before the Nine released Samal? Less than two days. The risk of losing his mind had to be weighed against the risk Samal posed to him.

Ren stood and dropped the now-curled piece of grass to the dirt. "Come, Tarrik, we have much work to do before the attempt to free Samal begins."

He grabbed her shoulder as she turned to walk away. For a change, she did not flinch from his touch, but Tarrik dropped his arm all the same. "You are not safe here," he told her. "The Nine want you dead. The Tainted Cabalists clearly distrust you—they just tortured you. How do you know they won't try to disrupt your sorcery? And Samal will know that you killed Lischen and Indriol—he will not be merciful. You know the far south, and you're able to make your way among the Orgol. You could go there and live. Here, we will be killed."

Ren's expression became resigned. "I have no choice."

And she strode off back to the encampment, away from Samal's prison.

For the rest of the day, Ren busied herself writing in her journal and sketching sorcerous diagrams. She frowned at Tarrik if he came close enough to interrupt her concentration, so he spent most of his time sitting at the entrance to their tent, wondering how to escape his looming fate.

"You know, you speak in your sleep sometimes. And not always in your demon tongue," said Ren.

Tarrik looked up to find her squatting in front of him, her head tilted to one side as if she were examining him.

"It's Nazgrese," he said. "Our language."

"How did Jaquel die?"

Her abrupt question threw him off-balance. Sadness threatened to engulf him, though Jaquel's death had happened long ago. He averted his eyes from Ren's gaze.

"She grew old, as humans do. I watched her wither. At the end, her mind was fragmented . . . sometimes she didn't know who I was. I buried her beneath an apple tree she'd planted as a seedling. Apples . . . disgusting things, but she loved them. How is it that a plant can last longer than a human life?"

Ren touched his shoulder lightly, as if expecting him to flinch. But he found her touch welcome. They'd begun to trust each other, and each had taken a risk. With a growing fear, Tarrik remembered that was how his relationship had begun with Jaquel. She had found a crack in the hard veneer he so often presented. And in the end, she'd died.

"She taught you how to care for humans."

It was a statement, not a question. But like so many assumptions sorcerers made about demons, it wasn't the truth.

"No. We care, sometimes too much. We also hate with an intensity that makes human emotions seem shallow. You humans are incapable of fathoming the depths of our emotions. When I love, I do so without reservation, with every fiber of my being. What Jaquel did, and Contian too, was make me love them. A path that can only lead to despair. For humans die, and love for them leaves a scar."

"What happens to your love then? Does it turn to ashes and hate?"

"It stays with me . . . forever. Don't you understand? Our emotions are like raging floods to your trickling streams."

I hate this world. I hate humans. But I don't hate you, not anymore.

Tarrik rose and padded away, wanting to be alone. He was weak. The demon lords had known it. Another reason for his exile. They'd labeled him a traitor to his kind for loving Jaquel, for working alongside Contian. A consorter, a revealer of demon secrets. All because he'd loved a human.

Tarrik spent a few hours wandering the encampment. The day was cold, and he wrapped his arms around himself for warmth against the chill.

Soldiers' campfires were pitched in depressions in an effort to keep any wind away and surrounded by rings of stones gathered from around the plain. The warriors spoke and joked in hushed tones, eating meals thrown together from whatever supplies had reached the encampments. Foraging was out of the question. Tarrik knew they were already butchering horses for meat, as equine screams rang out frequently. Soldiers had converted one tent to a smokehouse to preserve the horseflesh.

Men and women gathered around their feeble fires. Tarrik couldn't see any groups who weren't close by smoldering flame. It made sense that, this close to such darkness as Samal's prison, animals as fearful as humans would gather around pockets of light and heat. He smelled the fear on them, as sharp as rotting fruit.

As Tarrik wandered, he didn't go unnoticed. Men and women watched him and eyed his spear with hooded, cursory looks. It was not surprising, as he'd arrived with one of the Nine. One soldier, a robust man slabbed with muscle, glowered at Tarrik. A hard moment passed between them before Tarrik shook his head and moved on. He imagined it wouldn't have taken much to start a fight.

But despite wanting to burn off nervous energy and work himself into a frenzy to escape his meandering thoughts, Tarrik walked on. The soldier and his compatriots would die soon enough, through violence or accident or old age.

His care for humans had died a long time ago, buried under an apple tree.

A commotion woke them during the night. Detonations close to the pyramid cracked through the darkness, and eldritch lights flashed. Ren moved quickly to the tent's entrance and stood with one arm holding the flap open. Over her head, Tarrik saw sparkling lines scythe the night and heard a dozen pops like wood in a blaze. Screams reached them: human, and something lower, more guttural. Brief flashes of bright light bleached the side of the pyramid. After a time, the uproar died down.

"The Cabal's sorcerers encountered something," Ren said, "and handled it."

She said no more, just returned to her bed of blankets. Soon Tarrik heard her breathing even out as sleep overcame her.

He remained awake, wondering how someone as slight as Ren could be so fierce, so resistant to the torments that had assaulted her throughout her life.

She still hopes to break free of Samal's grip, he realized. *She hopes for a normal life. What would it be like for her? Could I work alongside her as I did with Contian?*

Once Tarrik finally fell asleep, he became caught in vivid dreams, an erratic jumble of sensations. Jaquel called to him, as if she were in another room. He entered but instead of finding her saw the apple tree they'd tended together. Its branches sank low with the weight of shining red fruit, and rotten apples lay on the ground underneath, chewed on by animals. Tarrik stopped, frozen with indecision, and a sense of foreboding surrounded him. Searching for Jaquel, he saw a worm-riddled corpse propped against the trunk of the apple tree, its skin wizened and tattered, its bones gleaming white where they were exposed. Inky ooze dripped from its rotted mouth, and its splintered fingernails were hooked into claws.

"I will teach you about power," said Ren behind him, speaking with a conviction as solid as stone.

Heat climbed Tarrik's neck. Despite her words, the belief in her tone, he knew she had been overtaken by madness, like all of the Nine.

He woke with a start, bolting upright. Sweat dripped down his brow.

This world brings suffering . . .

Ren seemed determined to do grievous injury to the Nine, knowing that when Samal was freed, it would cost her dearly. The Adversary would not be lenient. He would hurt her and continue to hurt her, never willing to forgive.

Tarrik wondered if a tiny spark of the original Ren remained, a spark that Samal couldn't extinguish. Whether, despite the evil she had perpetrated, there was still a part of her left untainted. Perhaps that was what drove her. Perhaps she wanted death, a release from her past.

Chapter Twenty-Four

The morning haze quickly cleared to an icy brightness that blinded Tarrik as he stood under the blue sky. For a few heartbeats he closed his eyes and imagined he was back in his realm, casting a final look at the hated daylight before hunkering down to sleep or amuse himself until he could set out in the darkness to hunt.

"Check what happened to the Cabal's sorcerers last night," said Ren from the doorway of the tent. "And do not let your guard down."

Tarrik nodded, knowing she probably only wanted him out of the way for a while. But he did as he was told, striding away past the soldiers and servants huddled around meager fires, burning precious fuel to heat water for their tea and boiled oats and barley. His stomach rumbled, but he would wait till he returned to sate his hunger. More of the salted rat meat could be found among the provisions in Ren's tent.

After the Cabalists had fought off whatever had come for them from the pyramid, they must have returned to the encampment for safety, leaving their dead behind. Nocturnal scavengers had been at the human carcasses; the ground around the tattered remains was splashed with liberal quantities of blood. Tarrik saw giant paw prints in the gore—they reminded him of the tracks of a gruul, a furred predator in the demon realms.

The carnage didn't seem to bother the two men he'd seen the day before. They'd moved their wagon closer to the slaughter and were shoveling remains into coffins. A dozen paces away stood three sorcerers, including the woman who had approached Ren yesterday, their mouths drawn into thin lines as they watched.

The men stopped and leaned on their shovels when Tarrik approached. Sweat streamed down their faces despite the cold air.

"How many killed?" he asked them.

"Don't rightly know. More than a few."

Tarrik prodded a gnawed leg bone with his boot. Something had cracked it open and feasted on the marrow. "What killed them?"

The taller man coughed and spat into the dirt. "Maybe a manticarr. Maybe something else. Tore through them like they were rabbits. The ones who didn't die ran for it. Can't say I blame them. You mess with unnatural sorcery like these people do, something's bound to get you one day."

The shorter man nodded. "That's right. Sooner or later the gods decide your time's over. Then we clean up and collect our coin."

"Everyone goes back into the dirt," Tarrik said.

"Ain't that the truth. Say, big man, you happen to know when they'll make the push into the tomb?"

"Tomorrow."

The taller man grinned. "Plenty of dead for us to clean up after that. Hopefully someone will be left to pay us for it."

Tarrik left the men and the remaining sorcerers and made his way back to Ren's tent. At its entrance the ground was newly scuffed, and there were wagon-wheel marks in the dirt. Inside, he saw a sizeable iron-bound blackwood chest by Ren's bed. It was secured with a heavy lock, and Skanuric runes had been carved into its wooden surface.

"What's that?" he asked.

"Nothing that concerns you. Come closer." Tarrik stepped toward her, and she stared at him, head tilted slightly to the side. "We need to talk."

He leaned his spear on a chair and went over to the table of food. What else had they to talk about? Was she going to confide in him further? His hands found a bottle on the table, and he drank deeply, the spirits scalding his throat. He wiped his mouth and chewed a piece of rat meat, in no hurry for this talk.

"Tarrik . . ."

He turned and spoke over her. "A few of the Cabal sorcerers survived, including the woman who spoke to you yesterday. They're spooked, though, and rightly so. Whatever creature came for them feasted on the corpses after the survivors fled."

Ren nodded. "They weren't careful enough. Exhaustion, probably. Well, they chose to join the Tainted Cabal; they knew what they were getting into. Come here."

Tarrik moved closer and saw that her eyes were red with fatigue. "Do you have another task for me?"

"Soon, yes. All my plans come to fruition tomorrow. After that . . . I don't know what will become of me. The heat of the forge is rising, Tarrik. But I have some surprises of my own. Still, that's not what I want to talk about. Have you succeeded in absorbing the demon you killed?"

Tarrik froze, a sinking feeling in his stomach. All this time she had known. There was no point in dissembling. "No."

"Not at all?"

"A little. If I had more time, I might succeed. But I doubt I'll get the opportunity before tomorrow."

"Is there anything I can do to help?"

Her suggestion shocked him and also baffled him. Why did she want to help him? And if he accepted her offer, what bond would that create between them?

Dare he push himself further?

"Well?" she said, her eyebrows raised.

Tarrik drew a breath. "There may be a way."

An unwillingness to say any more dragged at him. At first he thought the feeling was wariness. Then he realized it was, in fact, deep shame. He didn't want to ask a human sorcerer for help. The prospect ran against all he believed. But . . . here he was . . . on the verge of trusting a sorcerer again.

"The Wracking Nerves," he said, pushing through the resistance. "You must punish me with it. The demon essence within my mind will become distressed and fight against the protective shell surrounding it. If you apply enough pain, it will crack."

"And what then?"

"It will overwhelm me, or I will control it."

Ren frowned. "Is such a battle waged every time?"

"Yes. But usually demons absorb an essence gradually, gaining strength with each small portion. If I fail to control any part of the process, I will lose myself. I won't go mad, but I won't be the same being. I will be both myself and Ananias—a new entity. And, like a newborn babe, I will have no memories but considerable power, both physical and dark-tide power. If that happens, you should kill me before I kill you."

He looked around for something to grasp when the agony of the Wracking Nerves hit. Not his spear. If he became lost, having a weapon in his hands wasn't a good idea. He settled for a cushion, about as far away from a weapon as he could imagine.

Ren gestured to him to lie down on her blankets, his head resting on her pillow. He clutched the cushion tight in both hands across his stomach.

She knelt on the ground beside him. "Now?" Her dark-blue eyes were filled with sympathy—and determination.

He winked at her, then closed his eyes. She uttered a soft laugh and spoke a cant.

Tarrik's nerves erupted in searing pain. This time the agony didn't plateau but kept increasing. His mind reeled, and he screamed.

Don't lose control.

He clamped his thoughts into a tight ball. The Wracking Nerves sent waves of torment through his body and mind, shredding his consciousness. He gathered himself as best he could, battered by this sorcery designed to inflict maximum pain upon demons.

Ananias.

Tarrik fought his way through Ren's punishment; it crashed over him, buffeting him like a gale. When he found the shell surrounding Ananias's essence, he clung on for dear life, strangled by an ever-growing ache, his limbs a convulsing, grinding tangle.

A thought intruded upon his desperation. If he could barely hold off the Wracking Nerves, how would he cope with the surge when the shell broke?

Too late to worry.

With a tremor that lashed his mind, the shell cracked, unleashing a flood of essence. It hammered him, exploding through his flimsy defenses and attacking his mind like a snarling beast upon prey. Razors slashed at his being.

For an instant his mind recoiled from the alien presence within, giving it a breach to flow into. Then Tarrik's fury erupted, and he threw his entire being into the fray, sending out dark-tide threads to tear the essence into smaller shreds. He would lose some of its potency, but survival was paramount. He had learned enough from previous absorptions to know that greed would be his undoing. The essence was demon in its rawest form, and its ravenous brutality had to be lessened.

He lost track of time as his world became a burning, roiling sea of hostility. Tarrik was scarcely able to absorb one fragment of essence before another pummeled at his awareness. Threads wove through his mind, clotting his being with something not himself. A corruption, an intolerable baseness that scoured his own spirit with vitriol.

Tarrik fought as best he could, but Ananias's essence was too strong, and he was weak. It stripped his defenses and battered his spirit, diluting what made him Tarrik.

Fear crowded him. He had gambled and lost. Perhaps this was his lot, to die here in this human world and have his bones cast onto the piles surrounding Samal's prison. His mind would be torn asunder, and he would go mad. Like one of the Nine.

No! I will not surrender!

He threw himself back into the struggle and drew on the dark-tide power, weaving nets to trap the shattered essence running amok.

New threads intruded upon his thoughts, and Tarrik hesitated. They dove in like a heron into water, glowing white, silent and pure.

Ren.

Her sun power, shining bright, wrapped itself around fragments of Ananias's essence, and the pressing waves pulled back. Tarrik was able to gather himself, one errant thought at a time, until he'd regained some semblance of calm. But the respite was brief. He saw the white threads begin to snap and their cages unravel.

He attacked the shredded essence anew, splitting his thoughts to deal with the fragments not hampered by Ren's intrusion. He bound a few with dark-tide tethers, then focused on breaking off chunks for easier absorption. He took in three, then another two. As they dissolved, their energy flashed through his mind, searing him with brilliance. He felt his own essence expand.

His success and new energy strengthened his resolve. He would gain control over the essence. He would absorb Ananias and become something greater.

Tarrik fought as though he were a ravening beast surrounded by smaller creatures seeking to bring him down with their greater numbers. They were hunger, horror—tearing chunks from him with quick, vicious bites, hoping he would succumb.

He would not yield.

Tarrik thrashed wildly, tearing at fragments of invading essence, clawing, corralling, and finally absorbing them. He clutched at the scintillating slivers and pulled them into his own spirit, he who had not yet lost himself.

Darkness swirled around him as though it were a wind. A new sensation soaked through Tarrik's mind, warm, reassuring. *Ren*, he thought at first. But he could not sense her presence. He realized it was his own essence, stronger after absorbing part of Ananias's being. He had passed a threshold. He had succeeded. He had survived.

With a growing sense of relief and not a little pride, Tarrik breathed a sigh. At last he could ease back, take a few moments to gather his strength. He lurched away, leaving the dissolving essence to be absorbed and redefined by his subconscious, shaped to mirror his innate talents and augment his power.

He turned his attention to the physical world and found himself still on Ren's blankets, panting in the burning aftermath of the Wracking Nerves. He tasted blood in his mouth, and his whole body ached from his spasming muscles.

Ren lay on top of him, her hands on either side of his head, her blue-black eyes staring into his.

Though his mind swirled with chaotic thoughts and newfound promise, Tarrik's first impression was their closeness: his pelvis against her thigh, breast to breast. As lovers might lie.

He gazed at her penetrating eyes, her soft lips. He wanted to give in to the passion that rose within him. To exult in pleasures of the flesh.

"Are you . . . whole?" she murmured.

He nodded, not trusting himself to speak.

"Good." She removed her hands, withdrew slightly, and stood.

He remained lying there, focusing on his heartbeat, counting the thrums in order to give himself time to marshal his thoughts. The cushion he'd clutched was a few feet away, its cover shredded, the wadding from inside it strewn around the tent.

Tarrik got to his feet slowly and busied himself brushing creases from his shirt and pants. Ren had saved him from losing himself, and as a result he had grown, evolved. Potentially he could be confirmed to a higher rank. Without her intervention, he would be a mewling mess, lost in violence and hunger.

He drew himself up straight and met Ren's eyes. "I, Tarrik Nal-Valim, of the Thirty-Ninth Order, thank you."

Ren raised her eyebrows. Maybe she knew his advancement was self-imposed. "Don't thank me yet. We still have to survive the coming days."

"You helped me. I sensed you, in my mind."

"I didn't bring you this far to lose you before my plan reaches its culmination. And if something happens to me—which in all probability it will—you'll need all the strength you can muster to survive." She met his gaze, her eyes strangely gentle. "You are brave, Tarrik. And I sense there are depths to you that would be worth knowing. I did not expect to find such in a demon."

"I'm only trying to survive."

"I think it's more than that. Now get some rest. We both need to be strong for tomorrow."

With those words, she turned her back, shook out her blankets, and settled down to rest.

Chapter Twenty-Five

When Tarrik woke again, there was a damp cloth on his forehead. Elisa, the crone, knelt next to him, one wizened hand clutching his, crooning soothing words. Tarrik disentangled his hand. Even that minimal movement caused shooting pains in his head, and he clenched his teeth. His muscles ached as if they'd been pounded with a hammer.

Elisa cackled. "Awake finally, are you? I was going to rouse you soon. She ordered me to do it before she returned."

"You talk too much," said Tarrik. Whatever had brought about the change in the woman was unwelcome.

"You're the first person to say that." Abruptly, she seized his shoulder and leaned in close to whisper into his ear. "Don't consort with these people. Their sorcery cuts like a freshly sharpened razor. You will regret it."

"I already do," he said.

"The goddess is watching. She reminded me that the price of victory is often death."

Tarrik grunted. "Which goddess is this?" He'd never seen any evidence that these gods and goddesses the humans worshiped existed.

Elisa didn't reply, just removed the damp cloth. Instantly, Tarrik's forehead burned like he had a fever. A symptom of absorbing another's essence; he would need a few days for his body and mind to adapt.

A number of horns sounded in the distance. He sat up and looked around for Ren.

"Where is she?"

"Gone," said Elisa.

"I can see that. Where did she go?"

"To consort with the other evil sorcerers. It doesn't matter."

"You're unusually talkative. How long was I asleep?"

"It's morning now. Today is the day. The goddess has told me."

"I'm sure she has." It didn't take a great intellect to know the Nine's attempt to free Samal was planned for today.

He rose to his feet, ignoring Elisa, and picked through the food on the table. There were strips of smoked horsemeat, and he chewed one with relish.

Tarrik's thoughts turned to survival. He was unbound, which was good. So he had his free will, along with his innate talents and his catalyst. Unfortunately, the Nine were making their attempt in daylight, so he was somewhat limited.

Elisa tugged at his arm. "She told me to tell you to join her."

"Your goddess?"

"No, your master."

Oh, she means Ren. "Why didn't you say so sooner?"

"Make your peace with your god or goddess, whoever they are," she told him. "You'll likely die today."

"I hope not. I might, but I'll do my best not to."

"Death approaches. The abyss is on the other side of that void."

"What do you know of the prison?"

"More than most. Less than some."

Tarrik gave her a hard look. "You're no ordinary crone."

"Very perceptive. And you're no ordinary demon."

He only just stopped himself from bringing forth his shadow-blade and decapitating her. His position here was precarious enough without anyone knowing he wasn't human. But something stayed his cant and his hand. Maybe it was the gleam of amusement in the crone's eyes.

"Who do you work for?" he asked.

"No one you know. I just watch over the pyramid for the gods and goddesses."

"I'm sure you do. Do your gods and goddesses want Samal to remain imprisoned?"

But Elisa had turned her back and was busy folding the blankets Ren had slept on. And before he could ask any more questions, Ren herself entered the tent.

She wore her standard slim charcoal skirt and short coat, a crimson silk shirt, silver-buckled and studded belt, and black leather boots with silver side buttons. However, her hair was loose and untidy, as if unbrushed. And she'd pinned her two orichalcum brooches to her breast: the nine-pointed star of the Nine and the divided square of the Tainted Cabal.

"I see you're up," she said. "How are you feeling?"

"Like I was caught in a rockfall. But I'll survive."

Ren glanced at Elisa, who was now shaking Tarrik's blankets and folding them. "Have you gained in strength?"

Once again he was surprised by how much she knew of the absorption process. "I believe so."

"Good." She moved a stool closer to her bed and rummaged around in her gear to find a brush, comb, and black leather strips. "Today will be difficult, for everyone. I find myself on edge, and my hands are trembling. I'd like you to braid my hair—you do an excellent job on your own."

Tarrik's heart jumped, and he froze. *What is she . . . ? Does she know?* He tried to croak a reply, but no words came.

Ren frowned at him. "What is it? Are you still not recovered from last night?"

"I would prefer . . . not to braid your hair."

She sighed. "It is a simple enough request."

"No, it isn't. Between my kind, it is an act of intimacy to braid another's hair."

The sensation of her body lying next to his yesterday flashed into his mind—her hands by his face, her eyes penetrating his own. Blood and fire, he *wanted* to braid her hair! But he couldn't risk surrendering.

"Then it's lucky we're not the same race," Ren said, and looked pointedly at Elisa. She obviously didn't realize the crone had already deduced Tarrik's true nature. "Come now. It won't take long."

She sat on the stool and held out the brush, comb, and cords. Tarrik approached on wooden legs. *It doesn't mean anything*, he told himself.

Blocking all other thoughts from his mind, he brushed and braided Ren's long raven locks as quickly as he could. As he handed her back the brush and comb, he could still feel the silken ghosts of her hair on his palms and fingers.

"Have you finished?" she said.

Only then did he realize that he'd used the *ish-akhra* pattern, specifically for a warrior who went to certain death or sacrifice.

"Yes."

"Thank you." Ren stood and patted her head and fingered her braid. "Very neat. It's a shame I don't have a mirror."

Tarrik backed away on legs trembling with dread. Once again, his time on this world had sent him tumbling into confusion. The heat from the brazier felt stifling, though it was on the other side of the tent. A jumble of emotions whirled inside him: embarrassment and pleasure and desire. He stumbled and gasped, and somehow his hands found the table. He grabbed a bottle of spirits and popped the cork. Liquid scalded his throat.

He wiped his mouth with the back of his hand and turned to see Ren strapping her sword to her back, then buckling the baldric across her waist and chest. The steel hilt resembled feathered wings, and the silver snake entwined around the orichalcum pommel stuck out from behind her shoulder. He remembered how easily she had wielded the sword, though it looked too long and heavy for her.

She gave a grunt of satisfaction as she settled its weight on her back, then turned to him. "I need you to wait for me with the others of the Nine."

"At the pyramid?"

"Yes. Where we stopped yesterday. We are to all gather before the final cants."

"What will you be doing?"

"Preparing. Make sure you are ready when the time comes. For now, go to the others, but stay apart from them. I don't believe any would do you harm, but best not to antagonize anyone until I arrive."

"As you wish."

Few guards were stationed outside the pavilions now. The sun had fully risen and rested like a crimson bulb on the horizon. A chill wind swept down from the north and set Tarrik's teeth chattering. The soldiers' campfires were set with extra fuel and blazing merrily; they knew that soon they would be gone from this harrowing place.

More horns sounded, a signal to muster. The grand ordeal would be starting soon. Tarrik set out toward the pyramid, angling around tents and past doused cook fires.

Soldiers congregated in full armor, their weapons and gear polished to a high sheen. They marched toward the pyramid to join others that Tarrik could see had formed an arc around the entrance—the gate to another dimension, as Ren had put it.

The braying of horns and the beat of drums filled the air. Behind the cordon of soldiers, the rest of the Tainted Cabal's small army was gathered: a few squads of archers and all the servants and retainers a force needed to keep operating. Seemingly everyone wanted to witness the proceedings. The Cabalists probably thought an alliance with Samal and the Nine was a step closer to achieving their own desires and that the Nine could be ignored except when the Tainted Cabal needed to call on powerful sorcery. *Fools.*

When Samal was freed, he would bind the strongest of the Cabalist sorcerers and kill the remainder. The Nine would become the Twenty, or the Thirty, or more. And then there would be no stopping the Adversary.

No one stopped or questioned Tarrik as he made his way between squads of soldiers. He supposed that by now everyone knew he was Ren's bodyguard. The six remaining sorcerers of the Nine were congregated in a tight circle, deep in discussion. He stopped a good twenty paces from them, and no one seemed to notice his arrival. He glanced behind him but didn't see Ren.

Puck waved toward the pyramid, and the gesture was repeated by Marren. Puck stamped his foot, then his staff, on the ground. A disagreement. Tarrik sneered. They'd had years to plan this; you'd think they'd have sorted everything out by now.

Lera of the Fireflies, or the Betrayer of Shadows, stood to the left of Puck, garbed in the same thin white dress studded with rubies. The material was dirty and spotted with stains, as if the sorcerer hadn't changed at all since Tarrik had last seen her. Jawo-linger stood between the red-haired woman, Moushumi, and a man Tarrik didn't recognize. He must be the final sorcerer of the Nine: Ekthras. He was of mixed race with no defining features, though dressed in expensive tan pants and a matching coat with a cream shirt.

A man and woman loitered close to the group. The woman was as wan as a corpse and clutched the talisman at her belt. The man was towering and muscular, flamboyantly dressed in crimson velvet pants and coat with silver buttons and a feathered hat. Probably Moushumi's man, Ursael; and the woman might be Jawo-linger's apprentice, Rokkvi, though Tarrik couldn't be sure.

The Nine separated into two groups: Jawo-linger and Marren in one; Puck, Moushumi, Lera, and Ekthras in the other. Tarrik knew

Jawo and Marren held no enmity for Ren, so perhaps there were two factions, divided over their view of her. If he was right, that meant Puck, Moushumi, Lera, and Ekthras were enemies.

Marren clutched the artifact Ren had given him: a silver statuette in the form of a man covered with Skanuric script. Lera carried an identical artifact, presumably the one Tarrik had delivered to her. He frowned when he saw Ekthras holding the crudely formed bull statuette that Ren had swapped in Indriol's chambers. He wasn't surprised the sorcerer had it, as Jawo had revealed as much. But he must have brought the statuette from Atya after Tarrik and Ren had left. Ekthras had apparently traveled as fast as Ren's disc, which meant he was powerful. But he didn't know the artifact in his hands was a fake. The thought caused the hairs on Tarrik's neck to stand on end, and he rubbed them to ease his disquiet.

This must be part of Ren's plan. But these sorcerers were the greatest of their age. Surely they would be able to tell if an artifact wasn't genuine? Tarrik had the feeling that Ren's plan would only come to fruition once Samal was freed. And he had to be ready, whatever happened. His hands burned from squeezing his spear tight, and he made a conscious effort to relax them.

The Nine mounted several saddled horses close by. Tarrik heard hoofbeats behind him and turned to see Ren riding a brown horse and leading a spare animal. Her face lacked color, and she sat upon her horse without her usual grace. She halted beside him and held out the reins of the spare mount.

"I'm not hungry," said Tarrik.

Her lips twitched in amusement. "Ride beside me, for a while at least. Then I'll have a task for you."

"I'd rather not." If he had to fight, dismounting would cost him precious time.

"Suit yourself. Just stay close."

Tarrik followed Ren as she guided her horse toward the pyramid. The horns and drums stopped, and silence fell like a shroud over the

Tainted Cabal's army, broken only by the clinking of armor and weapons and the neighing and snorting of horses.

Tarrik kept his eyes on Ren's gray-cloaked, straight back. She rode to her death, he was certain. He had a sudden vision of her screaming in the throes of virulent sorcery, blood streaming down her face and bare arms. She should have tried to run when she had the chance, though such an act wasn't in her character.

Tarrik had been in tight spots before and survived. He hoped this was one more time he'd make it to the other side. He gripped the shaft of his spear: blackwood, immune to sorcery. The weapon's plainness and utility gave him strength. It had fought a thousand battles and was still whole. He tried to outline a basic spear form in his mind to settle his thoughts. But out here, in the shadow of Samal's prison, in the presence of seven of the most powerful sorcerers in the world, all stark raving mad, he could barely recall anything.

"We begin," Ren said to him, her eyes inscrutable.

Tarrik expected to see showy sorcery. Instead, he heard a faint sound that slowly grew in volume: a spoon-against-pot scraping that spread through his flesh and mind. It was, he realized, both physical and ethereal. The noise moved through the unseen aether where sorcery occurred until it seemed to latch on to his bones and gnaw at them like a ghoul. A putrid reek filled his nostrils, like the rot of scores of bodies. The insistent scraping grew louder. His bones rattled with the intensity, and his hands ached from squeezing his spear shaft.

All around him, soldiers staggered. Weapons dropped from their nerveless fingers, and they clutched their heads, covering their ears in a vain attempt to block out the discordance.

Ren reached a hand down to Tarrik, and he was surprised to find it held a brass key.

"It's for the chest in my tent," she said. "Open it, and bring me what's inside. Quickly—we are in mortal danger. If anything happens to me, keep them safe."

What she'd sensed eluded Tarrik. He nodded and jogged away from Ren and the pyramid. He glanced back to see more soldiers falling, their armor clattering on the hard dirt. The only figures seemingly unaffected were the dreadlords, and the sorcerers. None of the latter had raised shields yet and thus must have been some way from completing the ritual.

He broke into a sprint, easily balancing his long spear as he ran past moaning warriors. The arcane scraping noise wore at him too, intruding into his thoughts and weakening his limbs. A woman fell to the ground in front of him, retching bile. Tarrik leaped over her and kept running. He dodged around tents, their ropes laid out like traps for the unwary, and raced past more convulsing humans and their cries of disorientation. His foot struck a rock in the ground, and he stumbled but managed to right himself before he sprawled headlong. His urgency increased the more humans fell around him. This far from the pyramid, the effects of the sorcery were slightly weaker. One soldier retained enough wits to reach an imploring hand out to Tarrik. He ignored it.

Ren's tent loomed large in his vision, and he darted through the entrance flap. As earlier, the two dreadlord guards were nowhere to be seen.

Elisa cackled when she saw him. She was sitting at the central table with a goblet in one hand and a half-eaten apricot in the other. It seemed the debilitating sorcery didn't affect her, perhaps only disorienting those who were sane.

"I knew you'd be back! What happened? Are they all dead yet?"

Tarrik moved toward the blackwood chest. "They're alive."

"Not for long. The goddess is never wrong."

The lock on the chest was already open. Tarrik lifted the lid. Inside sat another sword, and a book. Ren's journal. The sword had a hilt of feathered wings and a silver snake entwined around an orichalcum pommel. It reeked of power, of eldritch forces barely held in check, masked by the blackwood. Tarrik's mind reeled, and he staggered back a step.

It was Ren's sword.

Then the one she carried was a copy. Why? Why would she weaken herself at this crucial time?

"Take them," Elisa crooned.

"No . . . I . . ."

His mind swam with confusion. Ren had sent him away. Whatever she'd planned, it was happening *now*. And she didn't want him around.

Tarrik whirled around and ran toward the exit before stopping. Ren had told him to keep the contents of the blackwood chest safe.

He hurried back to the chest and shoved the journal down the front of his shirt, then slung the sheathed sword across his back, fastening the buckles on the baldric to secure it in place. Then he dashed wildly from the tent and sprinted back to Ren.

Sorcerous cants reached his ears. The air vibrated like a drumhead, and a sound like the pattering of rain echoed through the encampment. As Tarrik rushed toward Ren, his ex-master, ex-slaver, his thoughts tumbled like stones downhill. Ren had left her precious journal and her sword to him for safekeeping. He could draw only one conclusion: she planned to die in her stand against the other sorcerers and Samal himself.

Chapter Twenty-Six

Run, a voice said—Tarrik's own inner betrayer. He should obey. He should turn his back on Ren, on Samal's prison, on the Nine. Now that he was unbound, he could return himself to the abyssal realms.

He reached for his dark-tide power, closed his eyes, and felt the niggling sensation of the beginning of return enter his mind.

And then he recoiled from the sensation.

Sharp pangs, cold as knives, sliced through him. He could not let Ren die. Not after coming to feel something for her. She had tried to use him to keep something of herself alive—her journal, her sword—to keep them out of the clutches of the Nine or the Cabalists. But he could not escape and leave her to suffer whatever plans the Nine had ensnared her in.

A clamor to save Ren inflamed Tarrik, but as he ran again toward the pyramid, a figure rushed at him from an avenue between tents. A dreadlord swinging its massive blade.

Tarrik leaped aside, and the sword severed a tent rope and bit into the earth. He grimaced as a corner of Ren's journal poked him in the ribs and thrust his spear at the orichalcum-eyed monstrosity. His blade screeched across its breastplate; the dreadlord hardly noticed the strike. Tarrik backed up a step, keeping his spear leveled at his attacker. The dreadlord was slow, but the armor was a problem.

The metal eyes went black for an instant before erupting in an orange glow. The great sword rose from the ground, and the dreadlord moved toward Tarrik as if possessing otherworldly grace. The massive sword spun up over its head and came slicing down at Tarrik's shoulder.

Tarrik pivoted and managed to raise his spear in time, deflecting the sword so its blade missed him by an inch. The dreadlord somehow arrested the weapon's momentum and swung it around for another hack. Tarrik tried to parry, but his spear was almost wrenched out of his grip with the force of the clash.

Too close. We're too close. His reach was his advantage.

He leaped backward and tripped over a tent rope. He tumbled to the ground, and before he could right himself, the dreadlord was above him, its great sword swooping down straight for his head.

Tarrik threw himself to the side, the hilt of Ren's sword digging into his back. The blade hammered into the earth, half of its steel buried. Tarrik kicked frantically at the rope around his leg to free himself. The dreadlord tugged at its blade, but the weapon barely moved.

Tarrik spoke a cant and brought his shadow-blade into existence. He slashed through the rope, releasing his leg. The dreadlord's blade came free from the ground, trailing dust and clumps of earth.

Tarrik scrambled to his feet as the dreadlord turned. He thrust his spear one-handed, fast and well-placed, aiming for the mailed gap between breastplate and thigh plate. The great sword moved as if weightless, the blade catching his spear tip and forcing it down and to the side. Tarrik's cut with his shadow-blade was fast enough to finish almost any opponent, but the dreadlord dodged to the side, and the dark-tide weapon scored a shallow cut along the vambrace protecting its upper arm. Sparks sprayed, and metal screeched.

Anyone else's arm would have been severed, but the dreadlord didn't pause. It came at Tarrik again, this time angling its great sword from shoulder to hip. Tarrik moved back in a crouch, letting the blade pass harmlessly in front of him. He risked a quick glance toward the pyramid. He was wasting too much time.

Finish this.

The great sword swung again—a feint. It altered direction midslice, and Tarrik barely avoided the blade. He jabbed his spear at the dreadlord's eyes, but even when its tip scraped across the helm's visor, the creature didn't flinch. The dreadlord attacked again, its blade moving in a blur, cutting and thrusting as if the weapon were as light as a feather.

Steel slammed into Tarrik's spear blade again and again. Somehow he managed to turn aside each blow, but the edge of the sword scored lines across his ribs, cheek, and thigh. In desperation he lunged at the dreadlord's legs. As the creature stumbled, its massive blade skittered off a rock, throwing sparks into the air.

Tarrik dropped his spear and thrust his shadow-blade through the gap between the dreadlord's breastplate and gorget. Black blood spurted as he tore the creature's throat out with a ripping gush. It slumped to the dirt, glowing orange eyes flickering and dying, leaving plain orichalcum balls. Tarrik saw the dreadlord's lips moving, but no sound came forth. Someone had sent the creature to kill Tarrik—most likely Ekthras, who apparently commanded the ensorcelled warriors. And whatever he'd done to them had altered their blood.

Tarrik grabbed his spear and raced toward the pyramid, his other arm clamping Ren's journal to his side. A swelling tide of eldritch energy washed over and through him; the screams of fallen soldiers mingled with an otherworldly hum.

A lone horn sounded, rising above the din, but the Cabalists' warriors had forgotten why they were there. They writhed and wailed on the ground, a chorus of suffering. Those closest to the pyramid were already dead. Only the Cabal's most puissant sorcerers, and the Nine, still stood.

Tarrik squinted at the standing figures as he moved closer, pushing through the mass of dead or dying bodies. Where was Ren?

There. Riding toward the churning black maw of Samal's prison. She halted her mount and turned to face the remaining Cabalists and the two groups of the Nine. At this distance, Tarrik couldn't see her face.

A luminous golden aura surrounded her, faint at first, then becoming stronger until she was bathed in ethereal light.

Tarrik urged himself to greater speed, all the while keeping an eye out for more dreadlords. If one had been sent against him, others might have the same goal. But why? Did Ekthras want him out of the way so Ren had one less resource to call upon?

The last few Cabalist sorcerers were singing cants now, their concentration focused entirely on the sorcery that would free Samal. The Nine spread out, still on their mounts, until there was a good twenty yards between them. Each was now surrounded by a spherical arcane shield, glimmering in the sunlight.

Tarrik slowed, then halted. He wanted to rush to Ren, to question her, but his interference might jeopardize what she was trying to achieve. Did that matter? Should he try to save her from herself, without thought to the consequences?

As he stood there, frozen with indecision, Ren raised her arms above her head. A tempest erupted between her and the other sorcerers—twenty-foot lances of searing shine as bright as the sun that speared into their wards. Tarrik blinked, his eyes adjusting to the brilliance of the unleashed power.

The Nine stood unharmed. Ren's dazzling spears had failed to penetrate their shields. But she had caught their attention.

"We are at the culmination of centuries of planning," she cried out in a voice that somehow reached Tarrik too. "Our lord, Samal Rakshazza, imprisoned so long ago, is close to being freed. But the demons themselves named Samal the 'Adversary.' And for good reason."

The remaining Nine exchanged frowns and puzzled looks but continued their cants. The arcane pulse humming through Tarrik increased in magnitude. The few warriors still on their feet fell to squirm in the dust. Three of the Cabalist sorcerers cried out in dismay and also collapsed.

Ren turned toward the pyramid, then came full circle to face the Nine again. "Samal made slaves of us, and so he will with all who inhabit our world," she shouted at them. "Our choice is simple. Open his prison and become his slaves again, or die fighting his demonic evil."

Surprised gasps rose at her words. Jawo-linger stood with her mouth open, a confused look on her face. Moushumi nodded vigorously, as if she'd known all along that Ren had somehow freed herself of some of Samal's bindings, for how else could she speak against their master?

Ekthras shook his head, and his mocking laughter rose over the tumult. "We are bound!" he cried. "All of us. There can be no return. Nor do we want one. This minuscule defiance is of no importance. You are Samal's creature, to do with as he wills. And when he is freed, your blood will be the first to spill."

Ren remained silent, a lone figure against the arrayed might of the Cabalist sorcerers and the Nine.

There was a flash of illumination—sunlight turned to milk—a searing light that gutted the Cabalists' spherical wards. Concussions cracked and hammered arcane shields into smoke. The air twisted into swirling tornadoes, raising columns of dust from the arid earth.

"*Nikerm Qualias!*" Ren shouted.

Golden lights smote the dozen remaining wards with the force of boulders, fracturing them into smoke and splinters. Sorcerers doubled over or pitched to the dust. Their clothes ignited. Blood streamed from their ears and noses.

More sunlight flared. Scintillating white lines, ruler straight, blasted the Cabalists. Men and women shrieked, all speared through as if made from tissue, shredded with a hundred razor cuts. Tarrik saw their skin blister and blacken.

The few Cabalists who remained fought back with shouted cants. Violet and sapphire lines arced toward Ren, forming through the haze of smoke and dust. Incandescent flares pounded her shield, skimming off to scorch the ground and leave burning slicks. Shock waves spread outward, sending gouts of dirt skyward. The ground under Ren steamed and glowed. Her boots began to smoke.

She raised a hand, spoke words Tarrik couldn't hear over the tumult, and rose into the air surrounded by a sphere of sparkling golden light. *Like a new sun*, he thought in wonder.

Ren soared over the devastation and the hostile sorcerers on the blackened ground, through the billowing smog and swirling dirt. Samal's pyramid reared behind her, the dazzling light streaming from her shield bathing its slopes.

A few flights of arrows arced toward Ren, but most burst into flame before they struck. The remaining arrowheads peppered her shield, drumming violet sparks from its golden surface and turning to molten blobs of metal that fell earthward.

Puck Moonan snarled cants from his froth-rimmed mouth. His apprentice lay prone behind him, her clothes smoldering.

Jawo-linger was on one knee, a hand outstretched toward Ren, her face a mask of rage and hate now. Her cants formed flaming balls that streaked at Ren and pounded her golden wards. Their supposed friendship was at an end.

Ren leaned her head back and answered the violence with cants of her own. A white mist shot through with lightning rose from the ground, somehow not dispersed by the turbulent air.

The sorcerers shouted with fear and dismay. Waves of sapphire and violet crashed against Ren's shield, splashing over her like water. They cascaded downward, washing over the dying warriors. Their skin blistered and cracked or was shorn away. Scarlet gore sprayed the dirt, and those still alive keened amid the carcasses of their comrades.

Ren floated above the carnage, a shattered circle beneath her. The Cabalists had sent their most powerful cants against her, and she had survived.

As Tarrik watched, she sent more hammering lights against the Cabalists, so bright as to throw shadows even in daylight. Their wards cracked and shredded into tatters. Ren could have wiped them out with another blast, but instead she turned her attention to the Nine, who were focused on freeing Samal. She shrieked, the sound amplified by sorcery, and began another series of Skanuric cants. Torrents of light raked across the Nine, their wards shrinking under the onslaught.

Red-haired Moushumi was the first to falter—her shield cracked like broken pottery. She groveled in the dirt, expecting to be obliterated, but another ward sprang up. Ekthras held a hand out toward her, and Tarrik guessed he had come to Moushumi's aid.

Jawo-linger took a few steps toward Ren, her mouth twisted into a snarl. She sent fiery balls cascading against Ren's shield, but they splashed off, ineffective.

Ekthras shouted, and the remaining sorcerers of the Nine moved closer, forming a circle with him in its center, their shields merging to form a single glistening dome. Moushumi rose to her feet again, adding her voice to the others'. Ren's blinding incandescences thrashed wildly across their wards, but they did not falter as the Cabalists' had. They chanted in unison, and their combined shield glowed brighter, the ground around burning with such fierce heat that it turned molten.

As one, the Nine turned away from Ren to face the void at the entrance to the pyramid.

Ekthras screamed a command and raised the silver bull above his head. It began to glow with a fierce light. Marren did the same with his statuette, and Lera with its twin. Jawo-linger held out a pearly cube and joined with them, all artifacts glowing brighter and stronger.

Ren shouted more cants, and more of her scything incandescent lines struck the Nine's wards. Again and again she smote them, but her might, the might of the sun, more powerful than either the dawn- or dusk-tides, wasn't enough. The Nine stood firm.

A long, low moan came from the disorienting void that was the entrance to Samal's prison. The wicked might of the Adversary was close.

Tears streamed down Ren's face. For all her strength, all her planning, all the secrets she had somehow withheld from her colleagues, the Nine continued with their goal to free Samal. She hung low above the plain, her knuckle between her teeth.

Tarrik almost laughed at the familiar sight, but his mirth was quickly replaced by a terrible chill that pricked his spine. Samal would be released. Ren would die. And so would he.

He heard the thud of boots, the clink of mail and creak of armor. Dreadlords. They formed into groups of three and, almost as one, raised their hands as if reaching for Ren. Brown discs shot from them, arcing at her wards, hitting them with dull thuds as if made from wet clay. Each strike dented her shield for an instant and sent shining violet motes skittering across its surface. One attack could be easily ignored, but they came in a relentless salvo. As Tarrik watched, Ren wobbled slightly and dipped in the air before recovering herself.

She descended steadily, straight toward the dreadlords gathered underneath her. The Nine ignored her, focused completely on freeing Samal, but the few remaining Cabalists resumed their attack. Searing lines again scored Ren's shield, and the pounding of the dreadlords' missiles persisted. The arcane ward surrounding her began to dissipate into smoke.

Move, Tarrik chided himself. He clenched his teeth and pushed against the heaving sensation of the sorcery around the pyramid, forcing himself to stagger forward. His body seemed to be tugged back and forth—a sense of falling, of being pulled across unseen dimensions.

He stumbled toward a horse, but just as he reached it, the beast uttered a terrible scream and collapsed, flailing its legs wildly in the dirt. He jumped back to avoid thrashing hooves, and when he looked toward the Nine, he found Ekthras staring at him. The sorcerer mouthed a word, inaudible to Tarrik at this distance. But then he saw dreadlords coming for him, slow and heavy, raising dust with each footfall.

He charged one of them, and it turned toward him, slow and heavy, its massive sword gleaming with reflected sorceries. The creature's blade hacked down at Tarrik, and he deflected it with ringing smacks of his spear. The great sword cut through the air to one side, driving deep into the dirt.

Tarrik leaped backward to give himself space and swirled his spear blade at two more dreadlords, swooping it around and out as he began his grim dance. He had no time to think; his vision was filled with waving blades and blank orichalcum eyes.

The time for dissembling was over if he was to survive. Tarrik shifted his spear to his left hand, then spoke a cant, and his shadow-blade sprang to life again. He reacted instantly, body and spear and blade moving in flawless movements. Swords were parried and batted aside, some shattering when struck by his shadow-blade. Iron-rimmed shields were cloven. Flesh was sliced and limbs punctured and severed. Booted feet slipped in gore.

Tarrik hammered his shadow-blade into a torso and tore it free. He darted to the side, moving out of the jumble of bodies and blood-slicked ground. Frantically looking around, he saw no more dreadlords close. Those that remained were racing toward Ren, as if they could somehow reach her lofty perch.

He crashed into another dreadlord, sending it staggering. His shadow-blade found its way through a joint in the creature's backplate, just above the hip. There was a brief resistance from the spine, and Tarrik pushed harder. The dreadlord uttered a coughing moan and fell.

The second swung its blade at Tarrik. He ducked under the sword, dropped his spear, found a hold on an arm, and twisted, wrenching with all his might. The dreadlord toppled to the ground with a crash, and Tarrik forced his shadow-blade into its neck.

He looked around to see the others still focused on attacking Ren. He grinned like a madman.

Tarrik threw himself at another two dreadlords. Filled with renewed vigor at the sight of Ren recovering, he hacked and slashed and thrust at the unnatural warriors until they were lifeless.

Ren's shield had renewed, and she raised a hand toward the Nine. White threads of energy shot from her fingers and pierced the united wards of the Nine. They connected to the artifacts held by Ekthras, Lera, Marren, and Jawo-linger. All four erupted into a brilliance brighter than the noonday sun. The sorcerers cried out, their cants forgotten, as their fingers and palms blackened and skin sloughed from bone.

Jawo-linger staggered and fell, and her face came too close to her artifact. Her hair erupted in flames, her eye turning white as it boiled.

Ekthras stumbled to the side, away from his artifact, and Marren and Lera followed. As Jawo-linger shrieked in anguish, the other three managed cants through gritted teeth, and Puck's and Moushumi's incantations continued unabated. A soft emerald glow surrounded their wounds, which began to heal before Tarrik's eyes. They stood straighter, eyes fixed on Ren, faces colored by fury.

Ren's sabotaged artifacts had bought her a short amount of time, but nothing more. The remaining sorcerers of the Nine chanted in unison Skanuric words of arcane power. Their eldritch sorceries joined with those of the Cabalists still assaulting Ren, and violet and pitch-black lances of energy slammed into her, buffeting her in the sky. Her wards cracked and shattered, and she plummeted toward the ground.

Tarrik dodged around a dreadlord, then kicked at the knee of another. The joint cracked, and there was a clatter of metal as the creature crashed to the ground. He sprinted toward Ren, reaching her just as she landed in the dirt. Her shields held, but tears streamed down her bloodied, grimy face, and her fingers were strangely curled. She snarled a cant, and a wave of pressure knocked dreadlords and Cabalists off their feet. Somehow Tarrik remained standing.

As did the remaining Nine, who had once again turned to face the pyramid.

"They are too strong," Ren said. "They know I am defeated. Samal comes."

Tarrik went cold all over. Whatever Ren's plan was, it had failed.

A keening moan flooded the battlefield. Tarrik realized it came from the void that was the gate to Samal's prison. The gaping maw wasn't swirling anymore. The gate had stilled, and in its center shone a flickering light, like a candle at the end of a tunnel. Around the edge of the blackness a crackling crimson fire shimmered.

"He comes," whispered Ren.

Chapter Twenty-Seven

All around them, the dreadlords and remaining Cabalists slowly regained their feet. Tarrik braced himself for another assault. But they all turned to the void, enthralled.

A sound came from Ren, faint at first, then with greater strength. Tarrik realized she was laughing.

"I broke your chains!" she screamed at the flickering light. "The sun cleansed me! You cannot torment me anymore! I am—"

The low moan coming from the void turned to an ear-piercing whine. A look of panic came over Ren's face.

"No, no, no . . . ," she whispered as she stumbled to her knees.

The light inside the void grew larger, resolving into the shape of a manlike figure.

"What do we do?" Tarrik asked.

"No!" Ren barked savagely—not to Tarrik, but to Samal. She staggered to her feet, and her hands tangled in Tarrik's shirt. "He is coming. I am not as free as I thought. He has me, Tarrik. I can feel his claws . . . inside me."

"Fight!" he urged her. "Fight or die; it's that simple." He could scarcely hear himself over the wail from the void.

Ren shook her head slowly. "It is never simple."

She shouted a word, lost to Tarrik in the cacophony. But his arm hairs stood on end, and a prickle niggled at his mind, the buzz of an insect. The glow surrounding Ren brightened until it was too strong for his eyes. Faint popping sounds came from high above, and then ahead of him a multitude of cracks opened in the veil that separated this world from the abyssal realms.

No!

Ren had summoned an army of demons, all bound to her will.

The air froze to white vapor, and snow fell from the sky. A sulfurous stench underlaid with rot poured through the breach between the worlds. Demons emerged from the tears in the veil, and the sight stole Tarrik's breath. Mighty winged monstrosities studded with horns, their terrible clawed hands huge enough to crush a horse's head; feathered predators with razor talons and bone-crushing beaks; seven-eyed, spiderlike beasts dripping with pestilence, their mottled hides shagged with wiry hair, their limbs longer than a human's entire body. *Siparankchigira, karat-skup, hishil-wurg, krux-alat,* and many others.

Tarrik knew these demons. They were unfettered hunger and debasement, full of bestial urges that overruled what little intelligence they had.

Ren had summoned these demons from the abyss and bound them with cruel sorceries that Tarrik loathed. His ilk, enslaved—and the sight brought him joy. How was this possible?

The shame he felt at his response was quickly overwhelmed by pride in Ren's strength. She had brought forth dozens of demons, surely a feat unsurpassed by any sorcerer of this world, living or dead. But how could she control so many minor demons at once? It was impossible. Only a higher-order demon could hope to—

Tarrik looked at Ren. Her face streamed sweat, and her eyes were red rimmed. He might be able to, now that he'd grown stronger from absorbing Ananias's essence. Somehow, he knew that Ren also understood this.

"I cannot control them," she said. "But you can. I know you can. Coerce them—compel them!"

He was dumbfounded, not believing what she was asking of him. "No. I cannot."

"You can. You must! Samal's grip tightens. If he controls me again, all is lost. You must do it, Tarrik!"

He would be sending scores of his own kind to die for Ren. How could he do such a thing? Tarrik knew he had to make a choice. What was worse: The death of many fellow demons or the return of Samal?

It was no contest.

Tarrik focused on his dark-tide repository and modified his scrying cant. Instead of just seeking, it would also deliver a message: *Kill the humans. Feast upon their meat. Sate your lust upon their corpses.*

Closing his eyes, he sent out his scrying tendrils.

Shrieking with hunger and desire, the winged demons descended on the sorcerers, the dreadlords, and any remaining soldiers. It was as if they fell from the sun itself, while others on the ground rushed toward a few feeble arcane shields and hundreds of prone warriors.

With the Nine having turned their attention to freeing Samal, the debilitating sound of their sorcery had all but disappeared. Tarrik no longer felt it gnawing at his bones, scraping against his mind. The warriors of the Cabal began to recover and struggled to their feet, hands searching for discarded weapons. Heads clearing, they gathered in ragged groups as they rallied, and the demons assailing them became manifest.

The inhabitants of the abyssal realms fell in arcs, some upon the Cabalists, while the bulk streamed toward the Nine.

Demons spread their wings wide to slow and control their descent. They swooped over the gathering at the base of the pyramid, screeching and chattering and bellowing. The Cabalists responded to the aerial assault with coruscating lines of energy. Fires blossomed, erupting against demonic flesh and hide.

A dozen or so arrows soared into the sky, most missing their targets. A feeble, probably final response of a beleaguered army. Cabal warriors chopped at demons with swords and axes. Shields weathered fists and claws, paint chipping and wood splitting.

A bearded man charged Tarrik, spit flying from his mouth as he yelled a war cry. Tarrik dodged the man's spear thrust, lunged his own forward, and impaled the warrior upon its point. The impact ran up his arm, and he twisted the blade up and free, ripping through leather and skin and muscle. The man screamed his foul breath in Tarrik's face. Tarrik punched him twice until he lay in the dirt.

Another soldier came from the left: a woman with a slender sword and round shield, her hair plaited into two braids. He shoulder charged her shield, and she staggered backward. He kicked hard, sending her shield's iron rim smashing into her mouth. Her lip split, and she fell, screaming. Tarrik killed her with a stab to her throat.

He looked up, panting. Dreadlords rushed at him from all directions, their orichalcum eyes blazing orange. He wondered how he was going to fight them all, then realized they were converging on the remaining Nine.

For a heartbeat, it seemed the Nine were dumbstruck. Then, as if one hand guided them, they congregated around a central point, still surrounded by their ward. The dreadlords stopped outside the dome and turned to face the oncoming demons.

The horde barreled into the dreadlords, howling and clamoring to get past them to the ward. The dreadlords' great swords swung relentlessly, severing limbs and rending flesh, sending purple blood spraying. But the demons were not cowed, driven as they were by heartless lusts. Their claws and talons scraped the dome's surface, sending sapphire motes skittering across it.

Ren sank to her knees and released a cry of torment. Her fists battered the sides of her head. "No! Not again!"

Although he wasn't directly targeted by Samal, Tarrik felt as if someone's fingers were rummaging through his skull.

He knew there wasn't much he could do to stop Samal. That fight was for Ren alone. But perhaps he could stem the tide and delay the Adversary, however briefly.

He drew on his dark-tide power and sent tendrils into Ren's mind. To his surprise, she latched on to them almost instantly. Just as she had helped him in his fight to absorb Ananias's essence, so did his awareness join hers now to battle Samal.

Black and crimson threads of Samal's dark-tide power invaded Ren. They were too numerous, and Tarrik couldn't disperse them. The best he could do was to block some and corral others for brief moments. But his intervention seemed to give Ren space to recover. Her defenses gathered strength, and her white and golden tendrils isolated and fractured the black and red of Samal. A surge of power flared bright, creating spheres of protection against which Samal's forces battered in vain. For now.

Tarrik withdrew quickly, not wanting Samal's attention to turn to him. He opened his eyes to see more demons assailing the Cabalists. Warriors fell under the weight of inhuman numbers as they were set upon with exultant abandon. The demons worked a grizzly slaughter, tearing out throats, ripping soldiers to shreds with their talons. One demon struck a big mail-clad man, and he simply dropped, his throat slashed. Three others were dismembered by a pack of taloned and feathered terrors. Human steel—blades and axes and spears—cracked against scales and thick hides, penetrating flesh to spill purple blood. Warriors shouted war cries and wordless yells. Only a dozen of the sorcerers remained, and they fought back, sending concussions and fiery balls and glittering incising lines in all directions, not caring who they killed.

Demons bellowed. Men and women cried out in fear and futile determination, brandishing weapons and shields. A horn brayed through the dissonance, a long, warbling note that trailed off as if it had given up.

The area around the pyramid was a screaming turmoil, humans and demons scrambling on bloodied dirt, slipping in ichor and innards.

Individual shields sparked and collapsed under the demonic assault. The flesh inside the vanquished wards was pummeled with abandon. Blue and violet shields dwindled to a mere handful. Brilliant explosions peppered the earth.

Demons screeched and swerved from the onslaught. Incandescent explosions pimpled the sky. Dozens of abyssal denizens were incinerated, their flailing or inert forms trailing smoke as they plummeted from the sky to hammer into the ground with loud thumps, sending up curtains of dust.

The Cabalists retreated toward the encampment, all the while pounding the demons with virulent sorceries. What shelter the Cabalists thought they'd find at the camp, Tarrik didn't know, but it was the way of humans to continue to hope when all hope was lost.

He turned his attention to the Nine, still protected by their ward. Shrieking demons threw themselves against the wall of dreadlords, who swung their blades to cut through scales and hide. But the mass of demons was too much. Their infernal claws and fangs scraped across the dreadlords' plated armor, penetrating joints, piercing mail. The dreadlords fell, torn to glistening chunks.

The Nine scoured the demons with violet fire. Those that didn't flee burned as if made of wax.

A great gust of air blasted across the battlefield. The wind scooped up dry earth and swirled it into a vast dust storm that boiled and churned, sending sorcerers and demons tumbling. So great was the detritus it occluded the sun and sent swaths of shadow across the ground. Within heartbeats the sky turned gray, and all was reduced to ragged shapes in the gloom. Ren propelled herself skyward again, surrounded by her golden shield. Tarrik lost sight of her completely in the swirling dust she had generated.

He made use of the obscuring storm to fight his way toward the Nine. If Ren was to win her battle, defeating them would surely be paramount. What he could do against them was another story.

Men and women and demons of all types scurried through the smoking and murky battlefield, moaning and crying, squealing and growling, either searching for a fight or fleeing like prey. The few Cabalist warriors that Tarrik stumbled upon mostly ignored him, though some tried to grab his arm and urged him to run away, their words uttered from faces gaping with horror. He passed unharmed between the demons' claws and pummeling fists, snarling at them in Nazgrese when they came too close. Some croaked back in their own tongues, and all skirted around him to search for human meat.

One of the few remaining soldiers fought a marfesh, blood streaming down his face from a head wound. Bubbling poison from the demon's mouth scored lines across the earth, and the man's left arm was covered with the vitriol, his flesh sloughing off in layers. Somehow he managed to drive his sword up through the marfesh's throat into its brain.

The man saw Tarrik and pleaded with him for help. Tarrik buried his shadow-blade in his chest.

A series of impacts shook the ground. "Finish her!" cried Jawolinger in a voice like cracking thunder.

The Nine chanted in unison, and a shock wave blasted out from their ward, clearing the haze that Ren had created to obscure herself.

Tarrik tottered, then righted himself. Only a handful of Cabalists remained standing, their glowing shields beacons for the demons. He caught sight of Ren. She hovered above the destruction but was on her knees, her arms hugged tight around her body, her face a mask of misery as she looked toward the pyramid.

There, highlighted against the backdrop of the void, stood Samal, a cloud of burning cinders swirling around him.

The others of the Nine whooped and cried out in adoration.

At first Tarrik thought enormous shadow wings spread behind Samal's massively muscled form, but as they writhed and twisted, he realized they were fleshlike tentacles, each studded with spikes and ending in talons. Glowing red eyes stared out from the Adversary's black visage, and horns curled down from his forehead, ending close to his chin. His mouth opened in four sections to reveal jagged fangs, and his roar smothered all other sound and set Tarrik's bones vibrating.

Tarrik shuddered with disgust and fear. This was not any form he'd ever seen or heard of. This was obscene. A caricature of a demon. A nightmare form created by a lord drunk on his own power. Or driven insane.

Samal's clawed fists pounded at the arcane window that still held him in the void. The talons at the ends of his tentacles struck at the barrier like snakes.

The keening wail returned and rose in volume as the Nine spoke their powerful cants. The invisible wall separating Samal from this world shimmered and swam with silver motes.

Tarrik fell to his knees in the dust, more afraid than he'd ever been. His spear dropped from his fingers. He reached a hand out to Ren, imploring her to retreat, to *flee*.

He called her name, and she turned to regard him. Violent sorcerous lines assailed her shield, which flashed with white brilliance where it was struck, lighting her face in brief spurts. For a moment Tarrik thought she'd heard him, that she had agreed to run. His heart wrenched as emotions racked his frame. The sobs rising in his chest made him feel impotent, pitiful. Had this world driven him mad, as the Nine were? As Ren was?

The Cabal's sorcerers, warriors, and servants lay dead all around. Oily smoke from their burning corpses poured into the sky in long plumes. And Tarrik knew, with a conviction that made him clench his jaw, that this was also part of Ren's murderous design. For even as she fell to the Nine's sorceries, the Tainted Cabal would be forever turned against them.

Popping sounds echoed across the battlefield. The cracks between this world and the abyssal realms once again opened. Tarrik's skin crawled, and his hair stood on end. Coldness seeped into his bones. What else would Ren bring through? Demon lords?

But he watched with amazement as the demons Ren had summoned disappeared into a swirling mist that was sucked back through the veil and returned to the abyss.

He sent his awareness inside her again. Only a few spheres of her consciousness remained: golden-white balls assailed by crimson-black sorcery. Tarrik threw himself at the invading threads and shredded some, but his effort wasn't enough. It would never be enough. It was a losing battle. Hopeless.

Ren rose into the air again, this time kneeling on her sorcerous platform, her arms cradling her body. Abruptly, a new shield surrounded her of a type Tarrik had never seen before, of a black so deep as to be impenetrable, making her form invisible. Crimson and pitch-black lances slammed into the strange shield, which wavered under the barrage. Swirling tendrils broke away and curled around the ward, as if twisting in a wind, before fading to nothingness.

For a dozen heartbeats the strange shield held.

The Nine paused in their assault, as if to regain their strength before a final offensive.

Ren's black sphere dissipated to reveal her swaying and clutching at her head with both hands. Tarrik's carefully woven braids had unraveled, and her tresses swirled in the wind.

Laughter came from the void. Samal. The sound rose in volume until it boomed as loud as an avalanche.

Ren's gaze fixed upon the demon lord, and her mouth curved into a smile. Her hands dropped to her sides. A look of resignation came over her.

Tarrik stared. For a moment it seemed that they both stood once more atop the derelict tower: Ren, damp and fearful; Tarrik, angry and confused from her summoning.

He stumbled toward Ren and shouted her name. His cry must have penetrated the fugue of Samal reasserting his dominion. She ceased her swaying for a moment and turned toward him.

She shook her head, then frowned. "Run, you foolish demon!" Her voice crashed around Tarrik like thunder.

She lifted her left hand and placed it against the back of her right shoulder. The same spot, realized Tarrik, where he'd implanted the artifact.

Blood and fire!

He threw himself flat into the dirt, landing on Ren's journal. Her sword hammered the back of his head, and he felt an eldritch shield press against his skin. Ren, trying to protect him to the last.

The earth heaved, and his body launched upward, breaking contact with the ground. A dazzling light pierced his eyelids, causing him to cry out in pain. He was slammed back into the earth, grunting as his breath was driven from his lungs.

Another detonation, and the earth heaved again, and again. Finally, the radiant glare faded, and the ground's shudders subsided to reveal a strange cracking and clicking underneath.

Tarrik staggered to his feet and gaped in dismay and wonder.

Flames had turned the battlefield into an undulating sheet of fire pluming noxious black smoke. The conflagration twisted as if alive. Gales swirled through the air, churning clouds of ash and fire into the sky, blotting out the sun yet again. The air tasted of charcoal and heat and roasted meat.

There was no sign of the Nine, nor of the Cabalists' warriors. A few scintillant spheres fled from the devastation. A tiny fraction of the Cabalists' sorcerers had survived, probably because they were outside the area of the detonation.

Ren and her artifact had rained down this destruction. She had used all of her remaining sorcery and whatever she'd stored to lay the battlefield to waste. All of the Nine were dead. Including Ren. But Samal Rak-shazza, the Adversary, remained safely locked within his arcane prison.

Tarrik blinked back tears as he acknowledged Ren's final stand against Samal.

He looked across the vast expanse of burning ground, searching for a way to escape. There was none. His gaze rested upon the looming mass of the pyramid and the shadows at one side of its base. Were they dark enough? They had to be.

He poured himself into the darkness and felt his essence dissolve into the void, re-forming far from the devastation wreaked by the Nine's attempt to free the Adversary.

EPILOGUE

Tarrik knelt in the dust, staring at the pyramid and the razed battleground, his blackwood spear discarded beside him. Flickering sparks of sorcery winked in and out of existence. He wasn't sure what they meant. The demon army Ren had summoned had been returned to the abyssal realms, and there was no one left near the pyramid apart from the few survivors of the Cabal's cadre of sorcerers.

He watched the conflagration numbly until the flames died down. The patches of molten ground fractured with sharp cracks as they cooled and hardened to slag.

Far above, though it was daylight, the white moon of this world was a blurred crescent, followed by the curved gash of the crimson moon. After the battle, the relative peace held an ethereal quality. Tarrik breathed calmly and slowly, steadying his heartbeat, but tears formed as he thought again of Ren's last stand. She had struck to his core and made him love again. Yes, love. A curse.

He wandered a few steps, feet dragging in the dust, then stopped, his eyes burning. For long moments he remained still, his hands clenched into fists, the only sounds his blood pumping in his ears and his breath rasping through his open mouth. Ren was dead. There was no avoiding the truth. There was nothing left for him here. He should never have thought otherwise. Once more this human world had made him care and then stripped him of all he desired, all he *needed*.

He reached for his dark-tide power, measured it, and decided he had enough to force his way home. He closed his eyes and soon felt a tug, a niggling sensation in the back of his skull. This time he wasn't going to fight it, as he had when she'd summoned him.

Invisible white-hot hooks jagged into his limbs, torso, and consciousness. He surrendered himself to the burning ordeal, embraced it, though it seared his nerves. The hooks sliced and clawed at his essence, unraveling him.

As his physical body was rent asunder, he bound three objects to himself.

His spear. Ren's journal. Ren's sword.

Reality tore, prized open by arcane forces. A blast of frost washed through Tarrik, a frigid wind he could sense ethereally but not physically feel. A conduit was created, joining this world to an abyssal realm.

The void beckoned.

Tarrik Nal-Valim surrendered to its song.

TO MY READERS

Share your opinion. If you would like to leave a review of any of my books, it would be much appreciated! Reviews help new readers find my work and also provide valuable feedback for my future writing.

You can return to where you purchased the novel to review it or simply visit my website and follow the links: http://www.mitchellhogan.com/.

There are also websites such as Goodreads where members discuss the books they've read or want to read or suggest books others might read.

Sign up for my newsletter to be the first to learn about new releases, news, sales, and upcoming projects. I send a newsletter every few months, so I won't clutter your inbox. Visit my website to subscribe: http://www.mitchellhogan.com/new-release-alerts/.

Send me feedback. I love to hear from readers and try to answer every email. If you would like to point out errors and typos or provide feedback on my novels, I urge you to send me an email at mitchhoganauthor@gmail.com.

Having readers eager for the next installment of a series, or anticipating a new series, is the best motivation for a writer to create new stories. Thank you for your support, and be sure to check out my other novels!

ABOUT THE AUTHOR

When he was eleven, Mitchell Hogan received *The Hobbit* and the Lord of the Rings trilogy, and a love of fantasy novels was born. He spent the next ten years reading, rolling dice, and playing computer games, with some school and university thrown in. Along the way he accumulated numerous bookcases' worth of fantasy and sci-fi novels and doesn't look to stop anytime soon. For ten years he put off his dream of writing; then he quit his job and wrote *A Crucible of Souls*. He now writes full-time and is eternally grateful to the readers who took a chance on an unknown self-published author. He lives in Sydney, Australia, with his wife, Angela, and his daughters, Isabelle and Charlotte.